Nick Santora has written for TV series including *The Sopranos* and *Law & Order*, and was the lead writer and co-executive producer of *Prison Break*.

F1FTEEN DIGIT5

The men who work in the print and post room at legal firm Olmstead & Taft are far too unimportant for anyone to notice. But the information that passes through their office is a goldmine: bank details, mergers, acquisitions . . . everything you need to play the stock market and win big. All of them could use the money. None of them can see how it would hurt anyone. They should have known that when millions of dollars are involved, all bets are off.

NICK SANTORA

◆

F1FTEEN DIGIT5

Complete and Unabridged

CHARNWOOD
Leicester

First published in Great Britain in 2012 by
Mulholland Books
An imprint of Hodder & Stoughton
London

First Charnwood Edition
published 2013
by arrangement with
Hodder & Stoughton
An Hachette UK company
London

A catalogue record for this book is available
from the British Library.

ISBN 978–1–4448–1628–0

Published by
F. A. Thorpe (Publishing)
Anstey, Leicestershire

Set by Words & Graphics Ltd.
Anstey, Leicestershire
Printed and bound in Great Britain by
T. J. International Ltd., Padstow, Cornwall

This book is printed on acid-free paper

For my parents:
I'm able to do what I love to do
because you did what you had to do.

Prologue

'The problem with all you lawyers,' Mauro lectured Spade, 'is you think the support staff's nothing but replaceable parts — just warm bodies in blue blazers running your files up and down the floors whenever you snap your fingers. You guys treat us like we're invisible.'

Rich Mauro sat back in the booth and took a pull on his beer. Spade studied him for a moment, then smiled a disconcerting grin — a Cheshire Cat That Ate the Canary kind of thing.

'And that's why you're where you are and I'm where I am,' Spade pointed out smugly. 'Where you see problems, I see opportunities.'

Jason Spade leaned across the table, over the half-finished Harp's and the untouched onion rings. In the crowded bar, between the blare of the Smithereens on the jukebox and the howl of drunk Irish electricians toasting some dead union brother, there was no need to whisper, but Jason Spade's was the kind of idea that demanded secretive tones. Even if whispers weren't required by the environment, they were called for by the very nature of what he was about to propose.

'The benefit of being *invisible*,' Jason whispered, looking straight into Mauro's eyes, 'is that people don't see you when you're robbing them blind . . . now, how 'bout you and I get rich, Rich?'

And with that simple question, a chain of

1

events began that changed, destroyed, and ended lives. People would be maimed, tortured, and killed. Millions of dollars would be stolen, then stolen away from the thieves themselves.

It was a question that would eventually make Rich Mauro, Jason Spade, Vicellous 'Vice' Green, Dylan Rodriguez, and Eddie Pisorchek suffer beyond measure. Some of them would die because of it.

After it all went down, to the ill informed, it appeared that it happened because of money. But to those who were involved in it, to the guys who were so deep in the mess that it covered their mouths and pushed up into their nostrils, they understood that it all happened for love — love that was pure and real or love that had never been there to begin with, but love nonetheless.

And all of it — every cry of agony, every drop of blood — it all began with that conversation between Rich Mauro and Jason Spade, a conversation that lasted less than fifteen minutes, on a summer night, over a couple of beers in a graffiti-stricken booth in the back of McMahon's Pub.

1

Rich Mauro dragged the razor deliberately
— starting just below his ear, continuing down
along the side of his face, moving across his
jawline. He rinsed foam and stubble away under
the faucet and then traced the plastic disposable
across his chin, careful to scrape off every
whisker. It was a big day; he had to look good.
Satisfied all facial hair was gone and forever part
of the Queens County sewer system, he splashed
cold water on his cheeks, mouth, and neck and
studied himself in the mirror.

Rich knew he wasn't a traditionally handsome
man, not like the guys you saw in the movies
anyway. But he had his father's chin and it was a
damn good one. Hell, the Marlboro man would
kill for his jaw. It was solid. Granite. It not
only gave his face character but had held up in at
least a half-dozen scrapes, and it wagged a mile
a minute so he could talk his way out of a
half-dozen more.

Other than a cream-colored 1977 Pontiac
Grand Prix and a leather tool belt, the jawline
was the only thing his father had left him when
he and Rich's mother were killed.

When shaving, Rich would sometimes stare at
himself, unaware of the minutes passing. If he
looked deeply enough and blocked out his
peripheral vision, the image in the mirror would
morph, and soon Rich would find his father

3

looking back at him. His old man would stare silently, almost with wonder at how his little boy had grown up so big — the father's eyes always loving, but also burdened with the slight weight of melancholia.

Then, and always too soon, his father's image would slowly fade away, leaving nothing behind but the reflection of a much younger version of the man, shrouded in a thin film of steam rising up from the sink.

Towel wrapped around his waist, Rich padded on his wet feet across the hallway's hardwood floor and entered his small bedroom to find his Uncle Jimmy laying a tie flat across the bed. Next to the tie was a pair of tan slacks and a white button-down shirt. All the clothes still had the tags on them.

'Whoa, Jack LaLanne,' Jim Mauro joked, jabbing his nephew a few times in the chest, 'I remember when I could take you down.'

'Ah, you can still take me, Unc,' Rich lied. The truth was, Rich was built like a brick shit house, five foot ten and two hundred pounds of muscle. He wasn't one of those guys who looked like they worked out, all biceps and six-packs. In fact, he hadn't been inside a gym in years. When you worked construction, you didn't need a gym — every day was a work out. He just had that trademark stocky, fireplug frame that was embedded in the genetic code of so many Italian men.

'What's this?' Rich asked, pointing to the clothes.

'That's nothing. Just, you know, first day of work and all.'

4

Rich picked up the shirt and inspected the tag.

'Mur-Lee's?' Rich scolded. 'We can't afford clothes from Mur-Lee's.'

'*We* don't need to afford them. *I* bought them.'

'Fine,' Rich countered, 'then *you* can't afford clothes from Mur-Lee's. We're returning 'em.'

Jim grabbed the shirt and the pants and ripped the tags off each. With a defiant smile, he tore the tags up and sprinkled the little pieces over his nephew's head like confetti.

'The shirt is going on your back, the pants are going on your ass, and as for the tie, you have a choice . . . either the tie or my *hands* are going around your neck. You decide.'

Rich brushed the paper from his hair.

'Fine, but no lottery tickets for two months.'

'Deal.' Jim smirked. 'But that doesn't even cover the cost of the tie. Sharp, huh?'

Rich looked at the tie lying on his bed. It was too skinny and had a paisley pattern that had been out of fashion since forever. It was hideous.

'Sharp as a tack. I love it,' he said, giving his sixty-four-year-old uncle a kiss on the cheek. 'Thank you.'

Jim's face flushed with pride, partly for his nephew and partly for having been able to walk into that snooty Mur-Lee's, pick out an outfit, and pay for it in cash. Jim would never admit it, but buying those clothes was one of the biggest thrills of his life. About thirty years earlier, when he worked for Garibaldi Construction, he had helped build the five-store commercial strip where Mur-Lee's was located. He'd hung the

5

drywall, done the ceilings — he even came up with the idea for the built-in mahogany display cases that became the store's showpiece and were still there.

A year of his life he worked on that job — his skill in every piece of floorboard, his heart in every driven nail. Thanks to an unexpected sneeze and a sharp Sheetrock knife, Jim literally gave his blood to that job. The store was perfect. Crown molding, solid oak changing rooms. He had never been so proud of a project. But as soon as it was completed, Mr. Murrel and Mr. Lee opened up shop, the union hall sent Jim to work on a housing project in Uniondale, and he could never afford to step back into what he had built.

But for a day like this, he didn't care about cost. He'd raised Rich, his brother Richie's son, since the boy was ten. And he loved him like he was his own. Jim had never married, since he realized early on that his two biggest loves — scotch and the ponies — would never take a backseat to any woman. He had a deep respect for people who fell in love, committed themselves wholly to each other, and built lives together. His own parents did it, and it was beautiful — so he swore he'd never sully the institution of marriage with his own bastardized version of it.

As a result, Jimmy had accepted the fact that he'd never have kids, and that was fine because having a child had never been a burning desire of his. The occasional romp with a young bar girl had always been enough for him — but the by-product of such activities was something he knew he could do without, so he always took precautions, despite what Father Dolan had taught him about 'wasting God's seed' during Jim's education at Our Lady of Mount Carmel.

But after the accident, Jim had a child to care for whether he wanted one or not. His nephew had no place else to go. The same week he buried his brother and sister-in-law, Jim moved all of Rich's belongings into his home. And despite the circumstances, it was never awkward or uncomfortable. Rich and Jim had been close before the deaths of Rich's parents, and they just became closer afterward — closer than Jim would have ever imagined almost twenty years earlier when he first took Rich in.

Jimmy once told a friend of his (after a snort or two of Black Label made such emotional displays by men socially acceptable), 'I loved my brother Richie with all my heart and I'd trade places with him in an instant if I could, and God forgive me for sayin' this, but his dying was the best thing that ever happened to me . . . 'cause it gave me my boy.'

But as Jim watched his nephew get ready, he knew he was no longer a boy; he was a man — and though Jim Mauro had been flying blind a lot of the time while trying to raise the kid, he couldn't have been happier with how that man had turned out.

'Lemme get my shoes and we'll see how I look in this getup,' Rich said, opening the closet door. He knelt and opened a shoe box to reveal a pair of thirty-dollar black dress shoes that he had bought three years earlier for the funeral of a third cousin he barely knew. He hadn't worn them since, but somehow, they shone like mirrors. Rich picked up the box and stood, raising his eyebrows suspiciously at Jimmy.

'I polished them last night when you were out with Elyse,' Jim confessed. 'Can't go to your first day with scuffed shoes.'

'Thanks, Unc.'

As Rich put the shoe box back in the closet, his eyes landed on a faded brass hook on the inside of the door. It was empty.

'Where is it?' Rich asked, all playfulness gone from his voice.

'You won't need it anymore — '

'Where is it? I want it.'

'What for? You're done climbin' scaffolds — '

'It's mine, Uncle Jim.'

'It's my brother's.'

'No, it's my *father's*, which makes it mine,' Rich said a little more forcefully than he had wanted to.

'Your old man wouldn't want you usin' it anymore. And neither do I,' Jim answered. He didn't get loud — Jim Mauro never turned up the volume; it wasn't in his nature. He was as big and thick as a cement mixer but also gentle as a lamb, especially with Rich. Rich couldn't remember a time when his uncle had yelled at him.

'It's not like I'm gonna throw it away or anything,' Jimmy promised. 'I'd never do that. It's just . . . it's just not an option for you anymore. I mean, you're wearing a tie to work

8

today, Richie. That means something.'

Rich regarded his uncle for a moment. He could see the pride, the hope, in his uncle's face. He didn't want to upset him, but he felt he had to try to clarify things.

'Look, I know it means a lot to you, but I'm just a glorified copy-boy — '

'It's a step to bigger and better, Richie,' Jim interrupted. 'A step to bigger and better.'

'Hopefully. We'll have to see, won't we?' Rich said, knowing he wasn't going to win this argument. 'But in the meantime, I'm gonna want the tool belt back.'

Jim sighed. 'Your dad was thick as a brick too, ya know.'

Jim exited the room. Rich stood patiently, listening to his uncle rummage around. He could tell from the sound that the tool belt had been hidden on the top shelf of the hall closet — most likely behind a bunch of videotapes of vintage 1950s TV shows that Jim never watched but refused to throw away.

Jim appeared in the doorway and tossed the tool belt onto the bed. 'Satisfied? Now hurry up and get dressed. You don't wanna be late.'

As his uncle moved back down the hall, Rich looked at the weather-beaten tool belt lying next to his brand-new dress shirt. It was cracked and faded and there was a faint chalky-white salt line in the leather where it had absorbed decades' worth of sweat that had rolled down his father's back. The belt had known his father better and longer than Rich had.

He reached past the belt and picked up the

shirt from Mur-Lee's. He slid his arms into the sleeves and fastened the buttons — they were those thick kind of buttons, the real high-quality jobs that don't ever fall off. The 180-thread-count cotton surrounded and caressed his skin. He had to admit — it felt damn good.

2

When Rich entered his three of the fifteen digits, he didn't have to think too long as to what they would be: 4-2-4. April 24 — the day his parents died. That was the day when his life as he knew it changed forever.

He knew that once he typed those three numbers, his life would once again change forever, so the numbers somehow seemed appropriate.

If he'd known then how things were going to eventually turn out . . . what was going to happen to his friends, what was going to happen to him . . . he would have never sullied his parents' memory by using that date.

He would have chosen something else.

3

The N/R Train dropped Rich off in the heart of New York City's financial district, just a few blocks from his ultimate destination, 55 Water Street. He was pretty early, but he walked quickly, wanting to start his new job, and his new life, as soon as possible.

Even though there was only two thousand feet of river separating Queens and Manhattan, for Rich Mauro, a kid from Astoria, the city might as well have been another world.

As soon as he exited the subway onto Broadway, he felt the difference. A different pace, a different energy — swarms of people walking in a hundred different directions, pressed closely together in ungodly narrow sidewalks lining ungodly narrow streets, white faces next to black next to yellow next to brown, all with the same thought: *green*. Simply put, the energy of the city was the result of one thing and one thing only — New York was where people came to make *money*.

Hell, that was why Rich got up that morning, showered, shaved, got dressed, and got on the train. That was why he'd left a decent, but far from spectacular, job in construction. That was why he had started night school, even though the tuition costs were making the slightest luxury, like a night at the movies with Elyse, an event that had to be budgeted sometimes weeks in advance.

Rich Mauro was in New York to start making some damn money. He knew it would be a long road, but he'd never been scared of hard work. His father had worked his ass off. His Uncle Jim had worked his ass off. Now Rich was ready to work his ass off. He'd be working at a desk *inside* a building instead of on a scaffold *outside* one, but it would be hard work just the same. Max Seymour had prepared him for that.

As Rich turned onto Water Street, he had nothing but business on his mind. *Business. Money. Work. Achieve.* He was taking the first step to becoming a lawyer and he was ready to knock down any barriers that got in his way.

He wasn't aware of it, but the intensity of his thoughts that morning caused his brow to furrow and his eyes to narrow.

Nothing was going to stop him, no matter how hard it was, no matter how difficult. He was laser-focused on the task at hand.

And then he spotted her.

And his brow relaxed. And his eyes opened wider. And he smiled.

4

In a city of eleven million people, Elyse Crane stood out. She was waiting by the front steps leading up to 55 Water Street, with scores of people moving past, by, and around her — yet amid all that chaos, she, as always, looked painfully beautiful.

Rich believed love at first sight was bullshit and anyone who said he knew as soon as he looked at someone that he was in love was either lying, delusional, or stupid. With Elyse, Rich always said, it was love at first *talk*.

He'd met her at Pete's Tavern when he was twenty-five and she was twenty-four. He'd been working on a job downtown and sometimes he'd go grab a drink with his uncle and some of the guys after work. Chauncey's, the place where they normally went, had been temporarily shut down by the board of health for an infestation violation. It seemed a tenant in the apartment above Chauncey's had let his pet boa constrictor out of its cage, and, via a ventilation duct, the reptile had found its way onto a plate of cheese fries on the bar downstairs. Pete's Tavern just happened to be the next closest watering hole to the job site, and that's where Elyse was working.

Rich wasn't particularly religious, but a few weeks after meeting Elyse he stopped inside Our Lady of Mount Carmel's, threw a buck in the poor box, lit a candle, and thanked God.

14

I know you sent Saint Patrick to drive the snakes out of Ireland, so if you had anything to do with diverting that serpent into Chauncey's to get Elyse and me together, much appreciated.

When Rich bellied up at Pete's Tavern, he knew instantly that the girl slinging beer on the other side of the oak was the most stunning thing he'd ever laid eyes on. He even told his Uncle Jim so, and he didn't use the word *thing* in a derogatory way. He meant it in the purest sense.

To Rich, Elyse was more beautiful than anything he'd ever seen — more beautiful than the sunrise peeking its weary head over the Atlantic when he was driving east on Ocean Parkway at five a.m. to get to a job down at Long Beach, Long Island; more beautiful than any rainbow arching over the East River after a downpour broke the oppressive humidity of an August day in New York; more beautiful than any thing Rich could imagine, any thing God himself had ever dreamed up. And Rich didn't even waste time comparing her with other women — that bout was over before the ref rang the bell.

She was a true beauty. A stunner. An angel with a pint of Guinness in one hand and a bar rag in the other.

So Rich Mauro was presented with a predicament — what to do with this woman pouring lager in front of him. If he spoke to her and she sounded like Fran Drescher with a head cold (a real possibility in New York), the love affair would be over before it started. But what if she didn't? What if she talked him up and was as smart as she was gorgeous? That would be even worse. What could he say that could possibly impress this goddess?

Hi, my name's Rich. I still live with my uncle, a man who likes eating Jarlsberg cheese smeared with peanut butter and arguing with TV newscasters. I have no money, no parents, and thanks to my uncle's love of the ponies, no inheritance coming my way. My dad and every man on my mother's side of the family went bald, so my forties should be interesting, and though I'm Italian, if I eat tomato sauce, let's just say you can't light a match within twenty yards of me for safety reasons . . . and, oh yeah, since I haven't had sex in almost six months, if we do ever become intimate, you can expect our first little romp to be quicker than a humming-bird's heartbeat.

Rich took a long look at himself in the mirror across the bar — his flannel shirt with a light cover of drywall dust, his hair pressed and matted from his hard hat, grease under his nails from oiling the skill saw. She was probably a grad student (he later found out he was right), wealthy (her parents were), and bartending to kill time between semesters (right again). Guys like him didn't get girls like her. So when Elyse approached him, he decided to keep it strictly business.

'Beam and Coke, please.'

Elyse smiled, grabbed a tumbler from underneath the bar, reached behind her, and snatched a bottle of Maker's Mark. She began to pour.

16

'I'm sorry, I said Jim Beam — '

'I know,' Elyse interrupted as she looked up to Rich. 'But a workingman deserves top shelf, and you look like you put in a full day.'

She had read Rich like he was the freakin' *New York Post* — his attraction to her, his insecurity in his own appearance, his acceptance of the fact that she was out of his league.

Elyse could tell he wanted to talk to her — she picked up that vibe from guys all the time. But unlike all those other times, for some reason, she wanted to hear what this particular boy had to say. There was something about him that she instantly liked — a sincerity that was practically visible. She was certain, almost instinctively, that this guy sitting at the bar didn't have it in him to ever hurt her, or hurt anybody for that matter. She could tell just by the way he interacted with his uncle that Rich Mauro was, simply put, a good man. But she could also tell he was, at that moment, a self-conscious man. So she said the absolute perfect thing — something that let Rich know that she not only understood his blue-collar world but *respected* it.

Love at first talk.

Rich was speechless. But Uncle Jim wasn't.

'Don't let her get away, Richie.' He snorted as he got up from the bar, patted his nephew softly on the back, and left the two of them alone. Rich turned red, since Jim had said this loud enough for Elyse to hear. But Elyse just laughed, and then so did Rich. They'd been laughing together for a long time now; her tractor-beam smile always pulling Rich away from whatever was bothering him (usually his lack of money) and pushing him toward a much happier place.

It was that amazing smile that greeted Rich in front of 55 Water Street.

'Hey, big shot,' she said, leaning in to give Rich a soft kiss on the lips. She wrapped her arms around him and pressed her forehead against his, grinning wildly. '*You excited?*'

'Clearly not as excited as you are, psycho woman.' Rich smiled back. 'What are you doing here?'

'I came to give you this . . . ' She handed Rich a greeting card.

'And this . . . ' She handed Rich a key.

'And this . . . ' She laid another kiss on Rich, and this was nothing like the sweet little we're-in-public peck she'd graced him with just moments earlier. This one lasted — her hand on the back of his head, her fingers moving ever so lightly through his hair. God, he loved when she did that — it was the fingers on the back of his head that got him every time.

'Thanks.' Rich smiled. 'But maybe it's not the best idea to have intercourse right in front of my new job.'

'That's what the key's for,' Elyse said with a gleam in her eye. She removed her fingers from his head and softly placed them on his chest, gently scratching. 'Come by tonight, so we can celebrate in a way that isn't accommodated by a public sidewalk.'

Damn, Rich thought, *I'm about to start the most important job of my life and I'm half considering skipping work to have sex with this woman all day long.*

'You're distracting me right before I start my first day?'

'Sorry.' Elyse winked devilishly. 'Now open your card.'

Rich did. It was a photo of a kid sitting on a training potty with his arms triumphantly in the air. Inside the card was printed: YOU DID IT! At the bottom was written: *I know you're going to do great. I love you. Elyse.*

'Wow, a semi-child-pornographic greeting card. Much appreciated,' Rich said, putting the card in his pocket.

Elyse laughed. 'Now go kick some ass.'

They kissed once more and said good-bye. Rich watched her go — her long chestnut hair bounced lightly with each step, almost joyously, like it was happy to just be part of the wonderful group effort that made up this exquisite creature. The hair, the legs, the face, the eyes — they all had their roles on Team Elyse and they were all all-stars. Rich hated being away from her, but he sure as hell enjoyed watching her walk away. The walk-away was pretty damn sweet.

Unfortunately, Rich noticed that a tough-looking Puerto Rican guy passing by was enjoying watching her walk away as well. The guy turned his head just slightly to get a good look at Elyse as she crossed the street, and when he turned back, he found Rich staring at him. Their eyes locked — for a second or two at most, but in New York, that's all you need. The look was more than long enough to let the guy know that Rich had seen him leering at his girl and that if

19

his look had lasted any longer, it would have been a problem.

Normally Rich wouldn't have been too worried — he never enjoyed fighting, but you can't grow up in Queens and avoid it. He'd spent the majority of his youth on the asphalt basketball courts of the inappropriately named New York City Department of Parks and Recreation — and since those fence-enclosed blacktops looked substantially more like penitentiary yards than parks, it was only logical that some pretty serious brawls would break out. Though he was the furthest thing from a guy who looked for trouble, Rich had always been able to hold his own when necessary.

But when the Puerto Rican looked back at Rich, his eyes made Mauro quickly understand that if things did jump off, Rich would have his hands full. They weren't the eyes of a street-tough kid who had thrown down with other street-tough kids throughout his youth. They were the kind of eyes you could earn only by doing some very bad things. *Really* bad things. The guy was about forty feet or so away. Rich tensed, waiting to see if their two-second eye-lock would lead to something else. He was sure it was about to. But then, to Rich's complete surprise, the guy just slowly shook his head from side to side, almost imperceptibly, as if to say: *Silly white boy, you have no idea what just almost happened to you.* And then he walked past Rich to a roach coach and ordered a café con leche.

Wow, I just somehow avoided a very severe

20

beat-down . . . today's gonna be a good day, Rich thought to himself as he turned and climbed the steps of the building where, he hoped, he'd be working for years to come.

He stopped at the electric revolving doors for a moment. His body was reeling a bit — the adrenaline that had kicked in from his near run-in with the Puerto Rican was mixing pretty hard with the rush of new-job excitement. He took a step and let the revolving doors guide him forward before momentum caused the structure to swallow him up.

Once inside, he looked around the lobby — the three-story-tall atrium, the gleaming brass elevator doors, the giant plants that reached ten feet high. As he moved toward the elevator he crossed the interlocking *O&T* in the center of the marble floor that let anyone who entered know, in no uncertain terms, that he was treading upon the hallowed ground of Olmstead & Taft — the biggest, baddest, toughest, and most powerful law firm in all of New York City.

It was a legendary firm.

It was a New York institution.

It was also where Rich would soon make choices that would get some very good men killed.

5

The offices of Olmstead & Taft were known in legal circles to be the nicest in New York. The firm owned the entire building, and the partners took pride in their home. Each office had custom bookcases with hand-carved crown molding, a personal thermostat for a climate-controlled work experience, and burgundy carpeting in a razor-thin crosschecked pattern that was replaced every four years whether there was even a hint of wear or not. Almost every office had a view of New York Harbor overlooking either the Brooklyn Bridge or Governors Island, and the lucky few, mostly partners and those associates being groomed to become partners, got the privilege of practicing jurisprudence under the watchful eye of the Statue of Liberty herself.

The marble-floored elevators were operated by old black men in gray wool suits who had to memorize what floor every attorney worked on. Considering that 55 Water Street serviced about four hundred of the more than one thousand worldwide Olmstead & Taft attorneys, this was no small feat. The elevator operators were instructed to say 'Good morning, Counselor,' or 'Good afternoon, Counselor,' or 'Good evening, Counselor,' and press the button for the floor of that lawyer's office. Some believed this practice was instituted to intimidate adversaries who were attending conferences at Olmstead & Taft — *If we demand perfection from our elevator operators, imagine how prepared our attorneys are.*

Others just figured the elevator policy existed so the lawyers wouldn't have to stoop so low as to talk to the help.

The hardest time of year for the operators was July and August, when a fresh crop of summer associates would arrive to work between their second and third years of law school. There would often be thirty to forty of them and even though only some would actually make the cut and get to be full-fledged members of O&T after they graduated, for those two summer months, the elevator crew was expected to memorize their floor numbers as well.

If an operator made too many mistakes or, God forbid, accidentally forced an inattentive partner to endure an elevator ride a whole two floors above the actual location of his or her office, that operator would be terminated.

Some lasted just a few days. Others lasted a few years. And then there was Chip.

Chip was a seventy-six-year-old sharecropper's son who had begun at O&T when he was seventeen. Rumor had it that it was Chip who actually created the floor-memorization policy. He allegedly knew early on that he didn't have many skills in life save for an uncanny memory, so he established the ritual back in the 1950s, knowing the status-seeking lawyers would instantly take to it. He also knew it would guarantee him a job forever: even though Chip was now well into his seventies, no one could outmemorize him.

The luck of the draw at the elevator bays

allowed Rich to step onto the car run by the legendary operator, but as soon as Rich was inside, the old vet looked offended.

'What you thinkin', copy jockey?' he barked, every basset-houndesque wrinkle in his dark face contorting in indignation. 'Get your khaki-covered ass off my litigator-conveyor.'

'Huh?'

'What? O and T's hirin' foreigners now? You don't speak English? Get out of my attorney-only elevator and take one of them lifts on the south wall.'

'Oh, sure, I'm sorry,' Rich apologized. 'Max Seymour just told me to go to the Printers and I didn't know where — '

'Oh, you're Max Seymour's boy,' Chip said, his affront subsiding a touch. 'I heard you were startin' up. Didn't know it was today. Okay then.'

Chip pressed a button and the door quickly closed, sucking them into the guts of 55 Water Street. The elevator, however, did not move upward and onward to the grandiose offices located high in the clouds over Manhattan. Chip had pressed B, as Rich's new job was located in a decidedly less glamorous section of Olmstead & Taft — the basement.

As the elevator hit bottom and the door opened, Chip left Rich with some advice.

'Blazers ride the south-wall elevators. I ain't been doing this fifty-plus years to be a chauffeur to no paper pusher, understand?'

'Yes, sir,' Rich answered.

'I don't wanna see you on my elevator again.

24

Don't care if you are Max Seymour's boy . . . I been here longer than him,' Chip said as the doors closed and he disappeared back upstairs.

'Blazers s'posed to ride the south-wall elevators,' a voice said from somewhere in back of Rich.

Mauro turned to find the voice belonged to a man standing just a few feet behind him. He was dressed in the same outfit as Rich (white button-down shirt, tan pants) except he was wearing a navy blue sports coat. The man was about five foot eight, a little bit husky but solidly built, and he had a mess of brown hair that was parted not so carefully to one side. From the slightest beginnings of crow's-feet at the corners of his eyes and the small recession of a widow's-peak hairline, Rich could see that the man was several years older than he was, probably in his midthirties.

It was also clear to Rich that the man was mentally retarded.

'Yeah, I know, I just found out,' Rich answered warmly.

'I'm Eddie Pisorchek,' the man said, extending his hand. Rich shook and almost fell to his knees. Eddie squeezed incredibly hard, driving Rich's index finger and pinkie together. Rich could tell Eddie wasn't trying to hurt him; he was just very strong and clearly unaware of his strength. 'And Chip is not your supervisor . . . *I am.*'

Now, Richard James Mauro wasn't a bigot or an elitist — he had been raised by his parents and his uncle to judge people only by their

25

deeds. That being said, if someone had told him when he was in high school that one day he'd be working in a basement and his supervisor would be retarded, he probably would have been a little concerned.

6

'How ya doin?' Rich said, delicately disengaging his now throbbing hand from Eddie's.

'No ties,' Eddie said.

'Excuse me?'

'*Blazers* don't wear ties. We wear tan pants, white shirts, black belts, and blue blazers. No ties. Only lawyers wear ties.'

'Yeah, I don't even really like this tie, my uncle gave it to me — '

'No ties,' Eddie repeated, clearly not interested in excuses.

'Yeah, right,' Rich said, quickly removing the tie and shoving it in his pocket.

'Follow me. You need a blazer. Only the supervisor can hand out the blazers,' Eddie announced, more as a way of bragging than as a statement of fact.

The ceiling of the drab, gray, cement-walled basement was a cross-section of air ducts and pipes, some of which dripped water onto the slab floor. They passed a group of maintenance men in gray jumpsuits who were heading in the opposite direction.

'Morning, guys,' Eddie said. None of the maintenance workers returned the greeting; none of them even looked his way — they just ignored Eddie and kept on walking. Rich thought it was pretty damn rude of them, bordering on hurtful, but he kept this thought to himself.

Eddie didn't mind, however. A thirty-five-year-old virgin who lived with his grandparents, who collected anything having to do with Green Lantern, and who had the cognitive ability of an eleven-year-old, Eddie Pisorchek knew what it was like to be ignored. He was used to it.

His retardation was mild enough for him to realize that people spoke to him — when they did actually speak to him — in different tones than they used with others; he knew that he was different. Yet his condition was also substantial enough that the challenges of raising a special-needs child like Eddie had made Ed Pisorchek Sr. catch a bus out of town, reportedly to Missouri, when his son was four, never to be seen again.

And it was this abandonment by her not-so-better half that tipped Mary Pisorchek into a chasm of severe bipolar swings and depression that earned her a small room and footwear with no shoelaces at Pilgrim State Mental Hospital. And it was both parents' flaking of their responsibilities that had earned Glenn and Edna Pisorchek the honor of raising their grandson just when they thought their days of child rearing were over.

Little Eddie was their blood, they couldn't turn him over to the state, but at the same time, they truly wanted no part of bringing up the boy. They took him on, an unwelcome burden, and proceeded to handle the responsibility half-assed and begrudgingly.

Eddie got the basics from his grandparents, but that was it. A bowl of Frosted Flakes in the morning. A peanut butter and jelly sandwich for lunch — a pickle on the side for a vegetable. Dinner rotated — SpaghettiOs on Monday, Wednesday, and Friday; Mrs. Paul's Fish Sticks on Tuesday, Thursday, and Saturday; and to top off the weekend, sloppy-joe Sunday. This was what Eddie ate every week. *Every* day of *every* week.

Eddie's room had a bed, a small desk salvaged from an elementary-school dumpster, and nothing else. He didn't have a closet, but there was an old dry-cleaning rack on wheels in the corner. On it hung six pair of tan pants from JC Penney (all bought on sale), six white oxford shirts (all identical), and one blue shirt with an extra-wide collar for Sunday services.

Eddie's grandparents didn't make him attend church; Eddie wanted to. He went by himself, and though he was technically Roman Catholic, he never stepped foot in St. Rita's. When he was about nine, heading home after having purchased the latest Green Lantern comic from Ernie & Esther's Stationery Shop, Eddie passed the storefront for the Chicken Shack. He waited for air heavy with the stench of deep-frying grade-D poultry to wrap his face, as it always did, like a hot, greasy barber's towel. But instead of the thick stench of trans-fat-covered animal flesh wafting out toward him, *music* filled the air. It was the most incredible sound Eddie had ever heard.

He pressed his face against the window, peering between a crack in the blinds, and saw the most amazing thing he had ever seen — a large group of black people singing and dancing and shouting and screaming.

It was loud.

It was energized.

It was *beautiful*.

Eddie was instantly hooked. Barely aware of his actions, practically hypnotized by what he was seeing and hearing, he opened the door, walked inside the onetime Chicken Shack, and sat down next to a muscular teenage boy, who looked at the little white boy rocking back and forth next to him like he was either insane or lost. Eddie just looked back at the boy and smiled. The teenager then realized that Eddie was neither insane nor lost . . . he was, as the teen's mother used to say, one of God's 'angels on earth.' The teen smiled back, and before long, Eddie was singing and clapping with the congregation as if he had always been one of them. After that, he went back to the First Baptist Church of Fourth Street every Sunday, the only white face in a sea of black and brown.

As the decades passed, parishioners came and went, pastors changed, the dilapidated storefront even got a new paint job, but the one constant at First Baptist was Eddie Pisorchek, singing and clapping and smiling along with everyone, every Sunday, rain or shine, in a button-down blue shirt with an extra-wide collar.

'Don't know why you spend all your time with them jigaboos,' Eddie's grandfather would say to him each week as Eddie was leaving for church.

Eddie didn't know the true meaning of that word or of the many other synonyms for *jigaboo*

30

that his grandfather liked to toss about. He thought it just meant people who liked to sing and dance — until one Thanksgiving mass when Eddie was twelve and Pastor Morris came around with a microphone, asking people what they were thankful for.

The music was blaring, the testifiers were testifying, and everyone was feeling a big, fat mess of the Holy Spirit when Pastor Morris reached Eddie. Eddie, grinning from ear to ear, just happy as hell to be surrounded by such happy people, grabbed the microphone and shouted loud, proud, and clear: '*I'm thankful I get to sing and dance with all you jigaboos!*'

The music stopped.

The singing stopped.

The testifiers stopped testifying.

Eddie's sentiment was from the heart — he was truly thankful that he got to sing and dance with these wonderful people; it was the only bright spot in his otherwise dark life. But it was his noun choice that was the problem, and for the rest of that particular service, a very understanding congregation taught Eddie the concept of prejudice. After hearing all the pain such words caused, Eddie promised never to use the offending terminology, or anything like it, again. And he never did.

The First Baptist Church of Fourth Street was the one place where Eddie felt like he belonged. His grandparents fed him, clothed him, and took him to the doctor when he was sick, but they never loved him because they'd never wanted him. Eddie grew up lonely. He grew up ignored.

The only time Eddie could remember his grandfather paying any attention to him was when he was eight. He had just watched an old black-and-white rerun of *The Mickey Mouse Club* on WPIX. He was captivated by the huge castle that Tinker Bell flew around at the end of every show and imagined the secret passages and hidden catacombs that awaited him inside.

He rushed to his grandfather. 'Can we go to Disney World?'

'No.'

'Please. I wanna go to Disney World.'

'I said no.'

'I wanna go to Disney World. I wanna go to Disney World. I wanna go to Disney World.'

Glenn knew the kid wouldn't stop — Eddie could be a stubborn son of a bitch — so he just folded his newspaper, slid it under his arm, stood up, and walked away. But Eddie trailed after his grandfather, right on the old man's heels, continuing his plea over and over. 'I wanna go to Disney World.'

Eddie followed the old man upstairs, down the hall, and toward the bathroom, getting louder: 'I wanna go to Disney World, I wanna go to Disney World, I wanna go to Disney World, *I wanna go to Dis* — '

The slap hit Eddie's face so hard he spun to the floor, landing on his hands and knees. He was so shocked and numb from the pain that he didn't even feel his grandfather pick him up and grab him by the shoulders.

Glenn Pisorchek shook his grandson as he yelled.

'We are never going to fuckin' Disney World! We don't have enough money to go to Disney World because we have to take care of *you! Don't ever mention fuckin' Disney World again!*'

Glenn looked at the stunned boy with a red handprint on his face. He wasn't proud of what he'd done, but damn it, he hadn't asked for this life. He had waited forty-two and a half years for retirement to come so he could leave his miserable job as a groundskeeper for the county so he could sit on his miserable ass in front of the miserable tube and watch the miserable world pass him by on the miserable news programs. Then, if he was lucky, one day his miserable heart would stop and end his miserable life. He hadn't asked for his son's retarded child to be dropped into his lap, but he was. So now he was Glenn's miserable problem.

After a moment, Glenn turned and went into the bathroom, closing the door behind him. Eddie just stood there, alone in the hall. He wasn't that upset that he had been hit because it was the first time his grandfather had actually had any physical contact with him in over a year.

At least he still knows I'm here, Eddie thought.

When Eddie graduated from the Staten Island High School for Special Needs, his grandparents were terrified. They didn't know what to do with the boy — Would he be with them *all* day, *every* day now? They couldn't have that — there was too much TV to watch and unhealthy food to cook; they couldn't have *him* around. So for the first time in their lives, Glenn and Edna Pisorchek actually did something for their grandson. They contacted government agencies and charities that aided the developmentally challenged and got Eddie into the Just Like You program, a nonprofit that placed special-needs citizens in paying jobs.

The job found for Eddie was not particularly glamorous but it came with real responsibility and a steady paycheck, which Glenn and Edna promptly told Eddie he had to cash each week so they could 'store it away safely.' Most of Eddie's money was stored away in car payments on a new Buick Skylark for Glenn and cheap jewelry and salon appointments for Edna, which did little for a woman who had canyon-deep grooves on her face consistent with a pack-of-Luckys-a-day habit.

Eddie had no idea he was being robbed by the very people who were supposed to be caring for him but he probably wouldn't have cared because Eddie loved his new job so damn much he would have done it for free. He got to work with computers, which he found incredibly exciting. And he got to ride the subway all the way to Manhattan, which, prior to his working, he had only seen on TV and from across the water. And there were even copy machines that each shone a bright green light that looked just like a blast from Green Lantern's power ring.

Eddie loved working at the Printers of Olmstead & Taft. On his first day there, when he was just eighteen years old, as soon as he walked in the door, he knew he'd never want to leave.

But Eddie would eventually leave the job he loved so much.

Almost seventeen years exactly from his first day of employment, Eddie Pisorchek would be dragged out of the basement's loading bay in the middle of the night — scared, bleeding, and crying.

7

When it was Eddie's turn to sit down at the computer and enter his three numbers, he was faced with a problem. He wanted to use 2-8-1-4, for Sector 2814, the section of the universe that Hal Jordan, the alter ego of Green Lantern, was assigned to defend with his superpowers.

But the guys said he could only use three numbers. Each of them got to use three numbers and that was it, they said. Jason even yelled at him and called him Special Ed and told him to hurry up.

Eddie hated being called Special Ed.

So he entered just the first three numbers — 2-8-1. It wasn't exactly what he wanted, but it was close enough.

When he was done, Eddie smiled. He was proud of himself.

8

The Document Production and Disbursement Department of Olmstead & Taft was universally referred to throughout the firm as the Printers. Though every major law firm had some version of the Printers, nothing rivaled O&T's. It had state-of-the-art equipment that put any Kinko's to shame. In that dungeon of a basement office, every week literally tens of thousands of pages of briefs, motions, appeals, and filings were copied, collated, and bound for some of the most powerful attorneys in New York. Each piece of machinery was computerized, and since New York and federal courts were broken down into multiple districts and departments, all of which had their own irrationally diverse rules as to the format of how pleadings should be submitted, the machinery had to be reprogrammed for each job depending on the type of filing and where it was to be filed. And that doesn't even take into account the various government agencies like the SEC, EPA, IRS, and countless others that needed their paperwork done *just so*.

It was complex, confusing work that would have taken any college graduate several weeks or more to master, but Eddie Pisorchek had it down pat. With Rich's hire, there were now four men working in the Printers, but when it came time to program the metallic beasts, everyone just let Eddie do his thing.

The work was not only complicated but also entirely thankless. A document was e-mailed down to the Printers, where it was formatted, printed, copied, velo-bound, and rushed upstairs to whatever team of condescending pricks had requested the job. More often than not, they would complain that the materials hadn't gotten to them quickly enough. Some lawyers even had the balls to complain that their papers had gotten to them *too* quickly — they'd argue that there was no way the boys in the Printers could have handled the document production with proper care and diligence and still gotten it to them so fast.

So Eddie knew which projects to sit on and which to rush; he knew who liked their briefs printed on high-quality watermarked stock and who wanted them on copy paper because he would just red-line the documents with notes anyway. He knew how to get the right job to the right lawyer looking the right way. He might have been mentally challenged, but when it came to his work, Eddie was a savant. He was the Master of the Printers and he didn't suffer incompetence from any of the Blazers working under him.

'Vicellous,' Eddie shouted to a rail-thin black kid hunched over a copier in the corner of the basement office and working furiously. 'You didn't bring these up.' Eddie pointed to a pile of SEC filings in a large wire-mesh basket with wheels that was sitting by the door.

'I'm doin' the briefs for Portnoy,' Vicellous shot back without looking up. 'He said they're a top priority. Where the hell's Ricky Ricardo? Tell *him* to wheel that shit upstairs!'

'Dylan's on a run. You have to follow the system, Vicellous — '

'C'mon, Special Ed,' Vicellous said, his head now buried in a cardboard box that he was filling with briefs fresh from an output tray. He had yet to bother to look at Eddie while he talked to him, but Eddie was used to that; it was just another way of being ignored. 'How many times I gotta tell you to call me Vice. And where the hell's that cracker that's supposed to start today? Make him do it.'

'Cracker's right here, Vicellous,' Rich said.

Vicellous slowly turned to face Rich and Ed.

'Son of a bitch, Special Ed, you gotta tell me when someone else is up in this mothafucka.' He stood and walked over to Rich, put out his bony hand, and gave him a multilayered bro-shake that no white man could possibly keep up with.

'Name's Vice Green,' Vice introduced himself. 'Don't take that cracker remark as an insult. I love me some crackers — Saltines, Ritz, even Britney Spears, once she let her ass get all nice and fat. I'm all about the love, baby.' He flashed a wide, gap-toothed grin.

Almost everyone in East New York, Brooklyn, knew that smile, and they all loved Vice for it. Twenty, black, and with a rap sheet thick as a phone book, Vicellous Green would have been a stereotype if he weren't such a great guy. Vice reveled in making people laugh; he *lived* for it.

If he saw a kid with a scraped knee crying on the corner, before Vice even realized it, he was pulling faces and mugging for the kid until the tears stopped. When his neighbor Miss Claire was dying from all the various things that make old people die, he visited her every day, swapped gossip about the folks on the block, and told her dirty jokes until she cackled her toothless smile that made them both just crack up.

He loved that he could help people forget about whatever kind of pain they were in . . . even if just briefly. The reason Vice loved making people laugh was that it helped him forget about all the pain *he* was in . . . even if just briefly.

Vice was a legend in East New York for not once but *twice* getting the cops to let him go just by being funny. No guns, no running, no weapon but his humor. The first time it happened, a couple of badges from the Seventy-Fifth Precinct had nailed Vice as he was climbing over the back fence of an electronics store he had just robbed. Earlier that day, Mr. Singhal, the owner of the business, told Vice in a heavy Indian accent and in no uncertain terms to get 'his sticky fingers and poor black country ass' out of his store, that his store was for 'paying customers, not welfare babies.' The ironic thing was, Vice actually had money that day and wasn't planning on lifting anything — granted, he had lifted the money from the handbag of a woman sitting next to him on the bus, but he had money nonetheless, and Vice was pissed because there was no reason for Mr. Singhal to embarrass him in front of the fine young ladies who were there shopping for iPods. So Vice struck back the only way he knew how

— he robbed the bastard.

But as he was hopping Mr. Singhal's fence, a pillowcase full of loot over his shoulder like he was some skinny, black reverse Santa Claus, he spotted the cops coming down the alley. Vice rushed his dismount, and sharp metal at the top of the fence caught his inner thigh, making a gash that instantly started to bleed. He fell to the ground and by the time he opened his eyes, the cops were standing over him.

'Get up, Vice,' Spano, the white cop, told him. Every cop in Brooklyn knew Vice.

'Looks like you cut your shit up bad, man,' Hughes, the black cop, said.

Vice looked down at his thigh. There was blood, but he knew he wasn't hurt that badly. So he didn't look at the cut as an injury but as an opportunity. He quickly scurried onto all fours and started searching on the ground.

'What the hell are you doin'?' Hughes asked.

'Shut up, brother, and help me find 'em!' Vice shouted back in mock anguish.

'Find what?' Spano asked.

In his best *Amos 'n' Andy* voice, Vice cried out, 'My *balls*, nigga! They gots to be round here somewhere!'

Vice knew when he was working for a laugh, especially when his ass was on the line, it was good to 'black it up.' Hell, he'd seen Oprah do it when she had black guests on her show, and Hillary Clinton sounded like Florence from *The Jeffersons* when she wanted to pander to an urban crowd, so Vice figured if it was good enough for a billionaire and a politician, it was

41

good enough for him. He'd black it up until he looked like Al Jolson if he had to.

It worked. The cops laughed.

'C'mon, we'll get you fixed up at the station.'

'Hell no! You best be ready to shoot me, Kojak, 'cause I ain't leavin' here till I find my *plums!*'

Vice's delivery and cadence were perfect — the absurdity and charisma of Chris Rock, the conviction of Bernie Mac, all rolled into one five-foot-six, 140-pound frame. The cops laughed harder.

Ah, the gazelles are hobbling, thought Vice. *Time for the lion to strike.*

'C'mon, use your flashlight, guys . . . if you see somethin' that looks like a couple bowlin' balls been rolled across a barbershop floor, those my nuts. Just roll 'em on back to me.'

Vice was shuckin' and jivin', steppin' and fetchin', whatever it took to not get in the back of that cop car. The cops were leaning against their cruiser now, crying.

Vice stood, clapped his hands together.

'Thank you, Officers, and don't forget to tip your waitresses.'

He looked hopefully at the cops, who were now regaining their composure. Vice waited for them to catch their breath, then said, sincerely, 'C'mon, guys, the asshole who owns this joint made me look like a punk in front of some fine ass today. It was a bitch move. I was just pissed.'

The cops looked to each other like parents processing some lame excuse their son had just given them for a bad report card.

'These girls were fine, huh?' Hughes asked.

'Brotha, they could fart in the tub and I'd still drink the water.'

Hughes chuckled again. He looked at Vice for a beat, then picked up the pillowcase of pilfered goods from the ground.

'Mr. Singhal will be happy that we got his stuff back. Shame the perp got away though,' Hughes offered with a knowing look.

That was all Vice had to hear.

'I *love* my boys in blue. Peace out!'

And Vice was gone before the cops could change their minds.

Just eight months later, Hughes and a new partner nailed Vice wheeling a shopping cart with a stolen air conditioner down Atlantic Avenue at 3:30 a.m. in the middle of July. Hughes just looked at Vice and said: 'You got five minutes, kid; make us laugh or you're goin' in.'

Lucky for Vice, Hughes's new partner, Dave Kang, was Korean.

Vice assessed his situation: one hot 5200 BTU Kenmore, two pissed-they're-workin'-night-shift cops, and three seconds to figure out how he was going to respond. Vice didn't need to check the stolen watch on his wrist to know what time it was — it was half-past Vice is fucked. Vice would have to bring the house down if he wanted to skate — the standard dick-and-balls jokes wouldn't fly this go-round. And since desperate times called for desperate measures, he rolled the dice. Hell, he threw them off the fucking craps table.

Vice started by riffing on how Kang was

everyone in East New York's favorite cop because he could never get a positive ID on a perp due to his horrible eyesight. Then he pulled on his temples with his fingers to make Asian eyes, bucked out his two front teeth, and even went so far as to say 'Me so solly' once or twice in a stereotypical Asian accent. It was totally offensive and politically incorrect. It was also funny as hell.

This time, the cops let Vice keep the air conditioner.

Any other perp who'd said the shit Vice had would've gotten Kang's billy club to the side of the head. But everyone in town knew what Vice's life was like. The cops had been called to his house so much when Vice was a kid, they'd practically watched him grow up. They knew why Vice stopped playing Little League — because the one time his drunk-ass father showed up to a game, he nearly beat the kid senseless for striking out. They knew why Vice always played shirts in pickup hoops — because he was ashamed of the scars that the belt had left on his back. And they knew why he was always playing the fool and laughing — because if he didn't, he'd probably be crying.

Vice had eight brothers and sisters, and they all lived in a house of fear. His parents had all their kids trained. Any bruise or mark on one of the children that was questioned by the authorities was quickly explained away by the child as a fall from a bike or a punch from a playground bully.

Vice was the oldest of the kids, so when he was in junior high, Social Services tried to get him to testify against his parents. Vice wouldn't play ball; he may have been young, but he was old enough to know how the system worked. If he turned in his parents, he and his brothers and sisters would be separated, sent to foster homes all over the city where things could be even worse for them. Then one day, his parents would get out of lockup and they'd get their kids back because the system was fucked, and what would happen next — well, nothing would be worse than that. Vice always thought it was best to take the beating you knew rather than risk the beating you didn't.

Even now, when Vice was a grown man, his parents had a hold on him. He still feared them. His father, at thirty-seven, was only seventeen years older than Vice, and since Vice had inherited his mother's small build, Cornelius Green still could, and often did, whip his oldest son's ass. And compared to his wife, Cornelius Green was a pacifist.

So Vice's life was what it was. He lived in the converted basement apartment of his parents' run-down house, took daily verbal and occasional physical abuse, and often lay in bed at night listening to his younger siblings upstairs going through the same hell he had gone through when he was their age.

So most of the cops felt for Vice. They could care less if Vice was a petty crook — everyone in Brooklyn was onto some kinda scam to survive, and Vice's was robbing. He never hurt anybody. He'd get busted once in a while, but half the times the cops would let him hang out in booking until his bail hearing so he wouldn't have to spend the day in county lockup. The cops had been around long enough to know there were a lot of real bad guys in East New York, and Vicellous Green was not one of them. He was just another victim.

But then he got arrested for something he hadn't even meant to do and everything changed. He *meant* to steal the gas for his moped, that was for damn sure. He just didn't mean to forget to take the gas pump's nozzle out of the tank when he sped off. And he sure as hell didn't mean for the irate attendant (who raced after him screaming in Urdu, except for the curse words that were in perfect English) to trip over the pump hose that trailed from the escaping dirt bike. And he certainly didn't mean to hurt Mr. Mohammed Al Mahmoud, but he did, in the form of a compound fracture of the right arm. Vice could have easily gotten away with it, but he couldn't just leave the man lying next to pump no. 3, clearly in pain, so he stopped to help him up.

Then Vice called 911.

And then he waited with Mr. Mahmoud for the ambulance to arrive.

And it did. With the cops.

And then Mr. Mahmoud served up Vice to the authorities.

And then the cuffs came out.

Mahmoud's injury had occurred during the commission of a felony. Under New York law, that meant that Vice, the guy who had been beaten more times than a piñata and had never

46

even raised his fist in self-defense, was arrested and charged with criminal assault.

Vice knew this wouldn't result in a few months in County like all of his other dalliances. With his record, he was looking at a fifteen-to twenty-four-month sentence at least. He knew he was going to do some time. But then he was assigned a very interesting public defender.

Neil Shapiro, Vice's court-appointed attorney, was fresh out of law school, passionate for the law, blindly liberal, and incredibly determined to save the world one oppressed, disenfranchised black man at a time. Vice was Neil's first case . . . *ever*. It was Neil's first day on the job and he had barely filled his pencil holder with freshly sharpened Ticonderogas when Vice's file was dropped on his desk.

What normally would have been a pro forma plea bargain became a lengthy lecture by Neil to Judge Rheingold on the inequities of society's and the court system's treatment of minorities and the disparity in suburban-versus-urban educational systems that gave men like Vice few options. Neil even blamed OPEC for what happened, because if they hadn't been unlawfully colluding to raise the price of a barrel of oil, Vice would have never had to steal the gasoline in the first place.

The ADA didn't know what had hit her. She'd been in the game over a decade and, like most prosecutors, had barely looked at the file prior to the hearing. It was a mismatch — the prosecutor was a veteran apathetic government employee who lived alone and had a bad case of shingles.

She was going up against a twenty-six-year-old idealist who actually thought he could make the city a better place; he was still too young and stupid to know better.

Vice watched his attorney's performance, amazed at what he was seeing. After one especially effective argument, Vice shouted, 'Yeah, you right, Mr. Shapiro . . . you're lawyerin' your ass off!' Vice wasn't trying to be funny. He was just thrilled as hell that someone finally gave a shit about him.

Every plea bargain from the government was rejected by Counselor Shapiro, who was itching to take his first case to trial so he could share his brilliant observations on injustice with a jury. Eventually Judge Rheingold pleaded with Neil, 'Son, the court's resources are too limited to try every case that comes across my desk, but I can't just let your client go. What would you suggest we do?'

Neil thought a moment, then said, 'Let's stop treating the symptoms and treat the cause. Society has made it next to impossible for Mr. Green to make a living. Let's teach a man to fish, shall we?'

So by the end of the day, Mr. Shapiro had made a call to Agatha Warren, a law-school pal whose father was a tax attorney at Olmstead & Taft. Agatha had passed her classes only because Neil shared all of his notes and outlines with her. Agatha owed Neil and now Neil was collecting on behalf of Vicellous Green.

By the end of the day, Vice was the newest employee at the Printers of Olmstead & Taft. In exchange for holding down the job and getting good employee evaluations, which would be forwarded to the judge, Vice got a suspended sentence.

Vice knew Neil Shapiro didn't come into his life by mistake. He was sent from God; Vice was sure of it. He'd always heard the Jews were God's Chosen People, and Vice was certain God chose Neil Shapiro to help Vice get out of the shitty life into which he'd been born.

The Printers offered a steady paycheck. It offered a way out. Vice knew it could change his life.

And he was right. He just didn't know how drastically.

9

Vice wasn't nervous at all when he entered his numbers. He'd committed crimes hundreds of times before — granted, nothing on this scale, but it's not like it was a new thing for him to break the law.

But this was a bit different. In a weird way, he was kind of pleased with himself. It was like he was graduating to a higher level of illegality — white-collar illegality.

Good-bye crowbar and ski mask.

Hello computer and offshore account.

It was just cleaner, higher class, more tasteful.

But despite his upswing in criminality, he didn't want to forget his roots, so he entered 7-1-8 . . . the area code for Brooklyn.

10

'Try this one,' Eddie said, handing Rich a navy blue blazer he pulled from a wall-mounted peg board by the door. Rich put it on. Eddie had a good eye — it actually fit quite well.

'Check out Thurston Howell,' Vice cracked. 'Hey, Dylan, whatcha think of the newest Blazer to join our crew?'

Rich followed Vice's gaze to Dylan, who stood in the doorway. As soon as Rich saw him, his mind was bombarded with a million different thoughts, and not one of them was good. In less than a second all of these thoughts boiled down to one simple idea: *Oh, shit*. And then another thought, this one in the form of a question, quickly arose: *Did this guy follow me in from outside?* And finally: *What the hell kind of name is Dylan for a Puerto Rican?*

Dylan's hand still held the café con leche from the roach coach, and his face still held the intimidating gaze he had flashed at Rich outside on the sidewalk. Dylan knew he had won the earlier showdown in front of the firm and felt there was no need for another, so he broke off his stare and stuck out his hand.

'How you doin'? Think I saw you outside,' he said with the quiet, slow cadence of someone who doesn't like to say too much. Rich could tell right away that Dylan Rodriguez wasn't a talker.

'Yeah, you did,' Rich said as they shook. 'That

was me . . . and my girl,' he added pointedly.

Dylan nodded respectfully, not wanting to make any trouble with the new guy, especially since Dylan himself had been at the Printers for just a few months.

As they disengaged hands, Rich noticed raised scarring on all of Dylan's fingers except for the thumb. Each scar was about the same size.

'Hey, beans 'n' rice, you wanna take this wagon upstairs?' Vice asked Dylan. 'I got my own shit to do.'

'You're up, Vice,' Dylan responded as he stepped to Eddie and helped him file away some papers in Redweld folders. That was all he had to say — the tone of Rodriguez's voice made it clear that he was not a guy you debated with.

'Fine, grouchy wetback,' Vice muttered. 'But I'm hittin' the head first. Gotta drain my nooky-stick. Damn lawyers can wait a few minutes.'

'Don't make them wait too long,' a voice called from the doorway. 'Lawyers can be a real persnickety breed.'

The Blazers turned to discover Max Seymour standing behind them in a gray-striped William Fioravanti with jacquard stitching that only a man who had made his mark in New York could wear. With his salt-and-pepper hair combed back and his aged but distinguished features, he looked like Jason Robards circa early 1980s.

A partner stooping so low as to actually visit the basement office of the Printers was rarer than Halley's Comet. Maybe once or twice a year a partner would send down some frazzled first-year associate to yell and scream and demand documents that hadn't been produced quickly enough for the partner's liking. The Blazers generally enjoyed themselves in these instances — they liked to watch the fresh-out-of-law-school attorney sweat and fret as they finished up the job, knowing that every minute that passed before the partner got his paperwork meant at least two minutes of tirade the rookie counselor would have to endure once he was back upstairs.

Partners liked to yell at people. They didn't really care who the target of their assault was — most just screamed at whoever was closest.

But as much as partners liked to yell, they also liked to beckon. They loved to sit on their thrones in their majestic offices and have things brought to them by lower life-forms. The senior partners enjoyed having briefs brought to them by junior partners. The junior partners enjoyed having documents handed to them by senior associates. The senior associates would demand junior associates carry the papers to their desks. And the junior associates would call down to the Printers and have the paperwork run up to them by the lowly Blazers.

It was Darwinian, a legal food chain.

And it was a system that was rarely, if ever, disrupted. And under no circumstances, not in the almost two decades that Eddie Pisorchek had worked at Olmstead & Taft, had a *partner* been down to the Printers. Not once. Eddie hadn't thought they even knew where the office was.

The Blazers stood slack-jawed. All except Rich.

53

'Hey!' he said, as if they were old pals, because they were.

'There he is!' Max smiled. 'Come on. Let's go up to my office for a minute.'

'Well, only if that's okay with my boss,' Rich said, turning to Eddie. 'That cool, Eddie? Can I run up with Max for just a sec?'

Eddie was almost too stunned to say anything; all that came out was 'Who's Max?'

'I'm Max, Eddie,' the partner said.

'Oh, okay, Mr. Seymour.'

'I'll make the delivery while I go,' Rich offered, moving toward the cart.

'Meet you at the elevator,' Max said.

Rich grabbed the cart's handles, cut the wheels sharply to his right, and headed to the door, but Vice grabbed the front of the basket with both hands, stopping Rich dead in his tracks.

'You high or somethin'?' he asked.

'What?'

'Bringin' a partner down here? This is *our* house. We don't need Suits comin' down here, sniffin' round and shit.'

'I've known Max Seymour since I was a kid. He's my friend.'

'Oh, now I get it,' Vice snipped. 'Same old story, ain't it? *You wash my white ass, I'll wash yours.* What's the word I'm lookin' for?'

'Asshole?' Rich offered.

'No, that ain't it. *Neapolitan*. It's Neapolitan bullshit.'

'It's bullshit from a city in Italy?' Rich asked sarcastically.

54

'You know what he means,' Dylan said. 'Nepotism. He meant *nepotism*.'

'Yeah, that's what I meant, *nepotism*. That's how whitey stays in power. Givin' the jobs to his own.'

'Whitey?' Rich responded. 'Have you looked around this room? Seventy-five percent of the staff down here is black, Puerto Rican, or . . . '

Rich looked at Eddie and decided not to finish the thought. But Vice pounced on the opportunity.

'Oh, now, don't you go insulting Special Ed 'cause he's a mongrel,' Vice snapped.

'The term is *special needs*,' Eddie said, defending himself. 'And yeah, Rich, don't insult me. I'm your boss.'

'I'm not insulting anyone; all I'm saying is, I'm the only powdered sugar on this brownie. And if making photocopies in a basement is what nepotism gets you, you can keep it. Now, if you'll get out of my way, I gotta make my first delivery.'

'Go ahead, Thurston Howell.' Vice stepped to the side, and Rich wheeled the cart past him and out of the room.

Max was waiting at the elevator.

'How do you like your new co-workers?' Max asked.

Rich just raised his eyebrows and shook his head to indicate it was better not to respond. Max got it.

'Yeah, well, don't worry,' he said. 'Before you know it, they'll be running documents to you.'

A bell signaled the arrival of an elevator. Once again, it was Chip's.

55

'Good morning, Counselor,' Chip said to Max, though his eyes never left Rich.

'Chip, I got my protégé with me. He's gonna ride with us.'

Chip didn't protest. He couldn't. But as Rich pushed his cart onto the elevator and felt Chip's glaring eyes burn through him, he couldn't help but think that he'd already made a few enemies in a very short time at Olmstead & Taft.

11

Rich carefully propelled the cart down the hallway of the twenty-third floor. He was literally, as Chip had admonished him earlier, a paper pusher. Max, a notoriously fast walker, was fifteen feet ahead, and Rich was having trouble keeping up. Olmstead & Taft had very wide corridors, but pushing the cart without striking a lawyer or smashing into a wall was not an easy task. The cart was an unwieldy metal beast, a stubborn conveyance with one uncooperative wheel that seemed to want to spin in the exact opposite direction of its other three brethren.

Rich was barely off the elevator before he picked up on how the lawyers at O&T regarded him. The attorneys clearly *noticed* him as he moved down the hall; they just didn't *acknowledge* him. Not a hello. Not a nod in his direction. Not even one of those phony half-smiles you give someone who holds a door open for you. Nothing. They'd just maneuver around him and his basket like people on the street sidestep a homeless man and his shopping cart — head down, no eye contact, disproportionately annoyed by the two-steps-to-the-left inconvenience presented. Some even looked a bit angry that Rich had provided a minuscule hassle to their already busy day.

What a bunch of uptight assholes, Rich

thought. But he was well aware of the irony because he wanted, more than anything, to *be* one of those uptight asshole attorneys in the five-thousand-dollar Zegna suits . . . and if Max Seymour, veteran litigator at Olmstead & Taft, had his way, he'd be calling Rich Counselor in a few years.

Max was a legend in New York — a *real* litigator in a court system that rarely heard the complex business cases anymore because almost all matters were settled prior to or during jury selection. But not when Max was the attorney of record. Max took *everything* to trial.

'A settlement is an official recognition of wasted time and effort. If you're going to go to war, you might as well shoot your gun,' he'd told Rich. 'If you don't go to trial, you're not shooting your gun.' Max was old school. He tried cases. He took verdicts. He threw his balls on the table and always got them back in one piece . . . except once.

Almost two decades earlier, Max represented the estate of a young couple who were killed when the charter boat from which they were fishing got rammed by a drunk boater off of Montauk, Long Island. Max had never handled a personal injury suit before, but Teddy Popodopilis, the small-timer from Suffolk County who had picked up the case through a hospital nurse he'd illegally paid to steer business his way, immediately knew that this particular matter, which dealt with complex maritime law and lost-earnings calculations and actuarial tables, was way too complicated for him. He figured it would be best to find a top-tier litigator to handle the case, so he reached out to Max. He didn't know Mr. Seymour personally but he'd seen his name repeatedly in the *New York Law Journal* and knew his reputation as a bulldog in the courtroom. Popodopilis would hand the client off to Max, Max would do all the work, and Teddy would get one-third of the legal fee for his referral. Plus, Max had always wondered what it would be like to slum in the world of ambulance-chaser litigation . . . and his firm could make a buck or two. It was win-win.

Except Max lost.

He got his balls crushed on that case, as well as his heart.

The intoxicated boater manning the twin-engine had no insurance, and Max couldn't get the charter boat's insurance carrier to pay up because he couldn't prove that the captain had failed to use proper evasive tactics, so at the end of the trial, Max had to tell the couple's ten-year-old son that no one was going to pay for his parents' deaths. What Max didn't tell young Rich Mauro was that his attorney had turned down a $1.2 million offer because he thought he could get more; because the guy who was used to high-end commercial litigation was convinced he could outmaneuver the low-end, no-name insurance-company defense attorney in the cheap suit. And because Max was cocky and sloppy, he was out-lawyered for the first, and only, time in his life.

After the verdict, Max swore to himself that he'd never let the kid down again. He became a constant in Rich's life. Every birthday, every Christmas, Rich got a thoughtful gift and a card with a hundred bucks stuffed inside. Over the years, Max had his firm sponsor Rich's Little League team; he went to Rich's confirmation and his junior high and high-school graduations; and when Rich told Max that he was thinking about following in Max's footsteps through the hallowed halls of the legal profession, Seymour made sure Rich got a blue blazer and a job in the Printers.

The plan was that once Rich finished his undergraduate degree he would take advantage of the Olmstead & Taft Law School Initiative — a program in which any employee who had worked at O&T for at least a full year prior to getting accepted to law school, who stayed gainfully employed at O&T throughout law school, and who kept a 3.0 grade point average would have half of every semester's tuition covered by the firm. And, rumor had it, a job at Olmstead & Taft would be waiting as soon as the ink on the diploma dried.

With Max in his corner, Rich knew that rumor would become reality . . . and it couldn't happen too soon. Though twenty-seven, Rich was just a year into undergrad — he'd gotten a late start on college because he'd had to spend several years working construction with Uncle Jim to save up money for tuition. The plan was that Rich would work at the Printers while finishing his last three years of school at Queens College, then ace his LSATs, get into a New York law school, and keep a 3.0 GPA or, Max said, he'd beat him senseless with a copy of *Prosser on Torts*.

Rich always found it a bit funny, and kind of comforting, that a kid who had lost his mother and father had somehow wound up with two parents anyway — his Uncle Jim, a gentle and caring man who, as far as Rich could tell, had never raised his voice at anyone, and Max Seymour, a gruff courtroom prizefighter who raised his voice at *everyone*. The men couldn't have been more different, but they were, as far as Rich was concerned, his family.

Rich parked the cart by Max's door and followed Max inside the office. He sat in a chair covered by Italian leather so soft, so perfectly crafted, it was as if God had cupped his palm and said: *Take a load off, son, and put your ass here.* A humidor sat in the corner, no doubt holding more than its share of illegal Cuban cigars whose identifying wrappers had been removed because, though Max Seymour was no Boy Scout, he was also no idiot. Artwork from some of SoHo's best young artists dotted the walls.

The place stank of fine leather, hand-rolled tobacco, and money. Rich knew it was going to take some doing, but he couldn't wait to start earning a lawyer's salary — he could *taste* the cash.

The bookshelves behind Max's desk were filled with treatises, case law, and binders of trial transcripts that Max kept as souvenirs of his hard-fought victories, like a cannibal sticking the heads of his victims on spear tips — remembrances of battles past. Framed diplomas hung

61

by the windows. Max had gone to Notre Dame undergrad and law school — he was what Fighting Irish alumni liked to call a double domer, a reference to the golden dome that sits on the top of the esteemed university's main building.

Whenever he was asked why a Jewish kid from Brooklyn had chosen Notre Dame, Max quipped, 'Those guys at Notre Dame pray to a Jew on a cross every day, so I figured if they love him, they'll love me too!' And the Notre Dame community did love Max. A born leader, he was elected president of his class as well as of the *Law Review* before moving back to New York to begin his impressive legal career. To date, Max was the only Jewish student to have held one, let alone *both*, of those honors.

Behind Max's desk were at least a dozen banker's boxers exploding with papers, briefs, depositions, and discovery documents. Each one had an Olmstead & Taft label on it that read KOLBRENNER ET AL. VS. ESTRIN MEDICAL.

'Looks like you got your hands full,' Rich noted.

Max regarded the boxes with disdain and grunted. 'About a hundred plaintiffs are coming after my client, a medical-supply company, saying there's a defect in its new wire scalpel for surgical correction of soft-tissue-contour defects. Been used in almost six thousand procedures over the past three years and ninety-nine percent of the time there has been no issue. The one percent where there is a problem, it's because the idiot doctor misuses the instrument.'

'You think you'll win?'

'Ah, the client wants this one to settle. They think a trial's bad publicity. I'm just building up as strong a case as I can to keep the number down. Should be wrapped up by the end of the year and I can't wait. I wanna get back in a damn courtroom already.'

Max collapsed into the chair behind his desk. He seemed exhausted just talking about the Estrin case.

'How's your uncle?' he asked.

'Good. He says hello.'

'Give him my regards.'

'I will.'

'Hey, how 'bout you and I grab lunch today?'

'I don't think that's a good idea. Kind of got the feeling that Blazers aren't supposed to fraternize with the attorneys.'

'That's crap . . . you come up here whenever you want.'

'I appreciate it, Max. I really do. But I just want to fit in down there, do my job, and keep my grades up so I can get into law school. I don't want any special treatment.'

'Okay, you got it. So get your ass off my chair and get to work,' Max said.

'That's more like it.' Rich grinned.

'But if I can be serious for a minute, Richie, I'm very glad you're taking advantage of this opportunity. I know how excited your uncle is too — he called me last night — '

'He called you?' Rich was beyond surprised.

'Yeah. Damnedest thing. In all the years I've known you, he and I have talked on the phone a

63

hundred times — almost always me trying to track you down. But I don't think before yesterday he'd ever just picked up the phone and called me. Not once. But he was so jazzed up about you starting up here — so thrilled . . . gotta be honest, kid, so am I. Can't wait for the day you and I can walk into court together.'

'You'd be second chair?' Rich joked.

'Already after my job.' Max cackled.

'Speaking of jobs, Ed's gonna have my ass in a sling if I'm gone too long so I better get moving. See you round the office, Max. And thanks, for everything.'

'My pleasure, Richie.'

As Rich moved toward the door, Max called out, 'And, Rich . . . you doing this . . . your mom and dad would be happy you're here. I know I am.'

A small smile curled the corner of Rich's mouth, and he nodded. 'Thanks again, Max.'

Rich left Max's office feeling pretty good about himself but that lasted all of two seconds before he saw that his delivery cart, and all of the important papers it was carrying, was gone. His heart raced.

He had left it right outside; what could have happened to it?

He spun around and saw a young male attorney at the other end of the hallway turning the corner with it. Rich chased after him.

'Hey,' he called out as he caught up with the lawyer, who looked no more than thirty. 'That's okay, I got it.'

The attorney turned toward Rich and sneered.

'No, you don't *got* it. Now I *got* it because I found it, abandoned, in the hallway. Do you know who these documents are for?'

'I assume they're for you,' Rich answered.

'No. I ordered them. But they're for Miles Spade, a partner here, and when they don't get to him on time — '

'He'll come down on you.' Rich finished the thought.

'That's right. And then *I'll* come down on *you*,' the lawyer said. 'You screw up again, you and I are gonna have a problem. Now get these to Miles Spade's office.'

With that, the attorney walked off, and Rich immediately became aware of three things.

One, he couldn't afford even the smallest slipup in this place. Max could protect him, but only so much — and Rich would never want to make Max look bad after he'd shown so much faith in him to begin with.

Two, he was going to have to swallow his pride along with some shit if he was going to work there. If some punk had talked to Rich on a job site like that lawyer had, he would have said about three words before getting himself a love tap across his smart fucking mouth. But this was a different world, and if Rich wanted to succeed in it, he'd have to check his ego at the door.

And last, from the moment he caught up to the attorney who had taken his cart, Rich knew that he knew the guy from somewhere. It had been a long time since he'd seen him but there was something about the man that was familiar. It wasn't necessarily the way the attorney looked

65

or anything he said; it was how he carried himself. The young lawyer seemed to be posturing when he chewed Rich out. He was just *pretending* to be brash. The guy may've had a law degree, but he was only *playing* lawyer. Underneath the veneer, Rich was certain, the associate was quite insecure. It was as if he were just acting out what he had seen others do when dealing with underlings because he himself had never actually had any power over anyone in his life.

Rich had seen that specific combination of insecurity and swagger before. He wasn't sure when, or in what context, but he'd seen it, been around it, and it had come from the same person who had just chastised him in the hallway.

Yes, he was certain he knew the guy from somewhere back in the day. And he was certain he didn't like him.

Rich wasn't sure why, but in his gut, he knew he needed to avoid that young attorney like the plague.

12

The problem was, the plague was everywhere. When delivering documents around the firm, Rich noticed that same lawyer on a few occasions, and the guy was always looking Rich over. Once, when Rich was getting into the elevator, he spotted the guy across the lobby standing in Chip's ride, staring at Mauro as the elevator doors closed, never moving his gaze. It made Rich uneasy. They had just had that single run-in near Seymour's office; why did the guy seem to have such a hard-on for him? Who the hell was this young attorney and what the hell was his problem?

The young attorney's name was Jason Spade, and his problems were many. And Miles Spade, the partner who needed the documents that Rich had been pushing around on the twenty-third floor, was Jason's father. However, Jason often looked at their relationship as nothing more than a legal technicality — something created by statute and legislature, not by blood and love. Their father-son affiliation was just another reason for Jason to hate the law.

Born to a West Virginia waitress, Jason Spade was taken from his mother's womb by the Marshall County Hospital doctor and handed over to a state social worker with tobacco-stained fingers who was waiting just outside the delivery room. The waitress never held her son, and that's how she wanted it, since she had never had any intention of keeping the child. She lived in a single-wide that shook when the coal trains passed — no place for an infant — and she wanted the boy to at least have a chance, even though the Mountain State's resources were limited and bastard children fathered by Wheeling Downs dog-track workers were low on the list of priorities.

But Jason Spade seemed, at least at first, to have a charmed life. Within a week of being born, he was adopted by Miles and Karen Spade, a wealthy couple who took him from the heart of Appalachia to a multimillion-dollar duplex apartment on Manhattan's Upper West Side. They wanted a white child, and the Spades did whatever they had to do to get one. They hired a private adoption service to help navigate the tricky process of bringing a baby into one's home; they retained the best family-law attorney in Manhattan who specialized in such matters, and Miles Spade, unknown to anyone but the Marshall County Social Services clerk who took the envelope full of cash, greased the right palms to make sure everything went smoothly.

The new mother showered the child with gifts and toys and all the things he could ever possibly need and a myriad of things he didn't. The new father tried. He tried to share in the enthusiasm. He tried to share in the love. He tried to share in the raising of Jason in ways other than paying the bills that made the boy's life comfortable.

But the kid wasn't his and he resented it. After all, it wasn't his fault that his wife couldn't bear a

68

child. They'd been to all the doctors, done all the tests. His sperm count was through the roof, twice the average for a man his age — a hundred million per shot; he practically had China in his balls.

But Karen couldn't cut it. At least that's what Miles told himself. Miles was an overachiever. Every challenge he undertook in life, he won. He'd graduated from high school a full year early. He lettered in football and track at Yale. He made *Law Review* at Columbia and was the youngest attorney to make partner in the history of Olmstead & Taft. He had a winner's genes. He knew that. His grandfather was the youngest lawyer involved in drafting the Panama Canal treaty. And he'd thought when he married Karen, a debutante from Great Gatsby country on Long Island's North Shore, that he was partnering with another thoroughbred.

But failed attempt after failed attempt at pregnancy made Miles face the truth — his genes wouldn't be passed on. He considered divorce, but old-money WASPs don't divorce. They cheat on their wives with their secretaries and paralegals, but they don't leave them — it just doesn't look good.

So five years after they were married, Miles found himself in the position of holding a child who was his son but wasn't his son. The kid was just weeks old and was already a disappointment in his father's eyes. And because of who he was, and who he *wasn't*, there was nothing Jason Spade could ever do to change that.

As Jason grew older, he felt the detachment

69

from his father. It was palpable. Early on, he thought he could fix the situation by simply trying harder. Jason played sports like his father had, and though Miles would pay outlandish sums to coaches for private lessons (and to league officials to get his son onto exclusive traveling teams), Jason didn't have the same natural gifts as his father. Where Miles was an A+ athlete, Jason, at the top of his game, was a solid B at best.

Academics were just more of the same. For Jason, understanding concepts and theories was like catching butterflies — you could see them right there in front of you, but actually *grasping* them was next to impossible.

Jason eventually reached a crossroads. He could try harder, put in more time and effort, in the hopes of achieving the impossible standards his father had set for him and thereby finally earning the man's love. Or he could do exactly the opposite of what his father wanted. He could rebel. He could not lift a book through four years of high school, spit on a teacher who dared try to discipline him, and show up at a varsity basketball game so drunk that he threw up on the court during warm-ups. That was the path Jason chose. If he could never please his father, why even try? And once Jason made this choice, a strange thing happened. He got the power.

As soon as Jason started screwing up, getting in trouble at school, getting suspended by various teams, he saw that he had leverage over his father. He saw that Miles Spade would move heaven and earth to make sure that no one bearing the Spade name would be seen as a failure. He refused to let his son embarrass him.

So when, at eighteen, Jason was found stoned in the park getting oral from the school principal's fifteen-year-old daughter (technically a felony in New York), Miles wrote a few checks and smoothed things over. When Jason was caught selling weed out of the back of a local diner, Miles had a talk with the cops, and a generous donation was made to the Police Benevolent Association. When Jason's grades went into the shitter, Miles bought his son's way into Yale.

Jason knew how much his father didn't care for him, but by this point in his life, Jason didn't care much for his father either. A kid can hear 'I wish we'd never brought you home' only so many times before he resents it.

So Jason Spade, the abandoned newborn from Wheeling, eventually became the poster boy for spoiled-rich-kid behavior, which always ended with him having his ass pulled out of the fire by Daddy.

But all of that changed with New Haven.

New Haven was the breaking point for Miles Spade. It had cost him a six-figure endowment gift to get his son into Yale and, by the time Jason was a junior, two more donations to keep him there. So when he got the midnight call that his son had, once again, been arrested by New Haven police, Miles Spade had had his fill. He was not about to get up, get dressed, and drive all the way from Manhattan to Connecticut only to see his son locked up in the drunk tank again, cuffed to a wall-mounted bar with the city's other winos.

'No,' he told their family lawyer, who had received a jailhouse call from Jason. 'Let him spend the weekend in there, teach him a lesson. I'll bail him out on Monday.'

But by Monday it would be too late.

Jason had gone out that night with some frat buddies, gotten way too coked up, and hit on the wrong girl at a bar. Her boyfriend was big, but Jason had coke muscles and went after the guy hard. When the cops arrived, Jason and the boyfriend had wrecked the place, and with at least a dozen witnesses saying Jason had instigated the fight, he was the one arrested. This didn't sit well with Spade, so while being cuffed, he jerked his head backward in protest, smashing his skull into the face of the arresting officer. You could hear the cop's eye socket crack from across the bar.

As soon he did this, Jason knew he had fucked up bad, but after the back-alley beating the cops gave him before hauling him off to the New Haven Correctional Center, he figured his troubles had ended. He was wrong.

He was put alone in a cell in the facility's underground lockups, known as the tombs, for several hours. Spade thought they had left him down there alone so no one else would see the bruises on his face, which were clear evidence of police brutality. He couldn't wait to sic his lawyer father on these bastards. He'd have their fucking jobs. But as the hours passed, Jason began to worry that his father wasn't coming.

Can the old man finally be taking a stand? Jason thought. But then he heard footsteps coming down the dark basement corridor. He relaxed, knowing once again Daddy couldn't allow himself to be shamed by having his only child prosecuted.

But the footsteps didn't belong to his father and family counsel. They belonged to an angry cop with a freshly sutured brow and an eye that had turned purple and swollen shut. The cop wasn't alone. He approached with another inmate — a six-foot-four black junkie with the unmistakable smell of meth on his clothes who weighed a deuce-sixty on a light day.

No words were exchanged as the other inmate was ushered into the cell. The cell door was closed and the cop left, but not before taking one last, long look at Jason with his good eye.

The junkie just studied Spade for a while. Spade stared off into the distance, not making eye contact, trying to look as tough and uninterested as possible. But Jason wasn't tough; he was very scared. And he wasn't uninterested. On the contrary, he was *very* interested in what this guy wanted from him. The heavy silence was eventually broken when the big guy spoke.

'Sorry, kid, but they told me to make it hurt.' Whenever he reflected upon the event, Jason couldn't understand why he jumped up and ran for the door. He knew it was locked — it was a jail, for God's sake. He knew they were alone in a basement cell. And he knew that there was no one out there to help him — in fact, the only ones who could have heard him yell were those who had set up this nightmare scenario in the

73

first place. But when *flight* wins over *fight*, you try to fly, no matter where you are. It's instinctual; reason doesn't come into play.

The junkie was powerful. He peeled Jason off the bars with a hard yank to the shoulder and had him bent over the cell's sink in one swift move. Jason tried to stand up but the weight of the guy was too much. He held Jason down with one hand on the back of his neck and yanked Spade's pants down with the other.

Whatever deal the junkie made with the cops, he was a man of his word. He made it hurt.

And it was not over quickly. The big guy was enjoying it. This was clearly not his first prison rape. He humiliated Jason, making him say aloud 'I'm a faggot' under the threat of even more pain. That was when Jason first realized he was crying: when he tried to speak.

But even then, with an animal of a man thrusting himself inside him, Jason had the clarity to know why he was crying. It wasn't because of the act itself. The physical pain was temporary. It would eventually go away. He was crying because his father had let it happen. His father had never come to get him; he had left him there. He was his son, for Christ's sake, and the son of a bitch had just left him there! *That* pain — the pain of betrayal — that pain would never go away.

Jason never told his father what happened. The cops had banked on the humiliation of the attack silencing the college punk, and they were right. Jason would never breathe a word of this to anyone.

When the cops were offered envelopes from Miles Spade, they happily helped the whole mess disappear, knowing that Mr. Spade's son had more than paid for his crime. The entire ride home, Jason said nothing. He had to sit there, trapped in bumper-to-bumper traffic on I-95, and listen to his father lecture him.

Years passed, and Miles Spade eventually bought his son a law-school degree as well as the unfulfilling job of working as an attorney by his dad's side at Olmstead & Taft. Jason didn't want to work with his father, but there had been another power shift in their relationship and once again the father had the upper hand. Miles had paid for his son's law-school education, but not until after Jason had signed a contract agreeing to repay the six-figure debt, with interest. Miles also held the mortgage on his son's condo and managed the Spade family trust, which provided Jason with an allowance that could be adjusted at Mr. Spade's whim. Jason wasn't capable of taking care of himself in the real world and his dad knew it. Jason became, for all intents and purposes, a kept man.

His life was not his own, and his working at Olmstead & Taft just secured his position under his father's thumb.

Jason often thought about that car ride back to New York from the New Haven police station. He thought about how he had remained silent, how he didn't say anything to his father about what had happened, how he sat there in the car and didn't respond once to any of the verbal abuse his father hurled at him during the entire ride home.

But Jason knew he'd have a response for his father one day. And it wouldn't be with words.

13

Jason Spade didn't have even the slightest hesitation as to what his three numbers should be: 6-6-6. He typed the digits with conviction.

Given what they were trying to pull off, he figured the devil was in the details, so he might as well be in the code as well.

Hell, Jason thought, the devil himself would have approved of what they were doing.

And that didn't bother Jason Spade one bit.

14

Rich's first few weeks at Olmstead & Taft were a blur. It seemed he spent almost as much time out of the basement office as he did in it. The pace was hectic, bordering on frenetic, and it was definitely a lot harder than he'd thought it would be. Working over white-hot copiers, humping twenty-pound boxes of paper across the expanse of the basement, hurrying up and down staircases and across hallways — Rich was breaking a sweat not unlike those he'd worked up in construction. But at least on a job site, the union guaranteed a certain number of breaks and a lunch hour.

At the Printers, they ate while they worked unless there was a brief lull in the paper traffic, which was rare. Documents were e-mailed to them at a pretty rapid pace, but amazingly, Eddie Pisorchek had the office humming.

He'd format each job as soon as it reached his computer. When formatting was complete, he'd send it to the right machine for printing, which depended on whether it was a straight-up text document, a document with visual aids, or a combination of both. Whatever the lawyers needed, the Printers provided.

Once the data was embedded in the right piece of equipment's hard drive, either Vice or Dylan would get to work. They'd press buttons, adjust paper stock, enter client codes (so O&T

could be certain to charge the client for the cost of the document production at a generous markup), and generally prepare the machinery to crank out the job in pristine condition. If there was so much as a smudge or a single typo in the final product, the lawyers would find it. They *always* found it. Then, not only would the Blazers have to do the job over again, but the attorney handling the case would rip them all brand-new assholes. Therefore proofreading was essential at the Printers, and for a group of guys who seemed to have little or no education, Rich's coworkers were amazingly thorough.

As the newest member of the team, Rich often got the grunt work: wiping down and cleaning the machines at the end of the day when the other Blazers had left, which was usually around midnight but could vary depending on the demands of the Suits upstairs. Some days Rich would double up his hours to make up for the time he missed when he had class, but some nights they were so busy he'd have to skip class and borrow notes from one of the students.

Rich knew he could have asked Max Seymour for a break in hours, and a call would have been made the same day and his schedule would have been accommodated, but Rich had already gotten enough of a leg up from Max and wanted to do the rest on his own — even if it meant fifteen-hour shifts followed by five hours of studying and, if he was lucky, four hours of sleep, not to mention seeing Elyse less and less.

And though he missed the time he normally spent with his girlfriend, Rich didn't mind the long hours or even the grunt work. He actually enjoyed it; it was a simple task — bottle of cleaning solution in one hand, scratch-proof rag in the other, spray, wipe, repeat. He'd spend that quiet time thinking about how one day he'd actually understand the documents these machines spat out, just like the men in the offices hundreds of feet above him did; he'd be able to tell his children about his humble beginnings in the Printers and working his way up to lawyer, maybe even partner.

On one particular evening, after getting some peanut butter off a console — Rich was pretty sure Eddie was the culprit — Rich cleared a paper jam, then crumpled the ink-stained pulp and took a fadeaway jumper at the corner garbage can. He bricked it off the rim.

'You never could shoot,' a voice said behind Rich, startling him. When he turned, he found the young attorney he had had the run-in with on the twenty-third floor.

Rich was instantly concerned. This guy had been giving him the stink-eye for weeks and now he was showing up in the basement, after hours. What the hell reason could he possibly have for coming all the way down there? Rich was certain he was about to be fired.

'I'm sorry?' he asked the lawyer.

'You were a great defender, tough as hell, but you could never shoot.'

Clearly the guy knew Rich — seemingly from their basketball days — but Rich was struggling to place the man's face. They hadn't played together on the same high-school team. He wasn't anyone from the playground games near his house — one look at the guy and you could tell he'd learned the game by shooting at hoops with glass backboards and white nets in some private school's gymnasium. He'd never played a city pickup game in his life.

Rich tried to remember if he'd done any document runs up to this attorney — but there were hundreds of lawyers in that building and you could go years without seeing some of them or coming across their names. No, he had no idea who the man was.

'I can see you're struggling. Lemme help you out,' the lawyer said, extending his hand. 'Jason Spade.'

And then it all came back to Rich. He had played ball against Jason in a few all-city basketball tournaments about a decade earlier, when they were in their teens. Jason was an average player and he shot way too much for a guy with his ability, or *inability*, to hit the mark. Rich never understood how Jason made some of the all-star teams he did — he just wasn't good enough. In games, he carried himself with the forced bravado of someone who knew that he didn't belong on the court with the other players, not unlike the false bluster he'd pulled in the hallway that day with Rich.

Rich received Jason's handshake. 'Rich Mauro.'

'Yeah, I know. Remembered the name as soon as I remembered the face. And I've been trying to place your face since the day we ran into each other upstairs. It's been driving me crazy.'

'Oh, man.' Rich shook his head, relieved. 'I've

81

seen you checkin' me out. I thought I was in trouble or something.'

'What? No.' Spade laughed. 'I'm just getting senile and I was trying to figure out how the hell I knew you. So, what are you doing down here?' Spade asked, though the answer was pretty damn obvious.

'Working,' Rich said, holding up the rag as proof. He knew where the conversation was heading and he didn't want to go there, but it was too late because Jason dove right in.

'Yeah, I mean, obviously. Just, how the hell did that happen?' The guy had the tact of a loud church fart.

Not all of us are born rich, you stupid asshole, Rich wanted to say. But he couldn't. Whether Rich liked him or not, Spade was a lawyer at the firm, so he couldn't tell the guy to go to hell. Also, Rich could only assume Jason's dad was O&T partner Miles Spade. Jason could do the math. Jason was, as Vice would say, a product of 'Neapolitan.' So Rich decided to be smart and kept his tongue in check.

'Well, you know, going to night school now, hoping to use the O and T Law School Initiative to get my JD one day,' Rich said.

'Oh, that's great. Good for you,' Jason responded, as if Rich were eight and had just told him he wanted to be president of the United States. 'Well, I was upstairs working on an LBO . . . do you know what an LBO is?' Rich didn't think Spade meant to be condescending, but he wasn't sure.

'No,' he answered.

'It's a leveraged buyout. Complicated stuff. Anyway, I was working on this LBO when it hit me like a ton of bricks — where I knew you from. And then I instantly felt horrible about the dustup we had. If I'd known it was you, a friend from back in the day, I would've never blown up like that.'

'Well, I did leave it unattended in the hall for a few minutes.'

'Oooh,' Spade said with mock distress. 'We should have you beheaded for such an offense. Let me be honest — I was a dick. So do me a favor and let me apologize the right way — I'll take you out for drinks tonight.'

'Oh, I appreciate it, but I don't really drink,' Rich lied. He was exhausted and had studying to do — the last thing he needed was a night out with a guy he hardly knew.

'Well, you can watch me drink then.' Jason smiled as he walked toward the exit by the loading-bay doors, where trucks dropped off shipments of copy paper and, sometimes, new equipment. He stopped when Rich hesitated. 'What's the problem?'

'Nothing. I'm just beat — I was studying all day between shifts; I got class tomorrow before my night shift; I should really get some sleep.'

'Sleep's for guys who get paid by the hour, Mauro.'

'I do get paid by the hour.'

'For now. But you just said we're going to be colleagues one day, right? So let's grab a beer. We'll catch up, and I'll fill you in on this place; it'll be good for you. You'll learn more about O and T in one night with me than you will in one year in this basement. I'll tell you everything about this firm.'

Rich knew he needed to get home and hit the books and then hit the sheets. But Spade was offering him something important — an insider's look at the firm. Max had told Rich volumes about it, but Max was older and had worked litigation only for over thirty years. But from Spade, Rich could get a young attorney's point of view on all of the various departments within the firm, who the best partners for a new associate to work with were and which were the ones to avoid, and how a rookie lawyer could get the plum assignments.

I'll drink my beer and then take off, Rich thought. He didn't figure he'd be out long, since there really wasn't much for them to 'catch up' on.

Besides, it was one night out.

What could be the harm?

The harm, it turned out, was substantial . . . more than Rich could have ever imagined . . . and it was beyond repair.

15

Rich and Spade exited the O&T building, and Rich instinctively turned right.

'Where the hell are you going?' Spade asked.

'I figured we'd go to one of the bars over on Maiden.'

'So we can hang out with lawyer losers and fund faggots?' Spade scoffed. 'I got a place, little bit uptown. C'mon.' Spade opened a door to a waiting Lincoln Town Car. Rich was slow to get in. 'Relax,' Spade said reassuringly, 'it's being charged to a client. Just ask me what Dionysus Corp. is.'

'What do you mean?'

'Just ask me what Dionysus Corp. is.'

'Okay. What's Dionysus Corp.?'

'It's the company I'm doing the LBO for. There, we just talked business. Now the car's a valid expense. So get in before it runs out of gas.'

Rich climbed into the back, followed by Spade.

Rich said, 'How ya doin',' to the driver, and Spade told him the address of where they were going, but the man didn't respond. Like most Slovakian drivers in New York, he barely spoke English and drove like he was still on the dirt roads of a small town in Eastern Europe — that is to say, way too fast and with barely a passing acknowledgment of street signs.

As they drove, Rich's cell rang. It was Elyse.

'Hey, babe,' Rich answered.

'Hey yourself. I thought maybe you forgot about me.'

'Yeah, sorry about the phone tag. I've just been cramming for this exam I have next week — Japan from Eve to Modernization — damn history requirement . . . '

'Well, why don't you come by tonight? I miss you. Between work and school I never see you anymore.'

'Can't. I'm going out for drinks with one of the attorneys . . . '

Spade gave Rich an *attaboy* wink.

'Wow, look at you, Mr. Big Shot.' Elyse laughed. 'Okay, but I want you in my bed, snuggled up watching reruns of *The Office* this weekend. And that's an order, Counselor.'

'You got it,' Rich promised. 'Love ya. Bye.'

As Rich hung up, he realized that the driver had boxed the car around and was heading up the FDR Expressway; they had already passed Houston and were well into the Thirties.

'I thought you said it was just a little bit uptown?'

'Don't worry about where it is.' Spade grinned. 'Just get ready to have a good time. And turn that phone off — girlfriends don't come into play tonight.'

Rich pocketed his cell phone, but he didn't turn it off. He watched the moonlight on the East River race alongside the car. No matter how fast the Slovakian drove — had to be close to eighty miles per hour — the moonlight kept up. Spade didn't say much — he spent most of his time texting or reading e-mails, commenting on the people communicating with him with such insights as 'What a putz this guy is' and 'Yeah, in your dreams, pal.'

But Rich didn't really listen. He was too busy watching the water. He was thinking what he often did when he stared at the river: If you followed it up past Roosevelt Island, around the northern tip of Queens, past the four hundred thirteen acres of prime waterfront real estate known as Rikers Island, under the Whitestone and Throgs Neck Bridges, into the Long Island Sound, past the mansions of Eatons Neck and Lattingtown that overlooked the water, and, finally, all the way out to just off the most eastern tip of Suffolk County and then used nautical measurements that make finding such seemingly ephemeral locations possible, at the intersection of a specific latitude and longitude, you'd get to the exact spot where his parents had died.

The current had long ago pushed along the specific water molecules that had wrapped around and embraced his parents' lifeless bodies, but Rich knew those particular microscopic bits of hydrogen and oxygen, bonded together by chemistry and bonded to Rich by tragedy, were out there somewhere, somewhere down below, swirling around — maybe sucked into the sky by evaporation one day only to be rained down like tears the next.

He felt that as long as he stayed in New York, near the water, he was always near his mother and father — he knew it was an illogical way to think, but it made him feel better. So he embraced the notion. And as a result, he often found himself comforted by the river and by holding his palm out when it rained.

He was so deep in thought, hypnotized by the swirling blackness churning away below the expressway, that he didn't notice that the car was turning off at an exit.

'We're past Columbia,' Rich commented. They had been in the car a good half hour, if not longer.

'We sure are,' Spade commented, amused. A few minutes later, they were getting out at 130th and Broadway. Rich had barely exited the car when the Slovakian peeled away, eager to get out of an area of Harlem he'd no doubt been told by his fellow expatriates was no place for a white guy after dark. Rich agreed.

'What are we doing all the way up here?' Rich asked.

Spade clapped his hands together and headed across the street toward an old brownstone. 'Just getting started, Richie, just getting started' was his answer as he gave Mauro an excited slap on the back.

They approached the building's broken-down stoop, where a very dark-skinned Dominican manned the door. The guy's hair had been treated; it was parted in the middle and combed straight down on either side of his head.

'What's the ticket price tonight, bredda?' Spade asked as if they were old friends.

'Three,' the man said sharply, indicating clearly that they were not.

Spade peeled off three hundred-dollar bills from a wad in his pocket and gave them to the

Dominican. Rich's face must've betrayed his thoughts because Spade said, 'Don't worry, I got it, bro. Least I can do after being such a douche in the hallway,' then disappeared through the door.

Rich took a quick look at the Dominican, who was busy adding the cash to a fat wad in his jacket pocket. As he did this, Rich saw the hint of a gun strapped to the man's torso. His gaze must've lasted a bit too long because when he looked back up he found the Dominican staring him down.

'Go with your friend, captain,' he said, a combination of order and advice that made Rich uneasy, so he quickly stepped inside.

It was like nothing Rich had ever seen before. The place was packed and even though you couldn't hear a sound when you were on the front stoop, as soon as you stepped into the foyer you were hit with oppressively blaring rap music. It wasn't that new hip-hop crap that was as much techno and sampling as it was rap; this was old-school eighties vibe — Rich was pretty sure it was Eric B. and Rakim, though he couldn't be certain, as he was more of an R & B guy.

He made his way through the semidarkness, the only illumination the flashing colored lights that corresponded to the beat of the music and the flicks of lighters torching up the occasional Treasurer, Dunhill, or other high-end cigarette. But despite the expensive tobacco, as well as the other smoking products whose scent hung heavy in the air, this was not a poseur, rich-kid rave for spoiled college brats so they could tell people that they'd partied in Harlem when all they'd really done was hang out with the same douche bags they always hung out with, just fifty blocks farther north than usual.

No, this was the real deal. Rich had worked on enough government construction jobs refurbishing low-income housing to know. The right clothes, the right tattoos, the right look and attitude of very hard men, not to mention some of the women, made it obvious to Rich that Spade had taken him to a legitimate gangbanger party. Granted, there was a spattering of white kids — some women who were clearly models, a few Wall Street types, even an actor from a bad police-procedural show Rich recognized. But they were there because they had money. Whoever ran this thing was smart; he let word get out to the wannabes that they were welcome, but there was a steep cover charge, and the booze, women, and drugs were probably marked up 50 percent — but that was fine for the Wall Street, private-school crowd. They just wanted a safe way to observe the wildlife — like a drive-through safari: you can look and get close, but make sure you keep your hands inside the windows.

Rich went to a bar, which was nothing more than an old door spanning the gap between two couches. He ordered a scotch from an incredibly attractive Asian bartender and got half a plastic cup's worth of rotgut for fifteen dollars. He gave the girl a twenty and she made change and dropped the extra five in her tip jar without asking.

'Another twenty and you get a tasty with that.'

'Um . . . okay.' Rich had no damn idea what a tasty was but he didn't want to seem like a guy who didn't belong there, though it was clear that he didn't. He dug into his pocket and pulled out another twenty. The Asian took it and then snatched a young girl who was helping her behind the makeshift bar. The girl couldn't have been more than nineteen. The Asian pulled the girl's head back by her hair and began making out with her. Rich didn't know what to do — he had figured a tasty was some kind of liqueur concoction with a piece of fruit shoved in it, not a girl's mouth with another girl's tongue shoved in it. He just stood there — he wasn't sure what Emily Post would suggest a party guest do when confronted with an unexpected interracial, barely legal lesbian sex show, but he assumed just walking away would be rude.

The moment ended with the Asian running her hand over the nineteen-year-old's breasts for a moment or two before finishing the kiss. She turned to Rich with a gleam in her eye. 'Mmmm.' She smiled. '*Tasty*. You wanna see a nasty? Forty dollars.'

'Yeah, yeah, give us a nasty,' Spade shouted, appearing seemingly out of nowhere. He threw his arm around Rich. 'See, you've already found something to do, you little pervert.'

'I didn't know what it was,' Rich said to him before turning back to the bartender. 'And I'll take a rain check on the nasty, but thank you.'

'You sure?' Spade laughed. 'It involves a drink stirrer.'

'I thought we were going to talk about the firm,' Rich shouted over the music. 'I can barely hear my own voice in this place.'

'We are, we will. I promise, bro,' Spade shouted back. 'Want you to meet someone first. C'mon.'

Before Rich could answer, Spade was off. Rich had to move quickly through the crushing crowd just to keep up with the lawyer, who seemed to suddenly be quite energetic. Rich couldn't be sure, but he wouldn't have been surprised if Spade had put something down his throat or up his nose during the few minutes they were separated. Spade kept looking back over his shoulder, waving Rich on like a little kid beckoning his pal to follow him to the swimming hole. But this party felt more like following Spade down the *rabbit* hole.

As Rich passed the kitchen he noticed two things. First, there was no faucet in the sink — the plumbing was missing completely, and from the corrosion around the little remaining piping, it appeared it had been torn out some time ago. Second, there seemed to be another Dominican, this one extremely muscle-bound, by the back table, a large Hefty bag at his feet. Two thin women in their twenties handed him money, and he reached into the garbage bag and handed them a small glassine envelope. A few stragglers hung out behind the two women, waiting their turn.

He caught up to Spade as he descended a back basement staircase. Rich followed; the walls leading down were covered with graffiti tags. At

92

the bottom of the steps, the same Dominican that had been at the front stoop stood guard.

How the hell did he get down here so fast? Rich thought. He hadn't seen the guy come in the brownstone upstairs, but then again, Rich had been kind of distracted by the tasty.

'He's with me,' Spade said, motioning to Rich. The Dominican mouthed, *Go 'head*, revealing a large gold front tooth. Rich realized it wasn't the same man from the stoop — but it was clearly his twin brother. Same complexion, same straightened, greasy hair, same terrifying eyes. If it weren't for the gold tooth, you'd never be able to tell them apart.

They passed into a room that seemed to have sofas everywhere. The furniture was definitely out of place — while the upstairs couches and furnishings were beaten up and clearly second-hand, the basement's leather sectional, away from the dancers and crowds, was distinctly more upscale. The liquor bottles, lined neatly along a side runner, were all top-shelf. And although the music had been blaring incessantly above, here it was absent — though you could hear the muffled thump of bass penetrating through the ceiling. The most conspicuous sound was a strange, droning hum that came from somewhere underneath the stairs amid the quiet tones of hushed conversation.

Sitting in the middle of the central piece of the sectional was the man who was clearly the boss. The boss of what, Rich had no idea, but the man obviously commanded respect. He was in his early thirties, several years older than almost anyone else in the building. He was tall, muscular, well shaven save for a soul patch and some stubble on his chin. He wore a black oxford tucked into designer jeans. A gold crucifix hung from his neck. Everyone in the room seemed to revolve around him, but he didn't move.

Jason Spade sat across from him. Rich remained standing.

'Manny Espinoza,' Spade said. 'This is an old friend, Rich Mauro. Rich, this is Manny. He's a promoter. He puts these parties together all over the city.'

'How ya doin'?' Rich offered, distracted as his eyes landed on what was making the noise under the stairs — a large generator with wires sticking out of it in all directions, all of them plugged into a fuse box. *A generator providing electricity. Plumbing fixtures torn out of the kitchen.* The brownstone had obviously been abandoned a while ago — likely one of the countless foreclosures sweeping through the city since the housing market collapsed.

'That thing there,' Manny said, 'a hundred bucks and it can provide enough electricity for a whole week's worth of crazy.'

Rich was instantly struck by Manny's voice. It was gravel mixed with knives; Barry White gargling stone — if a rock quarry could talk, it would sound like Manny Espinoza.

'So whose place is this?' Rich asked.

'Shit if I know.' Manny snorted. 'United Bank of Bullshit. Come six a.m. I'm outta here.' A bunch of Manny's boys laughed along. 'Mauro,

94

huh? Tell me, what's an Eye-talian from, lemme guess, *Queens* doin' all the way up here?'

'Askin' myself the same thing,' Rich said.

Manny laughed loudly. So Spade did too. In fact, everyone was laughing except for Rich, who noticed that the gold-toothed twin had moved from the bottom of the steps to a chair closer to the sectional. Rich figured if his brother outside had a gun, Gold Tooth would have one as well. The whole situation just made Rich uneasy.

'Whattya drinkin'?' Manny asked.

'Scotch.'

Manny motioned to Gold Tooth, who brought Rich a scotch in a heavy, etched Ralph Lauren glass and took the plastic cup that Rich was holding.

'Upstairs, I have the girls selling piss. That's the good stuff,' Manny said, raising his glass.

'Thanks,' Rich responded, as he motioned to Manny and Gold Tooth. 'You two aren't gonna offer me a tasty also, are you?'

Rich was just trying to lighten the mood, but when the room instantly went quiet he realized he had made a mistake. Spade paled. Rich, sensing he had seriously miscalculated, was about to explain that he was just kidding, but before he could get a word out, Gold Tooth was stalking toward him — 'You sayin' I'm a homo, white boy?'

He grabbed Rich by the shirt and drove him toward the wall. Rich could hear everyone yelling but his adrenaline was pumping so hard he had no idea what anyone was saying. He instinctively clutched Gold Tooth by the throat, squeezing as hard as he could. He could feel the man remove one hand from Rich's shirt; Rich was certain he was going for a gun somewhere in his waistband.

It all happened in less than two seconds. He couldn't believe this — he'd been in the Printers just an hour earlier, doing his job, minding his own business, and now he was about to get shot to death by a Dominican in the basement of an underground rave. *Fuckin' Spade*.

But at the exact moment Rich became certain that his future was not only quite bleak but quite short, Manny's voice rang out.

'Let him go. *Now!*'

Gold Tooth instantly let go of Rich's shirt with his one hand — Rich wasn't sure if the other hand had been going for a weapon or not. It may have been survival instincts or the inability of his body to process what his brain was telling him to do, but Rich's hands were still around Gold Tooth's neck. He was no longer squeezing hard, but he hadn't yet let go.

Manny stepped in, and gently peeled back Rich's fingers.

'The man was just making a joke,' Manny said calmly, staring Rich straight in the eyes. 'Ain't that right, Richie?'

Rich nodded. 'Just makin' a joke. No offense intended.'

'Now go get a drink and chill the hell out,' Manny told Gold Tooth, never taking his eyes off Rich. Gold Tooth reluctantly walked off, staring at Rich the whole way.

Manny studied Rich for a minute. 'My man, funny Eye-talian from Queens — just like Ray

96

Romano — 'cept here's the difference.' He leaned in and whispered into Rich's ear. 'Everybody *doesn't* love you here. You need to get your ass outta Dodge while your blood's still pumpin'. And do yourself a favor: don't ever kid about a Dominican's sexuality . . . and don't go north of a Hundred Twenty-Fifth Street again.'

Rich nodded. 'Deal.'

16

The French fries were thin slices of salty heaven.
And the Diet Coke washed over his taste buds
like a mouth-gasm. *It only takes one brush with
imminent death to make you appreciate the
simpler things in life*, Rich thought as he chowed
down on the diner food. But though happy to be
alive, he was still good and pissed at Spade.

'C'mon, man, I had no idea that guy was
going to go loco,' the lawyer defended himself.

'Yeah, well, he did,' Rich answered, sincerely
mad.

'I know. I almost pissed *my* pants and he
didn't even touch *me*.'

Rich kept eating and didn't look up.

'C'mon, bro,' Spade pressed, trying to lighten
the mood. 'You have to admit, that was just a
little bit epic. Now you have a story to tell.
You'll be dining out on that tale the rest of your
life.'

'You might like hanging out with drug dealers
and gangbangers, but it's not what I do.'

'They're not drug dealers. You think real drug
dealers would let us into their spot?'

'I saw a guy in the kitchen — '

'They sell a little X for the parties. So does
every NYU club in Greenwich Village,' Spade
argued. 'And, yes, there were a few bangers in
there, but Manny uses 'em for security — makes
sure the honkies feel safe comin' up to spend

their hard-earned Yankee dollars at the Cotton Club, so to speak.'

'Yeah, well, I didn't feel too safe when that metal-mouth freak grabbed me . . . *so to speak*. So I'm gonna finish my food, head home, and, as far as I'm concerned, you and I are officially *caught up*. Take it easy, Jason.'

Rich took a last bite and stood to go but Spade reached out.

'Hold on, man . . . I just wanted to show you a little fun tonight. Don't go . . . *please*.' It sounded as if Jason Spade hadn't ever said the word *please* before — like it was a foreign dialect that his mouth was struggling with, like the word was barbed and cut his lips upon exit. But there was something in Spade's eyes — Rich identified it: it was desperation.

Why the hell did this guy want Rich to stay so badly? Rich wanted to find out. He was curious. So he sat. And Jason talked.

'Look, Rich . . . I wasn't honest with you earlier, back at the firm. I knew who you were about five minutes after we ran into each other that day. I just hesitated to come see you because it was kind of weird — you know, I hadn't seen you in so many years, and then when I do, I chew you out . . . ' Spade paused, then continued. 'The point is, it was good to run into someone who didn't know me as Miles Spade's son, you know? Everyone at the firm, man, they look at me like I'm a freeloader, like if it wasn't for my old man I'd be giving grippers for crack behind the Winn-Dixie or something. I'm a good lawyer, I've worked hard at my trade, but I get less respect than Rodney fuckin' Dangerfield around the office because of my last name. I've been at Olmstead and Taft for three years now — wanna know how many times I've been out with someone from work? Once. And tonight was it.'

Rich was right; Spade *was* desperate — desperate for a friend. Rich was still pissed as hell at him, but he couldn't help but feel some pathos for the guy who had everything except a single person who liked him in a firm of one thousand lawyers. It was kind of like that one year when Rich was eight and his dad coached his Pop Warner football team. Every time the play called for Rich to get a handoff, kids grumbled that the coach was playing favorites. Not really a good analogy, but probably the closest thing Mauro could find that he and this rich kid from uptown had in common. His anger softened a bit.

'Tonight was stupid,' Rich started.

'Absolutely, man. Total miscalculation on my part. I wanted to show you something really cool. Something, I don't know, that maybe — '

'Something that maybe the rube from Queens hadn't seen before,' Rich offered lightly.

'Guilty.'

'I've seen crowded house parties before, and drugs, and chicks making out with each other. Well, that last one I've only seen on the Internet.'

Spade laughed, spitting some of his soda back into his glass.

'Look, Jason. I appreciate it. It was just not my speed. When I wanna go out, I hit a pub and watch a ball game,' Rich said.

'Message received — and I'm sorry, man,' Spade apologized sincerely. 'Let me make it up to you. That girl you were talking to on the phone during the ride up here, what was her name again?'

'Elyse.'

'Right. Let's you, me, and Elyse go to dinner. We'll hit the River Café in Brooklyn — food's as good as the view.'

'Jason, I appreciate it, but you and I are in *very* different economic situations right now. I can't sit down at a place like that . . . '

'It's on me. A way of saying sorry for almost getting you killed by some crazy Dominican . . . '

'I'm not comfortable with you always paying . . . '

'Fine, then we'll hit a hole-in-the-wall with bad pasta and rubber chicken. You gotta eventually say *yes* because I'm just gonna keep asking until you do.'

Jason Spade meant it. He really wanted Rich to like him. He *needed* Rich to like him. And since Rich couldn't help but feel sorry for the guy, he agreed to the dinner.

Besides, Elyse was always saying they needed to meet new people. Maybe she'd like Jason Spade.

17

Elyse hated Jason Spade as soon as she met him.

He was wearing horn-rimmed glasses, a designer belt, and shoes that were supposed to look 'shabby casual' but had clearly cost at least half a grand. And he was dropping his *n*'s and strategically replacing some *th's* with *d's* — a lame effort to ingratiate himself with Rich by copying his Queens accent.

Hey, Richie, what are you thinkin' about dat appetizer? I'm goin' with the asparagus.

It made Elyse sick, it was so obvious that Jason was desperate for Rich to like him — the boy of privilege who seemed to think it was novel to have a blue-collar friend. But for the most part she kept her opinion to herself. Since she'd known Rich, he hadn't really socialized much. He spent almost all of his time working, studying, or going to night school.

When he wasn't doing those things, he was with her. She had met a few guys he knew from Astoria, neighborhood guys, but they were acquaintances, not friends. She liked seeing Rich joke around with someone; someone who knew Rich when he was younger, an attorney who could look out for Rich in his new career long after Max Seymour had retired. So when Spade's smarminess oozed a bit too much for her taste, she bit her tongue.

Spade spent more and more time with them. If

it wasn't a dinner, it was a movie. If not a movie, a Yankees game. If not a game, something else.

But Rich made sure to get Jason to focus every so often. He'd have the lawyer bring some case books down from the firm library late at night, after hours, and Rich would make Spade show him how to read and brief a case, how to analyze and break down statutes, how to identify the specific legal issue in a particular fact scenario. Jason hated doing it at first, but Rich insisted.

'By the time I get to law school, I'll be ahead of the curve,' he'd argue when Spade would insist he was too tired to play tutor.

'By the time you get to law school, the students will think you're one of the professors.' Jason laughed.

'Ha, funny. Just for that, I want you to do two more cases with me before we go out.' Rich could always hint at the threat of no social activity if he didn't feel Spade was helping him enough with his informal pre-law studies.

Rich knew that Spade was using him, in a sense. The guy was lonely and, from what Rich could tell, he was Jason's only friend. Rich was content to fill that role, but he wanted something in return — just the smallest impartment of knowledge so that when Rich finally did make it to law school, he wouldn't be going in blind.

And after a while, even though Jason always complained about being the Miracle Worker to Rich's Helen Keller, Jason started to like it too. They'd talk about all the bizarre twists and turns the law could take, all the intricacies of modern-day jurisprudence, and for the briefest of moments, Spade didn't hate being a lawyer so much. But the feeling was fleeting and then he'd just want to hit a bar.

In fact, Rich quickly learned that almost everything he did with Jason eventually led them to a bar.

One night, at a club in the meatpacking district, just a half a block from the West Side Highway, Spade pulled Rich off to the side. They both had a few drinks in them. Spade lit up a joint, offered Rich a hit. For the hundredth time, Rich refused, but that never stopped Spade from asking.

That was the one thing that bothered Rich about Spade — the drugs. Rich had smoked pot a few times, had never ever seen cocaine, and was overall opposed to the notion of narcotics. But Jason seemed to like to dabble, maybe even more than dabble. But it's not like the guy was a junkie, and he never got out of control when they were hanging out — and Rich wasn't about to tell someone how to live his life. Spade took a hit and respectfully exhaled away from Mauro's face. He nodded to Elyse dancing with Cyndi, Jason's girl of the week, one in a string of rotating piece-of-ass bimbos he always seemed to have at his disposal.

'Look at them. Look at how hot they are.'

'Pump the brakes, partner — one of them's mine.'

Rich watched Elyse dance for a moment and damn it if it still didn't shock him that she was indeed his. After all this time, it never ceased to amaze him that this woman was with him. She

104

moved across the club — not the best dancer; she didn't have to be. But she had grace, and class, and natural beauty. Her gorgeous face partially lit by a strobe light, her long hair dancing along with her — she caught his eye for a moment as she spun around, and she gave him a smile. He smiled back. Spade noticed.

'Yeah, I know which one is yours. The sweet one; the educated one; the smart one. I got the idiot with tits.'

He pointed to Cyndi, who had somehow caught her heel under a bar stool. She tried to pull it free, looking like a deer caught in fencing.

'Yeah, well,' Rich said, 'that's your choice. You could get a smart girl if you wanted one.'

'Why would I want that? Girls like Elyse, they're hard to keep, my man. Hard to keep. But you know what I mean — I'm sure that thought's kept you up a night or two.'

The comment just hung there for a moment, but before Rich could respond, Spade was dancing across the room to his date, who had managed to free herself by slipping her foot from her shoe.

Rich wove through the crowd to Elyse just as some slow-groove remix of an eighties R & B love ballad began to play. It was bad rap over a semi-catchy sampled hook and lacked any semblance of creativity or artistry, but it was an excuse for Rich to dance with his girl and that was all he needed.

'Hey, you,' she said, wrapping her arms around his waist.

'Hey,' he said back, his mind elsewhere, still

thinking about what Spade had said. *Girls like Elyse, they're hard to keep.* Why would he say something like that? What did he mean?

Rich was sure it was nothing — the meaningless ramblings of a half-drunk, half-stoned twenty-something-year-old in a club. But as he swayed to the music with the woman he loved, Rich found himself holding Elyse just a little bit closer, a little bit tighter.

18

As the months passed, Rich got used to the pace at the Printers and got the hang of things there. He had figured out how to work the equipment to lighten Eddie's load a bit; he was quick putting the documents together, and he was never late with a delivery. When things got slow, he'd pull some boxes together to form a makeshift desk, lay out his books, and study for his night-school classes. When things got crazy, he always made sure to do more than his share — that way when he had an exam, the other guys would cover for him and let him duck out early.

In fact, despite the rocky first moments with his coworkers, highlighted by Max Seymour's visit to their basement lair, Rich had actually begun to enjoy working with his fellow Blazers. And even though they all busted his balls by calling him Counselor because of his desire to work on one of the floors above them one day, he was growing to like each of them more and more as he got to know them.

Rich learned that Eddie Pisorchek, despite his handicap, was far from stupid and actually used his situation to his advantage when necessary. One late Wednesday, for example, a paralegal scurried into the Printers angrily demanding Eddie give her some attorney's proposed jury instructions. That sounded like a simple document, but the truth was jury instructions

107

could run scores and scores of pages and were as important a part of the trial process as the evidence itself. The instructions were hours late, and the lawyer needed to catch a flight to Georgia, where he was first chair in an Eleventh Circuit toxic-tort litigation. Vice was supposed to have had the job done but he'd just plain forgot — a rare lapse in a worker who, despite his constant griping and complaining, was quite conscientious.

As the paralegal railed on, Eddie's eyes grew wide with fear and he began to smack himself repeatedly in the side of his head.

'I messed up! Eddie bad! Eddie bad! Eddie bad!' The paralegal screamed, 'Make him stop!' but nobody moved — none of them had ever seen Eddie so upset. The paralegal had to grab Eddie's hands and pin them to his hips. She apologized to Ed and said that if he could just overnight the instructions to the lawyer in Atlanta so he had them first thing tomorrow morning, everything would be fine. As soon as she left, Eddie turned to Vice and smiled.

'I just saved your black ass,' he said with a devilish grin.

A brief moment of shocked silence was followed by an explosion of laughter. Vice couldn't breathe and Rich had to hold himself up. Even Dylan, who usually said less than nothing in any given day, laughed until his eyes teared.

But that wasn't the only time Rich had seen Dylan's eyes get wet. Every month Dylan would bring in a new three-by-four-inch ultrasound photo of his and his girlfriend's unborn child and post it on the wall behind his work space; he'd take the previous picture down, fold it carefully, and put it in his wallet. And when he found out the baby's gender, he brought in cheap cigars with pink IT'S A GIRL bands around them. None of the Blazers smoked, but they all lit up and puffed away out of respect to Dylan. Dylan mentioned that they were going to name the baby Bella, after his mother, and his voice caught just a bit, his eyes got wet, and then Dylan grabbed a loaded doc cart and took off to make a delivery. Rich and everyone else acted as if it hadn't happened.

That was par for the course for Dylan — he was quiet, respectful, and the hardest worker of all of them. And even given the fact that after spending well *over* one hundred days working together, Dylan had said well *under* one hundred words to him, Rich could tell that Dylan Rodriguez was smart. But not just smart — he was *sharp*. He was the kind of guy who, in a different life, could have been a leader of men — he just had that air about him. But there was also something dark about the man, something he carried with him that he wanted no one else to see. Rich knew guys who played it close to the vest, but Dylan played it *under* the vest, and then he wrapped the vest around whatever *it* was and threw the vest in the fireplace and burned it to ashes.

But despite Dylan's laconic nature, Rich admired him for his work ethic and the long hours he was putting in to provide for his impending family. After Rodriguez passed out those cigars, Rich stared at the pungent gray smoke curling up from their amber tips and hoped that he could finish up school and get his law degree and then one day be able to pass out his own Tiparillos, whatever color the band might be, to celebrate his first child with Elyse.

And as for Vicellous Green, well, it seemed that he already had a brood of his own. Rich would watch Vice hand out money to all of his eight brothers and sisters who stopped by the Printers like clockwork on every payday. Vice explained that if he tried to do that at home his father would intercept the cash and head right to the liquor store. Vice never got into too much detail, but Rich could tell that his home was not a good place. In fact, it seemed pretty damn bad. But Vice never offered up too much information, and if you asked a question he didn't want to answer, he'd just crack a joke and move on to something else. It was clear that Vice was hiding some real pain.

But he'd light up like a jack-o'-lantern when his brothers and sisters came by. He'd playfully make fun of each one of them — ranking on their haircuts or their 'ugly-ass sneakers' — but he also gave each kid twenty bucks and a kiss on the forehead, even the teenagers. It was really quite beautiful to see. It made Rich wish he had brothers and sisters of his own.

Rich sincerely liked everyone he worked with at Olmstead & Taft. Even Jason Spade. Despite his insecurity, which manifested in a constant need to flash money and be a bit pretentious, he was a guy who just wanted to be liked.

And Rich knew that feeling. Growing up without parents instantly makes you different on the playground. Parents talk. Kids overhear. Within six months of the funeral, he'd gotten a new name — he was That Kid There, as in 'Hey, Mikey, see That Kid There? His parents got killed in a boat accident' and 'Hey, Big J, see That Kid There? I heard his parents got eaten by sharks.' Rich had heard it all, and he didn't like it, so he decided it was best to avoid it, the way some people just avoided him, the orphan kid. And even though playing sports broke down some barriers, he never really had the kind of bond with his peers that other kids had growing up.

But now, in the Printers of Olmstead & Taft, things had changed.

A retarded man, a black kid from the projects, a rich kid from the Upper West Side, and an intimidating but surprisingly gentle half-Irish, half-Puerto Rican guy had become something Rich had never had before.

They had become his friends.

The irony was that Rich had no idea how much pain he would eventually cause each and every one of them.

19

'Come on, let's go!' Eddie barked at Rich, who, if he was being honest, would've admitted he wasn't moving too fast. 'Baumgartner wants those exhibits ready in five minutes!'

Rich wasn't on his game — the night before, he'd been out late with Jason, Elyse, and a gorgeous African model that Jason had met at a D'Agostino's while he was buying cigarettes. This time he had taken all of them to a party at a SoHo art gallery that the firm represented pro bono, and Rich had had one too many glasses of free wine.

O&T did a lot of pro bono work for the arts — not because the partners gave a crap about their nonpaying clients but because such horseshit liberal programs enticed the still optimistic students at the top law schools during recruitment season. These wide-eyed academics would read about the firm's representation of some horrible comedy troupe (Improvisatiable!) in some free-speech case or about how the firm stopped a slumlord from evicting performance artists from a condemned warehouse that they were using as their theater.

The students figured that by joining Olmstead & Taft, they were embarking on careers of do-gooding and justice-providing. The reality was, as Max Seymour explained to Rich, as soon as the students signed on the dotted lines, their lives would become a continuous stream of demanding clients, all-night research sessions, and the never-ending tracking of billable hours. They'd be lucky if they got to take on one pro bono case in their first ten years at the firm. Pro bono cases were for partners who wanted free tickets to the opera and a source of good country-club stories.

And despite the hangover the previous night's cocktail party had provided, Rich kept rolling laminated posters, sliding them into cardboard tubes, and handing them one at a time to Vice while calling out a description of the exhibit.

'Engineers' Report Seven A.'

'Engineers' Report Seven A,' Vice repeated, writing exactly that on the tube with a black marker and then placing the tube in a large plastic bin on wheels.

'Engineers' Report Seven *B*,' Rich announced, but the slickness of the fresh lamination made the poster shoot out of his hand and strike a large pile of exhibits still waiting to be rolled. The whole pile slid slowly, then quite quickly, onto the floor.

'For shit's sake!' shouted Ed from behind his computer. 'Get it together, Mauro!'

Man, Ed can be a real dick sometimes . . . Rich thought.

'I'm faster than you,' Ed continued, 'and I'm retarded!'

. . . and he can also be funny as hell.

Rich and Vice cracked up.

'Laugh it up, a-holes,' Ed said. 'But when Baumgartner blows up — '

'When Baumgartner blows up, my man Richie

here's gonna call his boy Seymour or his boyfriend Spade and get the whole thing smoothed
over. So chill, Special Ed,' Vice countered.

'If we get chewed out, it's our fault. I'm not
calling anybody,' Rich said as he knelt and began
picking up the exhibits.

Vice knelt next to Rich and helped him gather
the posters. 'If we get chewed out, it's *your* fault,
ya wino.' Vice laughed. 'But I guess when you get
to hobnob with the Suits, you gotta go, right, my
man? Or should I say *slob*-nob, because the way
you been hangin' out with your boy Spade I'm
startin' to think you guys been headin' up to
Brokeback Mountain on weekends.'

Special Ed stifled a laugh.

'I know him from back in the day,' Rich
defended himself.

'You know him from back in the *gay* — ' Vice
quipped.

'Doesn't even make sense — '

'Love don't gotta make sense, baby.'

Rich shook his head as he and Vice stood up,
arranged the posters, and picked up where
they'd left off.

'Before ya know it,' Vice goaded him, 'we'll be
down here runnin' around to get you *your* shit
on time.'

'Shut up.'

'Yes, sir, Massa Mauro.'

Before Rich could tell Vice to kiss his hairy
Italian ass, he was interrupted.

'Hey,' Dylan barked without shouting. He had
just entered from the loading bay, where a few
pallets of paper were being delivered. 'Stop messin'

114

around and finish up. My girl's got a sonogram later and I ain't missing it 'cause I gotta run that stuff crosstown to Baumgartner at the courthouse.'

Dylan stared at them a second, and a second was all he needed. Message received, loud and clear. He grabbed a full delivery cart, checked the order slip, and wheeled it out the door.

'What's he all about?' Rich said after he knew Dylan was way down the hall and well out of earshot.

'Dylan Rodriguez ain't *about* nothin',' Vice explained. 'Dylan Rodriguez is, simply put, one bad mothafucka.'

'Yeah, he's one bad motherfucker,' Eddie added before laughing at his curse word and taking another sip of a Yoo-hoo he had gotten out of the mini-fridge behind his desk; he kept it well stocked with drinks, Reese's Peanut Butter Cups, and Big League Chew.

'How so?' Rich asked Vice.

'I don't know how so. I don't know shit about the man 'cause homeboy hardly talks. But he don't need to say much, now, do he? Hell, I saw that look in your eye when he walked into the Printers on your first day. You practically inked your pants.'

Eddie laughed again. Rich shot him a look, then glared back at Vice.

'Don't give me that Italian death-stare bullshit,' Vice jabbed. 'Your drawers probably looked like someone emptied a toner cartridge in 'em.'

Eddie kept laughing so Vice kept riffing, as it didn't take much of an audience for Vicellous Green to get revved up, even if his audience

115

consisted of only Special Ed Pisorchek.

'I mean, there was more ink in *your* briefs than in the *legal* briefs.'

Eddie was flat-out cackling now. He was turning red.

'I coulda wrung your underwear into the Xerox and made some stinky-inky documents for the lawyers,' Vice continued.

'Does *ink* mean . . . ' Eddie tried to, but couldn't, finish his sentence between bursts of hysterics.

'Does it mean *what*, Special Ed?' Vice prodded, loving every moment of this.

'Does it mean . . . ' Eddie could hardly talk. 'Does it mean . . . *diarrhea?*' Eddie barely spat out the words before collapsing onto a table, his purple face buried in his forearms, his body heaving, practically unable to breathe.

'Eddie's an easy laugh,' Vice said. 'Fart and doody jokes always get him goin', but diarrhea just slays the boy. But it feels good, don't it, Pisorchek!'

Eddie didn't answer. He couldn't answer. He raised his hand and waved off Vice as if asking for mercy just as Jason entered.

'What's his deal?' he said, motioning to Special Ed. 'He finally figure out why the chicken crossed the road?'

Ed and Vice stopped laughing — Vice because he didn't like Suits in the basement and Ed because he recognized Spade. The lawyer was always nice to him in the hallway, but there was a bite to everything the man said. Ed suspected that Jason was often making fun of him.

116

'What? Party doesn't have to stop on my account.' Spade smiled as Rich intercepted him and led him out into the hallway.

'What's wrong with you?' Rich chastised him when they were out of earshot. 'You tease a retarded guy?'

'What tease? I made a joke,' Jason defended himself. 'I didn't mean he couldn't figure it out because he's handicapped, you jackass. I meant it sarcastically — as if he'd really be laughing at the chicken joke — ah, you know what? Forget it . . . I've got a surprise for you. All lined up for tomorrow, so be free in the afternoon.'

'Can't. Elyse's parents are having a party at their place in Brooklyn and I have to be there.'

'Shit. Where in Brooklyn?'

'Brooklyn Heights.'

'You're kidding me, that's perfect!' Spade said, punching Rich in the arm. 'I'm gonna be downtown anyway. I'll meet you at the party.'

'Last time you had a surprise for me we wound up at a cockfight in Spanish Harlem.'

'We won money, didn't we?'

'*You* won money; I walked outta that disgusting shit.'

But Spade wasn't listening; he had turned and stuck his head in the door to the Printers and was shouting to Ed. 'Hey, Eddie, you take care of yourself, okay?'

Eddie nodded warily.

Spade hurried to the elevator bank for a ride with Chip.

'See you tomorrow, Mauro,' he called without looking back. 'And remember, it's a big surprise.'

117

20

Rich stood on the front stoop of the brownstone, the ugly tie Uncle Jim had given him for his first day of work at O&T tied snugly around his neck, causing him to sweat under his collar. Rich didn't want to wear the damn thing but Jim had seen him leaving the house and said, 'Hey, know what would look good with that outfit?'

A minute later the tie was on. And he had to *keep* it on because he knew the next time Jim saw Elyse he'd ask, 'Hey, what'd ya think of that sharp tie I bought your boyfriend?' And since Elyse was the world's worst liar, Uncle Jim would see right through her if she tried to cover for Rich. Plus, Elyse adored Uncle Jim and probably wouldn't have lied to him anyway, even if Rich had begged.

And that's how Rich wound up scratching his neck with one hand while knocking with the other, waiting to go into a party he had no desire to attend. The door opened, revealing a thin man with thin lips, thin hair, and a phony smile.

'Hello, Rich. Nice tie.'

Elyse's father couldn't have been more insincere. He stepped to the side and let Rich enter the home, which was, as usual, full of the kind of pompous assholes who would only be friends with a pompous asshole like Quinn Crane.

Elyse was from Brooklyn Heights, but not

Millionaires' Row — the cluster of four-story brownstones that sat on tree-lined streets and faced New York Harbor, some of the priciest real estate in Brooklyn and the place that at least a half a dozen O&T partners called home. However, Quinn Crane and his wife, Carol, were both optometrists, and even though much of their practice covered the underclass of Brooklyn, they lived a comfortable lifestyle and, through prudent saving and investments, had become moderately wealthy. They had high hopes for their daughter; they had a plan for her, and that plan didn't include her spending her life with a carpenter from Astoria who wore out-of-style neckties.

Though he was never the smartest guy in the room, Rich Mauro was far from the dumbest. He'd picked up on how the Cranes felt about him the first time they met. They'd been throwing a party back then as well, celebrating their wedding anniversary, and Elyse invited Rich. Quinn Crane and some of his phony friends were bullshitting in a corner, and Rich, at Elyse's prodding, tried to join in and be one of the guys.

Quinn made the introductions. 'This is my daughter's friend Rich. He's in the construction game.'

Handshakes and pleasantries followed, but the way Quinn had introduced him wasn't lost on Rich. First of all, he said Rich was Elyse's *friend;* not *boyfriend,* but *friend.* Truncating that compound word down to one syllable sent a clear message to Rich: *Don't get too comfortable here, pal; you're just a friend, nothing more. And friendships can end quite easily.*

Further, he said Rich was in the 'construction game.' That was also quite intentional. If Quinn were being honest, he'd have said, 'Rich is a carpenter,' but it was obvious that Quinn wasn't too keen on letting his moneyed pals know his daughter had taken up with a guy who wore work boots for a living, so he said 'construction game' and let the others assume Rich was in management, or building finance, or something else more palatable to people who sat behind desks instead of behind the wheels of Payloaders.

Finally, Quinn hadn't said Rich's last name. But as Rich met each of the men, he heard theirs: Williams. Smith. Thomas. Johnson. It was the damn passenger list from the *Mayflower*. Rich was pretty sure there wasn't a Longo or a Russo in the bunch.

Quinn Crane treated Rich like someone he had hired to fix his sink, not someone who loved Crane's daughter more than he'd ever thought possible. Rich hated the guy, and the feeling was mutual, but for Elyse's sake he was always pleasant to Quinn, kept his feelings to himself, and four times a year, when the Cranes had one of their seasonal get-togethers, Rich smiled and ate more shit than a dung beetle. He did it for Elyse.

'Um, Elyse's in the back, by the bar,' Quinn offered, which was strange because Rich hadn't asked. But when he glanced across the living room and saw Elyse talking to some well-coiffed schmuck who looked like he fell out of an Abercrombie & Fitch catalog, he knew why Mr. Crane was so eager for Rich to spot his daughter.

He wanted him to see the competition.

'Enjoy yourself, Richie . . . and don't forget to use a coaster,' Quinn snarked as he walked away, loving that Rich was obviously, instantly, threatened by the hairdo talking to his girl.

Rich eyeballed Quinn — God, he couldn't stand the son of a bitch. *Just for that*, Rich thought to himself, *tonight I'm gonna bang your daughter, and I'm gonna make it extra dirty*. He knew that was an infantile way to think, but hell, he just hated the bastard so much.

Rich moved through the room, brushing shoulders with bankers and lawyers and other people whom the Cranes collected to make themselves feel that they were of a higher social status than they really were. He recognized some poseur documentarian that the Cranes tangentially knew — he'd made a film about how plastic bottles were worse than Stalin or some ridiculous crap like that that the leftists ate up with a biodegradable spoon. The Cranes invited him to every event they threw and made sure that all their bottled water was hidden in the garage.

Rich approached the bar, taking a good look at the turd in glasses talking to Elyse. First thing he did was size up whether he could take the guy in a fight. Once again, he was well aware of how childish he was being, but when it came to Elyse all common sense went out the window. The guy was tall, slender, fit — but the kind of fit you get from taking spin classes with other metrosexuals at Crunch. Rich was climbing-scaffolds strong. No contest. Round one to Mauro.

Next question — who was better-looking? The

putz had newsanchor hair and a game-show-host smile. Rich had a semicrooked nose from catching too many pickup-game elbows, and a scar through his eyebrow courtesy of a level that had fallen from a ladder on a job in Flatbush. Round two to the asshole.

Now for the tiebreaker: what was going on in their pants. *That's* how crazy in love Rich was with Elyse — so head over heels that he would stare at another man's crotch to estimate what the dude was packing, see if it measured up to the old Italian *salsiccia* Rich kept tucked down in his boxer briefs, which, he had been told, was impressive.

'You know, I hear the bartender makes a good cock-a-tini if you're thirsty, big boy,' Spade said, surprising Rich.

'Son of a bitch . . . '

'Didn't mean to startle you, pal, but that's what happens when you're busy staring at some dude's lap meat . . . '

'I wasn't staring at — I was daydreaming.'

'Yeah, about schlong.'

'Shut up. When the hell did you get here anyway?'

'Before you. I've been helping your mother-in-law in the kitchen. She's a piece of ass for a long-tooth.' He grunted as he grabbed a beer from an ice tub being carried past by a caterer's assistant.

'Shut up, here comes Elyse,' Rich said under his breath.

'Hey, babe!' she said, giving Rich a big hug and kiss. She turned to Jason, gave him the obligatory peck on the cheek.

'Hi, Jason. Glad you could make it.' She didn't mean it, but she was civil.

'C'mon, now. Think I'd miss a chance to meet the people that created the most lovely girl I know?' he schmoozed as he snapped the bottle cap off his Anchor Steam.

'Where's today's car model?'

'On a rotating platform pointing to a Ferrari somewhere,' Jason said, oozing a potent combination of charm and self-deprecation. 'Nice to meet you; Jason Spade,' he said, putting his hand out to the guy Elyse had been talking to and who had taken it upon himself to interject himself into their threesome. Now that he was up close and Rich could get a good look, Rich was even more certain that he hated everything about this guy.

'Hi, I'm Terry Garhart. And you must be Rich. Heard a lot about you.'

Rich shook Terry's hand, dazed.

'You're Terry?' he said in a stupor. 'I've heard a lot about you too.' But clearly, he hadn't heard enough. A month or so earlier, Elyse had told Rich that friends of her parents had a kid who had just moved to New York to take a hotshot job in advertising. Elyse's parents asked her to show the newbie the ropes of the Big Apple, and Elyse, being the good daughter that she was, obliged. She took the new transplant to dinner a few times, around Central Park, and even to a show, if Rich's memory was correct. Elyse had said that the advertising whiz kid's name was Terry. She never once mentioned that Terry had

123

eighteen-inch biceps and a penis.

'So, Elyse tells me you started at O and T a while ago? What area? Commercial? Litigation?'

'Yeah, um, I didn't really get a chance to explain exactly what Rich does there — ' Elyse jumped in.

'I work mostly with Xerox,' Rich stated confidently. 'And a little bit with Hewlett-Packard.'

Spade almost spit out his mouthful of beer. It turned into a half swallow, half cough.

'Wow,' Terry marveled, impressed. 'Big clients. Just working with those two for now?'

'Yeah, well, I'm new, so starting at the bottom, you know, practically basement level.'

Elyse shot Rich a look.

'What do you do?' Rich asked, trying to direct the topic away from his fictitious career.

'I'm over at Pinnacle — advertising company — not the exciting creative end, the business end, putting together the deals. Nothing interesting . . . nothing like you're doing — '

'Terry,' Elyse interrupted. 'Can I steal Rich for a moment? I need to pay the caterer, and Rich is insisting on picking up the tab for my parents.'

'Steal away.' Garhart smiled before jutting his hand out toward Rich. 'We should grab lunch one day.'

'Absolutely.' Rich smiled insincerely while Elyse pulled him away and toward the back door. They exited into the small fenced-in backyard behind the brownstone.

'What the hell was that?' she asked. 'Why'd you lie?'

'Why'd *I* lie?' Rich said incredulously. 'Why

124

didn't you tell me Terry stands when *he* pees?'

'*What?*'

'*I thought Terry was a girl.* You've been running all over the city with him for weeks. I've been working away like an idiot while some guy is stealing you right out from under my nose!'

Elyse looked at Rich for a beat. She wanted to be mad at him for being so stupid, but she couldn't help herself — she laughed.

'Oh my God, you're such a moron.' She wrapped her arms around him and kissed him on the lips, then leaned back. 'He's a goofy tourist from Connecticut; his dad knows my dad from college and I'm helping him get his feet wet in the big city. That's it. That's all.' She leaned in and gave him another kiss, softly on the lips. 'He can't steal me away — because I belong to you, and you belong to me. Right?'

Rich pulled back and looked at her. Those beautiful eyes, twenty different shades of brown — chocolate, mocha, mahogany — all swirled together to perfection.

'Right.'

'Hey, you two,' Elyse's octogenarian Aunt Judith gurgled, startling Rich as she sidled up next to them seemingly out of nowhere. She kissed Elyse and Rich and clasped their hands within her own veiny, cold, liver-spotted mitts. She turned to Rich and playfully chastised him.

'Now, when are you going to make an honest woman out of my grandniece?' she asked. 'Do you know that my husband, Arthur, proposed to me on just our third date?'

Mauro's stomach fell. He hated that question.

125

A few times a year someone would ask — one of Elyse's friends or cousins or neighbors — and Rich always wanted to shout the same answer: *When I have some fucking money — now mind your own goddamn business!*

He decided, however, to take a different tack with dear old Aunt Judith.

'Three dates?' Mock aghast, Rich deflected the question. 'If I had you on my arm, I wouldn't have made it through the first. Uncle Arthur needed to clean his glasses and see what was in front on him.'

Aunt Judith flashed her dentures, blushed, and giggled like a schoolgirl.

'We're just not settled yet, Aunt Judith,' Elyse said, trying to protect Rich, which just made him feel worse. 'You know, we're both still in school — '

'So?' the old bat interjected. 'Your parents have plenty of money. They can help you along. Just give me a great-grandniece before I die.'

With her suggestion that Rich borrow money from the Cranes, Aunt Judith had no idea how close she came to getting punched right in her Pepsodent hole.

But lucky for her, she made a few clucking noises and then moved off.

'Okay. Now I actually do have to go pay the caterers,' Elyse said, pecking him on the cheek. She walked inside, nodding to Jason who was coming down the stairs.

'Thanks for leaving me alone in there with the Ad Sales Kid. It was riveting conversation,' he snipped at Rich.

'Sorry.'

'That's all right. He is pretty good-looking, ya know. I got lost in his eyes.'

'Go to hell.'

Jason took a contemplative swig of his beer, then turned to Mauro.

'Her parents are trying to set her up with that guy; you know that, don't you? They're gonna do everything they can to keep you away from their daughter. You better stay on your toes, King Richard, or you're gonna lose the hand of the queen, know what I'm sayin'?'

Rich didn't answer. He just stared across the courtyard into the back window of the house, looking at Elyse socialize with ease, socialize with people whom Rich had nothing in common with — people who'd never had to worry about not getting paid when bad weather shut down a job site, people who'd never clipped a coupon.

Rich looked miserable — he never took his eyes off the girl he loved.

Jason also didn't move his gaze, but he wasn't watching Elyse; he was focused on Rich. And in contrast to Rich, Jason seemed almost pleased with what he saw, and a small, practically undetectable smile began to form.

21

The rest of the party was horrible for Rich. The smallest things seemed to stand out and highlight the differences between Rich and the rest of the guests — the way they ordered their martinis ('Just swirl the vermouth, then dump it out'), made small talk ('I heard a piece about that writer on NPR last weekend'), and used the word *vacation* as a verb ('We vacation in Aspen every winter'). They were a completely different breed of human — a separate genus — so unlike what Rich was used to that every time he was at one of the Cranes' parties, he felt so out of place that he couldn't wait to leave. Spade picked up on Rich's discomfort and seized the opportunity.

'You wanna blow this pop stand?' he asked.

'I should stay. I haven't seen Elyse much lately.'

'Yeah, well, it looks like she's fine, bro.' Spade pointed across the room to where Elyse, Mr. and Mrs. Crane, and Terry were yukking it up like a couple of couples. Rich felt sick. Not because he was jealous or angry, though he felt both of those emotions in spades at that moment. He felt sick because the four of them looked great together. Mr. Crane in his Tommy Hilfiger casual wear, Mrs. Crane in a cocktail dress, both smiling with ease as they watched their stunning daughter talk to the living Ken doll that was Terry Garhart. It just seemed like they all *fit* together — a perfectly matched set. Terry must've said something particularly witty because Quinn placed his hand on Terry's shoulder and broke into laughter. While wiping a phony tear from his eye, his gaze locked on Rich, and damn it if the son of a bitch didn't give Rich a wink. There was a gleam in his stare, one that told Rich to start counting his days because they were surely numbered.

'Yeah, let's get outta here,' Rich said.

'Good, we can get to that surprise I told ya about. I'll drive.'

Rich said a quick good-bye to Elyse, had a cursory exchange with the Cranes, and effectively ignored Terry and was in Jason's BMW convertible and on the BQE in less than ten minutes. Jason drove like he did everything else in his life — *fast*. They wove through traffic and didn't talk — the top was down and the roar of wind made conversation impossible. But Rich was content to just close his eyes and rest his head on the seat back, letting the pink, setting late-summer sun warm his face.

For a moment, Rich felt relaxed. All thoughts of school, work, and Elyse, Terry, and the Cranes were washed away by the salty breeze whipping off the lower bay; it was as if his worries were being pushed out of his mind and over the back of the car, left to bounce along I–278 until they landed in a pothole or were run over by a semi. He relaxed to the point of falling asleep. When Rich finally awoke they had been on the Belt Parkway for some time and were actually getting off at Flatbush Avenue.

'Where are we going?' Rich asked, still groggy.

'You'll see,' Spade said.

A few minutes later they were pulling up at Gateway Marina, a private dock in Brooklyn that, if you hadn't just driven through the graffiti-covered cityscape to get there, you would've sworn was a boat slip off South Carolina. It was beautiful. The air was clean. The sun painted the water gold. Seagulls dove for a last snack and gently called to one another before turning in for the night.

They exited the car and Spade headed for a dock. Rich followed, saying nothing. Jason finally stopped at a boat that looked more like a small building.

'You like?' Spade asked.

'This is yours?'

'Well, kind of. My old man just bought it, but he's always working so I figure you, me, Elyse, some skank I pick up — we all go for a few day trips this summer. It's a Catalina Four Seventy two-cabin. This thing costs more than half the homes in Brooklyn.'

'The *Adage?*' Rich said, pointing to the name of the boat, painted in blue script on the stern.

'Yeah, Miles is into proverbs and old sayings. Here's one: He who has a kick-ass boat will party mucho the rest of the summer. Can you see us? Drinks on the bow, fishing off Fire Island, hitting the bars there at night. Elyse stretched out getting a tan, you and me steering this thing all around the island. It's gonna be great. Come on, check it out.'

Spade stepped onto the boat and disappeared

inside the cabin, but Rich didn't follow. He didn't want to go in. He was tired. Tired of being around people and conversations and boats and a million other things that made him feel like he didn't belong. He didn't fit in with that world. But he knew he didn't fit in back in Astoria either. He'd always thought he wanted the rarefied air of big firms and Manhattan living and all that went along with it, but now that he was getting a lungful of that air, he was finding it hard to breathe.

After a moment, Spade stuck his head out of the cabin. 'If you're waiting for a better boat, this is the only one I got.'

'Ya know, I'm feeling a little run-down, Jay. Can you just gimme a lift back to my place?'

'*You wanna go?* But what about the surprise?'

'It's great. It's a great boat.'

'Oh, no,' Spade explained as he climbed back onto the dock, 'the boat isn't the surprise. I have something much better for you.'

131

22

Rich sat in the back booth of McMahon's Pub longing for his bed, just a few blocks away. Jason had agreed to take him back to Astoria, but he'd made Rich promise to grab a beer once they got there. Jason had 'a proposal' and he said it couldn't wait any longer. Rich had grown to know Jason pretty well over the prior months, and he knew the lawyer wouldn't take no for an answer. Whether it was a particular movie Spade wanted to see or some young waitress's ass, when Jason Spade wanted something, he wouldn't let up until he got it. So Rich, too tired to protest, agreed to the drink.

Spade knew he had to talk to Rich that night. The timing was *perfect*. If he was ever going to convince Rich Mauro to do what he was about to propose, he'd have to lay it all on the line tonight. He had seen Rich's face at the Cranes' party — he was devastated, sincerely worried that Terry Garhart was moving in on Elyse.

Mauro's insecurities were at an all-time high. Spade had to play on them *now*, point out the obvious to the kid from Queens, even if the tough love hurt — even if it pissed him off. Spade had been working up to this moment for months and now it was time to seal the deal.

Spade paid for the beers and the onion rings — the bartender was a guy, so he didn't leave a tip. He walked to the booth where Rich was sitting and dropped a Harp in front of the aspiring attorney.

'Cheers,' Jason said, raising his beer.

Rich didn't say anything, but they clinked bottles. A pretty local girl in a Social Distortion T-shirt walked by. She smacked Rich on the shoulder — 'Hey, Richie, tell your uncle my dad says hi' — and kept on moving to the end of the bar, where her friends were waiting.

'You know that chick?'

'Yeah,' Rich said. 'She's a regular.'

'So you must be too.'

'My uncle comes here a few times a week to grab a burger, flip through the sports pages. I tag along. Sometimes I'll swing by and grab a beer if I get off work late.'

'You ever bring the other guys? Those guys you work with down in the basement?' Jason probed, trying to sound casual.

'Here? No. It's all the way in Astoria; why the hell would we come here?'

'I don't know. Just, ya know, do you like those guys? They good guys? The black kid, the other one . . . '

'Jesus Christ, Spade. You've heard me talk about them a hundred times by now — you don't remember their names?'

'C'mon, man, cut me a break — '

'The problem with all you lawyers,' Mauro lectured Spade, 'is you think the support staff's nothing but replaceable parts — just warm bodies in blue blazers running your files up and down the floors whenever you snap your fingers. You guys treat us like we're invisible.'

133

Rich Mauro drank his beer and contemplated the man sitting across from him. Spade was an okay guy, but every once in a while his arrogance shone through. Like not remembering the names of grown men he had met already, simply because their paychecks were his pocket change. Or in the way Spade was studying Rich right then, like he had a secret and pitied Rich because he wasn't smart enough to figure out what it was.

'And that's why you're where you are and I'm where I am,' Spade pointed out smugly. 'Where you see problems, I see opportunities. The benefit of being *invisible*,' Jason whispered, looking straight into Mauro's eyes, 'is that people don't see you when you're robbing them blind . . . now, how 'bout you and I get rich, Rich?'

Rich had no idea what Spade was getting at; he didn't even begin to suspect that the man was dead serious.

'How's that?' Mauro quipped. 'Your daddy gonna split your trust fund with me?'

Spade's expression changed. He didn't like it when people pointed out the obvious — that he was a grown man whose father was still picking up the tab.

'My mistake. I mean, what does a man making ten-fifty an hour need with money, right? In fact, I'm sure if you compared your bank account with Terry Garhart's, no one would be able to tell them apart.' Jason knew that was a low blow, but he had to get Rich's attention and picking at the fresh insecurity scab that was raw on Mauro's heart and soul was the easiest way to do so.

Jason's comment pissed Rich off enough that he put his beer down, looked Spade in the eye, and struck a blow of his own. 'Whatever, man,' he said as he stood up. 'But I'd rather earn my money than have it given to me.' Rich turned and headed for the back exit.

Jason was thrilled. He had hit a sore spot. Now Rich was acting emotionally. The next step was to get him *thinking* emotionally. He was certain if he poked that sore spot a few times more he could get Rich to be open to the opportunity Spade was about to present. But for now, he had to play it slow and just lay out the bait.

'Okay,' Spade called out after him. 'But you're sitting on *millions* and you don't even know it.'

This caught Rich's attention. He stopped at the door and looked back at the lawyer in the booth.

'Besides,' Jason continued, 'I'm not talking about having something given to you . . . I'm talking about *taking* it.'

'Taking what? Millions of dollars? What are you, a stickup man all of a sudden?'

'No, I'm not a stickup man. I'm a *businessman*. Now, why don't you stop being stupid and sit down so the whole damn bar doesn't hear us.'

Rich didn't move. He eyeballed Spade. He didn't like the condescending tone. Spade picked up on this; he didn't want to lose Rich now, not when he was about to get to the heart of his pitch — he couldn't afford to. So he smiled.

'C'mon, man,' he said, trying to lighten things

up a bit. 'I'm just talking here. Why do you have to take shit so seriously? Have a seat and I promise you, when you hear what I have to say, you're going to thank me. 'Cause I'm talking big money. *Real* money. Money you couldn't make in three lifetimes if you collated all the paper in the world. Just give me five minutes, that's all I'm asking.'

Rich checked his watch. It was 9:20. He'd give him until 9:25, then he was out of there. Rich slowly sat back down.

'The money piqued your interest? Man after my own heart,' Spade commented.

Jason knew he had Rich's attention, so, like most people who desire to command an audience but rarely manage to, he dragged it out, savoring the moment.

'So. How are you and Elyse doing?'

'Fine,' Rich responded curtly, annoyed the conversation had taken a detour. 'What the hell does that have to do with money?'

'Everything, Rich. It has *everything* to do with money,' Spade said, using his hands to frame the word *everything* as if he were holding it a few inches above the table. 'I've spent a lot of time with you guys now — gotten to know Elyse. Lovely girl. Beautiful. Classy. *Refined*. So lemme ask you something. You really think she'll be happy living with a fraction of the money she grew up on?'

'She lives on next to nothing now.'

'Please. She's in grad school, dummy. She's got her little studio and her little teacher's diploma on the way, but when she's all grown up

136

and married, she's going to want a big-girl life. She's going to want the life she grew up with. Especially when she sees all her friends have it.'

'You don't know Elyse; don't talk about her.'

'I know *people*. Rich. I know *her* kind of people. Her *parents'* kind of people. You think they're happy that their little girl wants to live a life where the mortgage payments for a small Cape in Rosedale depend on your back holding up and your knees not giving out?'

'Hey, I'm not doing construction anymore,' Rich said defensively. 'I'm in school — '

'*Night* school. So you'll graduate in what, six years, if you're lucky? And you'll have student loans up your ass. And if you're not top five percent of your class you're not getting into an elite law school. You'll wind up at a low-level firm because no matter what old Max Seymour is telling you, I promise that my dad and his partners aren't letting some Touro Law School reject step one foot into their firm. You're either top tier or you're working at a schlock shop in the Bronx doing car-accident cases at sixty grand a year. You think you can beat old Terry Garhart in the Elyse sweepstakes with sixty K? Not to mention the fact that her parents are clearly backing him — her old man was practically sliding the guy's cock inside her tonight — '

Rich reached out and grabbed Spade by his shirt, then yanked him halfway across the table. Their beer bottles fell to the floor and shattered. Everyone in the bar turned to look but Rich didn't notice. His eyes were locked with Spade's and he picked each word carefully as he spoke

137

slowly through barely parted teeth.

'You watch, *very carefully*, everything you say from now on. 'Cause I don't care whose son you are, I will lay you out right here.'

Spade looked back at Rich, unflinching, but definitely scared. He imagined for a moment what it would feel like if Rich smashed his curled left fist into his face. He was certain it would do some damage.

'Richie, everything cool?' the girl in the Social Distortion T-shirt called out. He didn't answer her. He just let go of Spade and walked out the back door of McMahon's, glass shards crunching under his feet.

23

It had rained while they were in the bar, and now the air smacked crisp against Rich's face, cooling it from an angry crimson to a more docile rose almost on contact. A few steps and Rich heard the door open behind him. He turned to find Jason stepping into the alley; he was already talking.

'Look, I'm not trying to be disrespectful, Rich. I'm your friend. I'm telling you the truth to make a point. I saw the hell you were going through at that party today — '

'Just back off — '

But Spade kept walking forward.

'Truth: Elyse has money, you don't. Truth: You need money but are a solid eight years behind the curve and might never catch up. Truth: Without money you cannot marry Elyse and we both know that's your endgame. Truth: Whether it's because she eventually realizes that she's become accustomed to life's creature comforts or because your own anger at your inability to provide them drives a wedge between you two *or* because Terry's charms become too hard to resist, you and she will break up if you don't do something about it . . . and I can help.'

Rich turned around, got nose to nose with Jason.

'*Truth*: You don't give a shit about me and Elyse. *Truth*: Helping me is the last thing you

139

care about. *Truth:* You need something from me, otherwise you'd never slum so low as to have a beer with me at a bar full of union workers.'

'Don't pull that class-warfare bullshit with me, Mauro. What *I* need, *you* need. Money.'

'The rich kid needs more money.'

'No, my *dad's* rich. *I'm* not. I have to crawl on my belly to that bastard every time I want an extra bowl of porridge and I can't take it anymore. Luckily I've figured a way out — for both of us. Aren't you even curious? Don't you want to know how you're letting millions slip through your fingers?'

'Just get to the point — I wanna go home,' Rich said, annoyed, his patience at an end.

'You say you want to be a lawyer and you've never even looked at what you're copying down there?' Jason scoffed. 'SEC filings, deal memos, the paperwork for multi*billion*-dollar transactions. You have *tomorrow's* Wall Street Journal in your hands every day and you don't even realize it. All these mergers and buyouts that send stocks flying through the roof or crashing through the floor — you have that information before anyone else in the world. Before the newswires. Before Wall Street. Before most of the people who work at the companies that are parties to the fuckin' deals! Hell, with all the checks and balances they have in the firm to protect against the lawyers engaging in insider trading, even *I* don't get to see that shit. But they overlooked *you*, Rich. They overlooked you because you're a nobody. You're nothing. You're *invisible*. And as a result, they gave you power and they don't even realize it. You, Rich Mauro, are one of the most powerful men in this city . . . and you barely make minimum wage. Let's do something about it.'

Spade was breathing heavy — excited that he was finally saying aloud what he had been thinking for months.

Rich didn't totally understand all that Jason had said but he understood enough. He knew that Jason was proposing something illegal. It had to be, or they wouldn't be talking about it in a dark alley in the middle of the night. He knew that it could get him into a lot of trouble. Spade's lips had quivered when he was listing all the documents Rich had at his disposal; his eyes had lit up like a drug user's right before he plunged in the needle — just talking about it made Spade's body experience the adrenaline rush that comes with the expectation of something big, the expectation of huge risk that could pay off in an even bigger reward.

Rich also knew that he *needed* a big reward. As much as Rich hated to admit it, Jason Spade was right. Rich could lose Elyse. Truth was, with all the time they were spending apart lately, he already felt she was slipping away — out of his hands and into Garhart's.

Rich almost couldn't blame her. They'd been together for more than two years and recently she'd been dropping hints about marriage, but he'd always found a way to duck the issue. He wanted to marry her more than anything in the world but he couldn't provide a life for her, not the life she deserved, because in his heart Rich

141

believed she deserved the best. And Rich knew that he was far from the best. He had nothing to offer her but his bedroom at his Uncle Jim's place, so he had nothing to offer her. He loved her, but that wasn't enough. He needed to make up for all the time he had lost — all the time, as Jason Spade had accurately pointed out, that had put Rich Mauro well behind the curve.

He needed money. He needed it sooner rather than later. He needed to make a big move. But doing something illegal wasn't an option.

'You want to use the documents we put together in the Printers to make money?'

'To trade on. To make smart stock picks. To get *rich*. Hell yeah, that's what I want to do.'

'Are you on drugs right now? Are you so whacked out of your fuckin' mind that you forget who got me my job? Max Seymour is like family to me and you want me to risk his firm!'

'Max Seymour is *like* family? Who the hell do you think Miles Spade is? You don't think I have some skin in the game too? Trust me, I've thought this out and if we're smart, no one will ever know. I've sold some stuff my parents got me over the years, cashed in some bonds — I've got the start-up capital; you've got access to information most lawyers in the firm don't get to see. We each bring something to the table. All we need is an offshore numbered account — '

'How fucked in the head are you that you're serious? *This* was the big surprise you had for me? A suggestion to commit federal crimes? Jesus Christ, Spade, I'm goin' home now. I'm goin' home, having a beer, and pretending we

142

never had this conversation. And from now on, you stay twenty-three floors above me. You and I are done.'

Rich turned to walk away. He hadn't gotten far when Spade called out, 'The *Adage* is a play on words. It's really the *Ad Age*. Pinnacle, the ad company Garhart works at — that's *his* company. The boat belongs to him.'

Mauro turned back to Spade, totally confused.

'I went to a meeting at his office in Stamford a few years back with my father, when he was trying to land Garhart as a client,' Jason explained. 'He clearly doesn't remember me — why would he? I was one of probably a hundred lawyers he met with when he was looking for new counsel.'

'Hold on. I thought he just moved to New York.'

'Yeah, he did. But he kept his mansion in Westport, and his lodge in Aspen, and his boat in Brooklyn that he couldn't stop talking about the entire time I was sitting down with him. That's how I knew about it. He has about ten framed photos of it hanging in his office. The guy's loaded, successful, and single . . . for now. Believe it or not, Richie, I'm your friend. I brought you to the docks because I wanted you to see what you're really going up against. The day trips to Fire Island, bikini tanning on the bow — Elyse's gonna do all of it. You just won't be there.'

Saying no more, Spade walked off. Rich remained. The moonlight, broken up by thick telephone wires, shone down onto him in stripes.

143

He just stood there, taking in all that just happened. The scam Jason suggested. The truth about Terry Garhart. The reality of the desperate nature of Rich's situation as laid out by Jason Spade.

As the moon rose higher in the night sky, Rich Mauro was alone in the alley with his thoughts.

And he was not in pleasant company.

24

The walk from McMahon's Pub to Uncle Jim's house usually took less than ten minutes even if you moved at a slow pace, but that night it seemed to take forever. A homeless man two blocks from McMahon's looked at Rich suspiciously, as if he had overheard the back-alley conversation with Jason Spade. Barflies stumbling out of some hole-in-the-wall joint stared at Mauro like they could read his mind. Rich knew his imagination was running wild, but he was worried just the same.

He was worried because Spade had seen something in Rich that made him think Rich was the kind of guy who, when desperate enough, would engage in something so dangerous and illegal. Or maybe Rich was worried because he was starting to feel that what Spade had said made sense.

Not the breaking-the-law part; that part was crazy — though Spade did make it sound possible . . . Rich shook his head sharply as if doing so would knock any thoughts of entertaining the proposition right out of his mind.

But Rich found himself more concerned about the *other* half of Spade's equation. The part about how long it would take Rich to get through undergrad and then law school on top of that. The amount of debt he'd rack up even with help from the Olmstead & Taft Law School

Initiative Program. The long-shot odds of getting into a top law school, and then the longer odds of landing a job at O&T if he didn't, because even though Max Seymour wanted Rich, Max was just one of over a hundred partners at the firm. Rich wanted to be in a secure financial position when he proposed to Elyse, so it might be close to ten years before he could pop the question. He knew she'd never wait that long. And she shouldn't have to — not with thoroughbreds like Terry Garhart and other jag-offs from the yacht- and country-club set breathing down her neck.

She wasn't the kind of girl to drop her panties for the first guy with a fat wallet who happened to walk by. She wasn't like that. But Terry wasn't just some guy. He had her parents' stamp of approval — she was being force-fed the guy and she didn't even know it. It was like her parents were pureeing spinach and mixing it in with Elyse's ice cream. It was bland, so she didn't know it was there, but she was getting a full dose of vitamin T and that was going to continue until Rich got down on one knee. And God only knew when that would be. Given enough time, Terry could win Elyse over. And it would be Rich's fault for letting it happen.

He thought about what Elyse had said to Aunt Judith, about them not being 'settled.' That was a euphemism for 'Rich has no money, won't have any for as far as I can see, and I don't know if we'll ever get married or have kids, Aunt Judith.' Every time he heard Elyse make an excuse for him, it stung like a bitch, made him physically ill, made him hate himself a bit more.

Because the truth was, Elyse was perfect. And she shouldn't have to wait for anybody — especially not for a guy with no pedigree, no parents, and no prospects.

By the time Rich ascended the three cracked concrete steps that led to his uncle's front door he had worked himself into a frenzy — his mind was racing; he was certain that he had severely miscalculated his ability to attain the future, and the woman, he had been hoping for for years. He slowly turned the key in the lock so as to not wake his uncle, who, as always, was passed out on the couch, *Daily Racing Form* across his stomach, no lights save for the bluish-green hue of a fifteen-year-old Zenith showing a replay of that day's Yankees game.

He turned off the TV and draped a blanket over his uncle. He sat on a chair next to the couch, looking at his father's older brother — a man who looked every one of his sixty-plus years and then some. Given Jim's penchant for alcohol, smoky OTB parlors, and deep-fried meatballs stuffed in half a loaf of Italian bread, Rich had to wonder how much longer he'd have the old guy in his life. Reaching eighty years old was probably too much to ask of the man — hell, seventy-five might be optimistic. At best, twenty years. Rich would be in his midforties when his uncle went — and then, just like those few days after his parents' death and before his uncle took him into his home, Rich would be alone again, lost, emotionally rudderless.

It was the scariest feeling Rich had ever

known, those seventy-two hours where neighbors and his parents' friends rotated staying with him at the house, all supposedly 'looking after the boy' when the truth was they could barely look *at* the boy. No adult wants to engage with a ten-year-old who has just lost his mother and father. They'd just put videotapes in an old VCR and left him in his room.

But after the accident investigation was over and the bodies had been returned to Jim and the wakes and funerals had been arranged, Rich's uncle stepped up and took the boy and never let him go. But those three days — when Rich was a lone, scared child — were as terrifying as any he'd ever experienced. He had found himself lying in bed, staring out the window, praying that it was all a dream or that he too had been on that boat with his parents and that he had died with them. But then, from a few blocks away, the rattle of the elevated subway let him know he was indeed alive, as subways don't run underwater.

Rich never wanted to feel untethered like that again. That fear was in the back, forefront, and both sides of his mind every minute of every day. And if he lost out on his chance with Elyse, that's exactly the situation in which he would find himself in not too long a time. He couldn't let that happen.

He stood and walked to his bedroom; the old wooden floor creaked loudly in protest under every step, but the empty scotch glass on the side table next to the couch made it clear it would take a lot more than squeaky wood to wake up Jim.

Rich entered his hundred-square-foot room, sat on his bed, and exhaled fully. His stomach churned a bit — it felt like it had those horrible days right after his parents died. He was scared now. Scared of doing the wrong thing. Scared of *not* doing the *right* thing. Scared of working toward a goal he'd never reach and not realizing he'd never reach it until it was too late. Scared of losing Elyse and once again being alone.

It terrified him to his core. He loved her without temperance, without governance, without reason. And he was willing to do anything to make sure he never lost her.

If he needed to get 'settled' before they could be together, then he damn well would do what was necessary to get settled — no matter what that was.

And that's why he picked up the phone and called Jason Spade.

25

Rich watched from a distance as Jason Spade emerged from underneath New York City, the A Line having just dropped him off near Port Authority Bus Terminal. One look at Spade's face and Rich could tell he was pissed. The lawyer hadn't deigned to ride the subway in years but Rich insisted during their phone call that Spade not take a cab or car service, since they kept records of pickups and fares. From here on in, Rich Mauro was all about being careful.

Rich kept his distance and followed Spade a few blocks to their arranged meeting place, Forty-Fourth and Eighth, right in front of the St. James Theater. Though Rich had insisted on this location, it wasn't because he was a fan of theater. The theater district in the heart of Broadway was a tourist trap — half the people on Forty-Fourth Street at any given time were from either Iowa or Hamburg, just there to take in a musical version of a bad Hollywood film, stay at a chain hotel, eat dinner at the Hard Rock Café, and then go home to tell everyone about how they'd 'experienced' New York.

But the tourists provided one benefit. Rich wanted to have this discussion where there was very little chance anyone would know them. And since they couldn't do it in Rich's house (Uncle Jim was home because his back was acting up) or

150

the law firm (for obvious reasons) and because Rich didn't want to meet at Spade's apartment (Rich had some demands and didn't want Spade to feel he had a home-court advantage), the patch of sidewalk underneath the iconic vertical sign that read ST. JAMES was as good a place as any.

Spade reached the sign, saw that Rich wasn't there, and lit a cigarette. Rich ducked behind a dumpster and watched him for a moment. Spade was anxious; that was obvious. But he wasn't scared. The guy was excited — very excited. You could see it in the way he rocked back and forth on his feet and in how he barely inhaled on his Marlboro before pulling it from his lips to quickly flick away ashes. Yeah, the guy was excited. Or a bit coked up, which wasn't exactly out of the question. Or perhaps a little of both. Rich took a deep breath, ran across the street, dodging a livery cab along the way, and approached Spade.

'What the fuck, Mauro? Were you following me?'

'No, I just got here. Did you take a cab?' Rich asked, even though he already knew the answer.

'No, you fuckin' psycho. I took the subway like you *insisted*. I had to sit next to some guy whose ass I could smell. Literally. Through the pants, into the air, up into my nose. Pungent homeless-man ass-smell is now inside me. It's disgusting down there — I don't know how people do it,' Spade complained as he tossed his smoke and quickly lit another. 'This cloak-and-dagger shit is ridiculous. We could've picked a corner downtown, a block from the firm — '

'I told you, can't risk being seen talking — '

'People see us talking all the time; they know we hang out sometimes . . . '

'You come down to the Printers. We rarely talk in the firm around other lawyers. But it's always *inside* the building. If we were outside during working hours and a group of O and T lawyers were walking from the Stock Exchange to the firm, what would they say?'

' "Hey, Spade'? And then they'd ignore you because you're a Blazer.'

'No, they'd *take notice* of me 'cause I'm a Blazer. They'd think, *Hmmm, why is a partner's son leaving work in the middle of the day to talk to a nobody outside of the office? That's queer.*'

'*You're* queer. Look, if we're gonna do this, you gotta relax or you're gonna blow a valve — '

'No, if we're gonna do this, *you're* gonna have to accept the fact that you can't do it without me and there are gonna be a lot of ground rules that I'm setting right now. One: no talking on the phone. You want to meet, call me and say you wanna grab a beer. We'll meet at McMahon's. I know people there; it's safe.'

'That's all the way in Astoria, man. I live on Eighty-Sixth and Columbus . . . '

'Deal with it. And no one can know about this except the people involved. I find out you're braggin' about this to one of your supermodel friends, it's not only over but I'll break one of your arms.'

'Easy, tough guy. The only people involved are you and me, and we aren't going to tell anyone.'

152

'Well,' Rich said, looking away for a beat before turning back and locking eyes with Spade, 'that brings me to my last condition. It's not just you and me. We have to bring in the other Blazers.'

'The welfare baby and the thug and the retard? No fuckin' way. They were our outs.'

'What do you mean, our *outs?*'

'If something goes wrong, we'll set it up so it looks like the black guy or the Rican did it; we got built-in scapegoats locked up in the barn, and you want to open the door? You're out of your mind,' Spade countered.

'I wouldn't let them take the fall if you tried it, so you can throw that reasoning out of the window.'

'Damn it, Mauro. What are you, a Boy Scout?'

'Yeah, from Troop Go Fuck Yourself. These guys need to be included from the get-go, stupid. The Printers is small and we're up each other's asses twelve hours a day, sometimes longer. If I start making extra copies of documents or letting you come in and poke around, even off-hours, odds of one of them seeing something are fifty percent. The chances of them turning us in are a hundred percent 'cause even though they won't know what I'm up to, they'll know I'm up to *something*. And they're smart enough to know that if something goes down, the rich, white, asshole lawyers will assume that *the black guy or the Rican did it*. So before they get pinched for something they didn't do, they'll narc on me just to save their own asses from the prejudiced bastards upstairs, you included. Either we let

153

them in and share the money or we do it ourselves and risk getting caught.'

Spade ran his hand over his forehead and bent at the waist in frustration. 'Why are you doing this to me?'

Rich knew why he was doing it. For the reason he had already stated — he thought it was the smarter move. But he also thought it was the right thing to do. Rich had barely started at the Printers and now he was looking to take a huge shit in the middle of the operation. Doing that without consulting the other guys there would be a punk move. Rich wasn't about to do it.

Especially since he knew Jason's proposal could help more than just the two of them, and more than just the two of them needed some help.

He had seen Vice struggle for months now, trying to take care of his brothers and sisters on a very small salary, always telling Rich how one day he was going to get his own place, move his siblings in with him, get them away from his parents. Rich knew that would never happen. Not unless something drastic took place. And if Spade's scam was anything, it was drastic.

And Rich had walked in on Eddie helping Dylan fill out some employer information for Medicaid forms. Rodriguez — too proud to show that he was getting assistance from the state — quickly covered up the paperwork, but Rich had seen the distinctive New York State Department of Health seal. The man busted his tail at his job every day, but after taxes and expenses he still couldn't pay for the delivery of

154

his child, let alone the medical costs as the kid got older.

Rich knew Dylan was thinking the same thing because Dylan was always asking Eddie: 'When's O and T gonna give us some damn health insurance?' And Eddie always gave the same answer: 'When Green Lantern starts using an ACDelco battery to charge his power ring.' Dylan didn't know what the reference meant, but he knew enough to figure out he wasn't getting insurance any time soon.

So Rich was jacking up Spade's blood pressure in front of the St. James because he knew that including the others was the proper thing to do, both strategically and ethically, though Rich realized how preposterous it was to factor in ethical considerations when planning a criminal conspiracy.

Spade stood up straight, accepting the situation, though not happy about it.

'You know, now we're going to have to whack the money up five ways,' he grumbled.

'Yeah,' Rich agreed. 'But I'm not telling Eddie Pisorchek what's going on.'

'You sure about that?' Spade asked sarcastically, his frustration showing. 'You sure you don't want to let Special Ed take the reins of a multimillion-dollar fraud?'

'I just don't want him caught up in all this, okay? He's a good person.'

Rich meant both statements. He sure as hell didn't want to involve Ed; the whole thing would probably just confuse and upset him. And Ed *was* a good person. The truth was, Eddie

155

Pisorchek was a very good person.

When he had to move around you to get to the storage closet, he said, 'Excuse me,' and if you sneezed, he said, 'God bless you.' Not 'Bless you' but '*God* bless you.' If you were coming down with a cold, Eddie Pisorchek would ask the Lord to bestow blessings on you so you didn't get sick. And despite the fact that he sometimes lacked patience with Blazers who worked slower than he did, Eddie had never failed to take the time to walk Rich through a task when he had first started at the Printers. Eddie fed the feral cats by the loading dock every morning, gave a part of his lunch to a bum who slept on a sewer grate every night, and donated a portion of his paycheck to his church every Sunday. Rich thought Eddie was one of the purest, most wonderful people he had ever met. He didn't want to dirty him with what he was about to do.

So it was settled. They would approach Dylan and Vice — guys Rich liked, guys who seemed to really need the money, guys who, despite their varying backgrounds, weren't too different from Rich himself.

And Eddie would be left out of the risk, but not the reward.

Spade reluctantly agreed to the terms. But he was pissed. He walked to the curb and defiantly hailed a cab.

He was done taking the fucking subway.

26

'What are you, some kind of plant? You tryin' to entrap us or something?' Dylan said, leaning forward in his chair, barely subdued anger filling his eyes.

This was not the response Rich had been hoping for. Dylan's scarred fingers were curling into a ball and he was eye-fucking Rich so hard, Mauro could feel his corneas getting pregnant.

Rich thought he had done everything right. He waited until he, Dylan, and Vice were alone in the basement and then carefully laid out what Spade had suggested to him the other night in McMahon's Pub. He started off with a sweetener, talking about how much he had enjoyed working with them, getting to know them, and so on. He complimented, commenting on how obvious it was that they cared about their families, those born and unborn. And he sympathized, commiserating with them over how hard it was to make a living on the wages paid by Olmstead & Taft. And then he presented — laying forth in clear language and quiet voice how they were going to use the nonpublic information that they had access to in order to make a killing in the stock market.

Rich was certain they'd jump at the chance before he was even done with his pitch.

He was positive they'd be ready to do what

needed to be done so they could care for their loved ones.

He was wrong.

Vice just stared back at him, saying nothing. Rich hoped he was at least thinking about the offer. But Dylan was clearly furious. He believed that it was a trap.

'I knew they'd never send some white boy down here unless there was a reason. They're lookin' to see if we're robbin' them . . . '

'No, man, I'm just talking here. I'm just trying to gauge interest . . . '

'They're settin' us up!'

Dylan sprang from his seat, and so did Rich — not to attack (he was still intimidated by Dylan) but as a defensive maneuver.

'You know what,' Rich said, worried he was about to get his ass kicked. 'Let's pretend we never had this conversation. This was a bad idea.'

'No, it's a *good* idea,' Vice said, speaking as if waking from a daze. 'It's a *damn* good idea.'

Dylan shifted his gaze from Rich to Vice. 'How the hell is riskin' our jobs and our asses a good idea?'

'Think about what we're doin'. We're just lookin' at paper we look at a million times a day anyway, right? 'Cept now we're gonna look at it a little more closely. That ain't illegal — '

'Right, exactly — ' Rich chimed in.

'Shut up, dumb ass,' Vice barked. 'I'm pullin' your Italian fat outta this Puerto Rican's fire, so don't interrupt.'

Vice continued. 'Then all we're doin' is we're buyin' stock. That ain't illegal either. Now, it bein' against the law 'cause we're doin' it with info that other people don't got — that just seems like some technicality bullshit to me. What was it that white dude with the hot wife said in that movie?'

Vice got blank stares.

'C'mon! The flick where he had his hair all slicked back and he had a cell phone size of a shoe box?'

'*Wall Street*. Michael Douglas,' Rich offered.

'Yeah, Michael Douglas. Brother said, 'Most valuable commodity I know of is information.' Well, I don't know what a commodity is, but I sure as shit knows what information is, and we're balls-deep in that shit right here.'

'I can't get in any more trouble,' Dylan said. 'I got strikes against me.'

'What do you mean, *more* trouble? What strikes?' Rich asked.

'None of your fuckin' business,' Dylan answered.

'Hey, if I'm gonna be teamin' up with you guys, I gotta know — '

'I never said I was teamin' up with anyone, *papi*,' Dylan said, taking a menacing step toward Rich.

Vice moved between the two of them. 'Hey, easy, muchacho . . . we throw down in the basement of O and T and we're all as good as fired. Now, hear me out. You don't trust him, but you trust me, right? You and me ain't that different — I'm just as broke and three times as brown and I gotta get somethin' more than hourly pay comin' my way if I'm gonna break my

159

shit cycle. And so do you. You got a girl and a kid and an ego that don't like takin' them government checks . . . '

Dylan shot Vice a look.

'Sorry, bro, but you left the Medicaid form in the copier a few months ago. But ain't no shame in your game; I've gotten more handouts than some dude runnin' down *The Price Is Right* aisle.'

Vice's analogy was met with silence.

'You know,' he explained, ''cause people are all stickin' their hands out and shit to high-five your Next Contestant ass when you run on down to Bob Barker.'

'Drew Carey hosts the show now,' Dylan corrected, stone-faced.

'Bitch, you know the point I'm tryin' to make,' Vice snapped back. 'Look, man, I done some fucked-up stealing in my life. I've swiped radios, parking meters — hell, once I boosted one of them UNICEF gumball machines they got in the front of drugstores. That's right, man, I stole from *UNICEF*. Didn't *want* to, but I *had* to. I got kids dependin' on me and you might not know that world yet, but before you know it your old lady's gonna shoot eight pounds, five ounces of responsibility outta her happy hole and you're gonna feel the pressure. This shit the Eye-tie's suggestin' — it ain't fucked-up stealin', it's *smart* stealin'. It's white-people stealin'. Stealin' with papers and computers instead of ski masks and guns. It's how the rich get rich and stay rich. You pickin' up what I'm layin' down, my man?'

Dylan didn't say anything for a moment. His

160

demeanor was still intense, but then again, there was always something intense about Dylan Rodriguez. His hands with their scarred fingers, which by now had uncurled, rested by his sides — this allowed Rich to breathe a bit easier. Then Mauro noticed the fingers on Dylan's left hand gently, maybe even subconsciously, tracing the outline of the wallet in his pocket, the same wallet in which Rodriguez kept the small ultrasound photos of his unborn daughter. That's when Rich knew Rodriguez was going to say yes.

'Okay, I'll do it,' he said, confirming Rich's instincts.

Rich exhaled, relieved, though the truth was he had almost wanted Dylan to say no. If just one of them hadn't agreed to it, then the deal was off, and a not-insignificant part of Rich had been hoping that was exactly what would happen. But it didn't. It was full steam ahead.

And he knew that even though he was scared shitless about the whole thing, he needed it to work. He wanted to make some money and marry Elyse, all the while moving toward his goal of becoming a lawyer. And once he had put a little folding money in his pocket, taken care of tuition bills, and slid the right ring on Elyse's finger, he would turn his back on this whole chapter of his life and never think of it again. It seemed easy enough in theory.

Rich exhaled again, harder than before, finally relaxed for the first time since he had called Spade from his bedroom and told him he was in. That relaxed feeling lasted all of four seconds.

'I'll do it too.'

Rich didn't even have to look to know that Eddie had just exited the storage closet.

And he had heard everything.

27

Rich, Dylan, and Vice just stared at Ed like deer in the headlights, if the headlights had caught those deer planning a federal crime. Eddie just stared back — he was holding a fluorescent green highlighter in each hand.

'No, Eddie, you misunderstood what we were saying — ' Rich started, but Ed didn't let him get too far.

'No, I didn't,' Eddie contradicted him. 'You guys are gonna buy stock in the companies that are doing big business deals. Like Donald Trump from *The Apprentice*. And you're gonna read the secrets in the stuff we copy. I want to do it too.'

Vice walked to Ed, put a hand on his shoulder.

'Listen up, Special Ed, this is some big-boy shit we're doin' here. You don't want no part of it, but that don't mean you gotta say nothin' about what you heard, right? I mean, you my man, Pisorchek.'

'Yeah, Ed,' Rich added. 'I always intended to give you a cut. I swear. It's just that — '

'It's just that you all think I'm *stupid!* Well, I'm not. I work the machines better than any of you. I get left out when the kids on my street play stickball; I get left out when Grandma and Grandpa go to the movies; I get left out when Pastor Morris does collections — and that's not even *hard*; it's just walking the aisles with a basket! I'm not gettin' left outta this!'

'Easy, easy, Ed. Take it down a notch, okay, pal?' Rich said reassuringly. Ed's voice was getting too loud for comfort, even if the chances of anyone hearing them down in the basement were slim to none.

'I've been here longer than any of you guys,' Ed yelled. 'I been here seventeen years! This is *my* office! Not yours! And Grandpa says we don't have enough money for Disney World!'

'What the fuck are you talkin' about, you crazy bastard?' Vice asked, exasperated.

'I want to go to Disney World but my grandpa won't give me the money,' Ed continued. 'So either you let me do it too . . . or I tell.'

For the first time in his life, Eddie Pisorchek was putting his foot down. The others knew there was no way they were going to dissuade the guy. It was too dangerous to play games with him — he was a wild card. He *would* tell.

So Eddie Pisorchek was in.

Vice spun on Mauro. 'Damn it, Richie, you didn't check this shit out before you started talkin'?'

'The storage room door was closed and the light was off,' Rich defended himself. 'What the hell, Ed? What are you doin' in there in the dark?'

Ed held up the fluorescent green highlighters. 'Colorin' Green Lantern stuff. These markers kinda glow in the dark,' he said, as if it were the most logical thing in the world.

'Oh, for shit's sake,' Vice said, shaking his head.

Two loud raps on the door made Vice jump, grabbing his chest. The source of the knock was

Jason Spade, looking intense as ever.

'*Jeez Louise, man!* What is this joint? A fuckin' surprise party?' Vice exclaimed.

Spade eyeballed Ed and then looked to Rich.

'Hey, man, thought maybe we could grab a quick lunch — '

'You can cut it out. I talked to them. They know. They *all* know.'

Spade paled. He looked at Ed, gave him a slight wave.

'Are you kidding me?' Spade exploded. 'You told the fucking retard!'

'Hey, take it easy, man,' Vice said, defending Ed.

'He overheard,' Rich explained. 'And watch your mouth. You talk like that again and you and I've got a problem.'

'We already have a problem. You let Corky here on the team — '

Before Spade finished the sentence, Dylan, who hadn't said a word since Ed appeared, grabbed him by his lapels and half pushed, half threw him across the room into a stack of at least twenty boxes of paper. Dylan then got eye to eye with the lawyer, whose back was up against the boxes.

'Get your hands off me,' Spade said, trying to sound tough but with his voice quivering. 'You know who I am?'

'Yeah, you're a crooked lawyer tryin' to steal a few bucks from the man — so that makes you no different than us. You watch how you talk to Ed, understand, *¿mi pana?*'

Even though Spade didn't speak Spanish, he

165

nodded his head that he understood. Rich watched as Dylan let go of Jason and he quickly realized the difference between him and Rodriguez. Where Rich threatened Spade and told him they would have a problem if Ed was insulted again, Dylan had gone from docile to überviolent in a matter of seconds. It was as if that violence was always right there, barely under the surface, and all that was needed was a flick of a spring-lock and the cage door would pop open, and God help whoever was in the way when it did. Rich was even more thankful that he had avoided that fight with Dylan outside the firm on his first day of work. He wasn't too sure he would have survived.

Dylan grabbed his coat and headed for the door.

'Eddie, I'm taking a sick day — I got two left this year. That cool?'

Eddie just nodded at his protector.

'Dylan,' Rich called out before he reached the hall. 'Are we still cool too? All of us? With what we talked about?'

Dylan pointed at Spade. 'I don't like this guy. But if you're all gonna do it . . . ' Dylan rubbed the back of his neck. 'I'm takin' the night to think about it.'

And with that, he was gone.

Rich watched him leave, realizing that the decision to go through with Spade's plan or not hinged solely on Dylan Rodriguez — a quiet man with broad shoulders, scarred fingers, and an obviously flashpoint temper; a man whom Rich knew next to nothing about.

28

The mercury-vapor lamps buzzed incessantly, as if they were complaining about their lot in life, saying, *Okay, we'll do our job, but our noise will be our protest.*

Their official job was to light the crossover bridge that spanned the train tracks of the 168th Street subway station, deep underground in a tunnel that had been blasted through the hardest of New York City's bedrock over one hundred years ago.

But their unofficial job was to act as a beacon for Dylan. He always rode up in the front of the train so he could look for the lamps. He knew when he saw them glowing, off in the distance, fighting the dark, he was home.

This day was no different. Dylan saw the amber kiss of the lamps and smiled. *Home.*

The subway car lurched and shook to a stop. Dylan couldn't wait to get off — he had caught the 1 Line, the local, and it seemed the train had stopped every minute to vomit a mass of humanity onto a platform, only to gorge itself again a moment later. By the time he reached 168th Street, Rodriguez had had enough of being underground. Even so, he let everyone near him disembark first, helped a woman get her stroller over the gap, and then ascended the stairs into a September night so unseasonably hot it felt more like July. He was sweating through his white dress shirt so much that it had become transparent in places.

As Dylan walked the three blocks to the small apartment he shared with Rosa, he could tell that people were staring at him. After all this time, they still stared. They still couldn't believe that Dylan Rodriguez was humping it on the subway, an hour each way, every day, like any other commuter. Like a mortal.

Dylan Rodriguez was the last person anyone in the neighborhood would've expected to find working in a law firm — a half-Irish, half-Puerto Rican former warlord of the PR Nation (one of the most powerful and deadly gangs on the East Coast; it kept headquarters just outside of Washington Heights). He'd made his bones and broken bones, had shot and been shot at, had led by fear and respect simultaneously. At twenty-seven, he felt like he'd lived several lifetimes. He was the kind of guy who never went civilian. Usually, when the word *former* was used to describe a banger from the PR Nation, it was just a euphemism for *dead*. Most members of the Nation were recruited at fourteen or fifteen, and they stayed in the Nation for life, which often meant until their midtwenties. Life spans were short north of 155th Street.

Dylan's father, Alvaro, was a founding member of the Nation — now he was a street legend serving three consecutive life sentences in Sing Sing, the prison on the Hudson thirty miles north of the city that was the genesis of the phrase *being sent up the river*. Alvaro was sentenced when Dylan's mother — a freckled

168

redhead, the daughter of Irish immigrants — was pregnant with the boy, so Dylan had known his father only as a man in an orange jumpsuit with a number stamped over the heart. But considering that a wall of scratched plastic had always separated them, they had a close bond.

Alvaro realized over the years, as he missed the joys of being a true part of his son's life, that the path he had chosen had led his tan ass nowhere except prison. He tried like hell to keep Dylan away from the PR Nation, but it was impossible — the Nation was drawn to Dylan as much as Alvaro had been drawn to the Nation. Dylan was the son of Alvaro Jimenez Rodriguez — aka *El Machina* — and the boy was destined to wear the Nation's colors.

Alvaro did everything he could to convince his son of the dangers of the Nation, but not much can be done when a son is in danger and his old man is in chains. Dylan, like all boys, wanted to be like his father, and Alvaro couldn't risk insulting the Nation by asking them to stay away from his son, as the loyalty and protection of Alvaro's prison *familia* was all that kept him alive inside Sing Sing. Rival gangs would have taken Alvaro out years ago had he not had the solidarity of the Nation brotherhood on the inside. So the man could only stand by and watch his son fall into the same abyss he did.

However, Alvaro's status afforded him certain privileges — so when his son, after thirteen years of bangin' hard for the Nation, after growing to be the gang's warlord, wanted out, out of the only real family he'd ever known, Alvaro was

169

able to call in *one* favor, and it was a big one, because Alvaro and Dylan both knew the Nation rules:

1. Blood in.
2. Blood out.

This meant that to gain membership in the Nation, you had to draw the blood of an enemy. Dylan got to 'plant his rose,' as the bangers called it, with a three a.m. drive-by that took down a midlevel soldier of the 4-1 Grid, a gang from Harlem that was creeping too far north for the Nation's liking.

It also meant that if Dylan tried to leave the Nation, they would *bleed him out*. There were only these two rules, but the Nation followed them to the letter. Everyone knew you could leave the Nation only in a casket.

But after a gun battle with a rival gang from Fort Lee about who controlled drug traffic coming over the George Washington Bridge had left a seven-year-old girl dead — the result of a stray bullet from Dylan's nine-millimeter — Dylan needed out. He couldn't live the life anymore, couldn't live with *himself* anymore. Though never diagnosed, Dylan became clinically depressed.

He tried every pill he could get his hands on, but nothing worked. It hurt Dylan to be alive; each breath was a reminder of the warm air escaping from the little girl's mouth as she looked up at him with big, black eyes. She didn't know Dylan was the man that shot her — she didn't know what had happened. She was quickly dying; you could see the life draining from her face, and in her eyes you could see she was confused. And scared. And, most surprising, *grateful*. She looked up at Dylan, this stranger who held her in his arms as she gasped for air — a sound Dylan still heard in his dreams — and damn it if she wasn't thankful: thankful that this man was there to hold her, thankful that he was telling her everything would be all right when in her heart she knew it wouldn't be, thankful that she wasn't going to die alone.

The child's death played over and over in Dylan's mind every day, slowly, in excruciating detail. The feel of the girl's blood-sticky cornrows pressed into the palm of his hand, the rumble of a nearby garbage truck's diesel engine, the way her blood snaked out of her side and through the divots and indentations of 159th Street like a crimson river flooding a gray canyon — it all repeated, again and again, the memory skipping as it replayed, as if the vertical hold in Dylan's mind were broken and nothing could fix it.

Dylan spent many nights alone on the roof of the corner check-cashing place, which over-looked the street where the girl died. It bothered him that he had had to leave her there, her body still warm, when he heard the sirens coming down Broadway. On a street lined with government projects whose windows were always dotted with dozens of tenants watching the urban play-house below because they knew the show on the street was better than anything the TV could serve up, there was no lack of witnesses. Every-one saw everything. But when the cops showed,

171

nobody saw nuthin'. So at 6:00 on the evening that Dylan Rodriguez killed a child, he was at home instead of in jail, sitting on the couch with his girlfriend, his hand resting on her stomach, praying that the baby inside, which had been confirmed only a few days earlier, would grow up to be nothing like its father.

That unborn child was the only thing keeping Dylan from spending one last nine-millimeter shell on himself. He swore to himself, but more important, he swore to that baby inside his girl, that he would never lift a gun again, that he was done with the life. The problem was, the only way the Nation let you end *the* life was by ending *your* life, and that's where Alvaro came in.

Alvaro had never thought that all the triggers he'd pulled and the lives that he'd taken, all the misery he'd caused during all his years on the outside with the Nation, could ever be worth it. But it was those years that allowed him to build his street cred, his rep, his name — and it was his name that allowed him to save his son. An agreement was made.

And on a morning when the air was cold, Dylan walked to the Church of Our Lady of Esperanza on 156th Street and entered quietly. It was hours before the first mass, but Catholic churches seemed to enforce silence on their own, through their very existence, so Dylan tried not to make a sound. He dipped his right hand into the holy water — every finger except his thumb had a letter tattooed on it. A *T* on the pinkie, a *P* on the ring, an *R* on the fuck-you finger, and an

172

N on his trigger-puller: *The Puerto Rican Nation*.

He pushed his hand deeper into the marble aspersorium so that each tattoo was completely submerged. He was hoping that through divine intervention the blessed liquid would burn the tats right off, peel the skin clean from his flesh. He didn't care how much it hurt; he prayed for it to happen. He took his hand from the water — no such luck, tats were still there. No matter — he'd get those damn things off if he had to take an electric sander to his paw and scar up his hand for life. He just wanted them gone. But he'd deal with that later — right then he just had to take care of what he'd come there to do. So he walked to a pew, knelt down, and prayed.

When he was through — it took all of five minutes — he left the church and walked all the way to the run-down warehouse on Dyckman, not far from the old train yard. A faded cinder block kept the double doors of the warehouse wedged open. After entering, Dylan kicked the block to the side and walked down a makeshift hallway created by cardboard boxes and industrial crates stacked ten feet high, about three yards from the exterior wall.

A few steps in and he heard the door slowly creak closed behind him. A few more, and he heard it snap shut with a dull, echoing *thud*.

At the end of the hallway, Dylan turned into the large open space of the warehouse. There the *gobernadores*, or governors, waited for him — twenty-two of his Puerto Rican Nation brothers dressed in their colors. There were

173

hundreds of PRN members in New York, *thousands* throughout the country, but there were just twenty-two chapters and, hence, twenty-two governors, one for each chapter. This was in recognition of December 22, the date the Puerto Rican flag had been adopted and officially flown over the island. The governors stood in a semicircle, facing inward.

Dylan walked through the opening where the circle was broken. As he did, he nodded to the men he had led for years.

'*We are the Nation,*' he shouted, loud, clear, a leader addressing his troops.

'*The Nation is ours,*' the men, on cue, barked back in unison.

Dylan stopped in front of Benito, his lieutenant for the past three years. Benito Guarez, or Benny G, as he was called, so as not to be confused with Benny Alvarez (Benny A) or Benny Benitez (Benny B), had been running with Dylan since he was fifteen. At twenty-three, with thick arms and a crown-of-thorns tattoo that circled his shaved head, Benny G hardly looked like the skinny kid with no money and a bad haircut that Dylan had taken to his side years earlier.

Benito made a fist and placed it against his heart. From his fingers, the letters *TPRN* faced Dylan. Dylan returned the gesture, showing his tats as well.

Benito looked Dylan in the eyes.

'I love you, jefe,' he said.

'I know you do,' Dylan responded.

A few seconds passed as the two men studied

174

each other. Then Benny G's upper lip curled in an almost undetectable sneer as his other hand, also in a fist, flew up from his side and caught Dylan flush in the jaw. The force of the blow knocked Dylan down; his skull struck hard against the warehouse floor. As his head bounced up from the impact it was met with the tip of Benito's boot, straight into Dylan's right temple.

This was the deal Alvaro had cut with the governors. As a token of respect for all Dylan's father had done for the Nation, his only son's life would be spared, but not without a cost. Dylan wouldn't be bled out of the gang, but he would be beat out — he would stand before the twenty-two men who had once been his soldiers and allow them to beat him to within an inch of his life. No weapons could be used, but none were needed. Dylan Rodriguez was properly known as the toughest Rican on the block — but even he couldn't handle almost two dozen street thugs coming at him at once.

Besides, the deal also stipulated that Dylan was not allowed to fight back. The deal stipulated that he had to take it like a bitch. The deal was bullshit. Alvaro founded the damn Nation; the governors could have just let Dylan walk. But they had to save face — the son of one their legends was turning his back on them. So the son had to pay.

After the kick to the temple, another fist, not Benny G's, slammed deep into Dylan's gut, twice, in quick succession, causing him to fold into the fetal position and spit up blood as another kick caught him square in the back.

Dylan's right eye was already swelling shut but he was able to see the semicircle closing in on him like vultures on road-kill. All of his brothers wanted a piece of him — each wanted to show he was man enough to beat someone who was curled up in a ball. Some spat on him; he could feel the phlegm smack wet against his face. Men who once worshipped him and did his bidding now spat on him; they spat on their jefe.

But Dylan welcomed the beating. He just closed his eyes and did what his father had told him to do: he prayed to the Virgin Mary to protect him until it was over.

Hail Mary, full of grace, the Lord is with thee . . .

As Dylan lay there, trying to stay conscious so he could keep his face and head covered with his arms, he savored the moment. He relished the pain, knowing every kick, every punch, took him one step farther away from the only life he had known and one step closer to the life he now knew he wanted. The life of a civilian. A life where he had a nine-to-five, where he punched a clock, paid taxes, where he'd feed his child with milk that wasn't bought with blood money.

Weeks later, after the swelling had gone down and only purplish-yellow bruising was left around areas that sutures had held together, Dylan had to lie at his job interview. He said he'd been an amateur boxer and that his latest defeat convinced him that a heavyweight belt wasn't in his future. The interviewer laughed. He liked Dylan's sense of humor — but then again, Eddie Pisorchek was always an easy laugh. And since Dylan really seemed to want to work, and another body was needed, Eddie gave him the job.

A week later, Dylan had the first legitimate day of work in his life . . . at the Printers of Olmstead & Taft.

The 'legitimate' part didn't last too long.

29

For the next few days they all waited on Dylan's answer. If he said yes, then it was a go. If he said no, then the whole plan was scrapped. The only way it would work was if they were all on board — either all in or all out.

Every day after work, no matter what time Rich left the Printers, and no matter how muggy it was underground, Spade was waiting for Mauro at the bottom of the subway steps, the shoulders and collar of his jacket darker than the rest of his suit from sweat.

'Did the wetback give you an answer yet?' Spade would ask every day.

'I don't know; why don't you ask him yourself? And a wetback is a Mexican, idiot.'

Rich knew Spade was terrified of Dylan and wouldn't go near him unless absolutely necessary. He sure as hell wouldn't push him for an answer.

It got to the point where Rich started walking a few blocks to the Rector Street stop to grab the W Line to avoid Jason altogether. Growing up in an environment where everything he ever wanted was usually provided promptly and without debate had made Jason Spade a very impatient man. That was probably one of the reasons he thought of the scam in the first place: he wanted his money when he wanted it, not when his father deemed it appropriate to dribble the funds through the cracks of some family trust. How was Spade supposed to get his coked-up whores and Japanese motorcycles *that* way? He could wait for the old man to die but that might be decades, and though Jason had often fantasized of killing his father, especially since that night in the New Haven jail, he didn't have the balls to go through with it. His lack of patience made sitting around waiting for Dylan's answer excruciating.

But he would have to wait because Dylan wasn't sure. He had gotten out of the life completely — he had paid a big price, with his body and his wallet and his street rep — so he wasn't about to reenter criminal activity lightly. He used to lord over Washington Heights, walking the streets like a boss, in charge of everything from the kickbacks to the turf lines to which fire hydrant the kids could turn on when it got too hot in summer. He didn't care what it said down in city hall — *he* was the fuckin' mayor.

But those days were over. Now he was an everyday hump like the rest of 'em, following the rules, paying for what he wanted instead of taking it, letting the government cut out its piece from his paycheck before he got his. And he was fine with it because he had a woman he loved who had a baby girl on the way and he wanted his old life to be no part of her new life. She'd have an honest father who earned honest money.

And even though young punks who once feared him now made comments under their breath as he walked, Dylan was fine with that too. And even though they had to move out of a sweet three-bedroom apartment into a one-room studio, Dylan could pretend to stomach that as well. And even though they had to buy a secondhand crib and wash it down with Purell in preparation for his baby girl, Dylan tricked himself into believing he could also live with that.

But when he came home one night to find Rosa crying at the kitchen table, one eye swollen and black, Dylan Rodriguez could lie to himself no more. Between sobs, Rosa explained that soldiers from the 4-1 Grid had accosted her just a block from their home. They smacked her around, told her that they were expanding, that 188th and Wadsworth was *their* territory now and that Dylan better not cause any problems.

'They said they don't believe you're out of the Nation! They think you're playin' the cops,' she cried. 'They said if you don't get out of Washington Heights, they'll come after me . . . *and the baby*.'

Dylan held her head as she wept into his chest. He stroked her hair and told her he would take care of everything. But the truth was, he couldn't take care of *anything*. Just months ago he would have grabbed all three Bennys and the rest of his soldiers and put half of the 4-1 Grid in the river for touching Rosa. But he didn't have any soldiers anymore — they wouldn't even make eye contact when he passed them on the street.

With no backup he knew he had to get out of Washington Heights, *but go where?* He could barely make his rent now, and Manhattan rents

180

were worse — he hadn't exactly saved any money when he was the jefe. Saving wasn't a concern when you were getting brown paper bags filled with five figures in cash every month.

He could try Brooklyn or Queens but there was heavy gang presence in those boroughs — if word got out Dylan Rodriguez was moving there no one would believe he was retired; they'd think he was looking to take over a new spot, and he and Rosa and the baby would have a *new* bull's-eye on them.

So Manhattan was the answer — America's largest gated community, full of white people and coffee shops and bookstores with their own coffee shops, small apartments that started at thousands per month, and no place to get good *cuchifritos*. But Dylan had more to worry about than fried pork. He had to worry about protecting his family.

So one Wednesday morning, at around eight thirty, Dylan entered the Printers, hung up his tan Dickies jacket, grabbed his blue blazer from a hook, put it on, and turned to Rich, Vice, and Eddie, who, as they did every morning, were waiting for Rodriguez's answer.

Dylan looked at them for a moment, then said, 'I'll do it.'

Then he checked the delivery log, grabbed a full document cart, and pushed it out the door without another word.

Simple as that.

They were now all co-conspirators.

30

Dylan Rodriguez wasn't much of a typist. His index finger had pulled many more triggers than it had tapped keyboard keys. He was embarrassed to hunt and peck with the other guys in the room — he didn't want to look stupid — so he pretended to be thinking hard about what numbers he should enter as his pointer finger surreptitiously and silently pushed down the little squares on the Mac that bore his chosen numbers.

The numbers had a very specific meaning to almost everyone in the world. But for most, that meaning was associated with pain and tragedy; Dylan associated the three digits with nothing but love and hope and new beginnings.

He wasn't sure if he was doing the right thing. He had his doubts.

But since fifteen dollars an hour before taxes doesn't really help new beginnings get off to a great start, he pressed Enter.

31

'My parents were sad you couldn't make it tonight, but they totally understand,' Elyse said over the phone.

No, they weren't, and no, they don't, Rich thought as he turned his back to Vice, Ed, and Dylan, who were standing on the other side of the basement doing the same thing Rich was doing as he talked to Elyse — *waiting.*

'But dinner was yummy,' Elyse continued. 'Chicken piccata, penne alla vodka — I'll pack some up and save it for you, bring it over tonight.'

'Yeah, I think I'm just gonna stay here,' Rich said. 'We've got a huge document production going out and then I have to study and it's just easier to hunker down at a desk for the night and then go home in the morning and catch some sleep before my late-afternoon shift.'

'Babe, listen to me for a second,' Elyse said softly, concerned. 'You need to take it a little easier. You're working around the clock, going to class all spring, then summer courses — you barely sleep — you're going to burn out.'

'I'm fine,' Rich lied. He was physically and mentally exhausted. 'Few more months and it'll be winter break — '

'*Three and a half* more months — '

'Look, I gotta go, the guys are doing all the work without me and they're gonna get pissed.'

Truth was, Eddie was now at his computer, Vice was pacing, and Dylan leaned against the wall, arms crossed, staring at the door. Rich hated lying to Elyse, but he had no choice. He couldn't tell her that they were having a clandestine after-hours meeting with an O&T attorney who was going to kick off their scheme to violate almost every law and regulation the SEC had.

'*Hey, your parents broke out Scrabble! Let's be a team — I'm horrible at this stuff and totally need help.*'

Rich heard the voice calling to Elyse and instantly knew who it was, but he asked anyway.

'Who's that?'

'Oh, my parents invited Terry Garhart to dinner — '

'That son of a bitch is *there* — '

'It's my parents' house, Rich, they can invite whoever they want.' Elyse whispered so no one on her end could hear. 'It was a last-minute thing.'

'So as soon as I told you this afternoon that I couldn't make dinner they run out and invite that dickbag. They are so transparent.'

'Rich, once again, he's a family friend. I'm not getting into this with you.'

'I really don't like him being there with you — '

'Then come over.'

'You know I can't. I have work. Man, I'm gonna kill that bastard — '

'Take a breath. You're just going to have to accept that tonight I will be playing Scrabble with another man, as salacious as that is. I promise I won't let him fondle my vowels.'

'If he goes near you, I'll scrabble his fuckin' brains.'

'You mean *scramble*.'

'Whatever.'

'I love you, Rich.'

'You have no idea how much I love you.'

Rich hung up, more motivated than ever to get things moving already.

'Where the hell is he? He said nine; it's ten thirty.'

'How the hell should I know,' Vice said, still pacing. 'He's *your* boy. Maybe he got cold feet.'

'Maybe you have 'em too,' Rich said. 'You're wearing a hole in the carpet. You having second thoughts?'

'Hell no, just a little nervous.'

'Why are you nervous?' Rich asked, suddenly nervous himself now that he'd heard Vice express some hesitation. 'I thought you said this was *smart* stealing, *white-people* stealing.'

'I did. And then last night I remembered all them white people I seen doin' perp walks after they'd been busted for Enron and Madoff and all that kinda shit. Just got me spooked a little . . . but I'm cool, *paesan* . . . I'm cool.'

Problem was, Vice didn't look cool. And even Dylan seemed a bit tense, though it was hard to tell because, like usual, he wasn't talking. The only one who seemed completely unfazed by the whole thing was Eddie, who sat quietly, sipping a Yoo-hoo, clickity-clacking away at his keyboard.

'Yeah, well, I'm cool too but if he's not here soon, I'm going home,' Rich threatened. 'I mean,

185

if he can't do what he says he's gonna do, then how can we trust him to run this thing the right way?'

Rich was *once again* looking for an excuse to not go through with this. The magnitude of the risk they were about to take would sometimes slap him across the face like a wet fish, shocking him into acute awareness of the dangers inherent in the plan. But then he'd think about Elyse, and how much he loved her, and how much she loved him, and how she was the only person in the world he wanted next to him when he'd wake up sweat-drenched, the result of his recurring nightmare.

At least twice a month for seventeen years, Rich dreamed he was standing on a rowboat watching his parents in the water below him as they clawed at the boat's side and then, unable to hold on, sank to their deaths. He'd gasp himself awake, as if trying to breathe for his mother and father, his heart tearing from its moorings, his soul crushed once again by a part of his psyche he couldn't run from, the part that liked to wait until Rich was asleep and peaceful and then sucker punch the shit out of him.

Elyse would curl in tight to him, wrap her arms around his chest, kiss his cheek, and stroke his hair — she was the only person who could make him feel calm and safe when calm and safe did not seem possible.

But despite that, Rich was torn. He knew if he didn't move forward with Spade's plan, he could lose Elyse forever. And if he did move forward and got caught, he could lose her just the same.

But whenever Uncle Jim decided against playing a horse that then didn't finish in the money, he'd smile knowingly and say, 'Sometimes the best move is the one you don't make.' So Rich, taking Spade's failure to show as a sign, took his uncle's advice and tossed his blazer on a hook and headed out.

'That's it, this whole thing is bullshit. I'm outta here.'

But before anyone could respond, and before Rich made it to the door, Spade entered.

'Gentlemen,' he stated formally. 'I hope you're all ready to make some fucking money.'

32

Spade put down his briefcase, popped it open, and laid out his laptop like a salesman setting out his samples. He pressed a button and the computer began to whir to life.

'You're late, Counselor,' Vice chided.

'Had to get a new wireless card set up on this thing. Don't want to use the firm's wireless server to do this, do you, dummy?'

Vice didn't really understand much of what Spade said after the word *new* so he didn't say anything in response.

As Spade typed and pointed and clicked away, he explained what he was doing, and amazingly, it was all relatively simple. He had opened a corporate brokerage account in an offshore financial institution in Wales that served as both a bank and a brokerage house. The name of the company Spade had created was BD Industries. He had buried it under more than a dozen LLCs, LLPs, and DBAs. The thing was hidden under more paper than the Canyon of Heroes was after a ticker-tape parade.

'Wanna guess what the *BD* stands for?' he asked.

No one wanted to play guessing games so when he didn't get a response, Spade answered his own question. 'Basement dwellers.' He smiled. 'I named it after you guys.'

No one felt honored by the sentiment.

Spade continued. 'Any individuals transferring

amounts of ten grand or more sets off alarms and then the banks have to deal with SARs, which we don't want.'

'That lung disease all them Chinese had a few years ago?' Vice asked, totally confused.

'Yeah, Vice, we don't want the bank to contract SARS. Jesus Christ: suspicious activity reports — *S-A-R* — *SARs*. If we're incorporated, we're good — corporations move hundreds of millions every day. We'll be moving a lot less, just my seed money, and then any trades we make, we keep the total value close to that number, which the Office of Foreign Assets Control will have in their system as our threshold. We stay within those parameters, no alarms. Just silence. And silence in this case is definitely golden.'

'How much seed money you putting in?' Dylan asked.

'Five hundred grand. Some from a savings account, and I sold some jewelry, watches — the few trinkets of my own my dad actually lets me have.'

Just hearing the number made Vice look over to Rich and Dylan and raise his eyebrows in the way you raise your eyebrows when you realize that whatever you're involved in is the real fucking deal.

This money would get to Wales via a wire transfer. It would bear no names, and neither would the overseas account — that would be identified solely by a password composed of fifteen digits. Any movement of the funds would be performed via this fifteen-digit number.

Since there were five of them, they would each

pick three numbers and keep them secret from one another. That way, no one could access the money alone. They were bound together by nefarious sin and numerical sequence.

If money was to be withdrawn, each one of them would have to enter his own code, which no one else knew, into a transfer order on the bank's Web site. Since Wales is part of the United Kingdom, the money could be transferred to the British Virgin Islands without any foreign taxes levied, and, hence, no international-transfer verification needed. And since a strange quirk in the international agreement between the British and U.S. Virgin Islands made the U.S. dollar the BVI's legal currency, the funds could be quickly exchanged back to American greenbacks quite easily. And because there was banking reciprocity between the two island territories, the money was easily exchanged between them — again, no paper trail. And once the money had left the *British* Virgin Islands and entered a *U.S.* Virgin Islands' bank, it could be wired to the continental United States and picked up at BD Industries' corporate bank account without having any identification other than a very specific fifteen-digit account number.

Damn, Rich thought, *Spade might be an asshole sometimes, but he sure as hell knew what he was doing when he set this thing up.*

After he explained how everything would work, just to be safe, Spade took some time installing firewalls and ghosting software so none of what he was doing could ever be traced back to his computer.

190

'It's like banging a girl from the hood; you throw on a second condom just to be prudent,' Spade said as he worked away at the laptop. 'No offense, Vice.'

'Fuck you,' Vicellous responded halfheartedly, too tired to get into it with Spade.

Truth was, they were all getting tired. There'd been the stress of waiting all day for this to begin, and with the almost-two-hour setup process by Spade, it was now well past midnight. But then, quite unceremoniously, Spade finished.

'So I guess I'll pop my cherry first,' he said as he spun the laptop around so its screen faced away from Rich, Vice, and Dylan. Eddie was about twenty feet behind Spade, his back to all of them, still hunched over his computer doing his work — he couldn't have seemed less involved or, frankly, less interested in what was going on. Rich actually envied him.

Spade entered his code: 6-6-6. The numbers appeared as asterisks on the screen, so when Vice switched places with Spade, he had no idea what numbers the young lawyer had entered. Vice entered his three digits, and then Dylan went after him.

Then it was Rich's turn.

His fingers rested on the laptop but he was unable to summon the strength to push down a single key, as if each little square of plastic weighed a thousand pounds and could not be budged. He thought about his Uncle Jim, an honest hardworking man who had sacrificed so much to raise his brother's son, and how

191

disappointed he would be with his nephew if he knew what he was about to do. He thought of Max Seymour, and the crime he was about to perpetrate in the firm Max had helped build. He thought about his parents in heaven — were they looking down at him now, shouting from the clouds for him to just close the laptop and walk away from all of this? Maybe it was they, through some kind of otherworldly intervention, who were making it so hard for him to perform the simple task of typing three numbers.

But then he thought about Elyse. And how at that very moment it was quite likely that Terry Garhart was not so innocently reaching across the Scrabble board to arrange her tiles — his hand *accidentally* brushing against hers. Elyse was too naïve, trusting, and unaware of her own beauty, and Garhart was too damn slick. Rich's hesitation jumped ship and he quickly depressed three keys.

'Okay, Eddie, you're up,' Rich said.

But Eddie was busy. He was still engrossed in formatting a document that had been sent down from the corporate department. He stared at the screen of his Green Lantern-sticker-covered monitor, double- and triple-checking all the margins and specs of the brief.

'Hey, Pisorchek, you're out of the on-deck circle, time to step up to the plate, baby,' Spade called out, but Eddie didn't respond. 'This is why I didn't want to clude-inay the etard-ray,' Jason pig-Latin-whispered into Rich's ear, making sure Dylan didn't hear him for fear of another confrontation.

Rich ignored Jason, though he noted to himself that Jason was becoming a bit bolder in his demeanor — insulting Vice, taking a jab at Ed; he was the master architect of what they were doing and he knew it. He was getting cocky and he didn't wear it well. Mauro wondered if a truer side of Spade's personality was starting to emerge.

Rich came up behind Eddie and gently put his hand on Ed's shoulder.

'Eddie,' Rich said, 'it's your turn.'

'Turn for what?'

'It's your turn to pick your numbers. For the account.'

'You do it for me. I'm busy, Richie.'

Rich began to think that maybe Spade was right, maybe letting Eddie in on this thing was a bad idea.

'I can't, Eddie. The whole point is that no one knows anybody else's numbers,' Rich explained patiently.

'I'll do it after I get this document formatted. The lawyers marked it *urgent*,' Eddie countered. He had turned to Rich and opened his eyes wide when he said *urgent* so Rich would understand the *urgency* of the situation.

Rich could only smile. Eddie was totally unaware of the irony of his wanting to do a good job for the very firm from which he was about to steal privileged information.

Rich turned to everyone and shrugged. There was nothing they could do about it. Eddie Pisorchek could not be rushed — he would steal on his own schedule.

Eventually, when he was ready, Eddie stood, walked over to the laptop, and entered his three secret numbers.

The account had been set up. Now all they had to do was use it.

33

The first company they hit was Paxton Industries, a Tempe, Arizona-based technologies company that was about to be the target of a takeover bid by a much larger outfit from Boston. Spade had searched through scores of documents, hundreds of pages of data — keeping them all at the Printers until past three a.m. — looking for what he called 'the perfect peach to pick.' When he skimmed the Paxton SEC filing, which was several days from being submitted to the government agency, his heart began to race. He read it more carefully and then read it once again. His eyes grew wide with excitement as he held it up and yelled, 'Fuck yeah!,' startling Rich, Vice, and Eddie, all of whom had fallen asleep — Eddie in his chair, and Rich and Vice on the floor, using industrial-size rolls of bubble wrap as makeshift mattresses. Dylan had stayed awake the whole time, sitting on a bench under the hooks where they hung their blazers, watching Jason. Years of doing it the hard way in Washington Heights had taught Dylan never to show your lids to someone you didn't trust, and he sure as hell didn't trust Jason Spade. He'd stay up all night if he had to.

For good measure, Spade turned over a small metal garbage can and began banging on the bottom of it. 'Come on, wake up, dummies! This is the one! This is *it!*'

Eyes were blinked and rubbed as everyone gathered around Spade, who explained that he had just found the perfect investment opportunity. Paxton was a midsize company with a market capitalization of $4.8 billion. That meant that it wasn't so big that it got a lot of attention, like a Microsoft, for instance, and it wasn't so small that significant stock trades would disrupt its regular trading volume enough that it would be obvious something weird was going on. The average volume for Paxton was a little over 731,000 shares traded per day, which meant that based on the stock price of $12.30 per share and the amount of money they had to invest, $500,000, they could buy about forty thousand shares of the company. That would account for only a bit above 5 percent of the daily volume, not enough to arouse suspicion.

'Tom DeGrassi's heading up this matter,' Spade said. 'I wanted in on it, knew it would get some good press in the *Journal*, but he's got his own little team of pet lawyers, only ones he'll work with . . . ' Jason said petulantly to no one in particular. 'Well, who's getting the last laugh now, huh, boys?'

Spade jumped on his laptop and pulled up the Web site for the bank in Wales. 'Okay, we all gotta put in our codes,' he said, typing in his three numbers.

'We already did that,' Vice said sleepily. 'Hours ago.'

'We gotta do it every time we wanna use the account,' Eddie said softly, tired himself.

'Glad one of you is smart enough to follow

along,' Spade snapped, 'but not really thrilled it's Eddie. Get your heads in the game, morons.' In the same order as the first time, everyone entered his three-digit code. Spade took the reins of the laptop once more and made the characters dance. His fingers moved like a concert pianist's, effortlessly but with conviction and an underlying passion. Jason Spade had been thinking about this plan for a long time, and he knew that in a matter of seconds, it would be real.

He finished the transaction and hit Enter. He looked at the others.

'Okay, we have an order to buy forty thousand shares tomorrow morning when the market opens; who wants to celebrate?'

'So are we done?' Dylan asked bluntly.

'Yeah, man, we're done.'

Dylan walked out, mumbling, 'See you tomorrow, Eddie,' without turning around. He was gone.

'Man, that is one Mexican who ruins the fiesta.' Spade snorted.

'He's not Mexican, he's Puerto Rican,' Vice corrected.

'Same shit, different donkey,' Spade cracked as he packed up his laptop. 'Now let's go get drunk.'

'I gotta sleep,' Vice said.

'Me too,' Eddie said.

'Shame, Ed, was really looking forward to picking up chicks with you,' Spade deadpanned as Vice and Ed exited.

'See you guys tomorrow,' Rich said. Vice and Ed grunted tired good-byes, and Rich and Jason found themselves with no one but each other.

'Good, didn't really want to hang out with the Island of Misfit Boys anyway. Now, in two phone calls and thirty minutes I can have us neck-deep in Taiwanese pussy,' Spade boasted as he dialed a number on his cell.

'I'm going home too, Jay,' Rich said, gathering his things.

'C'mon, man, it's me here. You don't have to play the Boy Scout. You'll be married to Elyse soon enough — how about you grab a little sushi roll when you still can. It'll stay between us — attorney-client privilege.'

'I don't do stuff like that.'

'Like what?' Spade said, amused.

'Cheat,' Rich said as he shut off all the lights in the Printers. 'I don't cheat.' They were now both lit only by the glow of the large EXIT sign over the loading-bay doors.

'You don't cheat?' Spade asked rhetorically and with more than a bit of pissed-off bite as he walked toward Rich. 'What the hell do you think you just did in here tonight? Wall Street is a board game — and it's full of people who actually read all the fine-print instructions inside the box. Some follow the rules to a tee — youngest player goes first; you can't move your piece until you've rolled doubles. Others pick and choose what they want to abide by — if the spinner lands right on a line you lose a turn, but we'll just say you can spin again. And then there are guys who wait until the other players have to take a piss and then grab an extra couple hundred from the bank. Guess which one you are, Rich.'

198

Rich didn't answer. Spade was up in Rich's personal space, challenging him. There was something about the way Spade was looking at him that made Rich uneasy, but he couldn't put his finger on exactly what it was.

'Let me tell you which one,' Spade continued. 'We just took non-public, material, inside information and traded on it. Now, I know you're really just a hammer-swinger who swapped your flannel shirt for an off-the-rack blue blazer, but even you know that what went down tonight makes you, at the very least, a *cheater*. You wanna keep your dick in drydock and be superboyfriend for your girl, that's fine. But don't stand there after what *we've all done* and say *you* don't cheat. Someone like you does not have the right to look down on someone like me.'

Jason, his eyes narrowed, glared at Rich, unmoving. Rich realized what it was about Jason that was making him so uneasy: it was the pure animosity Jason was displaying toward him; the unadulterated *dislike* Spade seemed to have for Rich. They had had arguments before, but this was different. It was as if now that the plan had been put into action, Spade's mask had been lifted off, tossed aside, and burned to ashes.

It was now amazingly clear that he had never really liked Rich at all. How could he? As Jason saw him, Rich was so far below him on the social ladder that he was only another rung, something to be stepped on to get where he wanted to go, and that's *exactly* what Spade had done with Rich. He'd *used* him. That was his plan all along

— to befriend Rich so he could have an in to the confidential information that was copied and bound in the Printers. It was so obvious now. All that talk he gave Rich about how hard it was for him being a partner's son at the firm; all the parties and events he took Rich and Elyse to; all the advice, *one friend to another*, about how Rich was going to lose Elyse forever if he didn't do something about it — it was all complete bullshit. Jason Spade didn't give a damn about Rich Mauro. He couldn't have given less of a shit if he had never eaten bran in his life. And now that Spade had the plan rolling and Rich was fully sucked in, Spade wasn't going to hide how little he thought of Mauro any longer.

'The first day you came down here . . . ' Rich said, a bit stunned from what he had just realized, ' . . . you knew. You knew what you wanted and you knew I was your way to get it. All these months — *this, tonight* — this was your plan the whole time . . . '

Rich didn't continue — he didn't have to.

'See?' Jason said as he picked up his briefcase, his laptop now locked up inside. 'And it only took you this long to put it all together.'

He walked to the door but turned back. 'And by the way, Rich,' he added, 'I've got an IPO that I'm sending down here in the morning. Make sure it's formatted and on my desk by two.'

And then Spade left.

34

They received a call the day after they put in the purchase order — *The trade went through* was all Spade said when Vice answered the phone — but that was it; they went about their business as if nothing had happened.

They put together the legal papers the lawyers wanted, just as they always had.

They delivered them promptly to the attorneys, just as they always had.

Chip stared daggers at Rich every time he got too close to the old man's elevator, just as *he* always had.

Everything appeared to be back to normal. Except it wasn't, because now Rich, Dylan, Vice, and Eddie worked in relative silence. And when they did speak to each other, it was all business.

Rich, John Sullivan's looking for his client memorandum, what's the ETA?

'Bout twenty minutes, Ed.

Eddie, we got that heavy card stock?

Top shelf, to the left, back of the storage closet. But don't print color on it, it smudges.

You wanna do the next run?

Sure, I got it, but then I gotta cut out for class. That cool?

All the camaraderie, the ball-busting, the fart

jokes that Vice served up with relish and that Eddie reveled in — it had all ended. They often worked without a sound for hours, the whirring of the machines their only sound track. They didn't talk about what they'd done; no one asked about it. Rich was fine with that. Perhaps if they didn't acknowledge it, it would just slowly disappear.

But Rich knew that wouldn't happen. The crime was the slug; their silence was the salt. But every morning, the slug was still there, farther along the stoop, almost at your front door. No matter how much Morton's you poured on it, it wouldn't dissolve. In fact, the more they *didn't* talk about it, the bigger it seemed to loom over them, because eventually, and they all knew this, one of them would have to bring it up.

As it turned out, that person was Eddie.

'Hey,' he said innocently one day while putting brads in scores of thick briefs that were requested on three-hole paper, 'when are we going to get our money? That money Jason said he was going to get us from the stock thing — '

'Shut the fuck up, man,' Vice said, rushing over to Ed.

'But it's been a while and I want to go to Disney — '

'Eddie, my man,' Dylan said in a quiet, calm tone in the hopes that Eddie's relatively loud voice would mimic his, 'it's not a good idea to talk about that in here. You wanna talk about it, we can all meet outside of work and talk about it until we turn blue, okay, bro?'

'I can call Jason and set something up,' Rich

added. 'He can fill us in on what's going on.'

Eddie looked at the other three Blazers; he could see from their faces that he had scared the ever-lovin' shit out of them by bringing up the topic. He kind of liked it. It wasn't often Eddie Pisorchek was able to scare anybody. Usually, he was the one being scared.

'Okay,' he said. 'Sorry, guys, I was just wondering.'

The others nodded and got back to work.

'Hey, Dylan?' Eddie asked. Dylan looked up at Pisorchek. 'What color does green and blue make?'

'Huh? I don't know, man.'

'Because you said that we'd could talk till we turned blue, and Green Lantern is green, so if he talked till he turned blue — '

'Purple,' Vice offered. 'The mothafucka would turn purple, okay, Ed?'

'That's red and blue,' Rich corrected.

'No, man, red and blue make brown.'

'No, red and green make brown,' Rich corrected again.

'Look at my skin and look at yours,' Vice countered. 'Which one of us knows more about the color brown?'

'I'm brown,' Dylan said. 'You're *black*. You're, like, *very* black. You're like purple mixed with black mixed with midnight.'

There was silence for a moment, and then Rich broke down laughing until tears came. Then so did Vice. Then Eddie got caught up in it and soon he was doubled over. Even Dylan fell in line, wiping his eyes with the sleeve of his blue

203

blazer. What Dylan had said wasn't even that funny, but it was as if they had all been waiting for any excuse to break the tension. Vice shook his head. 'Son of a bitch, you don't say shit for like eight months — you're like a goddamn Puerto Rican mime — and now when you decide to crack a joke, you're gonna crack all over my black ass?'

It felt great, like they had all just run a marathon together and crossed the finish line at the exact same time, all out of breath, all flush with endorphins releasing weeks' worth of stress that had built up inside each one of them.

The laughter served as an outlet. None of them had felt this good in weeks.

And then the phone rang.

Rich answered, barely keeping his composure as he spat 'Printers' into the receiver.

Rich listened to the voice on the other end and his laughter stopped immediately. His face changed; his jaw tightened. The others saw the look on his face and they stopped laughing too. Rich hung up.

'Spade says we have to meet him tonight. Something's happened.'

35

They sat in the same booth Rich and Spade had been in when Spade first reached out to Rich with his idea. Vice and Eddie sat on one side, Rich and Dylan on the other; Dylan insisted on sitting at the open end of the bench seat, facing the door, so he could see who came and went. Spade pulled up a chair and sat at the end of the table with his chair back facing front, like a high-school teacher who wanted his students to think he was cool. It was unnecessary — he more than had their attention.

Spade ordered a scotch from the waitress and didn't bother to ask if anyone else wanted anything. He barely made eye contact with Rich, which was the result of either the last conversation they had had or the fact that the scotch he was drinking clearly wasn't his first of the evening. Jason wasn't slurring his words or anything, but his eyes had a glaze, and Rich was pretty sure Spade was a bit stoned as well as intoxicated.

'Let's get into it, shall we, gentlemen?' Spade asked. In one quick motion he had his laptop out of his briefcase, on the table, chiming itself awake. He looked over his shoulder but there was no one sitting anywhere near them — it was a Tuesday night and McMahon's was dead; just a couple of rummies at the end of the bar and Jake the Take counting the week's receipts in a corner table by a cigarette machine that had been outlawed for years but was still used every day. Jake made book for the neighborhood and got his nickname from taking money from every gambler in Astoria with a system for picking games and beating spreads. Needless to say, he had a few of Uncle Jim's dollars in his pocket.

Spade quickly typed his three-digit code into the first three blank boxes on the bank's Web site and then slid the laptop to Vice.

'Why are we doing this?' Vice asked as he put in his numbers. 'We makin' another trade? I thought all our money was in that Paxton company.'

'It is,' Spade said, sucking down his scotch as the laptop made its way around the table. 'But not for long. We're divesting our position in Paxton, taking our profit.'

Eddie, who was entering the last three numbers into the Web site, looked up at Spade. 'We made money?'

Spade looked at the other three Blazers staring at him — they all had the same question.

'Shit, man, do you clowns read the papers? Did you see the *Wall Street Journal* two days ago?'

The blank looks he got in response answered his question.

'The tender offer statement to buy Paxton stock was filed. The stock jumped almost thirty-two percent on the news . . . '

He was met once again with blank stares.

'We made one hundred fifty-seven thousand four hundred and forty-four dollars without lifting a finger. We're each taking home over thirty-nine grand.'

The blank stares disappeared.

'It worked?' Rich asked.

'Don't sound so surprised.' Spade feigned being hurt. 'My shit worked like a fourteen-year-old in a Panamanian sweatshop on a double shift. Before you know it, our wallets will be choked with cash.'

'When?' Eddie asked. "Cause I want to go to Disney World.'

'Yeah? Well, now you got enough to pay Minnie Mouse to let you ass-fuck her, pal. Shit, throw the Little Mermaid into the mix and have a three-way.' Spade laughed as he polished off his drink and made a few more keystrokes. 'I just put in the sell order; it'll clear in a few days and I've already got in the request to send the money to our corporate account in the States.'

'A few days to clear?' Rich asked.

'At most, but after a couple more transactions the process will speed up,' Spade answered. It was the first time they'd addressed each other since they had all sat down. 'But we shouldn't go get the money yet.'

'Why the hell not?' Dylan asked, in a way only he could. Just four words from him and he had made his point: *You better have a good reason why I can't get to my money or I'll be unhappy, and if I'm unhappy, you're unhappy.*

'Because, amigo, that wouldn't be smart,' Spade responded. Rich was now convinced Spade was more than drunk because playing games with Dylan Rodriguez was like playing chicken with the 3 Train. 'I set up our corporate account at a small savings and loan in Colts Neck, New Jersey. It was established as an agricultural mutual loan association in 1857 and hasn't grown much since. Makes loans to farmers for equipment, land, that kind of shit. But it's in the middle of fuckin' nowhere and has minimal assets and it's not gonna ask a lot of questions when one of its few seven-figure depositors shows up with four other guys to enter the account code. Unless you guys want to just give me your numbers and trust me to get the money myself.'

'Fuck that,' Vice said.

'That's what I thought.' Spade smiled as he chomped on a piece of ice from his drink.

'What do you mean, seven figures?' Rich leaned in, whispering so Jake the Take didn't hear as he passed by their booth on his way to the bathroom. 'You said you put half a million in.'

'That's right, Richie. Good for you, you can count commas. But we've already topped six hundred fifty grand, and at the end of next month we'll be over a million. I don't want to go back and forth to that bank more than we have to; we should play it cool, take money out as little as possible, build it back up big, take cash out again. We're important depositors to that S and L — they won't bust balls, but the fewer visits to Jersey the better.'

Rich didn't argue because Spade was right. In fact, the way he had been handling the whole thing made Rich wonder how successful Jason could be as a lawyer if he'd just stop focusing on how unfair his pampered prep-school life had been and instead turned his energies toward practicing the law. If he'd done that to begin with, felt a little less sorry for himself, a little less victimized by his father, maybe none of them would have wound up in the back of McMahon's talking about how best to collect illegally obtained money.

But if Rich was truly honest with himself, the kind of honesty a person rarely shares with his own consciousness, and *never* with others, he was *excited*. Anticipation had replaced fear, and relief had replaced anxiety. Spade was right. It had *worked*. There was no debating that.

A few more stock trades, a withdrawal or two, and Rich could stop with all of this stuff — he'd propose to Elyse, get his degree, and start making babies with the woman he loved. A boy would be named after his dad, and a girl after his mom. On the nights when they'd been intertwined under the covers and love and cheap wine had allowed discussions of future lives and children who didn't exist yet, Elyse had always said naming their kids after Rich's parents would be a way to honor the people that gave her the man she loved. It was her idea.

She was a keeper, Elyse Crane. Of that, Rich was certain. But *could* he keep her? Of that, Rich had never been certain, and over the past several months, he had become more and more unsure.

But not anymore. Rich felt like he was on his way to getting things right, to where he could hold Elyse in his arms and never have to worry about her slipping through them. He was finally

209

starting to feel confident of that.

And the reason was simple: there was a shitload of money waiting for him in Colts Neck, New Jersey.

36

Aqualine Holdings — a commercial irrigation company specializing in the cleaning and maintenance of municipal pipes and conduits. Blackjack Films — an international distribution company that bought crap reality-show formats from country A and repackaged and sold them to countries B through Z.

Trison Construction — a heavy builder that put up transportation hubs for railroads and bus lines in midsize cities.

Those, and a half a dozen more, were all traded like bad baseball cards by Rich and the others. Each company fell into particular parameters or guidelines that Jason Spade had set in his mind, and each company paid off like a broken Reno slot machine.

Aqualine returned 25 percent. Blackjack Films kicked back 29 percent. And Trison was the big winner — 38 percent. That was still the one to beat.

Rich knew they were getting good, as well as greedy, when they were all disappointed with single-digit returns. When Agen Group, a chemical manufacturer from Fresno, gave up an 8 percent profit, Vice had the balls to ask, 'What went wrong?'

'That's almost ninety-seven thousand in four days, Vicellous,' Spade responded. 'That's not good enough for the guy on food stamps?'

'I'll *stamp* my foot up your ass.'

But Spade didn't pay him any mind. He was too busy reading through documents, as he had been doing nonstop for weeks. Every night after ten, when the maintenance workers had left for the night so there was no chance of their walking by the Printers and spotting a lawyer poring over paperwork, Spade would come in with one flask, two Red Bulls, and three hours of work ahead of him. He barely talked save for the occasional snide remark about the 'crack-baby music' Vice listened to or the noises Ed made when he slurped down a Yoo-hoo.

He would just sit at a corner desk and read through everything the Blazers had put together that day. Some days, he'd get up after fifteen minutes, say, 'Nothing but dogs with fleas' — another nod to the film *Wall Street* — and walk out. But other days he'd find a stock he liked and get so amped that he'd jump from his chair, pump his fist, and shout: 'Now, this little doggy can bark!' It appeared he liked canine analogies. But most of the time, he barely moved. He read, jotted down notes, looked up earnings and price trends on the Internet — say what you would about Jason Spade, but he took his stealing seriously. And when he'd start to slow down, rub his eyes, look like he was ready to call it a night, he'd go to the bathroom and come back two minutes later refreshed and ready to go. Rich didn't know what Jason was ingesting during those two minutes and didn't want to know, but he was sure that whatever Spade was doing in the bathroom was about as legal as what he was doing outside of it.

The money doubled to a million in just a few weeks. By mid-October, another million was in the account. By the time Dylan's little Maria was due, November 9, her father would be a very wealthy man.

Dylan talked to Rich and said it was time for them to go get the money. Rich agreed, as did Vice. They didn't even ask Eddie because the guy had been jonesing to go to Disney World for months. They knew how badly he wanted the cash. It was agreed that Rich would be the one to tell Spade.

As they had discussed that day in front of the St. James, Rich had Spade meet him at McMahon's. At this point, between all the buys and sales of stock, Spade and the rest of the crew had become regulars at the pub. They took their usual seats in the back booth and Rich said everyone wanted the money. To Rich's surprise, Spade agreed it was a good idea.

'It's about time we ring the register,' Spade said. 'How about we meet here on Saturday morning? I've got an Escalade — '

'Your dad's Escalade,' Rich pointed out. He sure as hell hadn't forgotten what Spade had said to him that night at the Printers — how Spade had admitted he had played Rich the entire time — so he enjoyed making note of the fact that Spade wasn't, at least not yet, his own man.

'You're funny, Mauro. I don't know if I ever told you that, but you're a funny son of a bitch.' Spade sneered. 'Funniest thing about you? Your optimism. We have well over three million dollars in the bank, did you know that?'

From the look on Rich's face, it was clear he'd had no idea their little nest egg had grown so much.

'After you take away the original five hundred K, shave off thirty-five percent for corporate taxes so the government of Wales doesn't come after our asses, and leave some in the account so we can keep having fun, you're still going to pocket over three hundred grand in a few days. More than your uncle could blow on ponies if he bet the exacta on every horse from Belmont to Santa Anita.'

Spade folded his hands in front of him and leaned across the table. He continued, speaking to Rich like he was a small child who needed to hear the truth about Santa Claus.

'And you think all that cash is going to change things for you. Lemme save you some time — it won't. Elyse will eventually realize who she'll have to walk down the aisle with: an orphan from a row house with bad aluminum siding. You could have a million dollars — and you will, soon enough — and you're still gonna lose her.'

Rich could've beaten the shit out of the smug bastard right there, but he figured it best to let it lie, at least until Rich had his money. Then maybe Mauro would show the poor little rich kid how hard the orphan from the row house could hit.

Spade got up and grabbed his jacket. 'I'll be outside the bar on Saturday at ten a.m. The bank closes at one on weekends and it's a drive, so

214

make sure the retard can tell time — and the other two, for that matter.' And then he walked out, leaving Rich with the bill for his two scotches.

Rich watched Spade go and knew the attorney had nothing to worry about. Rich would be on time, and he'd make sure everyone else was as well, because he just wanted to get his money and be done with Spade as quickly as possible.

37

'We're supposed to be on Four-Forty South, Jason,' Eddie called from the backseat of the Escalade in a voice that was way too excited and way too loud.

'I am on Four-Forty South, Pisorchek,' Jason called back, already at the end of his rope with Eddie, who had been reading a map and calling out directions every twenty seconds since they got off the Outerbridge Crossing.

'Yes, but you said we're taking U.S. Nine — '

'We are taking U.S. Nine, Eddie — we just haven't gotten there yet! Fuck me! Who the fuck let him bring a map anyway!'

'It's my grandpa's. I took it from the garage; don't tell him I took it, okay, Jason?'

Jason didn't answer. He kept his hands on the wheel and stared straight ahead, trying his hardest to ignore Eddie's prattle from the backseat.

'Jason? Jason, did you hear me?'

No one in the car did anything to dissuade Eddie from talking. Rich, Vice, and Dylan were too busy enjoying the bright red line of rage that was slowly creeping up Spade's neck. It had been entertaining them for the past half hour and had reached well above his shirt collar, which was held snug by a tie. They were all wearing suits and ties, as per Spade's instructions, which were very simple to remember:

1. Wear suits and ties.
2. Let Spade do all the talking.
3. Sit there and say nothing.
4. Enter your bank code when Spade tells you to.
5. Get rich.

'Jason? Did you hear me? I said, please don't tell my grandpa — '

'When in shit's sake would I ever see your grandpa? In what bizarre confluence of random events would the universe put me face to face with some old *fucker* from Staten Island? And if that million-to-one shot actually happened and I found myself with the old bastard, know what I'd tell him, Eddie?'

No answer. Eddie finally realized it was best to be quiet.

'You know what I'd tell him, Eddie? I'd tell him: *Your fuckin' grandson stole your fuckin' map from your fuckin' garage!* And then I'd pray to God that he went home and whipped your ass!'

Vice cackled under his breath. It was good; it helped break the tension, because they were all tense as hell. Just about thirty or so miles away, there was a bank, and that bank had a room, and that room had more than three million dollars that belonged to the five men in the car.

If they played it right today, if they pulled it off, they would walk out of that bank a lot wealthier than when they walked in.

If they messed up, they would walk out of that bank in handcuffs.

38

The bank was exactly as Rich had pictured it
— a small, one-story building with outdated,
barely matching furniture and walls covered with
wood paneling whose best days were years past.
It could have easily been an insurance office or
the regional branch of some horse-shit sales
outfit if not for all the money it had inside of it.
An old rectangular clock behind the teller
counter lit up green and was designed to look
like a stack of cash. The plastic trim around the
clock said COLTS NECK SAVINGS & LOAN — IT'S
TIME TO THINK ABOUT YOUR MONEY!

Rich found the clock's advice unnecessary.
The only thing he *had* been thinking about since
he could remember was his money — how to
earn it, how to increase it, and how to get it from
this fat lady with too much makeup who was
going through some paperwork with Spade. Her
nameplate read MYRA RAYBURN, and Spade sat
with her at her desk; the rest of them were at a
waiting area just a few feet away. They tried to
look casual but they were all getting nervous
because it was taking so long. Vice pretended to
browse a *Reader's Digest* from 2002, and Dylan
fake-texted on his cell, but they kept looking to
Rich for an answer, and the only answer he was
able to give was a shrug. Only Eddie, as usual,
seemed calm — he was busy watching an *I Love
Lucy* rerun on a TV that sat next to a coffee

station that sported a Mr. Coffee from the Joe DiMaggio-spokesperson days.

Rich leaned his body toward the desk imperceptibly, trying to hear what was being said. He got bits and pieces but a damn ceiling speaker was directly over his head and a Muzak rendition of Madonna's 'Crazy for You' made it difficult to hear anything.

He did pick up Spade explaining that BD Industries, which was in the vending-machine game, had just made a large investment in Change Changers. Change Changers were machines that gobbled up all of your coins and gave you paper money back. They needed to withdraw just under $1.6 million in cash to feed about sixteen hundred dollars into each of the almost eight hundred machines that were stored in their warehouse before they were shipped to supermarkets all over the country.

'Oh, like Coinstar,' Myra said, excited that a conversation about one of her customers' businesses didn't include talk of fertilizer and crop reports.

'Well, yes, except Coinstar charges seven percent for their service. We charge only five. So, you tell me, Ms. Rayburn, which of these two machines would you put *your* money into?' Spade asked. Shit, Rich thought, if Spade ever lost his law license he could make a fortune as a salesman.

The banker smiled. So did Spade. Rich almost relaxed for a moment but then he caught Eddie's actions from the corner of his eye; the guy was banging the hell out of the TV. *Loudly.*

'Ed,' Rich whispered intensely. But Ed kept pounding away. *'Ed.'* Though Rich tried to whisper again the second time, it was pointless — he was loud enough for Ed, Vice, Dylan, Spade, Ms. Rayburn, the geriatric security guard by the door, and the bank manager (who was helping someone at his desk) to all hear.

'It went off. The TV went *off*,' Ed said, frustrated.

By this point, Spade was approaching Ed with Ms. Rayburn right on his heels.

'Ed, buddy,' Spade said with all the patience he could muster, 'I'm almost done here and then we'll be on our way. Can you just be patient for me, my man?'

'When I hit Grandpa's TV, it fixes itself.'

'Oh, that TV's been giving us fits for weeks now,' Myra explained, clearly sympathetic to Eddie's 'special circumstances.' 'I can maybe see if the DVD player is working, put in a movie for you?'

'No, that's okay,' Spade said putting his arm around Ed. 'My brother has to learn that he can't get excited like this.' He stepped to Myra, pulled her to the side, and spoke so Eddie couldn't hear him. 'When my parents passed, I promised them I'd watch after him. I made him a full partner in my business — gave him real responsibility — and my other associates are fully supportive of it, but as you can see it presents its challenges.'

'My stepbrother's son, same affliction,' Myra whispered back with a knowing head nod. 'I just think what you're doing with him, keeping him involved, it's just so incredible.' She looked at Jason with fuck-me eyes. He was playing Ms. Rayburn like a big, fat violin that had on too much rouge.

'No. Just a little brother trying to make sure his big brother is okay financially if I go too soon, like Mom and Dad did; he needs to be able to take care of himself . . . ' Spade confided with such conviction that his eyes actually moistened just a touch, but they were not nearly as moist as Myra's crotch must've been at that moment — she was eyeing Spade like he was a basket of brisket. 'Speaking of which, we need to get to that cash to stock up our new investments, now, don't we? For security purposes, all of us have a portion of the account password — even Ed. We wanted him to feel part of the team.' He gave the banker a wink.

'Of course,' Myra said, winking back. She clearly wasn't used to flirting, because it looked like a moth had flown into her eyeball.

Within ten minutes the five conspirators had entered their collective password into one of those small keypads with no-peek mini-awnings that face where the customer sits. After Eddie entered his numbers, Myra gave him a thumbs-up and grinned. 'Good job, Ed.' Ed looked at her like *she* was the one that was mentally disabled.

Within fifteen minutes, they were handed $1.595 million, which Spade and Rich carefully put in two five-inch Zero Halliburton premier silver attaché cases, which cost $550 each and that Spade made clear he was being reimbursed

221

for. Spade had also made it clear on the way to the bank that only he and Rich were to handle the money. He claimed it was because they were the only two of the five with post-high-school education, and if anyone asked any unexpected questions, he wanted only them giving the answers.

Rich thought that was bullshit and was convinced the real reason was that Spade thought the sight of Dylan and Vice, a Puerto Rican and a black guy, loading stacks of hundreds into briefcases would subconsciously make the bank employees uneasy, and he didn't want *anyone* at the bank feeling uneasy.

Spade had asked for the money in a fifty-fifty split of tens and twenties, telling Myra that they were already set for singles and silver from a small video-arcade rental company they ran out of Delaware, where state taxes were lower. If lying were an Olympic event, Jason Spade was Bruce Jenner; if it were an opera, he was Pavarotti.

And once again, Spade proved himself to be quite the prepared thief as the two attachés held the money snugly and perfectly — one holding just Alexander Hamiltons and the other a mix of Alex and his pal Mr. Jackson. The cases were on wheels, which was fortunate because combined there were 79,750 sawbucks and 39,875 twenties, which totaled a little over 263 pounds of walking-around money — or in this case, *pulling*-around money.

The security guard, who introduced himself as Nate, had to be at least sixty-five years old, was fifty pounds overweight, and undoubtedly had multiple health problems — type 2 diabetes, at a minimum — but he insisted on 'providing safe passage to the car.' The man didn't even have a gun, and his billy club was circa 1972 so if they were jumped in the parking lot, there was nothing Nate could do but hope not to get killed.

They got in the Escalade, and it took all of Spade's willpower not to floor the gas pedal and peel the hell out of there. None of them could believe they had pulled it off.

Because Eddie's grandparents always took his paychecks from him, he had never really held any money of his very own. He couldn't wait to fold some up and put it in his pocket, just to know it was there and know it was his.

Rich would have had to drive home a million nails over a dozen years to get even half as much as was sitting at his feet at that moment.

Vice and Dylan were about to get $319,000 each, and neither of them had even said a single word in the bank — the very definition of *easy money*.

Spade carefully backed out of the parking space, put the car in drive, and pulled out of the lot. He made sure to use his blinker — last thing he needed was to get pulled over by a cop trying to make his ticket quota.

He gave a slight honk to Nate as they passed.

Nate waved good-bye, happy to see polite young entrepreneurs experiencing such great success.

39

Rich closed the door to his room and shut the blinds tight; only deli-thin slices of sunlight were able to con their way inside. The homes on his block were practically touching each other, like soldiers lining up for inspection. The narrow alley between Uncle Jim's house and Mr. Saffioti's next door was barely big enough to accommodate the garbage cans. Simply put, privacy was not easily found in Astoria.

Growing up, Rich always knew when old man Saffioti was having a hard time with Mrs. S.'s gravy because the toilet flush rang like a church bell in Rich's room all night long. And many a night when Rich was growing up, Uncle Jim would tuck him in, give him a kiss and a 'G'night, Richie,' and before Rich had even rolled onto his side, he'd hear from across the alley and through his window, 'G'night, Richie, sleep tight, sweetie,' courtesy of Mrs. S., who was clipping A&P coupons at her kitchen table, less than thirty feet from where Rich was lying.

Knowing all this, Rich decided to be supercautious. He hung a navy bath towel from the top of the blinds. It worked well — no way any neighbor going into the kitchen for a glass of water would accidentally see what Rich was doing. Problem was, it worked too well, and now Rich found himself in almost complete darkness. He fumbled his way toward the wall, arms outstretched like Frankenstein, banged his upper thigh on his bed frame, grunted the Lord's name in vain, and eventually found the light switch. Who knew counting stolen money would be so difficult?

He flipped the 80-watt to life and grabbed a bag that he had left on his desk when he had first entered. It was a brown paper bag from the same A&P where Mrs. Saffioti got the basil for her gravy — *If that sweet woman could see what was in this bag*, Rich thought, *she'd be as shocked as an inmate in the electric chair, and with her weak heart, twice as dead.* Spade had whacked up the money and put everyone's share into a separate, non-see-through bag. He kept his in the attaché cases.

Rich emptied the bag onto his bed; stacks of money landed like hail — *thud, thud, thud.* Rich picked up some bundles, looked at them, felt their weight in his hand, held a stack to his ear and ran his thumb down the length of the corners, making the money talk to him.

You did it, Rich! I'm really here, the money seemed to cry out joyfully. *Always knew we'd be together. It just took some doing, is all — but you should know, Rich, that I'm not much different than a gun. No point in having me unless you know how to use me.*

Rich put the money back in the bag, rolled it up tight, and held it to his chest as he lay on the bed looking up at the ceiling. He inhaled deeply through his nose and exhaled relief — years' worth of worry gone with a single breath and a simple crime.

The money had nothing to worry about — Rich sure as shit knew how to use it. He grabbed a stack of cash from the bag, threw the rest of the money under the bed, and hurried out the door.

He had a real estate agent to meet and a run-down storefront to buy.

40

'I told you the movie would be sold out; it's opening night,' Elyse teased as they ran into the bar, desperate to get out of a heavy rain. Hair matted wet against her head, makeup running, and she was still a knockout. She didn't know how not to be beautiful.

'See what happens when I don't listen to you,' Rich said as he helped her off with her coat and onto a bar stool. 'I wind up soaked.'

Elyse looked around Pete's Tavern — it had been a long time since she'd worked there. 'It feels like forever since I was behind that bar,' she said, eyes landing on a tattooed poseur throwing a few Amstel coasters in front of a couple of college kids at the end of the bar. 'Don't know the bartender; bet everyone that I worked with's gone.'

'Most likely.'

'It hasn't changed at all,' she said.

'Neither have you. You were perfect then, you're perfect now.'

Elyse smiled and kissed him softly on the lips. She pulled back just as her peripheral vision picked up the flickering flame of the candles being held by the poseur. He placed them on the bar next to them and then hurried off and began messing with the music on the sound system.

'Looks like Pete's decided to class up the place,' she joked, even though she knew her old boss, the guy who actually owned the bar, was named Eric.

'Amazing, the power of a twenty-dollar bill,' Rich observed.

'You got us candles?' Elyse asked rhetorically with a small grin.

'I knew that movie was sold out this afternoon. I mean, it's opening weekend, for God's sake.'

Tattooed Poseur finished messing around with the stereo and 'I've Been Loving You Too Long' by Otis Redding began playing over the speakers embedded in the bronze ceiling tiles. Poseur leaned back against the bar, his end of the deal finished, his twenty bucks earned.

The song was Rich's cue. He climbed down from the bar stool and got on one knee. He looked up at the girl he loved.

'This was where I first saw you, where I first fell in love with you,' he said. 'And this is the song that was playing . . . '

Elyse didn't respond. Her hands began to shake. Because if there is one thing a woman can feel in her gut, one thing about which her intuition is always correct, it is the moment when a boy in love is about to ask for her hand.

'I know I'm not good enough for you, and I know I don't deserve you, but I know I'm in love with you . . . Elyse, will you please marry me?'

Rich gently slipped the ring on her finger — it wasn't so big as to be ostentatious, but a family of rabbits could live well off the carats for years. Rich had thought long and hard about what to buy — if the diamond was too small, it wouldn't be good enough for her; if it was too big, then the questions would be too many. Like the third bowl of porridge, the stone was *just right*.

And even though the rock cost a bit north of ten grand, it was set in a ring that was gold-plated at best. The ring had once graced the finger of Rich's mother, the only thing her corpse had to offer when she was fished from the Atlantic.

It was a cheap little trinket Rich's father had given her when they were first dating. It was all Rich's dad could afford at the time, but his mother never took it off. It meant the world to her. And after Uncle Jim got it from the coroner and gave it to Rich, it meant the world to him. The Hasid in the diamond district had balked when Rich asked him to build a setting on top for the gem — 'You can't put a diamond like this on a cheap little nothing like that; it's a sin,' Mr. Abreveya scolded. But Rich's mind was set, so the stone was set. Rich's father had given that ring to the woman he loved, and Rich was determined to do the same.

Elyse was silent; tears ran down her face. Tattooed Poseur and the NYU kids who had clued into what was going on watched silently; this drama was much better than the overtime Rangers game on the corner TV — they knew the Rangers would lose, but the guy on his knee looked like he might actually have a chance. Rich looked up at Elyse. 'You can answer now, if you want,' he said, half kidding and half nervous that maybe he wouldn't get the response he hoped for.

Elyse smiled, nodded her head yes, then softly said 'Yes' as she threw herself into Rich's arms. It was the greatest feeling Rich had ever had. It was the feeling of the start of his new family — the first complete family he'd have since he'd been ten. But when it came to great feelings, Mauro was just getting warmed up.

When they arrived at Mr. and Mrs. Crane's house Rich almost had to suppress an erection — *that's* how excited he got when he saw the looks of sickness and disgust on Elyse's parents' faces. They tried to appear enthusiastic when Elyse barged through the front door screaming like a madwoman, holding her hand out in front of her.

But as hard as they tried to hide it, Rich could tell, both of his fiancée's parents were devastated at what was taking place before them on their imported sixty-thousand-dollar oriental rug. Elyse was crying and smiling and talking about wedding dresses already. Mr. Crane looked especially ill and that made Rich especially happy.

'Um, that's a heck of ring there, Rich. Where'd you get it?' he asked, dumbfounded. *You can't afford that, you dirty ethnic, where'd you steal it? That's* what the man really wanted to say.

Rich wasn't surprised by the query. He was keenly aware that after years of scraping by thanks to constantly turning paychecks into tuition payments, he couldn't just show up one day in Brooklyn Heights with cash, an engagement ring, and a wedding date. He knew there'd be questions. So he had made preparations, in the form of purchases.

Mauro had placed a down payment on a small but quaint two-bedroom apartment a few blocks from Riverside Drive, near the park but with no real view to speak of, a short walk from Columbia University. It was a converted one-bedroom, so the smaller bedroom had no closet, the kitchen was of the narrow galley-style variety, and the living room/dining area was large enough for one, but not both, of those intended uses. But it was a perfect spot for a young couple, and it had just enough room for a family to grow.

On the other end of the real estate spectrum was a piece-of-shit storefront in the Bronx that was in such bad shape it had been condemned two years earlier. The floor was warped with water damage, there was visible mold growing up three of the four walls in the front section of the store, and the back-office area had been a breeding ground for rats until they were evicted by a family of creatures that Rich could only assume, based on their ugliness, were possums. Rich had put about twelve grand down on it, and the Indian broker who sold Rich the property could barely contain his glee when Mauro signed the papers. Vishnu himself was smiling down on Mr. Kujibar that day, as he had been trying to unload the dump for almost half a decade.

Rich knew the questions would come fast and furious once he started throwing around engagement rings and starter apartments, and the Bronx storefront provided the answers.

He explained to the Cranes that he'd taken the few thousand he had saved and bought the

231

storefront, thinking he could fix it up with his Uncle Jim and a few of their construction buddies and make a small profit.

It was an armpit, so the price was right. But before he could even raise a hammer he got a letter from the state. The New York Department of Transportation needed to knock down his store and all the other buildings on the street to expand the Cross-Bronx Expressway. There was an eminent-domain battle looming over the fair value of the property, and the DOT wanted to avoid a drawn-out fight and knew it could do that only with money. So even though the building itself was almost valueless, the land it sat on was now worth a fortune. They offered him three hundred grand for a property that only cost him twelve! Rich went on to explain that the other property owners on the block were holding out for more money, and despite the DOT's efforts, the whole thing was now tied up in litigation that could take forever to unravel, if at all, so chances were the entire expressway expansion might not ever happen. But Rich didn't care so long as he got paid, and he did.

This is the lie he told Elyse and her family, and as far as lies went, it was pretty damn good. He had the paperwork showing he had purchased the storefront in case anyone asked, and he had several hundred thousand in the bank to back up his eminent-domain story as well. And when the expressway expansion never took place, Rich had given them a reason as to why not. Elyse asked why he had never told her about the storefront and he said he wanted it to be a surprise — the first investment in their future together.

He had thought of everything, of every possible contingency. And that was the problem.

Because the *possible* rarely trips you up in life. But the *impossible*, well, that can jump up and grab you by the jugular and bleed you out like a slaughterhouse hog.

And despite all of Rich Mauro's conniving, planning, and scheming, he had not prepared for what was impossible for him to imagine.

It was the impossible that would ruin it all.

41

The place on Avenue B was exactly twelve and a quarter miles from the apartment Rosa had lived in in Washington Heights, but it felt more like a million. She no longer had to look over her shoulder when walking back home from the corner bodega and she didn't need to have her keys already out and ready when reaching the street-level door to her building. She felt safe for the first time in a long time and that made Dylan feel happy for the first time in a long time. He had picked Alphabet City because back in the day it had had some Latino flavor, and it still did. Now there were as many artist hipsters and rich-kid fakers on their block as there were genuine brown brothers, but as long as everyone was chill and left his family alone, Rodriguez didn't give a shit. Rosa and their child were all he cared about; everything else took a backseat.

That's not to say that Dylan wasn't shocked at the staggering cost of bringing one tiny little human into the world. He spent a fortune on baby clothes; a breast pump; prenatal appointments (ultrasounds, blood tests, and pills to prevent blood clots because Rosa was missing some kind of enzyme that didn't really affect her but could affect the baby); baby books for baby (*The Goodnight Train*, by June Sobel); baby books for Mommy (*Dr. Spock's Baby and Child Care*, eighth edition); a bunch of black-and-white toys that supposedly were good for the baby's cognitive development; and an overstuffed rocking chair for nursing their little angel in comfort *and* style. And that barely scratched the surface.

The very fact that his daughter would shit and piss cost a fortune — he had to pick up giant boxes of diapers and baby wipes, a changing table, tubes of ointments and creams for rashes that invariably appeared, and something called a Diaper Genie for poops that invariably stank.

And he still had the staggering cost of the planned C-section, which supposedly was necessary according to the doctor but which Dylan was beginning to think was just an excuse to prolong and maximize the medical money grab.

As torn as he had been about jumping back into criminal activity so soon after leaving the PR Nation, Dylan was now thankful every day for Jason Spade's unlawful idea. His girl and soon-to-be-born daughter needed to be safe and provided for, and if taking Wall Street for a little bit of a ride was the best way to do it, then he had no problem with that.

But Rosa and the baby weren't the only women Dylan wanted to spend the money on. There were others.

The first one was a prostitute.

Marie Padilla's mother had died at the age of thirty-eight. Tuberculosis, almost all but gone in the United States, had been making a comeback in the inner cities and the Southwest for a while — a result of illegal immigrants carrying it across the border. Marie's mother violently coughed up

235

blood with her last breath as the deadly killer TB took her life, just a few years before Marie's brother, Jorge, a 4-1 Grid soldier, violently coughed up blood with *his* last breath as the deadly killer Dylan Rodriguez took *his* life.

Marie had no other family, and the money she made as a Duane Reade cashier was far from enough to keep her living in a New York apartment — even the modest two-bedroom in the projects she had shared with Jorge. Jorge had provided all the money, paid all the bills.

Soon after he died, Marie lost her home. Then she lost her job. Then she lost her willpower and hit the needle to cope with the pain. And soon thereafter, she lost her dignity. She turned her first trick after two months on the street.

Dylan saw her one night working the Point while he was driving with Benny A. Benny A eyeballed Marie, decked out in a black, sleeveless, sheer button-up that revealed a blood-red bra underneath it, and a denim mini that showed off half her ass when she walked and almost the whole onion when she bent at the waist. He smirked and thanked Dylan for icing Jorge Padilla because if he hadn't, Benny A 'never woulda been able to tap that fine ass.'

Dylan stared out of his car window and watched Marie, once one of the most beautiful girls in the neighborhood, now worn out and torn out, used up, working the cars as they crawled past, the drivers looking for the girl who was the least beat-up, or the most beat-up, depending on the john.

Dylan knew he'd caused that — he had

236

created Marie's new reality; he was responsible for where she was now. Throw a rock in a pond, lots of people get wet. Marie got drenched.

Dylan went to pick up Marie like any other john. He didn't have a car but he'd rented a Chrysler from a downtown Hertz and drove it up to his old neighborhood. He wore a hat pulled down to his eyebrows so he wouldn't be recognized, though he doubted anyone would believe for a moment the former jefe of the PR Nation was rocking a Sebring.

He saw her by a fire hydrant, one foot propped on it, adjusting a stocking that had twisted. He slowed.

'You wan' a date?' Marie asked, sounding exhausted.

'Sure.'

'You a cop?'

'No.'

''Cause if we have sex it's because I've determined I'm attracted to you. And if you gave me, say one-fitty, it's because you like me, not because it was in exchange of nothin', got it?'

Despite the size of her miniskirt, Marie Padilla knew how to cover her ass.

'Yeah, I just want to get to know you, have some fun.'

Marie didn't say another word; she just got in the car. Dylan gave her a moment to put her seat belt on but she didn't — Marie Padilla was not in the business of protecting her life; she was in the business of extending it the best she could and the only way she knew how, one day at a time.

Dylan drove down the Westside Highway a mile or two and found an old lot by the water where a broken fence and a NO TRESPASSING sign fought it out — the broken fence won.

He parked in the lot. Before he could take the keys from the ignition Marie had already rolled down her window and spit her gum out in preparation.

Dylan didn't say anything; he was nervous.

'You want a half'n half, BJ, or what?' Marie asked, impatient. She could handle about six dates a night before the soreness got to be too much, and this guy was just number two that evening — she needed to get back on the block.

'No, nothing like that,' Dylan said softly, staring straight out the windshield at the water. He couldn't make himself look at her — at least not yet.

'I don't give up the ass if that is what you're lookin' for,' Marie said, trying to sound tough but actually sounding a bit scared as she took in this quiet, imposing man across from her.

'No. I don't want that either,' Dylan responded.

Marie's instincts warned her; her adrenaline rushed. She could tell this guy didn't want sex from her, which could only mean one thing . . .

'Yo, if you try to hurt me, my pimp, Dibby, he'll fuck you up for life,' she said as her hand secretly searched for the door handle behind her.

'Just relax,' Dylan said as he reached into the backseat. Marie saw this as her moment and spun to open the door but Dylan hit the locks. She pulled on the handle, hysterical, as Dylan

238

grabbed her and yanked her back toward him. She screamed.

'No! No! Get the fuck off me!'

'I'm not gonna hurt you! Here! Take it! Here!'

Marie was so hysterical — heart pounding, chest heaving — that it took her a moment to even register the old, stained duffel bag Dylan was pressing into her lap. She looked back up to him, her heavy breathing now slowing down.

'If there's someone's head or some kinda shit in here — '

'No,' Dylan said. 'No. This is yours. Take it and go. You don't gotta do this shit anymore.'

Marie wasn't about to ask questions. She got out of the car with the duffel bag. Before she could take a step, she heard Dylan slam her door closed and peel off. Dust kicked up and blew all over her. She squinted, and by the time she could open her eyes again, the Sebring was almost a quarter mile away.

With her only companion the sound of the Hudson River gently slapping at the nearby rocks, Marie opened the bag. Inside was fifty thousand dollars. Inside was a new life. Inside was Dylan Rodriguez's penance.

The transfer had gone as well as Dylan could have hoped. He hadn't wanted to say anything of substance to Marie, so he didn't. But he knew the next one would be different. He knew he was going to have to say something at the next one. The problem was, at the next one, no one was home.

He rang the buzzer next to MORALES, but no one answered. He pressed the button, softly at first, respectfully, but then louder, repeatedly, more impatient. He had barely been able to psych himself up to approach the door in the first place — it had taken days for him to get the courage to even walk onto the block, let alone up to the building — and now it appeared he was going to have to leave and mentally prepare himself to go through all of this once again at another time. This didn't make Dylan happy — he wanted to get it over with as soon as possible, but it looked like that just wasn't in the cards.

He turned to leave and ran right into a woman carrying a bag of groceries into the building's alcove. Dylan knew immediately that the woman was Connie Morales, the woman he was searching for, because she looked just like her daughter. He also knew it was the girl's mother because her eyes were sad — she was too young and too pretty to have sad eyes, but when you lose a child, it stays with you, like a virus.

'Ms. Morales?'

'Yes?' she answered as she took a small step back through the doorway and onto the front stoop of the building. Connie had lived in Washington Heights her entire life — she knew a gangbanger when she saw one, and this particular gangbanger was holding a suitcase in one hand, a hand that had scars where tats clearly used to be.

She didn't know what was inside the suitcase, and she didn't want to know. She wanted nothing to do with it.

Dylan stepped outside too.

'I was wondering if I could talk to you for a minute?'

'Why? Who are you?'

Dylan glanced toward the preteens who had been playing hopscotch on the sidewalk. They were now looking at him. So was the clutch of old ladies drinking cheap coffee at an ancient metal folding table they had set up in the cement courtyard.

'Can we step inside? You know, for privacy?'

'No, we cannot,' Connie said, now moving down two of the three front steps at a faster rate.

Dylan was at a loss as to what to do. He had worn clean pants and a new button-down shirt. He had trimmed his hair and his fingernails. He'd shaved the thin mustache and the razor-thin beard that ran from his sideburns and down along his jaw until it met up and merged with his goatee. He had done everything he could to look as unintimidating as possible, but at the end of the day, Rodriguez knew, you could scrub a pig all you wanted but it would still smell like shit. And Connie Morales could have smelled Dylan's gangland stench from all the way down at the Brooklyn Bridge — it practically seeped through his pores, even though that wasn't who he was anymore.

Dylan hurried down the steps and caught up to Connie and blocked her path.

'I'm not here for any problems. I'm here to . . . I'm here to give you something.'

He reached out and grabbed Connie's hand. She let out a small yelp and tried to pull it away, but before she could, Dylan pried open her

241

fingers and shoved the suitcase handle into her hand.

'*Here,*' he said forcefully and Connie stopped fighting. She put down her groceries and put the suitcase on the top of the courtyard wall. She pressed the buttons on both sides of the Samsonite locks. They clicked and sprang upward. She lifted the top only a fraction before she saw the money inside. She closed it quickly.

'Who are you?' she asked, wide-eyed.

'No one important. I just wanted you to have that. I just want to say . . . I just wanted to tell you . . . '

Dylan couldn't finish the sentence.

'Tell me what?'

'Tell you . . . that I'm sorry.'

'Sorry for what?' Connie asked, confused.

Dylan said nothing. He couldn't. His throat was tight. His ability to speak was lost. He couldn't say the words. But he didn't have to. Connie stared deep into Dylan's now-wet eyes and she knew. She knew for certain. She knew who he was.

'Come inside,' she said; she took the suitcase and picked up her groceries and walked back up the steps.

Dylan was scared. For all he knew, the woman had a gun in her apartment and she was going to ice him as soon as he walked in. With a gangbanger piece of crap inside her home, she'd get off on self-defense, get her revenge, and get a case full of cash. But Rodriguez didn't hesitate. If the mother of the little girl you killed tells you go inside, you go inside. If she wanted to kill him, Dylan accepted his fate. He owed the woman at least that much.

But she didn't kill him. She silently made instant coffee and poured it into two mugs: one read VIRGINIA IS FOR LOVERS and the other BUSH/CHENEY '04. Even in the mental state he was in, Dylan couldn't help but wonder where she'd gotten the mugs, as he doubted this woman had ever left the neighborhood, let alone the state, and if she did vote in '04 it sure as shit wasn't for the Bush/Cheney ticket.

Then she sat and asked questions. It wasn't a conversation, Dylan could tell that much. It was a fact-finding mission.

Did she cry?

Was she in pain?

Did she ask for me?

To each question, Dylan gave a quiet, short, and honest answer. This was clearly what the woman wanted and he was not going to deny her.

No, she didn't cry.

She seemed to be in shock; I don't think she felt any pain.

Yes, she asked for you.

Neither of them touched the coffee. She'd made it either to stall while she mustered the courage to talk to her child's killer or because that's what you did when someone was in your home. In any case, the state of Virginia and the former president and vice president of the United States remained unmolested.

And then, she must have been done, because she stopped talking. Dylan had answered her last

243

question and she hadn't asked another, and after a while a silent minute had passed between them, and then five minutes, and at ten minutes Dylan decided it was probably best to go.

He got up, placed the suitcase on the table, and left.

He was about twenty yards outside of the building's courtyard when the first thick stack of hundreds hit him hard in the back. He turned and another quickly hit him hard in the nose. He barely blinked. He didn't wipe the trickle of blood that crept from his nostril down to his mouth.

'You want to pay me for my daughter?' Connie asked quietly through barely parted teeth.

'I just wanted to — '

The third stack of bills hit Dylan even harder, snapping the rubber band that held it together and sending money flying everywhere.

'You want to *pay me* for my daughter?' she shouted as she plucked another stack of cash from the pile she cradled in one arm.

'I'm sorry,' Dylan said as he quickly turned to go. Another stack of bills hit him on the back, sending even more money all over 145th Street.

'*You want to pay me for my daughter?*' Connie shouted again, now hysterical, her voice filled with grief and anger.

Dylan moved down the block. Every other step he was hit with another bundle of bills that promptly exploded, releasing paper shrapnel everywhere. And with each throw of cash, Connie bellowed her rhetorical mantra of anguish: '*You want to pay me for my daughter?*'

Dylan kept walking, blood and tears tracking down his face. After he'd gone about thirty yards, the screams at his back stopped and the angry words were replaced by a sound much worse.

Too scared to turn around, Dylan Rodriguez kept going, toward Amsterdam Avenue, leaving behind a grieving mother on her knees sharing her pain with the sky. Dylan would rather've heard the racking of a shotgun at his back than the sounds Connie Morales was making.

And while the mother cried, the children of the Booker T. Washington housing projects ran wildly across the street and between parked cars, chasing almost two hundred grand in windblown cash.

42

As the crane lifted the golden cross up and over Fourth Street to the waiting workers on the roof who were to affix it to the church, Eddie Pisorchek watched with Pastor Morris from the sidewalk, beaming. He couldn't help but think that the symbol of where Christ was crucified looked like a beautiful, glimmering addition sign. And this made sense to Eddie because Eddie *plus* the church *equaled* happy and Eddie *minus* the church *equaled* lonely. Eddie liked *plus* better.

The money for the new cross, choir robes, prayer books, and massive church renovation had been left in a green cardboard box on Pastor Morris's back porch with a simple note: *For the church*. There was a great deal of debate as to who the donor was. The note was signed *H. Jordan* and despite the best efforts of church members and even a few local reporters to track down the benefactor, it was impossible with just the initial *H* to go on.

Only Eddie knew the *H* stood for *Hal*, as in Hal Jordan, aka Green Lantern. Eddie loved spending the money on First Baptist. And the first donation was just the beginning. Soon after the green box turned up, a green trunk mysteriously arrived with new uniforms for the Christian youth basketball team, as well as new balls, nets, sneakers, gym socks, and even a whistle for Coach Korder. The team hadn't won a game in over two years, but at least now they could look good losing. A green envelope stuffed with green currency appeared on the altar one day, firmly wedged in the middle of a King James Bible.

It contained a note that read *For funerals*, and within a week Pastor Morris had purchased a new hearse so that those in Brooklyn who were dead broke as well as dead could travel to their final resting places in style.

Eddie knew Pastor Morris was an honest man and that he wouldn't pocket so much as a penny for himself. That's why, one morning when the pastor retrieved the newspaper from his front porch, he found a green piece of cardboard taped to it that said *Go to R. Taggert's* in sloppy print. R. Taggert's was the nicest men's shop in Brooklyn. It was in Bensonhurst. Everyone from actors to gangsters went there to get fitted. When Pastor Morris arrived there with the piece of cardboard and a befuddled look on his face, Mr. Taggert himself came running from the back office and explained that they had received a green shoe box of cash and instructions essentially directing them to outfit the hell out of whoever showed up with a green-cardboard note.

The next week the entire congregation smiled when the good pastor strutted out to his podium in perfectly tailored Italian elegance. But Eddie, sitting in his usual spot, smiled the most. He liked being able to finally give back to the church. He liked being useful. He liked being a superhero.

Even though the Blazers had been trading more stocks and doubling, tripling, and quadrupling their money, Eddie hadn't spent a dollar on himself. But that was about to change. He collected the little bit of money he had left hidden within his comic book collection — just a few grand — and walked two miles to a Liberty Travel office.

He had anguished over two possible destinations — and he almost couldn't believe it himself when, after all these years of pining to see the Magic Kingdom, he decided to put Disney World on the back burner. He knew in his gut that the other trip was more important.

Some nights the 747s out of John F. Kennedy International Airport flew so low over his house that Eddie was sure if he got out of bed a stewardess would tell him to sit back down. He'd heard the roar of every engine of every type of plane for years, he'd felt the vibrations rattle his bedroom windowpanes, but he'd never actually been on one.

But that ended when he boarded an American Airlines flight and went to his spacious first-class seat. When he sat down he made sure to ask the flight attendant, 'This is the kind of seat that gets ice cream, right?' Eddie had seen an episode of *Seinfeld* once where Jerry sat in one part of the plane and got free ice cream and Elaine sat in a different part of the plane and was all cramped and uncomfortable and didn't get ice cream. Eddie wanted ice cream. He wanted a Jerry ticket. And he'd paid an extra fifteen hundred dollars to get it.

At around thirty-seven thousand feet, Eddie dipped a perfectly warmed chocolate chip cookie deep into his ice cream, the cookie's warmth helping to pave its way. He used the cookie to scoop premium vanilla out of the bowl and into his mouth. Being on that plane was, figuratively and literally, the closest to heaven Eddie had ever been.

Since Eddie couldn't drive, he took a cab when he landed in Lambert — St. Louis International Airport, about one thousand miles from his grandparents' house. When he told the driver he needed to go all the way out to Lincoln County, the cabbie told him to get the hell out of his car. The driver changed his mind once Eddie handed him four hundred sixty dollars in twenties. Eddie rarely bothered to count his newfound money — instead, he used his own system: he estimated how thick a stack of cash to hand over. And he figured the thickness of the wad of cash he had just given the driver was enough to get him to where he wanted to go. He was right.

When the cab arrived at the destination, an hour later, Eddie was disappointed. It was ugly. Located in the middle of nowhere, right on Highway D in Hawk Point, the house was uglier than Grandpa's, and Eddie had always thought Grandpa's was the worst house in the world. But the place that the cab had just taken Eddie to was worse. It wasn't even a house, really — it was a bungalow, and the bungalow looked old, dirty, and tired of standing up.

It was smaller than the house Eddie lived in with his grandparents, and because of decay, missing shingles, and various bad paint jobs, it seemed to be at least three different colors. The front yard had a wheelbarrow that was overturned and rusted and a half-dead pear tree that, Eddie guessed from its sickly appearance, would bear only half-dead fruit.

'How long we gonna sit here?' the cabbie asked.

Eddie knew they'd been sitting there awhile, over an hour at least, but he was prepared to wait as long as it took. He gave the driver another hundred dollars and the driver shut up. About thirty minutes later, a tow truck pulled into the dirt driveway next to the house. A man in dirty overalls got out of the driver's side. A boy, about fourteen, got out of the passenger's.

Eddie exited the cab and walked toward them.

As the man headed toward his front door, he saw Eddie approaching.

'Hello,' Eddie said to them.

'Hi,' the boy replied.

'Go inside the house, Kyle,' the man told his son. The father's tone indicated this was a command, not a request.

'Dad?'

'I said get inside,' the man repeated sharply. The boy instinctively flinched. The way this man spoke to the kid made it clear that the tow-truck driver was not a particularly nice, or even good, person.

Kyle looked from his father to Eddie, then did what his father told him. Once his son was indoors, the man turned back to Eddie.

'Can I help you with something?'

'No.' Eddie was nervous.

'Then you should just move on.'

'I — I just wanted to tell you that I'm Eddie. Your son Eddie.'

Ed Pisorchek Sr. took a long look at the man in front of him. The last time he'd seen his son, Eddie was barely four years old. Now he was grown and on Ed Sr.'s front lawn.

'Figured as much. Not many people with your condition round here,' the father said.

'Uh-huh' was all Eddie could say in response. Eddie felt sick and as if he might cry. His emotions were confusing him and he suddenly wished he were back home. It was the first time Eddie had ever wished he were with his grandparents.

'My mom and dad send you here?' Big Ed asked, a bite to his words.

'No. I came by myself.'

'My parents, they dead or somethin'? 'Cause I ain't got the money or inclination to help out no one.'

'No. They're alive.'

Big Ed took in Eddie for a moment, his eyes looking him up and down. If Eddie had been capable of processing such subtle indicators, he might have seen a slight, fleeting glimpse of regret in Big Ed's eyes — but it was over before it started. Was it regret over abandoning his older son? Or regret over having a son with disabilities? Or regret over how he was reacting to seeing Eddie after all these years? Who the hell knew? Big Ed himself didn't know.

'Then get the hell off my lawn. You ain't my charge,' he finally said.

Ed Sr. turned and started toward his front

251

door. Eddie watched him go, this man he had thought about every day since he could remember being able to think. His bottom lip curled under his upper and anger welled inside him at the realization he'd come all this way just to be rejected again.

'Hey,' Eddie called out. Big Ed turned and looked at him.

'You are a very bad father,' Eddie said through tight lips, doing all he could not to let the tears that had collected at the bottom of his eyes fall down his face. But they fell anyway. Two big drops. No more.

Big Ed stood there, his hands in his overall pockets, with no retort to the truth his son had spoken. Eddie stared at the man defiantly. He refused to be the one to walk off first. After six very quiet and long seconds, Big Ed looked away and then went inside.

Eddie climbed back into the cab and stared out the window as the vehicle barely cleared a U-turn on the narrow street. He was looking at the pear tree on the front lawn when he saw Kyle running toward the car.

'Stop,' Eddie told the driver, and the driver complied.

Eddie lowered the window as Kyle arrived, breathing heavy.

'You're real,' he said. 'I'd heard rumors about you . . . you're real.' Big Ed's other son extended his hand, wide-eyed. 'Hi. I'm Kyle.'

Eddie extended his own out of the window. They didn't shake hands. Their fingers just curled around each other's, intertwined, and stayed there.

'I'm Eddie. I'm your brother . . . I'm older.'

They just looked at each other — each searching the other's face, looking for similarities, proof of the genetic code they shared. Other than the color of their eyes, they didn't look much alike. They said nothing for what seemed to be a long time.

'I have to go now,' Eddie said.

Then Eddie slowly disengaged his hand from his brother's.

Eddie looked at the fourteen-year-old standing outside the window — the boy almost in tears — and understood that of the two of them, Eddie was the lucky one. Eddie slowly lifted his hand up to the young boy to wave, but he didn't move his hand; he just held it there.

Kyle lifted his hand too.

'Bye,' Eddie said. Then he asked the driver to take him to the airport. By the time he landed back at JFK, Eddie had spent more time in the air than he had in Missouri. But Eddie didn't care.

He'd seen what he was missing: nothing.

And he had met his brother — a hurting kid who would be getting a green envelope in the mail soon, addressed solely to him. Eddie had decided during the flight, somewhere over Indiana, that he would send his brother a lot of those envelopes.

And as Eddie laid his head down on his pillow, back home on Staten Island, the thought of Kyle using that money to get away from Ed Pisorchek Sr. made Ed Pisorchek Jr. smile.

43

Dennis Dubroff was lucky. Of all the parentless children in the Miracle Home of Western Appalachia, he got the most packages, the best toys, the nicest clothes. He was the happiest ten-year-old orphan in Pennsylvania and he thanked his sponsor parent by sending him a letter and a photo of himself wearing the latest outfit he had received — a throwback Negro League Brooklyn Royal Giants baseball jersey.

'Look at this here; my boy Double D's lookin' fly!' Vice said as he proudly passed around the photo one night in the Printers.

Rich studied the photo.

'Come on, now, don't he look like a little pimp or what?' Vice asked.

'He looks happy,' Rich said.

'Damn fuckin' straight he's happy. Find me another mountain kid who's got a Wii.'

'It's stupid,' Spade said as he skimmed through paperwork.

'What's stupid?'

'All those charities,' Spade continued. 'You send money, ninety percent goes to administrative costs, you're lucky if the kid gets ten cents' of help. It's a scam. Actually, I give those guys credit, it's a good business model.'

'You know what's a good business model? Mindya. As in Mindya Own Damn Business. You're just pissed off a black man is sponsoring a

254

white boy. That's right, I bought me a perfectly good little white boy and it pisses you off.'

'You know there's an expression for black folk who spend their money in a certain way,' Spade said coyly. 'I just can't remember what it is . . . hmmm, what was the phrase . . . '

'Hey, you can call me nigga rich, porch-monkey rich, Richie Rich — so long as the word *rich* comes at the end of it, I don't give a pound of donkey shit, know what I'm sayin'?' Vice countered. He had gone from being intimidated by Jason Spade to disliking him to not giving a crap about him anymore. Now he just looked at Spade as a very necessary means to a very important end. Truth is, once the money started coming in, everything Vice had done had been in service of that one end. Because to Vice, that *end* was a new *beginning*, for him and his brothers and sisters.

Indeed, as much as Vice liked bringing a smile to little Dennis Dubroff's face, that Appalachian urchin was just a pawn in Vice's grand plan. Dennis was a chit to be played, no different from the parenting class Vice was taking at the New School or the first-aid certification he'd just received after attending the free clinic given by the firehouse down his block or the mini-library he had created out of the walk-in pantry of his new apartment in the West Village — an apartment that fell within one of the best public-school districts in the city.

Vice needed to do all of these things so he could show that despite his criminal record he had turned a corner. He needed to prove that he was a responsible citizen now, a charitable man, stable enough to raise eight children on his own because, with God as his witness, he was going to save his brothers and sisters from the hell he grew up with.

Vicellous Green was finally going to stand up to his parents.

Vice asked Rich to come with him to the courthouse. 'You're the reason I got this money, man. I know if it were up to Spade he woulda cut us outta the whole thing. I need my *paesano* up in the courtroom with me.'

Rich wanted to support his friend but as soon as he walked into the courthouse he wished he hadn't. It was one thing to steal from a distance — an offshore account in Wales, a transfer to the Virgin Islands, a wire back to the States . . . it was all *out there*, things he and the others were making happen with a few keystrokes but not really participating in.

But in the family court at 360 Adams Street in Brooklyn, Rich was right in the thick of it. He was sitting on an old wooden bench in the gallery as Vice stood next to his lawyer at counsel table perpetrating a fraud in the very legal system Rich was planning to belong to one day. The whole thing made Rich feel quite a bit uneasy and just a bit nauseated.

The process was a lot simpler than Vice had thought. He'd reached out to his old pal Neil Shapiro, the energetic public defender who had gotten him his job at the Printers, thereby unwittingly setting Vice off on the largest criminal enterprise of his life. Neil recommended a friend who had a family law practice, and before Vice knew it he was back in court, but for the first time ever, he wasn't there in handcuffs.

One of the biggest hurdles Vice had was explaining how he had earned enough money to pay for the apartment and take care of the kids. He told the judge that while working late at the Printers, he and the guys started playing poker when things were slow. He stressed it was only for fun, that no money had changed hands, as the last thing Vice wanted to do was admit to illegal gambling while he was trying to get legal custody of minors.

After a few weeks, Vice continued, he realized that he had an affinity for the game. Some of the guys said he was a prodigy. So he decided to take a trip to Atlantic City one afternoon to try his luck. He won twelve hundred dollars and instantly knew he had discovered a way to legally supplement his hard-earned Olmstead & Taft income.

Every weekend for months, he'd take the bus from Port Authority to Atlantic City, preying on tourists and novices who'd been watching a little too much *Celebrity Poker Showdown* on Bravo. He'd been cleaning up, he explained, as the court reporter dutifully took down every untruth. To support his claim, Vice had the bus-ticket stubs (though he'd never actually taken the ride) and an affidavit from a pit boss at Harrah's stating Vice was there quite often and was one of the best amateur players he had ever seen. The fact that Vice knew the pit boss's cousin from prison and had paid the guy three grand to sign the paperwork was conveniently left out.

Vice even got some of the cops to testify on his behalf. Officer Spano, who had let Vice go after he had robbed the electronics store, described to the court in detail some of the bruises and marks he'd seen on the Green children over the years and his suspicion that abuse had been ongoing for some time. Unfortunately for Vice and his siblings, that part of Vice's case wasn't fabricated.

Spano was a great witness — an honest cop with twenty-six years behind the badge — and he talked about how he had seen Vice grow up in a tough environment and that no matter how harsh things got, Vice always had 'a good moral core,' despite his occasional run-ins with the law. After his testimony, Spano walked over to Vice and shook his hand.

'Best of luck, kid,' he said. It was sign of sincerity and a sign of respect. It meant a lot to Vice.

His lawyer set up the plan. His two oldest sisters, who were seventeen and sixteen and had been forced to leave high school by their parents once they were no longer legally required to attend, would watch the babies every other day, alternating with their work schedules; at night they would study for their GEDs. The four middle kids would go to school and have delineated responsibilities in the home — washing the dishes, taking out the garbage, putting the babies to sleep — that were to be done every day after homework; everyone had a job and everyone was expected to do it.

The apartment, which had three small bedrooms and a den converted to act as a fourth, had already been approved by Social Services.

'How many bathrooms are there?' the judge asked.

'Just one, sir,' Vice's lawyer answered.

'How the heck are nine people going to share one bathroom?' the judge asked incredulously.

'Well, Y'Honor, it's simple.' Vice spoke up, though his lawyer had not asked him to say anything and in fact quickly put his hand on top of Vice's to keep him from continuing. But Vice didn't notice or perhaps didn't care — he kept talking.

Rich knew exactly what Vicellous was doing; Vice instinctively knew when it was time to perform, and this was one of those times.

'These are the potty rules,' Vice started. 'Boys can share and girls can share, but no mixin' it up 'cause I don't need to explain to Ginny what's hangin' offa her brother, know what I'm sayin'?' Some of the kids laughed but seven-year-old Ginny just seemed confused. 'If you gotta go number two, you crack the window — even if it's winter — 'cause that's just common courtesy. None of that lightin'-a-match business 'cause I don't want kids playin' with those things and truth is if Timmi lights a match anywhere near his ass he'll blow up the whole damn building.'

The whole courtroom laughed this time, except for Vice's parents, who sat stone-faced at the opposing counsel table. Even twelve-year-old Timmi cackled and fist-bumped his younger brother with a proud 'True dat.'

'And if I'm brushin', no flushin' — 'cause that's just nasty; no one wants to smell your funky business when their mouth's open,' Vice continued. 'And if it's yellow, let it mellow, if it's brown, send it on down — 'cause we gotta watch our water bills and be green and all that shit, right, Y'Honor?'

'Um, I guess so,' the judge answered.

Then Vice stopped riffing and clasped his hands together. He looked at the judge — the kidding had stopped. 'Bottom line, sir, we got a nice place — it's small, but nice. I've banked some money. Enough to care for these kids. And I work hard. So do my sisters and the little ones too. We'll make it work, 'cause we gotta. We got too many scars on our bodies and our hearts not to make it work. I love these kids and I can't let them stay with the people who call themselves our parents one minute longer if I know I can get 'em outta there. I'll make it work, sir. I'll make it work.'

Vice had turned and stared at his mother and father when he said that last part, and that was no small step for the man. During his entire childhood, Vice had always avoided looking his mother and father in the eyes. That's because if they felt the gaze lasted too long, or if they thought he was 'eye-ballin'' them or 'being wise,' a fist or an open hand or a belt buckle was sure to come across his face.

But at that moment, when Vice was finally standing up to them, calling them on what they'd done to him, to their other children, he knew he had to face them. This wasn't some legal document stating their abuse in typed black legalese on plain white paper. This was Vice doing it — his own mouth actually saying the words in front of his tormentors. He wanted to look them in the eye when he did it. So he did. And it felt fucking great.

The judge and the people from Social Services and the lawyers and the court-appointed guardian for each one of the children prattled on a bit. It was a bunch of crap that Vice couldn't understand, but he could understand the tone and read the feel of the courtroom and they both told Vicellous that he had won.

The judge entered something into the record regarding *termination of parental rights* and *criminal investigation*, and Vice knew that he was not only *protecting* his brothers and sisters but also *punishing* his mother and father, and that was just icing on the cake.

As everyone made his way out of the courtroom, Cornelius and Anna Green looked at their oldest child with pure hatred. But this time Vice didn't look back at them. He didn't need to. They didn't matter anymore.

He just walked out of the room, surrounded by his brothers and sisters, holding the hands of two of the younger ones.

He wasn't scared of his parents now.

The money he had stolen had made him brave.

44

Jason Spade used his money for substantially less altruistic reasons than the others.

His first purchase was a six-figure Shelby Mustang GT500 Super Snake with 800 horsepower that could do zero to sixty in four seconds, though it never actually left gridlocked Manhattan. He also picked up a hundred-inch, high-def, wall-mounted flat-screen with surround sound despite the fact that he was hardly ever home.

And between the women (who were many) and the drugs (which had become a necessity), most of his money went down his pants or up his nose. Luckily he and Rich and the fellas had been taking periodic trips to New Jersey to see Myra and the old security guard and the rest of the gang at Colts Neck Savings and Loan. They had traded wisely — Spade had made some very smart picks based on the inside information the Blazers now gave him unfettered access to — and the money was flowing like the Hudson.

The endeavor was so successful that when Spade said he was taking a double share for himself, no one really argued. He said it was to pay estimated taxes on their gains — he wanted to make sure the British government wasn't going to shut down their account based on failure to provide taxable revenue to the crown. He'd claim on the tax return that BD Industries was a U.S.-based holding company and pay with an untraceable money order. As long as the Brits got their pounds, they wouldn't look twice at it.

Dylan at first accused Spade of trying to rip them off, but Rich explained that if the account showed capital gains, then the government would want its piece, just like in the United States. If it didn't get its cut, eventually, even if it took years, the government would catch on, the account would be seized, and that could bring unwanted attention to them. Rodriguez didn't trust Jason, but he trusted Rich, and if Rich said it needed to be done, then it was accepted without further debate.

'But if I find out you're gettin' high on my money, boss, I'll spill you, *¿comprende?*' Dylan had told Spade at McMahon's the day Jason had explained the tax situation.

Spade just snorted a laugh and left — he had an important meeting to get to. He was about to make another purchase with his ill-gotten cash. It cost only six grand, quite small compared to his other indulgences — but it was by far the most important buy he would make; it was all he had really thought about since they had made that first stock trade, and he didn't want to be late.

As it turned out, the real estate agent was late. Spade took one look at her as she waddled in on bad shoes and a calf-length skirt that was a full size too small and decided it would be pointless to bitch her out. He just wanted to close the deal.

The office space was vacant. Almost half of the

drop ceiling's tiles were missing, exposing wires, and the majority of those that remained were water-stained brown. The windows didn't close all the way, and the October winds created a distinct draft.

'I spoke to the landlord,' the agent said, 'and if you want to do a longer lease he'd be willing to replace the carpet.'

'No,' Jason said, staring down from the third-story window to the narrow alley below.

'And the keys to the storage room — he hasn't found them yet but he promises to have them by the time you move in — '

'Don't need them,' Spade said, barely acknowledging the woman, still fixed on the alley.

It was the kind of alley you found only in the financial district of New York City, where massive corporate skyscrapers abutted century-old brick buildings in tight nooks and corners to create space where there was no space to be created. This L-shaped alley ran down from the street and turned into an area where dumpsters had been unloaded years ago but then apparently forgotten because they were rusted and eaten through in places by decay.

Spade had found the alley a few weeks earlier while smoking meth with a hooker whom he then left passed out against one of those very same dumpsters. It was quiet, so narrow a car could just about open its door when inside, and, most important, the little jag that gave the alley its L shape was totally invisible from the street. It was perfect.

'He also wants you to know that since you'll just be here a month, he only needs six thousand dollars: one month's rent and a thousand security deposit — '

Spade took a wad of cash from his pocket and tossed it at the real estate agent, who dropped it.

'Where are the papers?' Spade asked as she scrambled to pick up the money.

The agent quickly produced them. Spade signed them.

'Do you mind me asking, What will you need this space for, for just one month?'

'I'm a writer. On deadline. Need a quiet place to finish my work.'

'Oh,' she said, 'what do you write — '

'Bye,' Spade said, turning back to the window.

After an awkward moment — awkward for her — the real estate agent left.

Two nights later, at around ten o'clock, Jason Spade was standing in the same exact spot, in complete darkness. A pipe with some weed in it and a five-hundred-dollar bottle of Highland Park thirty-year-old scotch sat on the windowsill. He wanted a drug that didn't dull his senses too much and liquor that marked the importance of the occasion. It was a perfect combination.

He stood and sipped and watched and waited.

It was about ten after ten when the headlights' shine climbed along the brick walls, signifying their arrival.

A few seconds later, a faded Oldsmobile pulled into view and stopped about thirty feet below where Spade was watching.

A few seconds after that, four hard-looking

black men exited the car.

And a few seconds after that, they pulled Jason's father out of the backseat. Miles Spade was bleeding from his mouth, blindfolded, and terrified. He was still in his workout clothes, as he'd been abducted in the parking garage of his gym, where he always went from eight thirty to nine thirty on Wednesday nights to play squash.

Jason had organized the whole thing. He had even been down in the alley earlier that day and climbed on top of a dumpster so he could reach an arched, wall-mounted light on the back of one of the buildings that made up the alley. He unscrewed the lightbulb from the socket and replaced it with a brand-new one. He had no reason to believe that the original bulb was in danger of burning out any time soon, but he wasn't taking any chances.

He had waited too long for this.

He wanted to make sure he could see everything . . . and he did.

He saw his father struggle as the men held him down over the hood of the car. He saw his father's pasty-white ass after the men yanked down his shorts. And the best part was, thanks to the uncloseable windows, he could hear his father's muffled cries from below as each of the four men took turns raping him.

Jason could tell just by watching that they had taken his instructions to heart. They were making it hurt.

The best thing about this, Jason thought as he watched, *is he has no idea why this is happening, and he never will.*

266

Each one of them was a crackhead that Spade had met while buying his own intoxicants in neighborhoods and buildings someone of his upbringing would never be expected to visit. A grand a piece and they were more than willing to fuck a man they didn't know for a reason they'd never know. Spade found crackheads incredibly easy to negotiate with.

Jason poured himself a bit more scotch as the third man got up behind his father and did his thing. Jason took a mouthful of single-malt and savored it along with the moment.

It had taken six years and a total of ten thousand dollars for Jason Spade to finally get his revenge on his father.

But it was worth every minute.

It was worth every penny.

It was the best damn money Jason Spade had ever spent in his life.

45

Rich soon came to believe that the fifty cents he had used to buy that day's *New York Post* was the best damn money he had ever spent in his life.

He had just wanted to read the sports section and bask in his beloved Giants' dominant win over the Jets, but when he accidentally dropped the paper on the subway floor and it fell open to a small article tucked away on page 11, Rich believed it was divine intervention.

He came to recognize that it was a sign from God. But that wasn't until later. Initially, Rich didn't feel it was a gift from above.

He didn't feel it was a good thing.

He just felt sick.

'SEC Investigates Irregular Trading Patterns.' The headline punched Rich in the gut; his stomach instantly tightened, his heart immediately kicked into overdrive.

He reached down, retrieved the paper, and scanned the article. He was too flushed with adrenaline to comprehend it all so he just picked up the names of the companies, which stood out like they were on a Broadway marquee.

Blackjack Films. Trison Construction. Aqualine Holdings. Solomon-Kessler Systems. Sklar Technologies. And it went on.

The article read like a greatest-hits list of the companies Rich and the others had traded. He felt like he was going to vomit, and the rocking and jerking of the train car wasn't making him feel any better. He knew if he did it wouldn't be the first time a New York subway had been christened with regurgitation, but he swallowed hard and pressed his fist against his mouth to keep things in check. It worked. Breakfast stayed down, and Rich composed himself just enough to actually read and comprehend the contents of the news piece.

And soon he felt better.

The article set forth how certain companies that were involved in mergers, acquisitions, stock buybacks, and other corporate transactions had shown moderately increased volume over the past several months and how this increased volume had grown more substantial in pre-event trading over the past fifty days or so.

Rich looked at the figures laid out in the article and could tell that Spade had gotten greedy and was making trades that were too big, that were a much higher percentage of volume of shares traded than the first few trades had been. These were red flags for the investigators. But what was a red flag for Rich was that the trading volume discussed in the article was much more than anything Spade could have effected with the amount of money they had at their disposal. Rich knew the *smart money* must have figured something out and gotten into the game too.

By *smart money*, Rich meant brokers, fund managers, market makers, and everyone in between. They must have caught on to the fact that certain companies, about which rumors regarding potential impending transactions had been circulating, had seen acute spikes in their trade volume. And when they saw this, the *smart money* jumped into the action in a big way too.

The result was *lots* of people were getting rich off what was going on in the Printers.

And a side result was there was so much additional activity with these securities, so many more *millions* of shares traded than usual, the SEC, which often couldn't find its ass with both hands and a pair of salad tongs, found itself looking for a raindrop in the sea when it came to identifying the original fraudsters behind the trading irregularities.

Rich had played enough cards with Uncle Jim to tell a bluff when he saw one, and that's exactly what this article was — a bluff. Posturing. The SEC put it out there to frighten whoever was responsible for the inside trading.

We're onto you, is what they were saying, *so you better get your wrists ready for some government-issue bracelets.*

But what they were thinking was: *We aren't able to catch these bastards right now, so hopefully this article will scare them enough so they stop what they're doing while we figure out who the hell they are.*

Rich had been an altar boy for about six months but quit once he reached seventh grade and started playing ball for his junior high school. He wasn't allowed to be in the public-school league and the CYO league at the same time, and since the public schools provided better competition, it was a no-brainer. Less time at the church resulted in his hanging up his white vestments shortly into his ecclesiastical career.

But as he rumbled along on the L Train under Fourteenth Street, he couldn't help but think he must've done a hell of a job during his brief tenure at Our Lady of Mount Carmel. The Eucharist must've been placed perfectly in Father Frank's golden chalice, and, without realizing it, Rich must have let the communion wine breathe just right, because the newspaper falling the way it did, to that *exact* page, revealing that *exact* article — well, that could only have been a gift from God. A *sign* from God.

Rich had been feeling more nervous than usual lately about what he and the others were doing. He had gotten what he had always wanted — a future with Elyse. He didn't need anything more. He had been thinking that maybe they should cut bait on the whole thing, and this newspaper convinced him he was right.

When that paper landed the way it did, that was the Big Man telling Rich to cut the shit. He got the message loud and clear.

He tore the page out of the *Post* and folded it and put it in his pocket. The train slowed as it reached Rich's stop.

Rich exited and hurried along the platform. He was running late. He was supposed to have been at Beth Israel Medical Center almost a half an hour earlier.

46

Little Bella felt weightless when Dylan laid her in Rich's arms. The seven pounds, nine ounces seemed nonexistent — he was holding air; beautiful, brown-eyed, brown-skinned, brown-haired air.

'She's gorgeous,' Rich said. 'She's perfect.' Bella was swaddled tight in a white hospital blanket with a pink teddy-bear print; her dark locks peeked out from underneath a pink skullcap that fit snugly on her head.

Dylan smiled. 'Thanks. She looks like her mama.'

'She looks like Yoda,' Eddie chimed in as he edged closer to get a better look, scraping the plastic hospital chair on the visitors'-room floor.

'Don't be stupid, Special Ed.'

'*You're* stupid, Vicellous.'

'Guys, keep it down; we got exhausted mothers all over this floor,' Dylan gently reminded them before focusing on Pisorchek. 'Newborns just look kinda wrinkly, Eddie.'

'Oh.'

'Shit,' Rich said, adjusting slightly in his seat.

'What's wrong?'

'Nothing. It's just, I think I just heard her . . .'

'What? Make a poo-poo?' Dylan asked, suddenly very serious.

There was something about a guy who looked like Dylan saying *poo-poo* that made Rich laugh.

Vice and Ed laughed too.

'Kiss my ass,' Rodriguez said, almost panicked as Rich passed the baby back into Dylan's arms. 'Um, okay, let's see — '

Rodriguez fumbled with a wall-mounted fold-down changing table and pulled a fresh diaper from a bag the hospital had provided. He laid the baby down, carefully unwrapped her blanket, removed her onesie, and slowly tried to pull open the sticky tabs that held Bella's diaper in place. His hands shook like any new father's, terrified by the misconception that one false move could damage the child for life.

'Are you shittin' me?' Vice cried as he elbowed his way between Dylan and the infant and took immediate control. In one motion the diaper was off, rolled into a ball, and secured tightly by the tabs. He tossed the crap-filled Pampers over his shoulder without looking. 'Here, Ed. Catch.'

Ed reflexively caught the diaper and then instinctively dropped it with a small yell.

'See, no one realizes these newborns are inde-structible. They're made of fuckin' rubber — '

'Hey, watch the language,' Dylan said, indicating the baby.

'You're kiddin' me, right?' Vice chuckled as he quickly passed baby wipes over Bella's bottom. 'Fuckity, fuck, fuck, fucker,' he said in baby-talk tones as he leaned in close to the child's face. 'Is your da-da a wittle pussy-wussy who's scared of a wittle poopy-woopy?'

'Another wipe,' he demanded, putting his hand out like a surgeon waiting for a scalpel. Dylan pulled a wipe from the container and handed it over, grateful for the help. 'Important thing is to wipe in the direction of vaginey to heinie. Otherwise, you might accidentally get caca in her ya-ya, and that might give her an infection.'

He slapped the new diaper on in three seconds flat and had the baby dressed and reswaddled in about five seconds more. He handed Bella over to the new daddy.

'How'd you know how to do all that? You're like a Daytona pit crew.'

'Who do you think changed all my brothers and sisters? My drunk-ass parents? You're just lucky you got a girl — boys'll piss right up into your face and laugh while they're doin' it.'

Dylan sat down, holding a content and happy one-day-old daughter in his arms.

'Here,' Vice said, handing Rodriguez a wrapped gift the size of a shoe box. It had been in a brown shopping bag by Vice's feet.

The paper had pictures of flowers and bumble-bees on it, and the box, Dylan learned upon opening it, had an envelope with one hundred twenty thousand dollars inside of it.

'For Bella. From all of us,' Rich explained.

'Except Spade,' Eddie added.

Dylan didn't say anything for a while. He just looked down at his daughter, who was now sleeping. She was completely pure, wholly innocent — save for the original sin she was born with, but a splash of holy water and a twenty-minute ceremony at St. Mary's on Tenth Street would take care of that pretty easily. Dylan was more worried about the sin that was sitting in the envelope resting in Bella's daddy's lap, just a few inches from the child.

Rich could read the distress on Dylan's face. He knew it was the right time to bring up what he had seen in the *Post*.

'We should end this,' he said.

'Yeah, that's cool, I gotta get back to the kids anyway — two of 'em got soccer practice and one of 'em has a fever, so my day's shot . . . ' Vice said as he stood up, totally misunderstanding what Rich meant.

'No. I mean, end what we've been doing. End what we started.' Rich waited for a reaction, but at first he got none. Vice was motionless, taking in what he had heard. He looked to Dylan and Ed, then back to Rich.

'Please tell me you're fuckin' with me,' Vice said, eyebrows up. 'You see that *mucho dinero* we just passed to little Miss Rodriguez there? The critter's still shittin' raisins but she's already got her college done and paid for. Why you wanna stop the gravy train now?'

''Cause I'm scared,' Rich said.

'*So strap on a pair of balls and deal with it.*'

'I'm scared too,' Dylan chimed in.

That shut Vice up.

They had all gotten to know Dylan better over the past months — committing major crimes together tends to help people get to know one another — but they still didn't know him *that* well. His taciturn nature made it next to impossible to get too close to him. But despite how little they knew about the man, they were all certain of at least one thing — one thing they would've bet their lives on — that Dylan Rodriguez was frightened of nobody and nothing. Or so they'd thought. So when he said he was scared, that got everyone's attention.

'It's been too easy,' he whispered, still aware that if sleeping babies heard them there would be crying and if awake adults heard them, there would be arrests. 'I had harder times jackin' vending machines for twenty bucks than we've had pullin' millions outta thin air. Shit's not s'posed to ride this smooth — you gotta feel a bump on the road now and then, and I just get the feelin' that when we do hit that bump, it's gonna be big enough to knock us all on our asses.'

'D-Rod, look in that envelope,' Vice said. 'You got twelve hundred pictures of dead white guys on green paper and that can buy you a lot of peace of mind. So I suggest you get a massage and some aromatherapy and whatever the hell else rich people do to relax and chill the fuck out. 'Cause you rich now, ya dumb mick-spic, so act like it.'

'Just listen to me for a second,' Rich argued. 'Think about why we all did this. Dylan had a baby on the way that he wanted to take care of; Vice, you wanted to get your brothers and sisters away from your parents; Eddie, you didn't want to be left out. Well, we all got what we wanted — '

'What did you want, Richie?' Ed asked innocently.

'It's not important. What's important is, I got it. And what's even *more* important, I got *away* with it. We all did. So far. But I'm sitting here looking at this baby thinking about how I want to have one of them myself and how now that I'm getting married that's just a matter of time. But I can't be a husband or a father if I'm locked up. Vice, those kids of yours will wind up in foster care. Eddie, well, your *situation* kinda protects you; you won't go to jail but you'll lose the job you love so much — '

'I don't want that; I like my job,' Ed said nervously.

'I don't want that either. I don't want anything to happen to *any of us*. We all got a ton of money now, even after what we've spent, and a lot more that's still sitting in the account — hell, I got ten grand stuffed in my Phil Simms autographed football alone — '

'I don't have any money left,' Eddie mumbled.

'What do you mean, Ed? What happened to your money?' Dylan asked.

'I gave it away.'

'Gave it away? To who?'

'To good people.'

'Did someone take advantage of you, Ed?' Rich stepped up to Eddie, pumping him for information, suddenly worried. 'Did someone *make you* give them the money? *Did you tell someone about what we were doing?*'

'No, I'm not *stupid*,' Eddie fired back defensively.

'Bitch gives away almost a million bucks and then says he's not stupid — '

'Vice, that doesn't help,' Rich snapped.

'I gave it to good people . . . *autonomously*,' Eddie added.

'Well, technically, you did. But I think you meant to say you gave it to them without your name on anything?'

Ed nodded.

'All right, well, that's gonna stop. Because *we* have to stop. No more giving away money. No more taking money. No more nothing,' Rich stated authoritatively.

'I'm with him,' Dylan concurred.

''Cept it's not just you guys' call though,' Vice pointed out. 'There's five of us.'

'And *any one of us* can end this thing. You can't get the money without my three numbers, or Dylan's or Ed's . . . if one goes, we all go. But I think we should make this decision *unanimously*.'

'Like how I gave my money away,' chimed in Ed.

'Once again, you're real close, Ed; that's not it, but I know the word you mean,' Rich said encouragingly before turning back to Vicellous. 'You said you didn't want to stop the gravy train. But if you pour too much gravy on your plate, your potatoes get ruined. Then you're just hungry again.'

'Worst analogy ever,' Vice mumbled as he turned and stared out the fifth-floor window. New York City looked back at him. Vice sighed. 'We're just gonna leave all that money out there, aren't we?'

'I don't think we have a choice,' Rich said as he pulled the article from his pocket and handed it over to Vice.

'What the hell's this?'

278

Rich explained the article — not only its contents but his theory on what the SEC was thinking. 'I didn't want to show it to you guys unless I had to. I figured no sense in creating a panic if one wasn't necessary; and like I said, I don't think we have anything to worry about if we call it a day right now.'

There was silence for a while as the article was passed around.

Then they all agreed it was over. There was no more debate. Dylan reached into the box and took out Vice's share of Bella's gift. He handed it to him. 'You have seven more kids than I do. If it's the end of the line, you should keep this.'

Vice took the money. 'Sorry 'bout the mick-spic crack.'

'No worries, welfare baby.'

Vice smiled, then leaned in to Bella and whispered to the sleeping baby, 'Sorry 'bout the cash, kid, but I promise to keep you flush with hand-me-downs for the rest of your life.'

Dylan offered Rich and Ed their shares back too. They both refused.

'What about Jason?' Dylan asked.

'Still stuck in Tennessee; been doing due diligence on a merger for a week now. His old man's been in a shit mood for some reason, been crackin' the whip on his whole department. Spade hasn't been happy.'

Vice laughed. 'Not happy? When that asshole hears we want to pull the plug on this thing, he's gonna be *miserable*.'

47

'Oh, okay, um, sweetheart, please don't use your hand, there's a serving spoon . . . '

But Mrs. Crane was too late. Timmi or Darnell or TT or whichever one of Vice's little brothers it was was off with a handful of imported olives and had already begun sticking one on each fingertip.

'Sorry, Mrs. C.,' Vice apologized, 'but if you get between them kids and a plate, you're gonna lose a hand.'

Mrs. Crane forced a weak smile as she headed back into the kitchen, where she and her husband had been hiding most of the evening. This was *not* your typical pretentious Crane soirée. Of course, the usual group of assholes was there to celebrate Rich and Elyse's engagement — Mr. Crane's cabal of *Mayflower* pals; the environmentalist director who was completely unaware, or wouldn't admit, that from his shoelace tips to his Elvis Costello frames, he was wearing at least five different kinds of plastics; and, of course, Terry Garhart, who was looking quite glum, much like a kid who had been brought in to pinch-hit with the bases loaded but whose rocket shot into the bleachers had been caught by the left fielder in a perfectly timed leap: so close to winning but losing the same as if he'd simply struck out.

But there were also some new guests at the get-together, people whom the Cranes would normally never have invited into their home. Vice and his entire brood, who were just tearing up the joint; Dylan (Rosa was home with Bella, as both were suffering from lack of sleep lately); and Eddie Pisorchek, who was drinking root beer from a wineglass and talking to Uncle Jim, who was drinking wine from a beer glass.

Rich looked to the arched kitchen entranceway and caught his future in-laws peeking at his invitees with a mélange of repugnance, disgust, and abhorrence that made him incredibly happy. Between that and the Terry Garhart loss in the Race for Elyse Sweepstakes, Rich was downright giddy.

'What're you grinning at?' Elyse asked, curling into his side effortlessly, as if she had always been there.

'Them,' Rich said, nodding his head toward Elyse's parents. 'Maybe I should've been a bit clearer when I said I wanted to invite a few people from work. I'm pretty sure they thought I meant lawyers.'

'I'm pretty sure you *wanted* them to think you meant lawyers.' Elyse smiled as she leaned in for a kiss. 'Can you believe this is actually happening? Can you believe we're really getting *married?*'

She turned and watched as Vice's second-youngest sister, Cee Cee, poured apple juice down the back of her brother Darnell's shirt — not by accident but as a deliberate and malicious assault. Darnell screamed bloody murder as Vice tried to intervene.

'I want some of those,' Elyse said, pointing.

281

'You better be pointing to the bowl of smoked almonds.'

'I'm serious. I want a little brother and sister driving each other nuts. I want kids running around the house. I want a lot of them.' She spun back to Rich and looked at him with a naughty grin. 'Make some with me?'

Rich moved to kiss her but was interrupted.

'Whoa, you better not make them *right* here — there's still dessert to be served. Now, may I kiss the soon-to-be-bride?'

'Max!' Elyse beamed and she threw her arms around the man. 'We didn't think you'd make it!'

'I didn't think I'd get out of the office.' He sighed as he hugged her tightly and pecked her cheek.

'On a Saturday?' Elyse asked. 'Is that what I have to look forward to when Rich is a first-year associate? Saturdays alone while he's stuck at the office?'

'No.' Max chuckled. 'When he's a first-year you can look forward to Saturdays *and* Sundays alone.'

'What was it?' Rich wanted to know. 'Estrin Medical?'

'That case is going to be the end of me,' Max grumbled. 'But no shoptalk today! Now, gimme that dainty paw of yours, little missy!'

Elyse giggled, scrunching up her nose in the process, as Max grabbed her hand and inspected the ring.

'Mazel tov!' he shouted, a bit too loud, but Max could care less. He was happy as hell about the engagement — he had loved Elyse from the first time Rich had introduced them. He knew she was perfect for the boy he considered family. 'Quite the ice show, young Richard, quite the ice show. We must be paying you way too much! Maybe you should buy dinner at Peter Luger's next week? We're still on, right?'

'I'll be done with exams — I could use a night out.'

'Good!' Max bellowed as he grabbed Rich and pulled him into an embrace, pressing his lips against Rich's ear so no one else could hear. 'You did great, boy. You did great!' he whispered.

And with a hearty slap on the back, Max was off to talk to Uncle Jim; Elyse went off to calm her parents, and Rich had a moment to be alone in the corner. He looked around the room and he liked what he saw.

Vice cutting chicken into small bits for one of the babies . . .

Dylan, the gentleman gangster, helping the caterer move a buffet table a little closer to the wall . . .

Eddie secretively stuffing his pockets with cookies so he'd have something to eat during the subway ride home . . .

And Uncle Jim and Max smiling and laughing off in a different corner. He studied the two men who had helped raise him and felt closer to them than he ever had before. Rich knew that the topic of his parents would eventually arise between them, and their smiles would fade and either Jim or Max or both would say how much his mother and father would have loved Elyse and how happy they would've been to see how

283

Rich had turned out.

Rich couldn't agree with that latter part. He knew that how he had turned out — a lying, stealing serial felon — wasn't exactly what his parents had hoped for. He hadn't honored his parents with what he had done in the Printers. He knew that. But his parents hadn't been around — they hadn't been there when Rich cried himself sore years after they had died simply because some man in line at the deli was wearing the same aftershave as his dad.

They weren't around, and so he had had to smash his own finger with a hammer to get out of his junior high father/son bowling-night fund-raiser — Jim wanted to go, but Rich knew that it would just draw lingering glances and pathetic whispers, everyone feeling sorry for the parentless little boy who had to show up with his uncle.

And they weren't there when he was eleven and desperate and showed his teacher an article about a scientist who had stopped the heart of a zebra fish and then essentially turned the heart back on nine hours later — Rich wanted to know if it could work for people. The teacher coughed out a laugh and told Rich to 'stop being stupid.'

He was tired of it, damn it. He was sick and tired of the hollow feeling that was always there in his stomach — a feeling that disappeared only when he was with Elyse. He wanted his own fucking family already and he wanted it with the girl he loved. And he knew, even if *she* didn't, that she had been getting courted by a better-looking, more successful, richer man

— the same son of a bitch who was at the bar being served a drink by the only black person in the house other than Vice and his family.

Rich could feel his teeth clenching. The muscles in his temples tightened. The very fact that Terry was there offended him; it was the final bitch slap across his face from Quinn Crane. Mauro took a swig from his whiskey and Coke, trying to put out the fire before he said or did something stupid. The booze hit his belly and got into his bloodstream quickly. Another sip or two and he was almost calm.

And then he saw Spade, and his blood pressure shot back up and all pacifying effects of the alcohol were gone. Jason made his way through the crowd, half-empty tumbler in his hand. It would appear to others that he had had perhaps one belt too many, but Rich, who had seen the same look on Spade's face when they'd been at clubs, knew instantly that the lawyer heading toward him was stoned on pills or powder or something that went in his vein.

'What the hell are you doing here?' Rich asked through a forced smile.

'Celebrating your love.'

'Come on,' Rich said, leading Spade through the crowd and toward a back hallway. Dylan caught Rich's eye and shot him a concerned look. Rich held up his hand by his side and shook his head, letting Dylan know that he had things under control, at least for now.

They moved down the hall and into a bathroom. Rich closed and locked the door.

'How the hell'd you know I was here?'

285

'Got your message that you wanted to meet at McMahon's when I was back from Nashville. So I went to your uncle's place, and no one was home; went to Elyse's apartment, and nobody's there — so I swung by here. Gotta say I'm a little upset I wasn't invited.'

'I thought you were in Tennessee another week.'

'Was supposed to be but then I realized — I don't have to take his crap anymore, the shit assignments my father gives me, the menial pissant work. I said I was feeling sick and had to go back home to see my doctor. What's he gonna do, fire me? Go 'head. I got money now. Hell, few more trades and I might just quit the firm altogether.'

'One, you can't quit anything. Something in your glassy eyes tells me you're not saving too much of the money that's come in so far. And two . . . we all talked about it. We're done. We just want to take out the money that's in the account now and wrap it up before you get us all busted.' Rich pulled the *New York Post* article from in his pocket and slapped it into Spade's hand. Spade scanned it and paled.

He didn't say anything. He just sat down on the edge of the clawfoot tub and gripped it as if the room were spinning — and judging from Spade's condition, Rich thought he might very well have felt that it was. Spade stared at the floor, dumbstruck.

'Listen, we've all done well on this thing,' Rich said, 'so there's no reason to feel we didn't — '

Spade threw himself into Rich's midsection,

wrapping his arms around Mauro's waist, driving him across the bathroom into the sink. Rich instinctively punched Spade repeatedly in the back, trying to get him to let go, as Spade's fumbling left hand found a water glass on the vanity and quickly smashed it into Mauro's brow, shattering the glass and cutting Rich's forehead. Rich fell against the toilet and turned back to Spade just as he was stumbling toward him. Rich stopped him with a punch to the jaw. Spade fell to the floor, his lip bloody and already swelling.

'Get your shit together, you stupid junkie,' Rich whisper-shouted. '*This thing is over.* You'll never be able to make another trade without our codes. So we're finished. Sooner you get that stamped into your drugged-out brain, the better. We get the money that's left, whack it up, and then we all walk away . . . understand?'

Spade stood and smiled, blood covering his teeth.

'You think you can just walk away from this?' he growled. 'Always knew you were stupid.'

He spat a glob of blood into the sink, wiped his lip clean, and walked out of the bathroom and out of the house. Rich watched from the window and saw Spade's six-figure ride peel out of snow-covered Pineapple Street. He then picked up every shard of glass, big and small, and put them in the garbage.

He wadded up toilet paper and applied pressure to his cut, but it was no use — it was a head wound and it wanted to bleed. So Rich walked into the crowded party and joked about

287

how he had slipped on some water on the bathroom floor and fallen, his head hitting the vanity exactly where there was a glass — *what a klutz!*

One of Quinn Crane's cousins joked that Rich couldn't fake amnesia to get out of the engagement. Uncle Jim got him a clean dish towel from the kitchen, to Mrs. Crane's dismay. And Max made a few calls and got the top plastic surgeon in Brooklyn to meet them over at Woodhull Medical Center, even though it was a Saturday.

Elyse kissed her future husband on the cheek as he, Max, and Uncle Jim headed out the door to get Rich stitched up. He promised Elyse he'd be completely unscarred come their wedding day. She smiled.

Soon the party was back in full swing; everyone had bought the story. Everyone except Dylan, Vice, and Eddie. They had seen Spade show up at the party and they had seen him leave. And they had seen Rich's forehead.

All three men shared a look — something told them that this might be just the beginning of the bloodshed.

48

With Hanukkah coming early and Christmas only a few weeks away, things at Olmstead & Taft had slowed down considerably, and that couldn't have happened at a better time as Rich had his last two finals to worry about — though, miraculously, given all that had been going on, his grades had actually gotten *better*. He had learned he'd be getting two As and an A — in his first three classes; he was confident his pre-law exam would go off without a hitch, and his sociology grade was already locked in: a B+ minimum, and that was if he got a C on the final; if he scored any higher, he'd earn an A — . Somehow, some way, unless something went incredibly wrong, Rich Mauro, the multiple felon, was going to make dean's list.

But just to be safe, Rich hit the books hard.

The holiday lull let him study between shifts and on the job during downtime. Vice and Dylan took turns quizzing him from his notes, which Eddie had organized, tabbed, laminated, and placed in a massive three-ring notebook for Rich. They barely talked about anything else and after a while Rich began to think he could send any of them into the classroom and they would all be capable of passing his exams for him.

But Rich was looking forward to taking the tests himself — studying hard, learning the material, applying his knowledge to the questions; good old-fashioned hard work. Good *honest* work. Rich hadn't felt *honest* in a long time. Hell, he hadn't felt particularly *good* in a long time either. Not since they had started the scam.

He had done something wrong out of desperation, and some positive things had come out of it — that was for certain — but once the scheme had been declared dead and buried, he had never felt better. He was ready to feel *good* and *honest* again. And a few minutes into December 10, as he cleaned the machinery and looked around the Printers, watching his friends shut down the office for the night, he knew they felt the same way. They were good people. And good people sometimes did bad things — but they also knew when to stop doing them.

Having wiped down the machinery properly, Rich put the cleaning solution and the rags away in a metal cabinet in the rear of the office. His back was to the door when he heard the voice.

'Hey, it's the grape stomper from Queens.'

Rich didn't need to turn around to know who had just walked into the Printers. The voice was chunks of slate rattling around a tin can. It was deep. It was rough-edged. It was Manny Espinoza.

And when Rich turned, he was not surprised to find Gold Tooth and his twin brother on either side of Manny. A step behind them was Spade. Dried blood formed a line down from his left nostril to just above his Adam's apple. There were bloodstains on his shirt.

Vice and Eddie stood still — both of them instinctively knew that nonmovement was the safest course of action at the moment. Vice seemed particularly concerned — he shot a worried look to Rich but didn't hold the look long; he knew it was best to keep his eyes on the three badasses by the door. Growing up in East New York gave you a sixth sense and Vice's was on full alert. Dylan, who was in the supply closet unloading a few crates of toner, was unaware of the visitors.

Rich wasn't sure exactly what was going on but he knew it was nothing good.

'Manny,' Rich said warily with a small, forced grin — trying like hell to alleviate just the tiniest bit of the tension. 'What brings you south of a Hundred Twenty-Fifth Street?'

'My fuckin' money does, bitch. And don't think you're gonna cracker-shuffle your way outta this mess. Your little friend over here tried to do it and it just got him his ass beat,' Manny said, gesturing to Spade.

Before Rich could ask Manny what the hell he was talking about, Dylan exited the closet, taking off a thick weight-lifting belt the firm required they all wear when moving boxes of supplies, to protect against back injuries. Rich could tell immediately from Dylan's reaction that he not only knew Manny but also knew they were all in big trouble.

'Goddamn.' Manny smiled, bending at the knees and bouncing his body upward in a way that was supposed to convey his shock at what he saw. 'Spade told me that you were with this crew, so I knew you'd be around, but damn it if it ain't like one of them Freddy movies — you know the mothafucka's gonna pop out the woods, but when he does it still startles the shit out of ya! *Man, oh, man,* Dylan Rodriguez, the jefe, the king Puerto Rican shit, humpin' white paper for the white man. I'd ask you how you been, D, but it's clear life's gone and taken a great big shit right on your head.'

He turned to his men. 'Can you believe this shit, Caesar?' Gold Tooth's twin brother grinned. Rich still didn't know Gold Tooth's real name.

'Always knew you and I would be doin' business together one day, Rodriguez,' Manny said as he lit a cigarette and threw the extinguished match into a garbage can. Eddie watched it, worried, since the can had paper in it and smoking was strictly prohibited in the Printers. 'But never thought you'd try to fuck me. I had always heard you were straight up in yo' dealings.'

'I am,' Dylan said coolly, his voice steady and composed. Like the born leader he was, Dylan used a tone that gave and commanded respect at the same time. He stood straight, kept eye contact with Manny, showed no fear. 'So why don't you tell me how we're in business together and what your concern is, and I'll make it right.'

Manny backed up to a copier, put his hands on the top, and jump-lifted himself onto it so he was seated with his feet dangling over the floor.

'You're not s'posed to sit on the machinery,' Eddie scolded.

'Not now, Ed,' Vice snapped.

'But Vicellous — '

'*Not now.*'

292

Manny shifted his eyes toward Ed to make sure there would be no more interruptions. When it was clear there wouldn't be, he continued.

'See, this deal you had going with Spade — well, all this time, I've kinda been yo' *silent partner*,' Manny explained, motioning to Jason, who still stood by the door, eyes down, not wanting to make eye contact with Rich, who was now staring a hole through him. 'Little J over here's got all his money tied up by his Daddy Warbucks — it's been a hard-knock motherfuckin' life for the man. So when he told me about his plan to make some big cash, I was more than happy to bankroll his ass. For a cut, of course.'

Rich realized exactly what Spade had done. That first night when he and Jason had gone to the underground party was nothing more than a meet and greet for Manny's benefit. Jason must've told Manny that to have unfettered access to the information in the Printers he'd have to have at least one of the Blazers on board, and Rich, the hourly worker who desperately wanted to be one of Spade's colleagues one day, was the perfect mark. But Manny would want to feel the guy out first, get an idea of whom he would be working with.

Despite the fact that Rich and Gold Tooth wound up at each other's throats, literally, Manny must've signed off on Mauro and the whole project, giving Spade the cash to fund it all. Hell, maybe it was the balls the grape stomper from Queens had shown by standing up to Gold Tooth that made Manny think the plan would work.

Whatever the case, Spade told the Blazers that the start-up capital came from his own savings. And they bought it. And the thieving began.

When Jason said he needed the extra money to pay 'taxes,' it wasn't a complete lie — it was just that the money wasn't being sent to the United Kingdom. This tax was being levied by Manny Espinoza.

And Manny liked getting that money — his initial investment had tripled; this was substantially more cash than he'd ever made throwing raves and dealing drugs.

And when he heard from Spade that Rich and the other Blazers wanted to end the arrangement, that made him unhappy.

So he roughed up Spade and dragged his sorry ass to the basement of Olmstead & Taft at a little past midnight.

And there they all were.

'We can't do it anymore,' Rich said quietly but firmly. 'The SEC — Securities and Exchange Commission — they're looking at trades real close now, trades on companies that are making deals, mergers, stock purchases. They haven't found us yet, but if we do any more, we'll be shining a spotlight right on ourselves.'

'Then you figure it out!' Manny shouted, veins enlarging in his neck. 'Your partner promised me a certain amount of money! In return for that promise, I gave him half a million of my cash! And now I've made purchases based on his promise — *your promise! I owe now* and the people I owe don't visit and try to talk things out; they just pull triggers — '

'Maybe you don't understand!' Rich yelled back, surprising everyone in the room but no one more than himself. 'We can't do it! We trade on pending deals and we all go to jail! And if we go, *you* go!'

The words shot quickly from Rich's mouth, fueled partly by anger but mostly by fear. And as soon as he was done, he wished he had never said anything.

Manny spun to Gold Tooth and Caesar. He pointed to Eddie and then pointed toward the door. In an instant they were on him, grabbing him and pulling him to the exit.

'No!' Eddie struggled but it was no use. He was strong as a bull, but he was no match for two of Manny's men.

'Manny, you don't gotta do this!' Dylan yelled. 'We'll take care of business for you — let the man go!'

But Manny ignored Dylan. 'Y'all work in a fancy office, right?' he shouted to no one in particular. 'Ain't this just what you businessmen call an *incentive?*'

That's when it became clear Gold Tooth and Caesar weren't heading for the door. They were heading toward the industrial paper cutter next to it.

As Eddie yelled, Caesar slammed Pisorchek's hand onto the metal tray, and Gold Tooth raised the handle of the huge commercial blade that could slice through three inches of cardboard with one hard push.

'Don't!' Dylan yelled as he and Rich moved toward the men, but Manny had pulled a Lorcin

.380 from the small of his back and pointed it at the both of them before they had taken two steps.

'No!' Eddie screamed, but there was nothing they could do.

'Okay! Okay! Stop!' Rich begged. 'I'll figure something out! We'll get you money! Just let him go!'

For a moment, no one moved. Not even Eddie, whose face was pressed hard against the metal tray of the cutter. Caesar had him pinned down by the back of his neck with one hand, and he was holding Eddie's wrist with the other — keeping Ed's fingers directly underneath the waiting blade.

There was almost complete silence — the only sound being Eddie's heavy breathing. He had put up a good fight but had stopped trying to free himself; he had no strength left. Then Manny spoke.

'You're serious?' he asked.

'Yes. Absolutely,' Rich answered.

Manny cocked his head and stepped to Rich; no more than six inches kept them apart.

'Good,' he said. *'So am I.'*

And with Manny's slight nod to Gold Tooth, the blade sliced down on Eddie's hand with the sickening sound of sharp metal doing its job.

Eddie cried out, then fell to the floor. He gripped what was left of his wounded hand and writhed on his side, his legs kicking back and forth at nothing, his face a picture of surprise more than agony.

Dylan and Rich froze. They were both so

296

stunned at the surreality of what they'd just seen that they were beyond the ability to respond in any way.

Vice was in his own state of shock, but he scrambled on hands and knees, picking up all four of Eddie's fingers (his thumb had been spared) and putting them in a Styrofoam coffee cup, all the while whispering softly to his friend, 'It's okay, Eddie. It's gonna be okay.'

Manny moved toward the door with Gold Tooth and Caesar on his heels. He stopped by Spade, who had not looked up from the floor once since they'd entered the Printers.

'If this is what I do to y'all's little puppy, imagine what I'll do to you if I don't get my money.' He looked back at the rest of them. 'Imagine what I'll do to your brothers and sisters, or your baby, or your old-ass uncle or piece-of-ass fiancée. I been watching you — all it takes is me thinking *for a minute* that you're fuckin' with me, and your lives change on a dime.'

And with that, Manny left with his men.

The five inside traders were alone now. Rich hurried to Eddie, grabbed a sweatshirt from the back of a chair, and pressed it against the bloody hand. With the adrenaline starting to wear off, Eddie was beginning to feel the pain. He wailed in agony.

'Spade!' Rich yelled. 'Give Dylan the keys to your fuckin' car!'

Spade didn't say a word. He just quickly pulled out his keys and handed them over.

'Where is it?' Dylan demanded.

'In the alley behind the east side of the building,' Spade said softly.

'I'll be outside the loading docks in five minutes!' And Dylan was gone.

Vice and Rich helped Eddie off the ground, Vice being careful not to spill the contents of the Styrofoam cup. Ed's wails had turned to moans and cries and sounds that were more animal than human. His pain was primal.

'C'mon, Eddie, we're gonna get you to a hospital. C'mon, pal,' Vice said.

They all exited through the loading-dock door, letting it close behind them, leaving Jason Spade alone in the basement — just him, the soft whir of computers, and a paper-cutter blade that needed to be cleaned.

49

Even though New York Downtown Hospital was closer, Rich knew it was best to get Eddie to Bellevue's world-class trauma center, on Twenty-Sixth Street. He had had to rush there once before with his uncle after a lather doing a renovation job at the New York Life building had caught a foot of three-eighths-inch pencil rod clean through his shoulder.

Since it was well past midnight, Mauro figured the FDR Drive would be clear and that, with Dylan pushing Spade's supercharged Mustang to the limit, they'd spend only an extra five minutes in the car, tops, going to Bellevue instead of New York Downtown Hospital. He was right. From the time they lifted Pisorchek off the floor to the time the trauma doctors wheeled a still-in-shock Ed down the hall and out of sight, fewer than thirteen minutes passed.

Rich, Dylan, and Vice stood silently in the emergency room. They drew some stares because, for one, they had just brought in a screaming, six-fingered retarded man and, two, despite all the Kumbaya bullshit that went down after Obama was elected, it was rare to see a black, white, and Puerto Rican hanging out together unless they were all on the Yankees.

Vice dug into his back pocket, retrieved a wrinkled dollar bill, and shoved it into a vending machine. He was thankful when it wasn't spat back out at him. He chose a Mr. Pibb, which clunked its way down to the retrieval door. Vice grabbed it but didn't bother to open it up. He just put the can on the back of his neck and held it there, hoping the chill would jolt him out of the numb daze that engulfed him.

Rich motioned to Dylan, and they stepped through the automatic doors and into the cold night air.

'We got a problem,' he said to Dylan, shoving his hands in his pockets.

'Hell yes, we do.'

'Seems you know this Manny guy.'

'Yeah.'

'Fill me in.'

So Dylan did. Manny Espinoza had always been a player — never part of a gang, always a freelancer with a hard crew around him at least ten men strong, but it might have grown stronger since Dylan had quit the life. Manny was a thug and was capable of being very violent when necessary — as they had already seen — though he preferred to think of himself as a businessman who had the balls to cut to the chase in a way legit businessmen never would. He'd started throwing raves when he was a teenager, made some nice cash, and soon determined that if he was inviting people to warehouses, foreclosed buildings, and abandoned lofts to get crazy, he might as well provide them with the inebriants to help them along their way. Meth, weed, speed. Coke, crack, smack. He had it all at every bash he threw, and he threw four to five a week, all over the city, every week of the year. And since he was keeping his sales off the corner, he avoided most of the gunplay and made it hard for cops to bust him since the party locations constantly changed.

'But he wasn't a distributor,' Dylan explained. 'He was a retailer — buying from the big boys and selling directly to his customers at a healthy markup. Manny was rich by the time he turned twenty. But now that he's older, he clearly wants more — '

Dylan's cell rang, cutting him off.

'Hey, baby . . . yeah . . . I know but someone got hurt at work . . . Eddie . . . I don't know . . . his fingers got caught in some machinery . . . I don't know, look, I gotta go . . . yeah, I'll grab a box — Swaddlers by Pampers, got it, but I gotta . . . and Desitin — tub, *not* tube — got it, now I gotta . . . baby, you're killin' me, *I'm in a hospital here* — okay, sorry, but the sooner you let me go the sooner I can come home to you. Okay . . . love you too, *mami*.'

He hung up the phone and rubbed his eyes with the heels of his hands. '*Dios me dé fuerzas.*' He looked up at Rich with red, stressed eyes. 'Where the hell was I?'

'Manny was looking to get big.'

'Right. I mean, the crazy bastard's takin' product *on credit*, Rich . . . no wonder he's buggin' out and cuttin' off fingers and shit — the guys *he* owes, they'll do to Manny what Manny did to Ed.'

'Espinoza's desperate,' Rich said quietly, almost to himself.

'And he'll come after us hard if we don't get him paid.'

'You need to figure something out, Rich.' They turned to see Vice exiting the hospital, the Mr. Pibb now open. He had picked up the last bit of their conversation.

'Why me?'

''Cause you're the one who's always got his nose buried in a book; you're the one who wants to be a lawyer so damn bad. You gotta think of a way out of this thing, man. I don't wanna wind up running from New York with all them kids, and Eddie's got a routine here — he can't handle a life on the run.'

'Runnin' won't do no good, *papi*. Manny's plugged in. Wherever you go, he'll find you eventually — you and your family,' Rodriguez stated.

Rich slumped onto a bench next to a NO-LOADING ZONE sign. He leaned forward, rubbed the side of his head with his hands. He filled his lungs.

The air had a bite to it; he rubbed his hands together to keep them warm until the irony of what he was doing struck him. Eddie was probably under the gas right now, getting his fingers, at least those that could be salvaged, sewn back onto his mangled mitt. What an asshole Rich was to allow himself to be bothered by the fact that *his* hands weren't warm enough. He stopped rubbing them. He let them be cold.

He thought about poor Eddie lying on the table, his face so calm and peaceful, like a sleeping child's, while just inches below and to the right a flurry of doctors and nurses and technicians tried to Humpty Dumpty his hand together again with science and skill and shiny metal instruments as sharp as the blade that maimed him in the first place.

And it was this last thought that gave Rich pause.

It was this last thought that caused him to stand and pace and consider.

Vice could tell that Rich was onto something. 'What? What are you thinkin', man?'

But Rich waved him off. He didn't want to talk. He wanted to focus on the idea. Get it clear in his head. Think it through. Work it out.

Because if the idea was half as good as Rich thought it was — it very possibly could save them all.

50

The porcelain plate was sizzling when it was placed in front of Rich, the sirloin still popping and hissing at him. Their waiter, Chuck, had described the steak as *impeccably prepared*, and he hadn't exaggerated. It was a work of art.

'Watch yourself, it's over four hundred degrees,' the seventy-year-old server warned.

Rich pulled his hands back as Max swirled and tasted a sample from their second bottle of wine. 'It's great, thanks, Chuck.' Chuck nodded and began to pour. 'Truth is,' Max said to Rich, laughing, 'I don't know anything about wine — no idea what goes with what or which end is up. But pinot's always tasted good to me, so that's what I get.'

'Well, it was an excellent choice, Mr. Seymour. You always make excellent choices.'

'Ah, you're paid to say that, Chuck.'

'Yes, I am,' the waiter replied with a smile. 'I'm going to go serve the less important diners now.'

Max grinned and patted Chuck on the arm as he moved off to the kitchen.

'Love this place.' Max beamed. 'Though the best steak I ever had was in California. Joint called Mastro's in Thousand Oaks. Go out a few times a year on business, always stop in. But in New York, you can't beat Luger's. Can't beat it with a stick. But enough about the food; I hear

304

congratulations are in order.'

'For what?'

'Dean's list? That's nothing to sneeze at.'

'It's just dean's list. It's not like making *Law Review* or something.'

'What do you mean, *just* dean's list? It's things like that — dean's list, the pre-law classes, working at a law firm, a great letter of recommendation from a brilliant lawyer like me — those all add up. And you know what they add up to? A *top* law school.'

'At this point, I just want to get accepted anywhere.'

'You will. Just keep doing what you're doing and we'll be here celebrating your first court win before you know it.'

Max raised his drink. Rich reached across the table with his and they tapped glasses. Rich didn't savor the wine; he gulped half of it down in one swig. He wanted to deaden the pain of what he was about to do.

He'd hated himself for even thinking of it and now he hated himself even more for going through with it, but he had no choice. People had gotten hurt already and more would be hurt, *even worse*, if Rich didn't implement his plan. He didn't want to do this to Max; he didn't want to betray him; but his back was so far up against the wall he'd gone through it and come out the other side. Max had treated Rich like family since he was a child. Rich loved the man. But there was no other option. In a perfect world, Max would never even know what happened. That's what Rich prayed for as he steeled himself and began talking, trying to sound as nonchalant as possible.

'So, other day at the engagement party, you said you were trying to wrap up the Estrin Medical case. How's that going? 'Cause you had said when I started at O and T that you figured it would be done by year's end.'

'It will. We're working on a settlement agreement now, still dotting the i's and crossing the t's. Pain-in-the-ass case.' Max took another sip of wine.

'But you think it'll get resolved?' Rich asked, once again trying to not give away his real intentions.

'Oh yeah, next week or so. Parties want it wrapped up before Christmas. Can't wait to close that case and forget it ever existed.'

So Rich now knew that there was a resolution in the works and that it would be finalized in the near future. There was just one last piece of information he needed. Rich knew he had to play it cool.

'You happy with how it turned out?'

'Yeah. 'Cause it's *over*.' Max snorted as he chewed.

'No, I mean, was it a satisfactory outcome for the client? For Estrin Medical?'

Max laughed. 'Satisfactory? Those sons-abitches should put a statue of me in their lobby! They're getting away with a two-million-dollar payout — they make that in an *afternoon* at Estrin.'

'From the chef, Mr. Seymour,' Chuck said as he placed a plate of extra-thick-cut bacon with a side of homemade blue cheese dressing in front of one of his best customers.

'Wow, look at this. Please tell him thank you for me,' Max said, biting into a fat chunk of swine.

Chuck nodded and walked off.

'See, one of the benefits of coming to the same place for thirty-five years. You spend twenty grand in meals, they give ten bucks' worth of free pig,' Max joked.

Rich didn't laugh, but Max didn't notice. He was too busy slowly looking around the restaurant, taking it in. The Peter Luger Steak House was over one hundred twenty years old, but Max wasn't contemplating the eatery's history; he was reflecting on his own.

'You know, Chuck served me and my dad here the day I got sworn into the bar. At the New York State supreme court — appellate division — first department. Great old building, great architecture, amazing history,' Max reminisced. 'Same place you'll be sworn in, kiddo.'

He looked down at Rich's plate, then up at his protégé.

'The cow doesn't get any deader. *Eat*.'

Rich took knife to flesh and carved into the perfectly cooked medium-plus cut of beef. Next to the meat rested the restaurant's famous German fried potatoes and creamed spinach. But despite the incredible feast before him, Rich didn't want to eat. He had no appetite after what he'd just done. He forced some steak into his mouth, polished off his wine, and quickly poured himself some more.

Max continued. 'I remember, after the swearing-in ceremony, my father and I went for a walk in the park across the street. He and my mom, they had me late, so he was getting on in years by then, and he wrapped his arm around mine to steady himself a bit. I didn't say anything; we just walked and he just kept patting my hand and saying things like *What a day* and *That was some ceremony, wasn't it?* and *Did you see all those judges up there?* It wasn't until we sat on a bench and he said, *We did it, Ellie, our boy's a lawyer*, that I realized he was talking to my mother, who had died eight years earlier. He was just so damn proud of me.'

Max looked up from his wine; his eyes were red and wet.

'I feel the same way about you, son. I knew you were special when I first met you. When you were *ten*, I knew it. What you're doing, how hard you're working — at the firm, at school. You're getting married now, to a princess . . . you know my situation. I got daughters, good girls, great girls, but one of 'em's a stockbroker, the other's a full-time mom . . . '

Max's voice got softer; the hefty wine pour had made him vulnerable. 'No one, ya know, wanted to come along with me into the law. But then you . . . well, I couldn't be prouder of you if you were my own.' Max's voice caught as he choked up. He lowered his eyes, a bit embarrassed by his display, and pretended to be absorbed in cutting his meat. 'I just wanted you to know that,' he said quietly.

Rich didn't say anything. What could he say?

The man from whom he had just garnered information so he could commit more crimes had told him that he thought of Rich as a son. Rich hadn't thought it was possible, but now he felt even worse.

'Thanks, Max. I appreciate all you've done for me' was the best Rich could come up with.

They small-talked their way through the rest of the dinner. Max asked about Ed, still shocked that his grandparents had allowed a mentally challenged man to dislodge ice that had collected around the fan of a snowblower. Rich and the others had decided that saying Ed's injury happened at the Printers would result in too many questions, too much paperwork, and too big of a risk. So a lie was fabricated and they all stuck to it. Dylan's girlfriend, on the night of the incident, had been told that it occurred at work, but since she had never interacted with anyone from Olmstead & Taft and probably never would, they figured they were okay. Rich explained to Max that Ed's pointer finger and pinkie had been reattached successfully, but the middle finger and ring finger were lost.

'But Ed's in good spirits,' Rich lied. 'We're teaching him how to whistle.' Rich put his pointer and pinkie in his mouth and mimed whistling.

After dinner, Rich saw Max to his car, in the parking lot across the street.

Mauro watched the veteran lawyer drive off in his Lexus toward Sixth Street and the water. Max had tried to give Rich a ride but Rich begged off, claiming he wanted to meet up with some friends at a bar on Driggs Street. But the truth was he wasn't feeling well.

It wasn't the food or the wine or anything medical.

Rich had made himself sick. The person he had become had made him physically ill.

As he walked along Driggs, thinking about what he had gotten himself into, what he had gotten his *friends* into, what he had done to Max, his head began to throb, and his stomach tightened and soured.

Within a half a block, Rich doubled over and threw up his impeccably prepared sirloin in the shadow of the Williamsburg Bridge.

51

Rich and Jason descended the multitiered staircase that took them down the equivalent of three stories to Morningside Park, the thirty-acre piece of nature carved into the heart of Harlem.

The stairs seemed to take a lot out of Spade, who was gaunt and pale, his eyes deep in his head, his cheeks sallow and gray. The drugs were clearly getting the better of him, Rich thought — though if there was ever a time to get high, it was now.

To their right, a massive masonry retaining wall seemed to grow taller and taller with each step down that they took. The lampposts were few and far between and one of them was flickering its last breaths of light, so the blackness grew with every stair they put behind them, as did Rich's anxiety. He was beginning to wish that he had insisted Dylan come with them. But when he had asked Rodriguez, the former gangbanger explained that he was not really welcome that far north in New York City anymore and that if he went with them and was spotted, it would cause a lot more trouble than what Rich was trying to avoid.

When they reached the bottom of the stairs, Rich turned and looked back up. High above them, the lights of New York shone carefree, unaware, and safe from the dangers Rich was about to walk into. The retaining wall had a

311

spiked iron fence that ran along its top. It looked and felt like the outside of a prison — or the inside of one, depending on how you thought of yourself. Rich felt it looked like the inside of one.

They walked silently along serpentine paths land-mined with patches of black ice that leaped up and bit you, sabotaging your traction. Rich almost fell twice but was able to maintain his footing, just barely.

He heard what he thought was the sound of cars driving really fast. Then he thought it was an audience applauding loudly. As they got closer, he saw what the sound was coming from. At first he thought the dark was playing tricks on his eyes, but the dark can't screw with your ears, and Rich could hear it loud and clear.

You can live in New York your entire life and feel like nothing will surprise you — you've seen it all. And then one day you come across something you never knew was there, something beautiful and amazing that can't possibly exist in New York City, but there it is, right in front you, and you can only marvel at it. And that's how Rich felt when he found himself at the base of a beautiful twenty-five-foot waterfall.

He knew if he'd been with Elyse instead of Spade, they would've whipped out their iPhones and searched the history of this wonder — was it natural, man-made, a combination of the two? How many times had developers tried to ruin it and how many times had protests from the citizens protected it? Did the waterfall have a name and if so, was it named after some political hack or someone who truly deserved such an honor?

He and Elyse loved discovering things together, whether it was a quiet little nook on Breezy Point beach or a nameless falafel cart on Varick Street that served the most addictive food you could imagine, and for only three dollars. Being together was what they did, and they did it well.

But as he comprehended that the dark and the sound of water crashing into water made him effectively blind and deaf, he began to worry that they had walked into a trap and perhaps he wouldn't be able to *be together* with Elyse again.

The glare took him completely by surprise. He took two quick steps back before he registered that it was the shine from a flashlight about fifty yards away.

Gold Tooth held the flashlight.

Caesar held the gun.

And Manny held court.

There were no pleasantries or preambles. The thugs quickly closed the gap between them and it was right to business.

'You gonna get my money or is the Parks Department gonna find someone facedown in this pond come sunrise?' he asked. It didn't come across as a tough-guy threat. It came across as a businessman presenting two options to associates — either option was acceptable to Manny; that was clear from the tone in his voice. It scared the hell out of Rich.

Rich explained his plan. The SEC was on high alert for abnormal trading pertaining to companies that were involved in certain transactions

313

and deals, like mergers or stock splits or the selling-off of subsidiaries. Rich figured they could shake up that pattern and avoid SEC detection by investing in Estrin Medical — a company that wasn't doing anything sexy like making a front-page-of-the-news acquisition. It was just settling a boring, years-old run-of-the-mill product-liability litigation for a couple million in nuisance value.

'So?' Manny asked, dense. 'How does a company giving away millions make *me* millions?'

'It takes away uncertainty in the market,' Rich said. 'Investors won't hesitate to buy Estrin stock now because there's no longer the potential for a huge judgment against the company. When those investors start buying, it drives the price up.'

'He's right,' Spade added quietly.

'No one asked you, junkie,' Manny snapped.

'I'm just sayin', it'll work — '

'Why don't you just take your ass back to Promise Medical before I put you in a *real* hospital,' Manny spat back.

Promise Medical was an upscale, private rehab facility in the Murray Hill section of the city. It catered to actors and musicians and prep-school kids who had to be pulled out of Dalton before Mommy and Daddy were embarrassed. It also seemed to be where young lawyers were sent by their fathers when the young lawyers' sudden influx of cash converted recreational weekend drug use into a dangerous habit and then into an unbreakable addiction.

Spade had never been in Tennessee, Rich realized. His dad had told everyone at work that his fuck-up son was doing a lengthy document review there, but in fact his dad had been trying to sober the kid up. One look at Spade, and Rich knew that Promise Medical hadn't kept its promise.

'Okay,' Manny said. 'Do what you're saying. But it better work or more than fingers get cut off next time. Some lobsterman's gonna pull your head outta one of his traps — you follow, bredda?'

'I follow,' Rich said nervously.

'*Buenas noches, mis trabajadores,*' Manny said with a sadistic smile. It meant 'Good night, my workers.' Manny wasn't being cute — he was laying claim to them; they worked for him now, belonged to him. And they needed to know it.

As Manny stepped away, Caesar raised his gun and Gold Tooth sharply produced his own from his waistband, quickly firing multiple rounds toward Rich and Spade. They instinctively hit the ground, covered their heads as if that would somehow stop the bullets, and waited to die — but the barrels were pointed way over their bodies, and the ammo sailed high into the blackness, disappearing into the waterfall and embedding in the rocks behind it.

It was just a second or two before Rich did the math and figured out he was still alive. But he lay there, face in the dirt, waiting for the gunfire to cease. Manny just wanted to put a little scare into them, let them know how serious he was — though after Manny had cut their friend's fingers off in front of them, Rich felt this display in the park was a bit of overkill.

The noise ended and Rich waited a moment before he lifted his head. Manny and his boys were gone. Rich imagined them hiding in the dark, behind the trees, having a good laugh at their expense.

But then he figured they probably weren't watching because, despite the relatively steady stream of crimes that took place in Morningside Park, extended periods of gunfire were uncommon enough to get the citizens of Harlem up and out of bed and to the phones.

Cops would be there soon.

Rich grabbed Spade and pulled him along, shouting at him to move his ass.

Rich hated Jason, but if Jason got busted, Rich knew he'd flip like a pancake on all of them.

So they ran like thieves in the night — because that's exactly what they were.

52

In the back of McMahon's Pub, Spade entered the letters *EST* into the laptop — the New York Stock Exchange symbol for Estrin Medical. Spade then typed in *220,000* — the number of shares they were buying. When the *Journal* and *Barron's* and CNBC and all the other money watchers released the news that Estrin's dark cloud of potentially massive payouts had been lifted via settlement, the stock wouldn't just run, it would *sprint*. Rich was sure of it. So was Spade.

Spade entered his digits first. Vice and Dylan went next. Then Rich. Eddie went last, hunting and pecking with the pointer of his left hand because his right was still wrapped in gauze and in no condition to do anything but hurt when the codeine wore off.

Spade hit Enter and it was done. Seven figures pilfered over two Fat Tires, a Corona, a water, and a root beer.

'When will we know if this worked?' Dylan asked.

'Not sure,' Rich answered. 'But Max said the case was getting wrapped up soon.' It hurt Rich even to say Max's name aloud. He was being so disloyal to him. But he saw no other way.

'I know a couple of first-years that were doing grunt duty on Estrin,' Spade said between nervous drags on a Marlboro Light. 'One of them was just sent to Brussels for some international shipping matter; the other got crammed into this software antitrust case that every rookie lawyer is getting pulled into. No way Seymour would give up bodies unless he knew his case was closing.'

'Good,' Vice said, finishing up his water as he stood. 'Then we're done.' Lately, Vice was always rushing home, partly because being the dad to almost a baseball team's worth of kids kept his schedule full and partly because, after what happened to Ed, he just didn't want to be around the Printers or any of them anymore.

That was kind of the feeling they all had, though no one said it aloud. They all, save for Spade, of course, cared for one another, but they had done such bad things together, had *caused* such bad things, and looking at one another reminded them all of their moral corruptibility, of the worst parts of themselves.

'So we just wait now,' Dylan said, more a statement than a question.

'Yup,' Rich concurred, sliding from the booth. 'As soon as the stock jumps, we'll sell.' Rich turned and placed two of his fingertips on Spade's chest so the lawyer couldn't follow him out of the booth. 'And then we're giving all the money to Manny and we're done.'

Spade looked at the four men staring back at him, instantly recognizing the faces of a unified front.

'You fuckin' guys have been talking?' he scoffed. 'This thing was *my* idea. *My* idea — '

'And you blew it up,' Rich growled under his

breath, up in Spade's face. 'We're gonna clear more than one point one million on this trade. Plus all the money that's sitting in the account right now. Manny considers himself a business-man, so I'll appeal to that side of him. He can enjoy all of the cash, plus everything's he's gotten so far, pay back his suppliers, and make a mint dealin' or stealin' or whatever the hell it is he does. Or he can keep pushin' this thing until we all get busted, which I don't think is that far down the road if the SEC already has its antennae up.'

'You guys can't just do this.'

'But you see we are,' Rich said with no small measure of satisfaction. 'If Manny agrees, we give him the money and we're all out of this thing. If he doesn't, we're all willing to give him our digits. Then he'd just need *yours* to get any future money. And since we'd all quit our jobs, it would be up to you to provide whatever inside information you could glean from the cases you handle during what I'm sure will be a long and distinguished legal career.' Rich's words were deep-fried in sarcasm because one look at Spade and it was obvious that if he didn't get clean soon, neither his legal career nor his *life* would be long and distinguished.

'Manny will have you killed. All of you.'

'Maybe. But I think after I explain things to him, he'll just wanna ring the register and get out with a fat final payday and no bracelets on his wrists. He'll be pissed at you though. You promised him a cash cow that never ran out of milk. But Bessie's dead.'

Rich wasn't nearly as confident as he sounded. He knew there was a chance Manny would shoot him on the spot when he heard what Rich had to say. But he wasn't going to let Spade know he was concerned. Spade, by contrast, was sweating like a fat guy on a slow buffet line, although most of the perspiration was drug induced.

'This thing can still work,' Jason pleaded. 'We can still get what we want.'

'I want my fingers back, you son of a bitch!' Ed shouted, causing the smattering of patrons to look their way. Vice gently placed his hand on Eddie's arm to calm him and they all just waited it out until the regulars went back to their beers and sports arguments and debates over which crooked politician did which crooked thing.

When the attention was off them, Spade lasered in on Mauro. 'Rich, look, I know you and I have hit a rough patch in our friendship, but we go back a long time — '

'We were never friends. You *pretended* to be my friend so you could use me. And now you're pretending to be my friend because you're desperate — you're a desperate addict who knows the clock's ticking on his money supply, his drug supply, his girl supply, ticking on his trust fund and Daddy's patience. And now you want me to keep something going that could get us all killed or locked up just for your sake?'

Rich cupped his hand behind Spade's head and pulled him close. 'It's over,' he said, and then he turned his back on Jason and walked out.

The others left as well.

Spade slumped in the booth and ran his hand through his sweat-drenched hair. He knew Rich was right — he was desperate.

And he felt ill. He needed to self-medicate. As he washed some Oxycontin down with what was left of his beer, he wondered if the drugs or Manny would kill him first.

53

Rich brushed snow off the top of the headstone. The stone was covered in ice so he smashed the bottom of a gloved fist into the frozen water, about a quarter-inch thick, covering the New England granite that shared with the world the last few thoughts about his parents.

Loving mother, devoted wife.
Loving father, devoted husband.
Caring and kind to all.

Other than the dates of birth and death, that was all it said. Uncle Jim wanted to keep it simple. Rich thought he did a good job. It was accurate and to the point.

Rich turned as the sound of snow crunching underfoot behind him grew louder.

'These might be good,' Elyse said, holding out her mitten-covered hand. She had two nice-size rocks lying in her palm.

'They're perfect. Thanks.'

He took the rocks and put them on the top of the tombstone. It was something the Jews did to let other mourners passing by know that those six feet under that particular piece of ground had people topside who loved them, people who cared enough to visit and record their time there with stones. Uncle Jim had learned the tradition from a Jewish contractor he knew and always thought it was nice. So he started doing it when Rich's parents died, and Rich always did it because his uncle did it, and now two Italians went to St. John Cemetery off Metropolitan Avenue and honored their dead like the Israelites had been doing for thousands of years.

A light snow fell, kissing the tops of all the monuments. Snow at Christmastime could make even a cemetery seem pretty.

He knelt in the snow and gently touched his mother's and father's names before speaking to them.

'Hi. I know I should've done it sooner, but time and things have a way of slipping away, ya know,' Rich said, his eyes welling. He always tried not to cry when he visited his parents, and he always failed. But he wanted to keep his composure this time. This time was more important than the others.

'But I figured better late than never, right?' he said softly. 'So, Mom, Dad, this is Elyse. I love her very much. She's the one who's gonna give you your grandchildren.'

Elyse let out a small laugh that was much closer to a cry. Tears had been making their way down her beautiful face from the moment Rich knelt. She loved him so much and she knew how much it hurt him to be without his parents. She knew he loved her, but she also knew she served a purpose for Rich — she filled a void in his life that needed to be filled. She was happy to do it.

'I gave her your ring, Mom — I know you'd love her. She'll take care of me. She already does.'

Rich thought long about what to say next. With all that was going on — the danger he was in with the SEC and Manny — he needed help, and his parents were the most direct channel he had to God, so he had to ask. He just didn't know how to phrase it with Elyse right behind him. He decided to keep it honest but vague.

'I know I haven't always made the best decisions, I know that. But I'm going to be better; I promise. Just help me. Watch over me. I need you.'

He took his glove off and kissed his hand and touched his parents' names one more time. He was crying now. He had failed again. Elyse watched, a bit perplexed by what Rich had said. She wasn't sure what decisions he was talking about, but she knew that Rich very much wanted to have a family and be a good father, like his own was. She assumed he was asking for their guidance and love from heaven. She thought it was a beautiful request.

In reality, Rich knew he was going to have to meet with a violent man in the near future, give him millions in cash, and hope that, as a result of that transfer, Rich would get to end his crimes without ending his life.

Rich wasn't praying for guidance in family and love.

He was praying for protection from pain and death.

54

The resolution of the Estrin case hit the press on December 17. The stock jumped 12.5 percent. The next day, another 11 percent. At the sound of the closing bell on December 20, EST settled 28 percent higher than it had been just three days earlier. Manny would be getting millions. Rich had to deliver some power-of-attorney papers to the firm's trusts and estates department, which was just down the hall from Spade's office, and Rich planned to use the opportunity to check in on Jason. He had called Spade a few times to invite him for a 'beer at McMahon's,' but Jason hadn't returned his calls. Rich was starting to get worried, as were the other Blazers. They just wanted to get Manny his money and lower the curtain on the whole thing. So, despite the huge risk of talking about their crimes up on the higher floors, where lawyers prowled, they all agreed someone had to go up there and do something. If Manny had seen the business pages, and they were sure he had, he'd be expecting his payout soon, and they'd better have it when he wanted it. So they needed Spade.

Rich got on the elevator, pressed the button for the twenty-third floor, and rode upward. But at the lobby, the elevator stopped. The doors opened and wouldn't close again. Rich pressed every relevant button, to no avail.

'That thing's been misbehavin' all mornin'. C'mon, ride with me, youngblood.'

Rich looked up from the elevator buttons. Across the lobby, watching him, was Chip. It seemed like years, not months, since he'd first met the old guy.

Rich picked up his cardboard box of documents, walked across the O&T logo embedded in the floor, and climbed into Chip's movable office.

'Who ya goin' to see?' he asked, indicating the box.

'Michael Zucotti.'

'Ah, twenty-third floor, trusts and estates. Mr. Zucotti. Always busy helping the rich keep their money.' Chip hit the appropriate button, and the elevator began to move.

'Yup,' Rich said, not in the mood to talk. He was exhausted on all levels.

'He's a nice man. Helped me move some of my stuff around, get cash to my grandchildren, avoid that gift-tax thing and bunch of other ways Uncle Sam tryin' to take what I've earned.'

Rich raised his eyebrows. 'You got estate issues?' Rich said in wonderment.

'I been in this box longer than you been alive, son. Whatcha think they pay me in, chewin' gum and buttons?'

'Yeah, no, I didn't mean to offend — I just didn't think what this firm pays would be enough to warrant — '

'It ain't. But every month since I been twenty I've taken some of my paycheck and bought stocks that pay dividends. Nothing fancy. None of that tech bullshit. Coca-Cola. Con Ed. Bank

326

of New York. That's where my money went, and that shit *grows*.'

The elevator stopped and Chip pulled the lever that opened the door. He continued. 'In this country, anyone can make it. Just gotta work hard and believe you're good enough.'

The words struck Rich like a haymaker from a heavyweight. He could work hard. He always worked hard. Whether behind a nail gun or a textbook, Rich had always been willing to put in the hours and spill the sweat.

But did he believe he was good enough? The hard truth was, he didn't. Perhaps he never had. Maybe because he grew up lower middle class, then watched kids his age start at Fordham while he was pouring cement outside its gates.

Maybe because his parents' death made him feel like he was being punished for something. If he was *good*, why would God take his family away? He asked himself that question for years after the accident, and though he didn't consciously ask himself that anymore, he had never come up with a satisfactory answer.

Rich had believed all that Spade told him about losing Elyse to Garhart. Believed it easily. Believed that Elyse could, *and would*, be swept away by a richer, more handsome version of what a husband should be. Rich had been insecure about his relationship with her from the day they met. She was too beautiful, too smart, too perfect to fall for a parentless night-schooler from Queens. That thought was on a constant spin cycle in his brain, even though he didn't always acknowledge it.

As he was about to step off the elevator, Rich understood that he'd done what he'd done — broken the law, lied, gotten people hurt — because he'd never thought himself good enough. He felt that since he was a kid. He wasn't good enough to have parents. Or to have a wife who loved him. He wasn't good enough for anything.

Dazed at this realization, Rich nodded to Chip before turning to leave, but Chip stopped him with a hand on the shoulder.

'Boy,' he said. 'I know you're with Max, and I know you wanna be a lawyer here and all, but some people ain't cut out for the stress of this place. Look at you, you can't even handle movin' the papers.'

'Huh?' Rich asked, still a bit out of it.

'You ain't even been here that long yet, but this job has aged you. You look like shit, kid.'

Chip pushed a button and the doors to his office closed.

Rich walked off and delivered his box of documents. *Damn.* When a seventy-something-year-old elevator operator tells you that you look worn down, you know things aren't going well. But he felt better about his own appearance when he found Spade huddled in his office.

The door had been closed but Rich let himself in to find Jason lying on his couch with the lights off and the shades pulled. There were bottles of prescription pills on his desk. Maybe Promise Medical had gotten him some meds and was trying to wean him off the hard stuff. Or maybe Spade had just found another kind of drug to abuse. Rich didn't care.

He woke Spade up with a kick to the leg. Spade groaned, and after a minute of prodding, Rich got him to sit upright. He was ragged. Rich was surprised his father hadn't sent him on another 'business trip' to avoid the questions that were sure to come if enough lawyers saw Jason like this. Maybe Miles Spade, like his son, had just given up.

Rich grabbed Spade roughly, fixed his tie, and slapped him hard across the face. 'Get your shit together, stupid. We're *this close* to getting out — don't fuck things up more than you already have.'

Spade didn't protest. He nodded as if he not only understood Rich but agreed with him.

Rich grabbed Spade's laptop and pulled him into the hallway. Luckily, it was lunchtime, so a lot of O&T lawyers were in the dining room or out with clients, judges, adversaries — somewhere nice with linen tablecloths and checks that got expensed. The important thing was that very few of them were around to see Spade looking like the product of a hangover fucking an ass-kicking.

Rich shuttled him into an empty elevator, which, thankfully, was working properly. They hit the basement in just over thirty-six seconds and were safe.

In the Printers, Spade poured himself some coffee and popped a loose pill he fished from his pocket. Within a minute, he had perked up a touch.

'Okay,' Rich said, 'so tomorrow we'll meet in

329

the alley behind McMahon's at ten a.m. We'll go to Colts Neck, close out the account. Everyone bring duffel bags, lots of 'em. We're gonna have a lot to carry.'

'Okay, but how we gonna get all that cheddar to Manny?' Vice asked. 'I ain't goin' up to Harlem with that much cash. Might as well wear a shirt that say *Please Shoot My Black Ass*.'

Rich agreed. 'Morningside Park's out of the question. He fired on us last time we were there — no knowing what he'll do now. I want someplace public but with little chance of security or traffic or ATM cameras picking us up.'

'Can't be too secluded,' Dylan countered. 'Not when you're planning on telling Manny Espinoza that it's all over.'

'Yeah,' Vice chimed in. 'Gotta do it like breaking up with a lady, do it somewhere that decreases the odds of a scene — but in this case, I'm talking *crime scene*, know what I'm sayin', paesan?'

'Yeah, I do,' Rich answered. 'That's why you guys aren't coming. I'm doing this alone.'

'Fuck that,' Vice protested. 'I'm no bitch. I ain't leavin' you out there like that.'

'Rich, it ain't safe to do it solo,' Dylan added.

'No. Vice, you've got those kids counting on you. Dylan, you have a brand-new baby, and Ed, you've been through enough. I can meet Manny on my own,' Rich insisted.

Vice and Dylan argued and Ed said he wasn't scared but he clearly was. Spade didn't offer to tag along.

'I brought this thing to you guys. It's my fault

you're involved at all. It's my mess. Please, let me clean it up,' Rich said, a statement more than a request.

The other Blazers begrudgingly acquiesced.

Dylan suggested a drop spot near his Alphabet City apartment — a patch of grass behind a chain-link fence, called Orchard Alley Park. He would sometimes take Bella in the stroller there on weekends, and, by habit, he checked to see where the security camera was, even though his days of conducting illegal activity in parks were behind him. There was only one — on a lamppost by the swing set — but birds had shit all over the lens, and it was useless. There was a girls' prep school across the street that always had weekend events, and Manny wouldn't start firing with all those people around. And even though the school had security cameras on its brick façade, they were all pointed at the door to show who was coming and going. Also, since Dylan knew the area, he could watch from a distance and jump in if anything bad went down — but he kept that to himself, because he knew Rich would fight him on it.

Rich said it sounded good.

'I'll tell Manny that's where we'll do the transfer,' Spade said. 'But what if he says no?'

'Then he doesn't get his money,' Rich said matter-of-factly.

Rich opened Spade's laptop, and Jason got to work. They had made so many trades over the months that his fingers glided from key to key like a dancer remembering the most familiar of steps.

Within moments, all the money from the overseas account was on its journey. Because they had cleared so many transactions already, and because the numerical account was such an 'important customer,' the waiting periods had been dropped by the banks, and the money would be available in Colts Neck in a little less than twenty-four hours.

Rich couldn't wait to get to Jersey. He had never wanted to give money away so badly.

The rest of the day passed like any other. The holiday lull was getting more pronounced but Ed saw that as an opportunity to get the machinery operating better through cleaning and maintenance, because even after all that had happened, Ed Pisorchek still cared about his job. He worked silently. He hadn't been talking much since he'd been assaulted, and the others had noticed. Vice tried repeatedly to make Eddie laugh but Ed's laughing days were over. Now he was 'a cripple to boot,' as his grandfather told him the other night.

'Didn't think it possible,' old man Pisorchek said to his grandson, 'but you actually managed to make yourself even more useless. Losing those fingers was the fart on a shit sandwich.'

Then he asked Eddie to check with the county to see if he was entitled to any additional disability payments.

Then he changed the channel.

Rich would never forgive himself for what happened to Eddie. It pained him every time he watched Ed take his antibiotics (to prevent infection under the still raw sutures) or leave for physical therapy (to prevent the loss of range of motion in the still stiff joints).

So that night, around seven, Rich told Ed to go home. He told them all to go. He'd finish up with the machines and see them tomorrow. They all took him up on his offer and left.

Rich spent the next several hours cleaning and scrubbing and wiping and polishing. The only break he took was when Elyse called to ask if June was too soon to have the wedding and if they should wait for the fall and do it in October. She wanted to give family enough time to prepare if they had to travel.

'I don't really have family to invite,' Rich pointed out. 'Just me, Uncle Jim, Max, and the guys from work, of course. You think we can have Vice's family and Dylan's girl too?'

'Of course,' Elyse responded. Rich could tell she was smiling at the other end of the line. 'Of course your friends should be there. I gotta run, call me tomorrow!'

She hung up, too busy with calligraphers and florists and wedding-band auditions to let any call last too long.

God, he loved her.

At a little past midnight, Rich was done, and as he shut off the lights to leave, Spade entered. He looked much better than he had earlier but still appeared bone-tired, the dark bags under his eyes making him seem years older than he actually was.

'What's going on?' Rich asked.

'Nothing,' Spade replied. 'I just — I know this got all fucked up — I just wanted to say I'm sorry. I lied to you from the start, you know that, and I — I don't know what I'm saying, I don't know . . . ' Spade trailed off.

Rich looked at him with disbelief. After all this, after all the deception, the son of a bitch still wanted to be friends. That was never going to happen — Rich was done with Jason Spade — but he couldn't help but marvel at the innocence of Spade's childlike request when he asked Rich, 'You wanna walk out together?'

'Sure,' Rich said. What other answer could he give? They were both walking out the same way anyhow.

The wind off the water made sure to remind them it was December as soon as they stepped outside.

On massive poles outside the firm, flags — the state of New York's, the bar association's, Old Glory — all snapped loudly in protest of the blustery weather.

They walked down the steps toward the street, and the cracking of the flags' fabric got louder and louder.

Rich didn't realize the sound was actually that of footsteps running toward him until it was too late.

He was blindsided and tackled to the ground. His assailants were the real deal — his hands were behind his back and cuffed before he could even catch the breath that had been knocked out of him.

He turned his head and saw that Spade was getting the same treatment.

As freezing air ice-picked his lungs upon entry,

334

Rich listened to his rights being read.

Poor Elyse, Rich thought.

Her wedding plans had been over before his head bounced off the sidewalk.

Not June.

Not October.

Not ever would they be married ... and marrying her was why he had done all this in the first place.

55

Turns out, the boys from the basement had seriously underestimated the SEC. Traditionally, the federal investigators would run a company that had raised a red flag under a microscope. They'd look at the target's internal directors, officers, executives, department heads, and anyone else who would know that certain transactions were going to take place and who could then trade on that information.

But in this case, *several* publicly traded companies were showing irregularities. And as more and more companies displayed suspicious trading over the period of a few months, the investigators realized there was a connection. They knew someone on the *outside* of these companies was getting ahold of classified data.

So they looked at *everyone* affiliated with each corporation. The engineers. The manufacturers. The suppliers. Perhaps there was overlap — maybe an R & D firm hired by one company was doing work for some of the other companies as well, and perhaps an unscrupulous person within that R & D firm was making the unlawful trades. But the corporations that had been traded covered too broad a spectrum — they involved operations as diverse as construction and entertainment and pharmaceuticals. There was no way that one engineering company or one supplier could work for such a wide range of businesses.

But one law firm could.

And the investigators eventually noticed one name that came up quite often during their inquiry was that of the venerable old-school, white-shoe firm of Olmstead & Taft. The firm didn't represent one of the primary corporations involved in the transaction in *each and every* matter, but when the investigators dug deeper, they found that in those instances when O&T didn't directly represent the particular corporation, it had provided legal counsel to the investment bankers on the deal, or to the deal's underwriter, or to the deal's accountants, or to one of the dozens of other players who got involved when multibillion-dollar enterprises decided to play Monopoly for real.

And the lawyers in these deals would be in contact with classified material that could be used to take Wall Street for a ride. Hell, they were the ones who were *putting together* those materials.

But that begged the question: Which of the over one thousand employees at one of the world's biggest legal firms was breaking the law? There were different attorneys working on each of these matters — many were from corporate, but some were from patents and trademarks or finance or litigation. There was no way, the investigators knew, that so many lawyers from so many various departments had *all* agreed to break the law and be in on the conspiracy.

And they quickly dismissed the notion that information was somehow being leaked *accidentally* within the firm. Olmstead & Taft, like all top

337

firms, took precautions to make sure the lawyers in its employ did not share inside information, even unintentionally. Code names were given to clients so no one outside the cases knew what particular lawyers were working on; 'war rooms' were set up for sensitive cases and only team members were granted access; and in the most sensitive of situations, O&T instituted Chinese walls — stringent rules governing conduct that forbade lawyers who represented clients with competing interests to even *talk* to one another until the case was resolved; in some drastic instances, they couldn't even be in the same room or elevator together.

Eventually, the SEC realized that the only people in the entire building who had access to all of the information necessary to do what had been done were those you'd least suspect, the ones you never even thought to consider — *the group of kids working in the basement.*

They pulled the card on each of the Blazers. Nothing of note — a carpenter, a petty thief, a mentally challenged future ward of the state. The only one who showed any type of leadership ability to put something like this together was the gangbanger, but he didn't have the educational background needed to digest the dense legality of the paperwork he processed every day. In fact, none of them did.

The Blazers would have needed someone to decipher the legalese of the briefs and filings and motions. So the investigators reverse-engineered the Blazers' lives to see if any of them had had any previous contact or relationships with any of

338

the lawyers in the firm. Surprisingly enough, they got two hits on the same Blazer — Rich Mauro.

Public court records almost two decades old showed that Max Seymour, a partner at O&T, had represented Mauro in a wrongful-death suit when Rich was a child. But Seymour was a Boy Scout — commended and honored by every bar-association chapter from Astoria to Albany. And his finances checked out; he didn't need the money — so he didn't have a motive.

But the other lawyer did. A run on Jason Spade showed he had next to nothing in his name — only a very expensive recently purchased automobile. He was broke. And computerized medical records kept by the city's health department showed that both Jason Spade and Rich Mauro had passed physicals to play in the all-city basketball tournament almost a decade earlier, when they were teens.

Spade and Mauro knew each other from childhood, and they each brought something to the table — one had access to valuable information, and the other had the ability to understand it.

They knew they had their guys. A review of their finances didn't show any big deposits in bank accounts, but they figured Mauro and Spade weren't dumb enough to put stolen money in a domestic account under their names. They assumed anything that was done was overseas, numerical, under dummy corporations — the SEC knew that finding the money would prove to be a hell of a lot harder than finding the culprits had been.

But the investigators had enough to get the FBI involved.

And the FBI had enough to bring to a U.S. district judge.

And the district judge had enough to issue arrest warrants.

And the Jacob K. Javits Federal Building at 26 Federal Plaza always had staff eager to process the most recent arrests.

Rich and Jason were fingerprinted and photographed. Rich's picture had to be taken three times. After the first time, the photographer asked Rich not to look down when his picture was taken. Rich said okay and then proceeded to do it again, not to be difficult but because he was so damned ashamed that instinct took over and made him hide his face, no matter how illogical it was. After the second time, the officer manning the camera didn't *ask* — he *threatened* Rich with separate additional charges of obstructing justice and resisting arrest. Rich didn't know if the guy was blowing smoke or not but he wasn't about to find out. He turned into a statue and stared straight ahead. *Click.*

Spade went through the motions without expression — he had been arrested for everything from bar fights to DWIs. He knew the drill.

They were separated and put in rooms down the hall from each other. As Spade was being led away he said just loud enough for Rich to hear, 'Don't say shit.'

A federal agent named Alfredo Barrios sat down with Rich in a midsize room that looked bigger than it was because it was basically empty — only a wooden table and a few government-issue chairs. Rich couldn't help but think that the guys who wrote for *Law & Order* and all those other cop shows got it pretty much right — it looked like every interrogation room he had ever seen on TV, except for a long, waist-level bar that ran the length of one wall. It looked like a ballerina's barre, but Rich knew no one was going to be doing *ronds de jambe* on the thing unless he liked dancing while handcuffed.

Mauro waited for the vitriol to spew from Barrios. He was a cop, and Rich was a criminal, and once Rich asserted his right to speak to counsel, he figured he'd get an earful of abuse, maybe even a face-full of fist. He'd seen movies, he knew what was about to go down, and he braced for it.

But Barrios was a decent guy. He offered Rich water, which Rich refused. He offered him something to eat, which Rich accepted; he had skipped dinner and was, despite the circumstances, quite hungry. Barrios pulled a protein bar from inside his suit jacket pocket.

'Peanut-butter-chocolate. That okay?' the agent asked.

'Great. Thanks.'

'Okay, the formalities,' Alfredo continued. 'Rich Mauro, you've been placed under arrest for the crimes of insider trading, conspiracy to commit insider trading . . .'

Rich didn't hear the words. The same thing had happened when he'd had his rights read to him outside the Olmstead & Taft offices an hour earlier with a mouthful of New York City sidewalk and a back-full of cop knee. It was as if his ears were protecting him — if he didn't *hear* what was going on, maybe it wasn't *actually* going on. But Rich caught bits and pieces: 'Right to remain silent . . . '; 'If you can't afford an attorney . . . '; and so forth.

Once Rich was fully Mirandized, Barrios leaned forward, hands clasped in front of him, and said, 'So I want to make sure you understand your rights.'

Before Rich could respond, Barrios's cell rang. He answered it with urgency.

'Hello? Yeah, okay, that's great. Look, I'm working — yeah, I know, but it never ends — okay, I'll call in the morning . . . love ya, bye.'

He hung up.

'My sister. She's down in Florida with my dad; he had knee surgery and was running a fever after the operation and the docs think it was a bad infection but they got it under control now,' he explained as he pulled at some lint on his suit sleeve. The lint was stubborn, so Barrios continued fussing with his garment; he didn't even look up at Rich. 'So anyway, you understand what I said to you, about your rights?'

Rich almost laughed. Here it was, the worst moment in his life, but it was just another day at the office for Agent Barrios. Sick dads and uncooperative lint were as important to Alfredo as Rich was. Rich's life as he knew it was about to end, but for almost everyone else in the world, life went on.

'Yeah, no disrespect, Agent Barrios, but I think

342

I should talk to a lawyer first.' Rich tried to sound as polite as possible.

'You *think*? Does that mean you are invoking your right to counsel?'

'Yeah, I guess it does.'

'You *guess* it does, or it does?'

'It does.'

Without a word, Barrios stood up and moved to the door.

'Wait, hold on, what happens now?'

'Once you invoke your right to counsel, I'm not supposed to have any kind of communication with you that could in any way elicit information about your crime. But if you're asking me the next procedural step, you'll head over to MCC and spend the weekend. On Monday you'll be arraigned. MCC's just down Worth Street and around the corner. A minute ride.'

But Rich didn't need directions. As soon as Barrios explained what the acronym stood for, Rich knew he was in for a long forty-eight hours. Any kid growing up in New York — watching the news, reading the *Post* — knew what Metropolitan Correctional Center was. It was where almost every notable defendant at one point or another rested his head once his due process came due. Mob bosses, fraudsters, terrorists — they had all called MCC home.

John Gotti.

Bernie Madoff.

Ramzi Yousef.

And now Rich Mauro.

Wouldn't his parents be proud?

Barrios opened the door and was halfway out when Rich stopped him.

'Hey,' Rich said. Barrios turned. 'I hope your dad feels better,' Rich said sincerely, wanting the agent to know that he wasn't his typical amoral scumbag criminal.

Barrios's face registered a bit of surprise — probably wasn't often that men looking at decades in prison wished their captors or their captors' families well. 'Thanks,' he replied. Then he closed the door on Rich and arranged for Transpo to take him to a cell less than half a mile away — because that's what Agent Barrios did with typical amoral scumbag criminals.

Before leaving, Rich was allowed to make his call. He picked up the phone and instinctively began dialing Uncle Jim. But then he stopped — he wasn't sure if Jim could do what needed to be done. His uncle was wonderful, but Rich needed someone who could meet with bail bondsmen, secure assets to post bond, retain an attorney, and take care of a score of other things that required immediate attention; he was certain that would be too much for his uncle to handle. Also, it was late at night, past two a.m., and the glass of scotch Jim had surely polished off, combined with the noise from the TV, which Rich was sure was on because he hadn't made it home to turn it off, might ensure his uncle wouldn't hear the phone when it rang.

He considered Elyse for all of three seconds. He wouldn't know what to say to her. He dreaded the confession he'd be making to her sometime over the next few days, either face to face or face to Plexiglas-visitors'-room window. He just wasn't strong enough to do that now.

Finally he realized that the call he had to make was the one he feared most of all because Max Seymour, unbeknownst to himself, was involved in this scam. It was his client Estrin Medical that Rich had traded on in their last stock purchase. Max was going to be devastated. So when he answered the phone, half asleep, and Rich explained he had been arrested, he couldn't bring himself to respond to Max's question: 'What the hell for?'

'Just ask for Mr. Barrios when you get here. He'll explain everything' was the best Rich could come up with.

'Richie, what happened? Are you okay? Are you hurt?' Max's concern was as pure and fatherly as if one of his own children had called.

'I'm fine, Max. I gotta go.' And Rich hung up.

And soon he was off to MCC.

Thankfully, though Rich's seven-and-a-half-by-eight-foot cell had bunk beds, Rich didn't have a cell mate. Spade was placed in the cell next to Rich.

This wasn't done by accident. The Feds knew that if they were put in the same cell they might possibly make plans, in inaudible whispers, about what to do with the millions that had yet to be found. However, if they were in cells next to each other, they might speak loudly enough for what they said to be overheard. Or maybe they'd fly a kite back and forth — prison slang for using a string or some other device to pass a note to another cell. If they did that, the note could be confiscated and read.

But even if they'd been put in the same room with a romantic candlelit dinner, they still wouldn't have said shit to each other. They knew what was at stake and they knew the best move was to keep their mouths shut. They hadn't said a word to each other on the ride over from the federal building and they weren't about to start now.

Rich lay down. It was almost three a.m., and like most guilty people who've been caught, he found that once the stress and pressure of keeping a secret was finally alleviated, it was easy to pass out and sleep like a baby.

But it didn't last. He had the dream again — the one with the row-boat out at sea. He tossed, sweating through his brown MCC-issue jumpsuit, as in his mind he leaned over the side, searching in the charcoal waters for his parents. A hand emerged from the waves and Rich reached for it; this time he was determined not to let them die. But as he got closer, he saw the face of the person bobbing among the white-caps — *it was him*. He was the one drowning now. And then suddenly, somehow, Rich's point of view switched and he was in the water, looking back at the boat. His parents stood inside it, safe and dry. He called out to them for help but they did nothing. They just watched him; sadness painted their faces. And as the tide carried them away, Rich went under.

At 6:00 a.m. all the lights in the cells automatically came on but Rich had been awake for a solid hour already, unable to go back to

346

sleep, not wanting to return to the sea.

At 6:30 a cart with breakfast arrived at his cell. Banana (brown in spots). Oatmeal (decent, but how can you fuck up oatmeal?). Bread with margarine (inedible). Milk (warm). Coffee (cold). He asked the guard when he'd be able to speak to his lawyer but the guard was already shoving food at Spade and was then on his way down the hall.

Hours passed. No one came. Rich was nervous. What was Uncle Jim thinking? By now, he'd seen that Rich had never come home. Did he just assume Rich spent the night at Elyse's? Or did he call her, ask if Rich was there? If he did, when Elyse said no, did they call the Printers? And what about the other Blazers? They'd be waiting outside McMahon's Pub in a few hours, expecting to go to Colts Neck. Were the Feds waiting to nail them? Or had they done that already? Had Dylan and Vice and poor, terrified Eddie been rounded up and processed, and their paths just hadn't intersected with Rich and Jason's? Or maybe the government had no idea that they were even involved.

Rich's mind ran away with possibilities, then it circled back, thought of some more scenarios, and then kicked him in the ass. Rich started pacing, which was next to impossible to do in a cell that was a little over fifty-six square feet and had less than twenty-eight square feet of walking room once you factored in the space gobbled up by the bed and wall-mounted sink and toilet. He dropped to the floor and did push-ups. He didn't feel the first ten. The next ten were a blip. He

347

started to slow at thirty, and his chest burned through forty. At fifty-one his arms gave out and he collapsed onto the floor, though his heart pounded so heavily that it seemed about to catapult him back upright. He lay there catching his breath.

'Get up.'

Rich scrambled to his feet. 'What's going on?'

'Arraignment,' said the guard outside his cell.

'But it's Saturday.'

'Arraignment,' the guard, who clearly wasn't much of a talker, repeated.

Rich was cuffed and taken from his cell. Another guard was already moving Spade along the hall.

Rich knew he was in trouble because after just one night in lockup, he was already finding the ten-foot-wide prison hallway luxuriously spacious compared to his cell. He already knew he didn't want to ever go back in. Not good news for a guy who was facing a long bid.

They took an elevator down to the basement, where Rich and Jason were presented to federal marshals. There they were both put in four-pieces: cuffed at the ankles, chained at the waist, and cuffed again at the hands. Rich wanted to explain, *Hey, this really isn't necessary. I'm not a bad guy, not like the ones you normally deal with.* But he didn't say anything. He was told to walk, though that was impossible in the four-piece. So he shuffle-hopped through a forty-foot-long tunnel under Pearl Street. He wondered if anyone in the taxis or on the sidewalks above had any idea that this tunnel was down there.

They passed through electronic security doors that were remotely controlled by officers watching Rich and Spade through cameras.

At the end of the tunnel, they reached a prisoner elevator. Spade was told to stay and only Rich was let on. He wasn't sure why until he saw the locked cage. He was told to step inside and he did. He was locked up like a dog in a pet carrier on a plane. On the way up to the courthouse, Rich's throat tightened and his eyes teared. Not from the indignity of it all, but from the realization of how he was being viewed, of how everyone would look at him from now on. Like an animal. Like a person who took what wasn't his.

Jesus Christ, what have I done? Rich thought.

He was taken to a room where he was uncuffed and allowed to dress in his civilian clothes, which were waiting for him. Before he was done, Spade was led in, and he got dressed as well. They didn't talk to each other. They changed and buttoned up in silence, under the watchful eyes of men with guns.

They were then led across the hall to a courtroom.

There were four people in it. One of them was Miles Spade. And one of them was Uncle Jim. Max Seymour wasn't there. Two of them Rich didn't recognize.

Uncle Jim was sitting in a gallery bench and he stood as soon as Rich walked in. His face was drawn with worry; he looked horrible. He wore an expression that Rich had never seen before — his uncle looked terrified and anguished and lost, all at once.

Rich stood there, unsure of where to go or what to do, but then one of the men whom he hadn't recognized hurried over to him.

'Hello, Richard,' the man said in a quiet, intense voice. 'I'm Lyman Dratch. I'm your attorney and will be representing you and Mr. Spade in your bail hearings if you are comfortable with that.'

'Where's Max?' Rich asked.

'He asked me to be here. He also asked that you not mention his name in open court.'

Rich nodded. He looked to Jason, who by now had stepped up next to Rich.

'Mr. Spade, I am your counsel — '

'Yeah. Sure.' Spade cut him off. He'd been arraigned before; he knew what to expect. He just wanted to get home and get high.

Lyman pointed out the other man Rich didn't know.

'That's Craig Finger. Federal prosecutor. I know him. He's very fair, but he's also very aggressive. He's going to fight bail.'

Before Rich could digest the no-bail concept, a small-statured duty magistrate wearing a suit entered from a door in the back of the courtroom and walked to the bench. He seemed very serious-minded and made no eye contact with anyone. As there was no court officer to announce him, he announced himself.

'Okay, everyone. I'm Magistrate Michael Jaffe. I'll be handling this hearing. Forgive my informal attire but I didn't expect to be working on a Saturday morning, so my robe is in the cleaners. That being said, let's begin, shall we?'

Rich and Jason sat at defendants' table with Mr. Dratch. Rich was just a few feet in front of his uncle, and it took all of his willpower not to hurdle the three-foot-high wall separating the courtroom well from the gallery and hug him with all his strength, burying his head in Jim's chest the way he had at his parents' funeral. But Rich just stared ahead as other men discussed his fate and his freedom, or the potential lack thereof.

Just like when he was Mirandized, Rich heard only bits and pieces — most of the dialogue was drowned out by the sound of blood rushing through his head, courtesy of a heart beating as hard as if he had done another fifty-one push-ups.

He is a flight risk, argued Finger.

He has strong ties to the community, countered Dratch.

He has access to the millions that are still missing, accused Finger.

Those are allegations. My client has entered a plea of not guilty, in case Mr. Finger didn't hear, snapped Dratch.

Not guilty. Rich must have missed that part of the proceedings. He couldn't believe he was even allowed to plead not guilty. He was guilty as sin. Guilty as a fox in a henhouse flossing with a feather. It was laughable that his lawyer could speak those words and not be arrested himself.

But Rich didn't care. He wanted a life with Elyse. He wanted the life he'd fantasized about since the first shovel of dirt landed on his parents' coffins. If he had to lie, then he'd lie.

Any character that his father and uncle and Max may have instilled in him over the years was gone. He just wanted to survive.

The magistrate agreed with both lawyers. Rich was a flight risk. But he had no priors, was engaged to a local girl, and what money he had — if it was even dirty, which had yet to be proven — had been seized in the search at Jim Mauro's home early that morning.

Hearing this, Rich spun to his uncle — one look from the man and Rich knew that Jim's morning had been much more complicated than Rich had imagined. Rich filled in the blanks: His uncle had been awakened by pounding on the door, had climbed off the couch, and was greeted with a search warrant in his face before the sun had even risen. Men in gloves tore the home apart as Jim tried to make heads or tails of what the hell was going on. Rich could only imagine what his uncle thought when the Feds walked out of Rich's room with bags and bags of cash.

Magistrate Jaffe continued, presenting a compromise — an ankle monitor that would alert authorities if Rich left the state of New York, and a bail so big it could choke a donkey.

Rich would wear the monitor around his neck like a fucking dog collar if it meant he didn't have to go back in his cell. But the bail was a different matter entirely. The guy who had been buying diamonds and storefronts didn't have a pot to piss in now thanks to an early-morning raid by the FBI. The bail was undoable, or at least that was what Rich thought.

'That's acceptable to my client,' Dratch said, placing his hand on Rich's to remind him to stay the fuck quiet. Rich sat silently as the same song and dance was done for Spade. Then Dratch and the U.S. attorney went into the magistrate's chambers, and Rich was alone with his uncle, Jason, Miles, and two U.S. marshals and their .40-caliber Glocks.

After about twenty minutes, Dratch exited and said, 'You're free to go, gentlemen. We just need to get your jewelry on.'

Another man had entered the courtroom as Dratch was speaking. Rich never found out if he was with the FBI or the marshals or what, but he had an ankle bracelet on him and one on Jason in less than five minutes.

Dratch, Uncle Jim, Rich, Spade, and Spade's father rode the elevator in silence until Miles said with a grunt, 'We should've left you in Wheeling, you fucking piece of garbage.'

Jason just closed his eyes and remembered what he'd had done to his father in the alley. It was the only thing that gave him peace.

As soon as they stepped outside, Miles and Jason quickly peeled off. Dratch asked Rich and Jim to follow him to his car. They did. Rich soon wished they hadn't.

Because inside the car sat Max Seymour.

The engine was running. Max lowered the window. He stared straight ahead and wouldn't look at Rich.

'Mr. Dratch did me a favor by coming today. The magistrate did me a favor holding a hearing today. But that's all I can do. You'll need to find

353

your own counsel. I covered your bail, but no one will know that. No one can know I helped you. You compromised my firm and my clients.'

Rich began to cry. He didn't make any noise, but tears moved steadily down his face. He wiped them with his sleeve. Max finally turned to him — the man's eyes were almost as red as Rich's.

'I love you, son,' he said. 'But I can't ever see you or talk to you again.'

Rich audibly sucked in air, as if to help steady himself after what he'd just heard. Before he could respond, Max was facing forward again and the window in the car was proceeding upward — then it slid shut.

Mr. Dratch shook Rich's hand and Uncle Jim's. He advised Rich to find a new lawyer as soon as possible. Then Dratch got in the driver's seat, and the car pulled away.

It was the last time Rich ever saw Max Seymour.

56

Vice bounced up and down a bit on his toes, trying to stay warm, but the wind tore through the alley behind McMahon's like a group of rioters, knocking garbage cans over for the fun of it and making you want to run inside and hide.

Despite the cold, Dylan didn't move to keep his blood flowing. He stood still, hands shoved deep in his coat pockets, as if he'd find enough warmth down there. His eyes were focused on one thing — the time-and-temperature clock that sat outside Astoria Federal at the end of the alley and across the street.

Rich and Spade were late. Very late. And Rich was never late. If it had just been Spade who was late, Dylan would've chalked it up to the drugs. But not Rich. Not Rich. And Eddie hadn't shown up either. Something was wrong. He felt it.

'Let's just call him,' Vice said, freezing and frustrated.

'Already told you *no*. Rich said we shouldn't be callin' him on his cell phone outside of work, especially not on weekends.'

'Yeah, yeah, I know, too suspicious,' Vice said, repeating what Rich had told him a hundred times. 'Know what else is suspicious? A black guy and a beaner hangin' out in an alley behind a bar in the morning. Five-O's gonna drive by and hassle our ass.'

'Just give 'em another minute.'

'Fuck that. I'm callin'.'

Vice dialed his cell.

Dylan opened his mouth to argue but decided against it — maybe it was best to make the call.

Rich's cell rang, but he was in the car with his uncle heading home. He saw it was Vice and was relieved. If he was calling, odds were he hadn't been arrested. That meant Dylan and Ed were most likely okay too. He knew they wanted to know where he was, but he didn't want to answer. He had had a rough night and morning. He silenced the ring.

'No answer,' Vice said ominously. 'I don't got Spade's number. I'm tryin' Ed.'

Ed answered on the fourth ring. 'Hello.'

'Special Ed, where the hell you at?'

'I didn't want to come. It's too cold today.'

'Too cold? We can't do it without you. We need your digits, ya dizzy bastard. What the hell's that noise?' Vice heard a dull roar in the background.

'The bus. I found my long johns so I decided to come. I'm on the bus now.'

'Don't bother — Rich and Spade didn't show. Did you hear from them?'

'No. Where are they?' Ed asked, worried.

'I don't know. That's why I asked if you knew where they were, Ed.' Vice was crazy about Eddie but sometimes the guy could drive him up the wall.

'Something's wrong, man. We should go,' Dylan said, now blowing on his hands. 'Tell him to stay low.'

'Listen, Ed,' Vice said, 'we think maybe Rich and Spade got in trouble — '

'With the *police?*'

'No, with the fuckin' Super Friends. Yeah, with the police.' But then Vice caught himself. 'Sorry, Ed. I'm bein' a dick. Just be careful. And don't say shit to no one about nothin'. When we find out what's going on, we'll call you.'

'Okay . . . and, Vice, the Super Friends wouldn't be a problem, because they're all good guys, and they only go after the Legion of Doom and, like, ya know, *bad* guys — '

'Buddy,' Vice said softly, hating having to break the news to Eddie, 'we *are* the bad guys.'

57

Rich and his uncle didn't talk in the car. They said words to each other, but they didn't *talk* — not about what had transpired. Jim was mostly concerned if his nephew was all right.

Did you eat? Did you get any sleep? Are you hurt?

He was just like Max, Rich thought. His initial instinct was to worry for Rich's well-being — not to ask why Rich had done what he did.

Max had explained Rich's crimes to Jim over the phone. The call had come in the midst of the search of Jim's home. The carpenter was so shaken by what was taking place before him — drawers pulled to the floor, furniture turned over — he was not even sure if he was allowed to answer. He asked one of the agents if he could pick up his own phone in his own house.

As Max was giving a quick summary of the situation to Jim, Rich's uncle wished he'd just let it ring. He couldn't believe what Max was telling him.

Rich had never been so happy to walk up the steps to his home — and never so sad to enter. The house looked like it had been burglarized. The search warrant allowed the Feds to look for proof of or fruits of the crime. Cash fit both categories and since it could be hidden anywhere, the Feds could search anywhere.

The couch cushions had been sliced open, and

foam was everywhere — at first blush, it looked like the snow had made its way inside. Paintings had been pulled down from the walls and their backs torn off. The china hutch in the dining room, which thankfully was only full of books and old *Racing Forms*, not actual china, had been emptied all over the floor.

Rich silently stepped through, and around, the mess.

'I'll get the vacuum,' he finally said.

'No, you look tired. You need sleep. I'll clean. We'll talk when you wake up.'

'I'll get the vacuum,' Rich repeated, softly. He had brought this literal and figurative mess into his uncle's home. He wasn't going to ask him to clean it up. He moved to the hallway but stopped when he heard his uncle say quietly, 'I'm sorry.'

Rich turned back to Jim. The man's face was contorted, pained. His eyes were redder than at the courthouse and he gently wept as he spoke.

'I'm sorry, Richie. I tried. I tried so hard, but I never knew how to raise a kid. I worried from the moment I set your room up for you that I was gonna mess things up . . . I don't know what I did wrong.' Jim slid his fingers from his temples across his eyes, wiping the tears to the bridge of his nose. His broad shoulders heaved up and down as he silently cried.

Rich hadn't thought it was possible to hate himself any more, but now he did. His poor uncle — a man who had sacrificed everything to give him a safe home, a loving home, a home where food was warm and laughter abundant and where hugs were dispensed with abandon

359

— was now blaming himself for doing a lousy job. He was blaming himself for *Rich's* choices. He was blaming himself for nonexistent missteps he believed he must have made as a substitute parent. He was blaming himself for the piece of crap Rich had decided on his own to become.

'You did everything right, Unc. I made the mistakes, not you,' Rich said. 'You did everything right. It's on me. It's only on me.'

Rich stepped over a pile of papers toward the hallway closet but stopped when he turned the corner. The closet's contents had been spilled across the hall. Shirts and coats with pockets turned inside out. Shoes and work boots. And his Uncle Jim's video collection of 1950s TV shows.

And in the rubble — half buried, half exposed — was his father's leather tool belt. Rich picked it up. There was a shoe print on it, courtesy of the federal government. He brought it to the bathroom, wet a hand towel, and scrubbed. He scrubbed as hard as he could. One minute passed, and then another — he wanted the dirt gone. He eventually stopped; the imprint had been washed off. It didn't matter. Rich still knew it had been there.

He heard the vacuum turn on in the other room. Uncle Jim was stubborn. He wanted Rich to sleep. So Rich went into his room, briefly surveyed the damage. They had found the cash that was hidden under his bed. He couldn't help but be impressed when he noticed his Phil Simms football had been cut open: *How the hell did they think to look in there?*

He collapsed onto his bed and fell asleep in his clothes. This time he didn't dream of the sea.

He dreamed of Elyse. She was beautiful as always, in a sundress and barefoot; she was struggling to read blank pieces of paper that Rich kept handing her. When he woke up, hours later, Rich had disdain for his own subconscious; it was trite — the paper was clearly his loss of words for what he had done. It was one thing for his conscience not to be able to justify what he had done; it was another for his subconscious to dramatize it so obviously.

Rich knew he had to do better than blank pages when he saw Elyse for real. They had agreed to spend the rest of their lives together, and he had just thrown the rest of their lives away.

But he had no idea what he could possibly say to her.

And that was a problem, because at that very moment, she was waiting for him in the kitchen.

58

Usually Rich's heart quickened when Elyse surprised him with a visit; he'd grin like an idiot when she'd show up on a job site with a special lunch she'd made or when he discovered her waiting for him outside of school when night class let out.

But now, seeing her sitting next to Uncle Jim at the table, his heart just stopped. The empty cups and saucers in front of them and four spent Lipton bags made it clear they had been drinking tea for a while. The lines down Elyse's face and splotched mascara made it clear she had been crying.

'Hi,' Rich said.

'Hi.'

She got up from the table and threw herself into his arms. He held her. And she sobbed. And Jim cleaned up the teacups.

Then they all sat and talked, and Rich held nothing back.

He told them every detail — about Spade coming to him with the idea, and Rich agreeing to the deal. He explained how the other Blazers were involved and how he had misappropriated information about Max's Estrin Medical case for the latest big score.

When Rich mentioned this last fact, Uncle Jim just looked down at the plastic tablecloth, shook his head, and whispered, 'Oh, Richie,' almost to himself.

But Rich didn't let that stop him. He poured it all out, unburdening himself of the secrets he'd held on to for months. He continued about how they'd set up accounts and how there was still money out there that the Feds were looking for and even how the diamond Elyse was wearing was bought with tainted funds.

Elyse subconsciously traced her finger over the diamond's facets when she heard this.

Rich didn't bring up Manny or the violence against Eddie or the threatened violence against all of them. Jim and Elyse were worried enough and he didn't want to make things worse. Manny had threatened all of their families, but that was if they didn't go ahead and make another trade. Well, they had done that — they had followed his orders. The government had just caught on. Besides, when Manny found out what had happened, which was inevitable, he'd probably surmise that the Feds would have an eye out on everyone and everything having to do with Olmstead & Taft. There'd be too much heat for Manny to risk making a move against one of the Blazers' family members.

Finally Rich explained why he did it. He didn't edit himself. He told Elyse about how much he loved her, how scared he was to lose her. He talked about her parents and how they were pushing Garhart at her and his insecurities and fears of being alone again, just like when he was a boy.

He just wanted to be good enough *for* her so he could always be loved *by* her.

Elyse listened until Rich was done. And when

he was, she took off her engagement ring and slid it across the table to him.

Rich felt ill. It was over. After everything he'd done to keep her, it still hadn't worked.

'Take the diamond. Give it to the FBI. Give it to charity. Throw it in the river. I don't care,' she said. 'But I want the ring. Because it belonged to my fiancé's mother.'

Rich stood and grabbed Elyse from the table and held her. He couldn't believe she was sticking with him.

'I might be going away for a long time,' he said.

'I'll get money from my parents; we'll get you a good lawyer.'

'Your parents hate me.'

'But they love me,' she said. 'And I love you.' She kissed Rich again, gathered her things, and said she'd call later.

Rich watched her go, so thankful yet amazed that such a woman would ever choose to love him.

He could still smell her perfume from when she had leaned in to kiss him good-bye.

He didn't know it then, but it was the last kiss they'd ever share.

59

Elyse's parents must've hated Rich a lot more than they loved their daughter because they refused to cough up a penny. Instead, they pleaded with her to break off the engagement, and Quinn Crane threatened to call the authorities and tell them about the diamond still in Rich's possession if she didn't.

'They'll revoke that little wop's bail and throw his olive-skinned ass right back into lockup when they find out he still has assets bought with the dirty money!' he shouted at his only child.

But Elyse held firm. She promised that if her father made a single phone call or said a solitary word to anyone about anything he knew or even anything he *theorized*, he would lose his daughter forever. And she meant it. So Quinn said he'd keep his mouth shut, but he wouldn't budge on the money issue. He figured he'd stay quiet for now and enjoy Rich's demise from afar, reading about it in the paper and watching it on the news.

Except that twenty-four hours after Rich's arrest, the press had yet to get wind of the story. That was not by accident. Despite all the talk and flag-waving in America about freedom of the press, the truth was there were about six monopolistic companies that owned almost everything that could be seen, heard, or read. Network news, cable news, online news, AM and

FM radio, satellite radio, magazines, local and national newspapers — they all fell under the auspices of one of those six corporations. And Olmstead & Taft, as powerful a law firm as had ever existed on the island of Manhattan, represented all of them. If a story was leaked from the federal courts (a slim possibility at best, considering the magistrate had graduated from Cornell with an O&T partner, and the U.S. attorney had asked six months earlier about any job openings at the firm), it would instantly be killed.

Rich had no idea why his home hadn't been surrounded by reporters yet but he was thankful, for two reasons. First, it meant less embarrassment for his loved ones. And second, it meant Manny didn't know there was a problem. Rich knew Manny would come looking for his money soon, but at least he didn't know that they had been pinched.

Without the press harassing him, Rich could concentrate on his defense with his new lawyer.

'I spoke with the prosecutor and he might be willing to deal,' Ari Greenburg said to Rich and Uncle Jim. He tapped his pencil eraser in time to the salsa music emanating from the Cuban restaurant located directly below his office on Thirty-Fifth Street, between Ditmars and Twenty-First.

Ari seemed like a decent enough guy, but he didn't instill confidence in Rich — his shirt collar was frayed, his tie was outdated, and his office had stacks of paperwork and folders everywhere — on his desk, on top of file

366

cabinets, in the corners, on the radiator. The furniture was old and worn and, in places, stained.

But the fifty-year-old, six-foot-tall attorney with long, slicked-back hair was all Uncle Jim could afford. He was going to pay Ari with a second mortgage he was about to take out on his house. Jim had found him in the yellow pages under *Attorneys*. Ari had a quarter-panel ad that boasted of his ability to handle not only criminal matters but also workers'-comp claims and immigration problems. On top of that, according to the ad, Counselor Greenburg could *¡habla español!*

'What kind of deal?' Jim asked, curious.

'With what your nephew is looking at time-wise, he'd be almost your age when he got out,' Ari explained. 'But eventually this thing will get out to the press. I don't know what strings your former employer is pulling to keep it quiet but you can only stick your finger in the dike for so long before other leaks start to spring. And when they do, the government doesn't want any articles written about the ill-gotten millions out there that are still unaccounted for. They'd look like idiots. So they're willing to recommend a ten-year sentence in exchange for the location of the cash. That's what they're saying now, but I think they'd come down a bit, maybe seven or so; with good conduct you'd do six years and a few months.'

Rich exhaled audibly. Six years was a long time. A real long time. But he'd still be young when he got out. Young enough to live a life.

Young enough to have kids if Elyse still wanted him, and incredibly it seemed she would.

'But you have to give up the cash. Every dollar, every ruble, every shekel. Every asset you bought with the money. *Everything*. No games. They catch you holding out, they will tear up the agreement and tear up your ass in that courtroom. Understand?'

'Yes,' Rich said. 'I can do that.'

'Listen to me.' Ari leaned in, changing tone. Suddenly he wasn't a schlubby putz in a bad shirt in a bad office. Now he was actually a bit intimidating, and the thought crossed Rich's mind that maybe his uncle hadn't made such a bad choice after all.

Ari pointed to Jim. 'This man right here, he called me yesterday, on a Saturday, and he *begged* me to come in today to see you. He's a *good man*. He's putting up his house to pay me to save your black ass — sorry, habit — to save your white ass, and I won't take a dime if I think you're going to fuck around and hurt him more than you have. It's Hanukkah, for Christ's sake, I should be home with my family, so if you want to play games, go somewhere else. I won't let you waste my time or your uncle's.'

Rich knew the speech was an act performed by Ari for the benefit of every mother who sat in front of him with her teenager who had just caught his first criminal mischief or assault charge. But it was effective. Rich could tell Jim felt better already — he believed in Ari Greenburg, and in a weird way Rich did too.

Rich was shocked to find his mouth slowly

creeping up at the corners to form a small smile. For the first time in a long time, things were looking up.

'I'll tell them where the money is,' Rich said with conviction.

'Good . . . and they're not stupid,' Greenburg continued, jabbing his finger in the air in Rich's direction. 'They know the other guys working with you down there had to know something was going on. So you're gonna have to roll on them too.'

And that's when Rich's smile disappeared.

60

Rich popped Uncle Jim's truck into neutral, disengaged the parking brake, and gently pushed the Ford down the slightly sloped drive-way between their house and the house belonging to Mr. and Mrs. Bellatone. Even though Jim slept like the dead, one thing would always jolt him awake, and that was the sound of some punk trying to jack his 1981 Ford F-100. The ice helped the truck along the way and even though Rich almost lost his footing once or twice, he got the Ford to the street without incident and was inside and driving less than thirty seconds after he'd crept out of the house at 4:07 a.m.

Anyone who wasn't sneaking to or from a mistress's house, working the night shift, or doing something illegal was warm in bed, so there was no one on the road. When traffic is light, New York is a small town, and Rich was out of Queens, across the Williamsburg Bridge, and pulling into Little Italy in less than twenty minutes.

He stopped on Broome, a few blocks from his destination. The streets were desolate that time of day — probably quieter than any place in the city — and Rich didn't want to be seen. And he didn't want the others to be seen either. He reached the corner of Broadway and Prince, where St. Patrick's Old Cathedral School stood. A ten-foot-high hundred-year-old brick wall that blocked in the school's property stretched all the way down to Mulberry Street.

If you pressed up against the brick and looked all the way down the length of the wall, along Prince Street and toward Broadway, the structure serpentined in and out of flush from decade upon decade of settling, decomposition, and ground shifts. From that viewpoint, the wall appeared to be a brick ribbon that could fall over in either direction at any time — but day after day it stood there, overseeing the good people of Little Italy and protecting the children of St. Patrick's from those who were not so good.

Rich looked to see that no one was watching; it seemed as if the whole island were asleep. He got a toehold in a groove of a large stone that made up a corner pillar of the wall and pulled himself up and over into the private property of the Archdiocese of New York. He'd wanted to get there early, before the others, so he could work on what he had to say, but when he hit the ground and looked up, he saw Dylan, Vice, and Eddie staring back at him.

They all had scores of questions but they kept them to themselves. All three of them figured it was best to let Rich talk and fill them in on what was happening, and then if anything needed to be asked, it would be.

Rich told them all that had gone down, in minute detail. The other three were silent, except for Vice, who let out an occasional, quiet *Damn* under his breath. Rich thought it would be quick, but when he was almost finished he realized he had been speaking for fifteen minutes nonstop.

'And the last thing,' Rich added, not wanting to say it but knowing he had to, 'they know you guys had to be involved. There were too many trades, too much activity going on in the office for no one else to notice — '

'Are you hot, Rich?' Dylan asked.

'What? It's almost the end of December, I'm freezing my ass off.' Rich was thrown by Dylan's non sequitur.

''Cause you look hot. You look like you're gonna pass out. You should take some layers off, know what I'm saying?'

Rodriguez stared at Rich and it was *very* clear what he was saying. Rich had just said aloud that they were all involved. None of them had confirmed it yet. But if they did, and Rich was wired, they were all toast. So Dylan wanted Rich to strip. He was too smart to say why, in case Rich actually was miked, but it was 28 degrees Fahrenheit and Dylan wanted Rich to get naked. And since Dylan had the same look on his face that he had had the first time the two of them met, outside the law firm, Rich unzipped.

'This is ridiculous, man,' Rich said as he dropped his jacket to the ground. His teeth began to chatter as he removed his shirt, and his balls were practically in his stomach when he dropped his boxers.

'Satisfied?' Rich asked, his freezing, naked body illuminated by a combination of moonlight, streetlights, and red and green Christmas bulbs hanging from a nearby tree.

'More satisfied than Elyse'll ever be,' Vice cracked, pointing to Rich's ice-cold dick, which

372

looked like it was trying to crawl back into its shell.

'Fuck you, it's freezing,' Rich said as he pulled his clothes back on.

'Sorry, man,' Dylan said, sincerely, 'but I had to.' He hated suspecting Rich but he couldn't take any chances. 'This whole thing's a mess and I'm scared shitless they're gonna take me away from my baby.'

'You should be scared,' Rich admitted as he zipped up his coat and felt warmth coming back to his body. 'Because they want me to serve up all three of you. If I do, I get time off — a lot of time. If I don't, I'm going down for a while.'

Dylan, Vice, and Ed didn't say anything for a moment. It was quiet — just the sound of winter at 4:45 in the morning, which is basically no sound at all.

'What are you gonna do?' Vice asked, concerned.

'He's doin' the right thing,' Dylan answered knowingly and with no small sense of relief and gratitude. He looked to Rich. 'No way you'd meet me behind some secluded wall in the middle of the night if you were gonna fuck me over. 'Cause you'd know I'd hate to do it, but I'd do what I had to do, Rich. If you wanted to sell us out, you'da done it already in a warm room with warm coffee with white guys in suits.'

Rich nodded. 'I'd never do that to you guys. But Spade might. He could be cuttin' a deal right now, for all I know, but I'm gonna make a deal of my own . . . '

'How? Whatcha got beside us?' Vice asked.

'The money,' Ed whispered to no one in particular.

'That's right,' Rich concurred. 'It's the one thing the Feds want more than your asses. I sign a confession implicating me and Spade, and tell 'em where the money is.'

'Can't they eventually find that shit out for themselves?' Vice asked.

'Yeah, they can. But my lawyer says it could take 'em a couple years to track it down, what with the offshore maze, the numerical accounts, the phony corporations, and everything else Spade set up — and then once they find where it *is*, they're gonna need court orders to actually have the money released. It's a bother wrapped up in a hassle inside a giant pain in the ass. And the whole time the press'll be all over 'em about the cash. They'll eventually find it — in about two years, if things go real smooth, and maybe more. End of day, they just wanna avoid the whole mess. I can help them do that. And if I do, I do six years instead of possibly four times that.'

'That's a long run,' Dylan said. 'And I don't have the juice to get you help or protection on the inside. White-collar boys rarely get the country clubs anymore — not since Madoff — and even medium-security houses can be fucked-up places.'

'I know. But I don't have any other options.'

'We could visit,' Eddie said sweetly.

'Thanks, pal, but no visits,' Rich replied. 'I tell these guys you weren't involved, last thing we need are jailhouse visits. This is the last time we see each other. Ever.'

Eddie processed this thought for a moment.

Dylan put his hand out. 'Thank you, Rich,' he said as they shook. 'You're helping keep my family together, and I won't forget it. I owe you.'

Rich looked down at their hands, particularly at the ragged patches of skin on Dylan's hand where black-ink letters had once lived.

'You know,' Rich said, 'those scars are the best thing that ever happened to you. Good luck, Dylan.'

Vice gave Rich a bro-hug. 'White man takin' the fall for a brother. Now, ain't that some backward shit,' he joked weakly with wet eyes and no hint of a smile.

Eddie stepped to Rich and hugged him, linking his good hand and his injured one behind Rich. He cried.

'I'm sorry, Rich.'

Rich was taken aback and it was all he could do not to cry himself when he looked at Eddie's red face, a puff of breath shooting from his mouth with every sob.

'You have nothing to be sorry for, Eddie,' Rich said. '*I'm* sorry for mixing you up in all this. You're the best boss I ever had, you know that, Ed?'

Eddie laughed softly as he wiped his nose with the back of his bandaged hand.

Rich turned and climbed the wall again. When he had straddled the top, Eddie called to him.

'Merry Christmas, Rich,' he said, waving his gauze-covered paw in the air.

Rich nodded, took one last look at his friends, and was over the wall.

61

Rich was in no rush to get home. If Jim had heard him leave with the car, he'd want to know what Rich was up to, and the last thing Rich wanted to do was get into a debate with his uncle as to why he wouldn't testify against the others. He didn't really want to talk to anybody.

He just wanted to walk around the city, enjoy the energy as people started to wake up, move about, get the day going. He bought the *Post* — its sports section was the best in the world. It was something he knew he wouldn't be able to get his hands on that often on the inside.

He decided to get two tickets for a matinee. He and Elyse hadn't seen a movie together in a long time and he knew it could be six years until they got to do it again. There was a comedy, a family holiday film, and a small indie. Rich chose the comedy and bought tickets on his iPhone. He figured he could use the laugh.

Before heading home he stopped at Mollo's — a little Italian joint the width of a train car and half as long. It was hidden away, tucked between two much larger buildings. Rich had eaten there once or twice before, and since he was looking at a run of over twenty-two hundred days of shit food, he decided to step in. His mind had been wandering while the clock hands spun, and it was now deep into the morning, and the breakfast crowd was already in high gear.

He ordered almost everything on the menu — *cugootzeel* with eggs, sausage and eggs, eggs and eggs; he had pastries and jams and half a loaf of Italian bread with goat cheese. He savored every bite and cursed his stomach for not having room for him to stuff down more.

When he was done, he walked to Lafayette Street and watched firemen work on engine no. 4 at a historic firehouse between Walker and White Streets.

Later, he wandered into a record store near NYU, amazed that such a place still existed.

He enjoyed freedom while he had it.

But eventually, hours later, he drove home. During the ride he called Elyse. They talked. She cried. He told her he'd love her forever and that he'd never do anything again that could separate them. She said she'd wait for him even if he got a million years. Rich smiled because he knew she meant it. They made plans to meet up in a few hours to see the film.

Rich parked the Ford in the driveway and engaged the emergency brake. He grabbed the paper that was in the bushes — maybe the paper would take Jim's mind off things for a half an hour or so.

But he never got to give it to him. He was walking to the front door when the pain hit. It was a hot pressure that seemed to shoot through the back of his head and out of his eyes.

Then the feeling of the stairs meeting his face quite hard.

It wasn't until he was being lifted up by his arms and dragged off that he managed to figure out, despite his blurred vision and growing daze, that he had been struck by something.

What he'd been struck by, he had no idea.

Who he'd been struck by was answered quickly — because after he was dumped next to a spare tire and while he was watching a car's trunk close above him, Rich caught a brief glimpse of the sun.

And it was glimmering off a singular bright gold tooth.

62

Rich spent a long time in the trunk of the car, it seemed, going in and out of consciousness, disoriented, attempting to figure out where he was being taken. He tried to keep track of the turns — a left at the end of his block, then another left — but he lost count eventually. At one point, from the acceleration and speed, he could tell that they had gotten on the BQE. He prayed that his captors would go over the Verrazano-Narrows Bridge and into New Jersey, because once they were out of state his ankle bracelet would set off alarms in some agency office somewhere and the Feds would think he was making a run for it. They'd follow the signal and he'd be rescued — assuming, of course, he was still alive when they found him.

But Rich's hopes were dashed when he felt the car slow and veer right — the movement of a vehicle getting off at an exit. They hadn't been in the car nearly long enough to get to the Verrazano. The trunk rumbled over what Rich could only assume were cobblestone streets.

Shit, he thought. *We're in Brooklyn. They're taking me down by the water.*

Then he heard seagulls. He panicked.

They're gonna dump me in the bay.

Another few minutes and the car came to a stop. The sun was barely peeking through December clouds but the light seemed blinding to Rich when the trunk was opened and his dark world was obliterated.

Gold Tooth yanked him out of the car. Caesar was with him, like usual. Rich looked around quickly, trying to get an idea of where he was. It didn't take long. Straight ahead of him was the Red Hook Grain Terminal — a massive structure consisting of a grain elevator over one hundred feet high and fifty-four concrete silos, all joined together by buildings and walkways.

Built in 1922, it had housed almost all the grain and wheat and barley that came from the western states via the Erie Canal, then sent it on to the East Coast breweries and distilleries. But once the containerization process was perfected, the terminal was no longer needed, and in 1955 it was shut down.

And for over half a century, it sat on the piers of Red Hook, rusting and decaying, a useless concrete giant lording over piles of abandoned debris and polluted water.

There were weeds, rats, and the occasional daring urban explorer, but other than that, the place was unoccupied, a ghost town that was no use to anyone.

Until now.

Manny Espinoza found the abandoned terminal perfect — it was tens of thousands of square feet of space that almost no one would dare go into. The tip of Red Hook was surrounded mostly by water — an Ikea was down the road but too far away for anyone there to hear the screams that he knew he would be causing in here.

They could stay as long as Manny needed — and he wasn't going to leave until he had either his money or the information that could get it for him.

Rich had gotten his footing now and he could walk on his own, but that didn't stop Gold Tooth from pushing him hard in the back.

'Move.'

Rich moved. He looked at the current lapping against the pier and wondered if any of the water that had touched his parents had made its way all the way down to Red Hook. Maybe it had, just to say good-bye, because Rich Mauro was convinced he was being led to his death.

He was shoved through a small doorway at the base of a tall, faded red smokestack. The wooden door had been nailed and locked shut, closed up tight like the rest of the terminal. But Manny and his boys had business to do, so they figured out a way to get the door open.

The first thing Rich saw after he stumbled inside and was pushed through the wide expanse of the abandoned building was Eddie, bloodied and sitting on a crate that read CARGILL GRAIN but in colors so faded it was difficult to make out. Ed was rocking back and forth, his pants wet. The poor guy was so scared he had pissed himself, and with good reason.

In front of him, just a few feet from the crate, lying on the cracked, cement floor, was Vice. His face had been badly beaten and was already swelling, and he was shaking from the pain; his breathing was labored, and each inhale rattled as his lungs filled with blood. Near him was a pile

381

of scrap, five-eighths-inch rebar that was decades old and cut down to all different sizes, from a few feet long to a few inches. The two pieces that had been driven into Vice's thigh looked about six inches long. Rich knew instantly his friend was in real bad shape. The very sight of him made Rich ill. And frightened.

Vice's and Rich's eyes met. Mauro couldn't tell if Vice even knew it was him, as one of his eyes was so puffed up it was almost closed and the other was full of blood.

Standing a few feet from Vice were Manny and two more of his men. One was the guy who'd been selling drugs at the underground party Spade took Rich to when he'd first met Manny. The other one Rich had never seen before but he fit in with the others perfectly — ripped, tattooed, mean, terrifying.

Manny's two thugs had Dylan by his arms and pressed up against a giant concrete mushroom-topped pillar. Manny cracked him across the face with a sock-full of something very hard — Rich guessed either rocks or batteries.

Dylan's head slumped to the side. He spit up some blood as his head bobbed like a newborn's. He didn't seem to notice Rich.

But Manny did.

'Good, you found him,' Manny said to Gold Tooth. 'He's next.'

Caesar pushed Rich down to the floor. He landed hard in a pile of rotted lumber. The noise of the fall seemed to shock Vice into awareness and he seemed to notice for the first time that Rich was there with him.

'I told them,' Vice sputtered softly on seeing Mauro. 'I'm sorry.'

Rich instantly knew exactly what Vice meant: he had told them his code, his part of the fifteen digits needed for Manny to get his money, and now Manny was trying to get the same information from Dylan.

Manny threw a vicious backhand, swinging the sock up and under Dylan's chin. It struck him right in the Adam's apple. Dylan let out a sickly sound — the sound of breath being cut off — and fell to his knees.

'*Hey!*' Rich shouted.

He got a kick to the stomach from Gold Tooth for his trouble. He keeled over, holding his gut. As he sucked air in hard and expelled it even harder, trying to keep from vomiting, he saw across the room, by weather-beaten and rotted wooden pallets, Jason Spade. It was as if he were trying to hide, standing with his back flush against a brick-red wall next to an ancient two-foot-wide conveyor belt that ran parallel to the floor before turning sharply and inclining up toward the rafters, at least thirty to forty feet.

His face was slightly battered — he'd been roughed up a bit also, but it was nothing compared to the others.

Even in his current state — pained and fetal-positioned on the floor — Rich was able to put together how this had all gone down. Manny had gone by Spade's place and demanded his money. Spade told him they hadn't gotten it yet. The fact that Spade was still alive led Rich to assume he hadn't told Manny about their arrest.

Spade couldn't take Manny to get the money because he didn't know everyone else's codes, so Manny's boys batted Jason around. It probably didn't take more than a few slaps across the face for Spade to spill about how the account number was joint property and he had access to only 20 percent of it.

So while Rich was taking his one last walk around New York City and purchasing movie tickets; Jason was calling the personnel office at Olmstead & Taft, asking for the home address of each of the Blazers, making up some lame excuse about wanting to send them each a gift basket for a job well done on an important case or some bullshit like that.

And while Mauro was enjoying his luxurious Italian breakfast in Little Italy, Manny's thugs were rounding up his friends as they were leaving their homes or walking to the subway to get to work.

And while Mauro was bouncing around in the trunk of a car, Manny, Vice, and Ed were being beaten and tortured until they gave up their codes. From the looks of it, they'd tried to hold out as long as they could. They might have been willing to give Manny their digits in the context of a mutually agreed upon business arrangement, but they had been violently abducted; the game had changed. Sociopathic gangbangers didn't kidnap people and let them go. Once Manny had the code, he had the money. And once he had the money, they were all as good as dead.

On the interior wall next to Spade, there were

three sets of numbers scratched in white — the product of a rock being scraped hard against the brick: *666; 718; 281.*

Those must be the others' codes, Rich thought.

He knew from looking at Vice — whose breathing was becoming more labored — that the skinny, wiseass kid from East New York had put up a hell of a fight, but he'd eventually broke.

Rich wasn't sure about Eddie, but from his urine-soaked pants, Rich figured the odds were good that he'd been broken with minimal effort.

As for Spade, the few bumps and bruises on his face made it clear he hadn't tried at all. He handed over his code on a serving tray with linen napkins and tartar sauce.

So it was down to him and Dylan, and Dylan wasn't looking so good. The hits kept on coming and they all landed hard on Dylan's face. Rich knew it would be his turn soon.

The beating was brutal to watch. It anguished Eddie.

'Just tell them your code!' he cried to Dylan.

'Listen to your little puppy dog over there, Rodriguez,' Manny said, stepping close to Dylan and yanking him up off the ground by his coat. He slammed him back against the column, causing Dylan's wallet to fall out of his pocket.

It landed open, in a small pool of Dylan's own blood. Manny looked down and saw a photo of Rodriguez's girlfriend and child looking up at him.

'You want to see that family again? Hold your

little girl again? Then you give me your *números, papi.*'

Dylan stared deep into Manny's eyes.

'I give you . . . the numbers,' he said, each word sounding like a dagger through his badly damaged larynx, ' . . . you still kill me. We both know that.'

'Maybe.' Manny grinned. 'But if you play nice, then I won't have to go get this pretty little girl, tear her from her mama's hands, and feed her to my three pit bulls. I've seen what they can do to a chicken carcass — and she's no bigger.'

Now it was Dylan's turn to smile.

'Soon as things . . . went bad for us,' he said, 'I sent them away. They don't come back . . . until they hear from me . . . Good luck finding them.'

Frustrated, Manny grabbed Dylan by the hair and slammed the back of his head into the pillar. Then again. And then again.

Eddie cried out, but Dylan remained silent. His head hung low again.

'What do you mean, went bad?' Manny asked, confused. Rich knew then for sure that Manny had no idea about the arrest. At least Spade was smart enough to keep that much to himself.

Dylan slowly raised his head — it took all of his strength — and glared at Espinoza.

'Figure it out for yourself . . . *papi,*' he sneered before spitting a mouthful of blood at him that sprayed Manny's face and clothes.

Oh no, Rich thought.

Manny's eyes grew wide with rage — he was a man of power, a man who commanded respect. Being spat on like that, in front of his men,

386

demanded a decisive response.

So Manny stepped back, pulled a gun from his waistband, and responded.

'No!' Rich screamed, but by the time the word had left his mouth the bullets were already deep inside Dylan. The speed of death was faster than the speed of sound.

Dylan's body slumped to the ground and landed so that his face was turned away from the wallet and the photo of his family — almost as if he didn't want them to see him like that.

Despite all his efforts to better his life and to avoid this fate, Dylan Rodriguez still died in a blaze of gangster gunfire.

Manny spun and charged toward Rich, furious, his gun out, his face painted crimson with anger and Dylan Rodriguez's blood.

'*What about you? You want to die today too?*' he screamed as he closed the gap between them in seconds.

'Four-two-four!' Rich shouted. The numbers exploded from his mouth like gunfire. He knew that giving up the code, and hence the money, could seal his fate, but when a crazed, blood-covered Dominican is racing at you with a snub-nosed special pointed at your face, you don't think about the consequences, you just give him whatever the fuck he wants.

He had held out shorter than any of them — he was sure of it. But he felt no shame. Only a desire to survive. Besides, none of them had seen a friend gunned down in front of him before he was asked for his code.

Manny pressed the gun under Rich's chin. He

was scared to even swallow, so he didn't.

'Good,' Manny said, breathing heavy.

He turned and moved across the expanse of the grain elevator floor toward Spade, who was pale and frozen with fear. On the conveyor belt rested Spade's laptop.

He grabbed a fist-size rock that lay next to the computer and scratched it on the brick wall to write *424*.

'Now get me my money,' he barked at Spade.

'I c-can't,' Spade stammered. 'You killed Dylan. He was the only one who knew his code.'

'There are only three numbers left! Fill 'em in until you find what the code is! One-one-one. One-one-two. One-one-three. *Do it!*'

'That'll take forever,' Rich said.

Manny spun to him. 'I'm not talking to you.'

'But three empty spaces — and including zero, ten possible digits for each space — that's a thousand possible combinations!'

Manny digested this information for a moment. Rich could see in Espinoza's eyes that he was just then realizing the mistake he'd made in the heat of passion. He'd let his anger and machismo get in the way of his reason and killed Dylan before he got what he needed from him. He stepped away from Rich, put his hands on the back of his head, and screamed into the rafters in frustration.

The yell bounced around the emptiness.

He turned to Rich, eyes burning.

'You. Mr. Math. Figure it out.'

'I can't.'

'Figure it out!' Manny shouted.

'I can't!' Rich shouted back.

Manny grabbed Rich and pressed the gun to his temple.

'Get me my goddamn money!' Manny screamed as loud as he could, his face pressed up against Rich's.

The man had completely lost any semblance of composure. Rich didn't answer. He was afraid if he once again said he couldn't get the code, he would wind up on the floor next to Dylan.

Manny threw Rich to the side and pulled Eddie off his crate. Eddie cried out as Manny pistol-whipped him across the head. Eddie's nose poured blood like a faucet left on.

'Don't!' Rich pleaded.

'Then you figure out a way to get that money!'

'The numbers are missing!' Rich shouted back.

'Figure it out!' Manny ordered with another crack to Eddie's face. Blood shot everywhere.

'*It can't be figured out, you fucking idiot!*' Spade screamed, terrified. Prior to that, he had been so quiet, Rich had forgotten he was there.

Manny, still gripping Eddie by his bloody collar, turned slowly to face Spade.

'You already gave me your code, right?' Manny asked.

'That's right,' Spade answered, confused.

'Then why am I talking to you?' Manny's gun barely recoiled as it discharged a round straight into Jason Spade's forehead. He fell onto the conveyor belt and then face-first onto the floor.

Manny quickly turned to Vice, who was so weakened he could barely raise his hand in front of himself before the bullet tore through his palm and into his chest.

Vicellous Green squirmed a bit and took two breaths, which rattled blood around his lungs for a moment. Then he stopped moving. Then the rattling stopped as well. He was gone.

Rich shook. Three men had just been gunned down in front of him in less than five minutes.

Manny pulled Eddie toward Rich.

'The retard's next if you don't get me that code!' He pressed the gun tightly against Eddie's temple.

'Stop it, I don't know!' Rich begged.

Manny looked at Rich, disgusted — as much with himself as with Mauro. He knew that killing Dylan Rodriguez made it impossible to get the code. And it was clear Rich didn't know it. Furious, he tossed Eddie to the floor.

'Go get the cars ready,' he said to the drug dealer from the party. He pointed the gun at Eddie, still lying on the ground in pain. 'They don't know anything, they're useless.'

Rich turned away; he couldn't stand to watch the death of another one of his friends. But when he did so, his eyes landed on Dylan's lifeless body to the side of him. No matter where he turned, he couldn't avoid the bloodshed.

He shifted his gaze slightly and it settled on Dylan's wallet — beautiful Rosa and Bella looked back at him. And that's when he realized it. That's when he knew.

'Wait! I know the code!' Rich shouted.

Manny looked at Rich, unsure.

'You playing games?' he demanded.

390

'No. I think it's his kid's birthday. It's all he talked about. November ninth.'

Manny looked at Gold Tooth, who shrugged as if to say, *It's worth a shot.*

Manny moved his gun from pointing at Ed to pointing at the laptop — Rich's signal to get to work.

Rich slowly walked over and looked at the computer screen. The account site was already online and Jason's, Eddie's, and Vice's codes had been entered, presumably by Spade, who lay dead near Rich's feet.

Manny watched over Rich's shoulder as he slowly typed his number — 4-2-4 — and then 1-1-9, for November 9. He hit Enter.

INVALID ENTRY.

'You're done, *blanco*,' Manny snarled, raising his gun.

'Wait!' Ed shouted from the floor. 'He coulda done it day first, ninth of November. Nine-one-one.'

'Try it,' Manny ordered.

Rich tried to hit the keys but his hands were shaking so much his fingers didn't cooperate. But somehow they eventually landed on the right numbers and he slowly pointed his index finger toward the Enter key. He knew if he was wrong he'd be shot in the head in a matter of seconds.

He pressed it.

The screen went white for a moment . . . and then the account access page appeared.

It was the most beautiful thing Rich had ever seen. Even Manny smiled.

'All right.' Manny laughed, clapping Rich on

the back. The other men grinned and commented to each other in Spanish. Rich picked up the word *dinero* a few times.

'Okay. Looks like we're all taking a ride down to Colts Neck, boys,' Manny cackled. 'How much we movin' out of there? We gonna need some big bags, no?' he asked Rich casually as if they were old friends and the killings and pistol-whippings had never happened.

He was giddy with the euphoria of sudden and unearned fortune. Rich knew the feeling well.

Mauro clicked on the account information tab.

Rich looked at the screen that appeared and prayed to God it was a mistake. It wasn't.

It read BALANCE: $0.00.

63

'You motherless pigs took my money!' Manny bellowed, his gravelly voice ripping through the cavernous grain factory.

'No! It's impossible!' Rich cried, hoping Espinoza would believe the sincerity in his tone, as Rich legitimately had no idea what had happened to the cash.

'Kill them!' Manny shrilled to Gold Tooth. 'Kill them and dump all their bodies in the river! The rest of you, get the tarps outta the car.'

So this is it, Rich thought. *I'm going to die in a grain terminal, then get wrapped in a tarp and tossed into the same New York water my parents died in.*

He looked for a way to get out of the building but there was only one doorway that he could see, and Manny and three of his men were walking to it.

Gold Tooth readied his Lorcin .380 and stepped to Eddie, whose difficult life was about to come to an even more difficult end. Eddie cowered, his hands over his head, but Gold Tooth had barely moved when a hand *sprang up* and jammed a sharp piece of rebar steel into the thug's calf.

Gold Tooth screamed, completely surprised by Vice, as he, and everyone else in the room, had been under the impression that the bloody, motionless heap lying on the floor was dead. But Vicellous Green had the smallest bit of life left in

393

him and he was determined to use it to try to save Eddie Pisorchek. He had pulled one six-inch-long piece of steel from this thigh and returned it to the man who had put it there in the first place.

Manny and his crew, who were now by the door, spun back on hearing the scream, just in time to see Rich, forty yards away, seizing the opportunity and tackling Gold Tooth to the ground, bringing him down hard. The .380 fell from Gold Tooth's hand, landing near Eddie.

'Eddie, the gun!' Rich shouted. Eddie grabbed the gun, and as soon as he did, Rich wished he hadn't. Pisorchek, terrified, began firing wildly toward Manny and the others. The problem was, Rich was between Eddie and the bad guys, and Ed's third shot hit Mauro dead in the arm. Rich collapsed and then scurried the best he could to safety behind a concrete pillar.

Ed hid a few feet away behind a pile of rusted pipes, and Manny and his men took shelter behind some industrial pallets.

'You fuckin' nigga *hijo de puta*,' Gold Tooth cried as he pulled the thick steel shank from his leg. He then picked up his good foot and lifted it over Vice's head. The force of Gold Tooth's boot easily crushed Vice's skull with a sickening crack. And though Rich was hiding and couldn't see the brutality, when he heard the sound, he knew that Vice's brothers and sisters would need to start taking care of one another from now on.

The second stomp sounded wet and almost made Rich throw up. The third stomp never came, because the bullet from the gun Eddie

Pisorchek was holding tore into the right side of Gold Tooth's head, killing him instantly. He fell dead, next to what was left of Vicellous Green.

'Bartolo!' Caesar wailed at the sight of his dead brother.

Rich could see Eddie from where he was hiding, and Pisorchek looked frozen — unable to comprehend what he had just done.

'Eddie!' Rich yelled to snap Pisorchek out of his stupor. 'Eddie, stay where you are! Don't move!'

But Ed couldn't respond. Manny and his men had begun unloading their guns in his direction — their shots were pinging off the pipes. Eddie slouched behind them, crying, scared to death.

Rich sat on the floor, his back against the pillar. He pressed his hand against the gunshot wound to his arm, but the bleeding was bad. He knew he'd be getting light-headed soon and then he'd be as good as dead. He had to think of something.

'I'll kill you, you fucking mongoloid!' Caesar shouted, desperate to avenge his brother.

Rich looked to Ed, who was cowering — the only thing between him and death was the slim protection afforded by the pipes and the old conveyor belt, which angled so high above Ed that it barely protected him at all.

Rich's eyes landed on the conveyor belt for a moment; he saw how it sloped down from Ed's location until it stopped and leveled off right behind the pillar where Rich was taking refuge.

The gunfire stopped for a moment.

'Just drop the gun, puppy dog, and you won't get hurt. I'll let you walk right through that door,' Manny called out.

'Don't listen to him, Eddie. Stay where you are!' Rich shouted.

'Fuck you, *blanco*,' Manny yelled at Rich.

'Fuck you!' Rich screamed back.

'I'm hurt, Richie,' Eddie cried. 'I just want to go home!'

'You gotta stay cool, Ed!'

'You stand up and give me your gun and I'll let you go home, Eddie,' Manny promised.

'If you stand up, they'll shoot you, Ed! Do *not* stand up!' With the blood loss, Rich was finding it harder and harder to yell. He knew he had to get out of there and to a hospital quickly.

'How 'bout this?' Manny suggested. 'I come out with my hands up and walk to you, Eddie. I just want to talk about how we can end this so we're all happy and safe at home, okay?'

'Eddie, if he so much as sticks his head out from behind those pallets, you blow it the fuck off his shoulders! Eddie, look at me! Look at me, I want to know you understand me!'

Eddie looked across the hundred feet or so between him and Rich. Manny and his men couldn't see either of them from where they were. The locations and cover had made all of them a Bermuda triangle of deadly stalemate.

Rich motioned to Eddie, moving his fingers in the shape of a gun. He pantomimed firing his weapon and then placing it on the conveyor belt. Eddie shook his head, confused. Rich did it again. Amazingly, somehow, Eddie seemed to understand.

Rich nodded and counted down to three with

his fingers — one, two, three. '*Now!*' he yelled.

Eddie fired in the direction of Manny, causing all three of the criminals to fire back at Ed's position. Ed then quickly reached up and placed his gun on the conveyor belt over his head. Because of the incline, the gun slid down the conveyor belt, across the expanse of the room, into the waiting hands of Rich behind the concrete pillar. The gunfire Eddie had drawn upon himself muffled the sound of the weapon's downward skid.

Manny, Caesar, and Drug Dealer were focused on Eddie's position — firing off shots in the hopes of getting lucky and nailing Pisorchek through a gap in his cover or scaring him so much he'd get up and run. It was their attention to Eddie that allowed Rich the few seconds he needed to get up and sprint, as best as he could, the fifty feet he had to go in order to be parallel with the pallets, about ten yards away from the gangbangers.

He unleashed a flurry of gunfire. Drug Dealer dropped first, and then Caesar. They were both dead or dying within seconds. Caesar's body fell into the pallets, causing them to topple over. Manny used the opportunity to turn and run off into the darkness of the building, disappearing.

Rich hurried to Eddie. Now that he was up close, he saw just how bad Eddie had been beaten. He had blood all over his shirt. His face was a mess.

'Are they dead?' Eddie asked, shaken.

'Two of them,' Rich answered. 'But we need to get out of here.'

He grabbed Pisorchek and helped him up, no small feat considering Rich had a bullet wound the size of a fifty-cent piece in one of his biceps.

They shuffled to the door, Rich holding Ed up, trying to look *forward* while aiming a gun *backward* in case Manny decided to show his face. But Rich was pretty sure he was off in the bowels of the terminal, probably on a different floor, or under a staircase or hiding in a crevice with the other rats.

At the door Rich had to lean Ed against the wall and pull hard on the handle to open it. But it was old and warped and the hinges were so badly oxidized from a lifetime on the docks that they barely moved. Rich's one good arm wasn't enough to pull it inward. Rich had no strength — the door had moved only a fraction of an inch.

'Eddie, ya gotta help me,' Rich pleaded. 'Hurry.'

But then the crack of the shot bounced around the empty space and Rich knew he was hit before he felt it. Same arm, just an inch or two above the first wound. He fell but had the wherewithal to spin as he did, propping his back against the door to keep himself from completely sliding down.

He saw Manny exiting the shadows, framed by sun rays that stretched down from high-set windows, dust particles dancing in the amber.

The second shot missed Ed's head by mere inches. Ed whimpered, covering his ears. Rich instinctively raised the gun with his good hand and pulled the trigger. He missed, but Manny

398

froze. They were fifty yards apart, their guns pointed at each other.

Rich's hand shook and his arm felt like there were ice picks being driven through it and he wasn't even sure if he had the strength to pull the trigger again with his good hand, but there was no way he was going to lower his piece.

Manny had already killed two of his friends — he wasn't about to let Eddie die at Manny's hand too.

But the truth was, Rich wasn't about to let Eddie die at *his* hand. Manny or one of his boys had pulled the actual trigger, but Dylan and Vice had died because of Rich. Rich couldn't deny that to anyone, especially not to himself and especially not now, with Eddie's life still salvageable. Rich was the one who had brought them the plan. He was the one who insisted they be included. He'd told them it could be done. He'd told them it would work. They had been treading water and surviving just fine until Rich grabbed them and pulled them under with him, down deep to where the sunlight doesn't reach. And they had drowned down there. Down where Rich had taken them.

But he wouldn't make Eddie drown too. No fucking way.

'Eddie, pull open the door and run,' Rich said as calmly as he was able.

'It took two of my men to open that door,' Manny pointed out. 'He's going nowhere.'

Eddie just froze. There was no place to hide. If he ran, Manny would fire at him. So he didn't move.

399

But Rich did. He slowly straightened his legs, sliding back up along the door until he was standing again. He began inching forward slowly, figuring every bit of ground covered gave him a better chance of hitting Manny when he fired.

'Don't leave me here,' Eddie pleaded.

'When the gunfire starts, you get down,' Rich ordered softly as he continued moving closer to a dangerous man who wanted to kill him.

'You shouldn't have been greedy,' Manny chastised. 'It's gonna cost you your life.'

'I told you already, I didn't take the money. I don't even care about the money,' Rich answered. They were now forty yards apart, their guns still pointed at each other.

'Everyone cares about money,' Manny said as he too stepped a bit closer.

'I don't,' Rich said. 'Not anymore.'

And he meant it. He could've cared less about money or security or any of the things that he once thought were so important — all the things he thought he needed to have love in his life. He just wanted to protect Eddie. And then, hopefully, leave that grain terminal. He wanted to hold Elyse, tell her he loved her, and talk about the family they would have one day.

But with every small step Manny took toward Rich, that family became less and less likely.

Rich steadied his gun. 'I wouldn't get any closer,' he said.

Manny stopped. They stared at each other a bit.

'If you don't want the money, what do you want?' Manny asked, curious.

400

Rich thought about it a moment. It was quiet — a pigeon flew from one rafter to another, high above them.

'I got movie tickets this morning. I wanna go to the movies,' Rich answered.

Manny looked at Rich for a second, then he snorted out a laugh. So did Rich.

Then they went quiet and looked at each other again. And then, because they both knew there was nothing else left to do, they both fired.

It would have been impossible to determine who had fired first, but they both hit the ground at the same time.

Manny Espinoza was dead.

Rich Mauro lay on his back on the dirty floor, gasping for air. He found breath, with difficulty. Eddie ran over.

'Rich! Rich!' He knelt beside his friend. Eddie could see into Rich's chest.

Rich looked up toward Eddie but his eyes searched past him to the beautiful sunlight still shining in through the windows high above them.

He remembered a day at the beach once, when he was seven: his parents each held one of his hands and lifted him into the air when the waves broke at his ankles. He remembered looking up at his parents, who were smiling, and the sunlight shone down on them at the beach that day, just like it was shining down on Rich at that very moment.

He tried in vain to suck in air as he thought of his mother and father. God, he had missed them for so long.

He prayed that he hadn't messed things up so bad that he wouldn't be able to see them now that his time had come.

That was the last thought Rich Mauro ever had.

He died with his head resting in Eddie Pisorchek's hands.

After a few moments, Eddie could tell his friend was gone, and he slowly laid Rich's head down on the floor. He stood and looked around.

Eddie was alone, except for the eight dead bodies that surrounded him.

64

Eddie Pisorchek found a bathroom in the back of the building and, amazingly, there was a ceiling pipe dripping semidirty water. Ed broke the pipe and caught the water in an old tar bucket. He used it to clean himself up the best he could. Once the blood was off his face, neck, and ears, he looked substantially better. His nose was swollen and he had a bruise on his cheekbone, but he could easily pass for someone who had been in a car accident as opposed to someone who'd been involved in a mass homicide.

He took off his shirt, which was quite bloody, and swapped it for Manny's, which was pretty clean, as Rich's shot had gone right through Espinoza's head. He also took Manny's coat, which was black — any blood splatter on it was hard to see . . .

It took Ed twenty full minutes to open the door.

Then, limping badly and dizzy with pain, Ed Pisorchek walked. He walked for hours. He staggered down the pier and went north toward the Brooklyn Bridge. Each step was agonizing, but he knew he couldn't go to a doctor — at least not yet.

Late afternoon had come, and the little bit of sun New York offered in December was already starting to diminish. Eddie pulled his coat closed tight.

The entire walk, Eddie thought about all that had happened. He had liked the guys from the Printers. He liked them all so much. They were the only real friends Ed had ever had. He missed them already.

It was taking him twice as long to walk as it would have if he weren't injured. Hours passed and it seemed he'd barely made any progress. The snow wasn't helping, as Eddie often slipped and fell. Each landing sent lightning bolts of pain through his leg.

By the time he got over the Brooklyn Bridge and into Manhattan it was night. He headed downtown toward Whitehall to catch the Staten Island ferry, but he just missed it. He had to wait thirty minutes for the next boat.

He sat inside during the ride across the harbor. The wind coming off the water was way too strong, and Eddie was freezing. There were a handful of other passengers on the ferry but no one paid him any attention. Eddie was used to that.

When he reached the house he was looking for, it was dark. He walked to the backyard, where there was a small garden. Though he didn't have the strength, or all of his fingers, he knelt down and began to dig.

As he did, he wondered if it was his fault. He didn't think it was. He was sure it wasn't. But still, he wondered. Manny was going to kill them once he got the codes, Ed told himself. He was going to kill them no matter what.

Eddie reached into the hole he had dug and pulled out a large hockey bag. He unzipped it and looked at the cash inside. Millions. All his. And he refused to feel guilty about it.

He had paid a higher price than any of them — well, at least until a few hours ago. He had had his fingers cut off — *he had been maimed, damn it*. And if he hadn't overheard them talking that day when he was in the supply closet, he was sure they would have cut him out of the deal in the first place.

And besides, he had given all of his money away, and the more he thought about it, the more he wanted some of his own. Well, now he had it.

He zipped the bag back up and thought about how everyone had always treated him like a mascot, never like a person, never like someone who had to be *considered*, someone who had to be *dealt with*.

And because no one ever paid attention to him, he'd known he'd be able to sit at his computer screen that day when everyone punched in his code and they'd all be totally unaware that he was watching them in the reflection of his monitor. They all assumed the retarded kid didn't grasp the concept of what they were doing. But the truth was, they didn't understand what *he* was doing. He was reading their digits. He had known all fifteen the whole time. That's how he knew Dylan's code was day first, then the month. He gave it up to spare Rich's life. He tried to save him, he reassured himself. He refused to feel guilty.

When Vice called him that day from the alley behind McMahon's to see where he was, it was easily believable that dumb old Eddie was just late. No one suspected that he wasn't on a bus from Staten Island to Queens but was instead on a bus coming back from Colts Neck with a hockey bag full of money at his feet. The woman at the bank was so proud of him — going to the bank and making a withdrawal for his brother all by himself.

Eddie was proud of himself too.

Rich once told Eddie that Spade had said, 'The benefit of being *invisible* is that people don't see you when you're robbing them blind.' Eddie always remembered that. He thought it was a good saying.

So he refused to feel guilty or sad.

He had been crippled.

He had been beaten.

He had been abandoned as a child and raised by bastards and treated like shit most of his life.

He had waited his whole life for this. He had *earned* it.

As Eddie stood and slung the almost-one-hundred-pound hockey bag onto his back like a knapsack, a yellow glow lit the garden and he looked up to find Pastor Morris standing in his robe by the porch light.

The pastor took one look at Eddie — exhausted, bruised, and covered in dirt and some remaining dried blood.

'*My God*, Eddie. Are you okay, son? What the hell are you doing out here?'

Eddie, bag of millions now securely on his back, limped toward the driveway that led out to the street. He stared straight ahead, not at the pastor, as he walked out into the dark night, and he gave his answer.

'I'm going to fuckin' Disney World.'

Acknowledgments

In the acknowledgments for my first novel, *Slip & Fall*, I commented on how recognizing everyone that makes a project come together is impossible because so many people contribute advice, expertise, and encouragement. Well, it seems it doesn't get easier the second time around. But once again I'll try, with the knowledge that I will most likely fail.

I dedicated this book to my parents for a simple reason — I owe everything I have in my life to them. Always knowing that I have an infallible safety net of love and guidance to fall into has made some of my risk-taking over the years a lot less risky.

And underneath my parents' fail-safe is a secondary net that has been dutifully manned by my sister since the day I was born. Kristine, I wish I were half as good a brother to you as you've been a sister to me.

This book would never have gotten published without my managers Jeremy Bell and Lindsay Williams at Gotham Group. While they were looking to sign me as a client, they harassed John Schoenfelder of Little Brown/Mulholland Books until he read *Fifteen Digits*. Well, he did, and now the joke's on all of them — I signed with both companies, and they're stuck with me. *Suckers*. They now know the pain that my great agents Ari Greenburg, Jay Mandel, and everyone else at William Morris Endeavor have felt for the past eight-plus years.

Thanks are also due to Miriam Parker at Little, Brown, who helps 'get the word out,' and my talented copyeditor Tracy Roe, who helps 'get the words *right*.'

Sincere appreciation is also owed to my lawyer and, more important, *friend* Patti Felker (and the entire firm of Felker Toczek Gellman Suddleson), as well as to Brian Lipson and George Jones — the men who made me a novelist.

I also want to acknowledge Pethra Turro, my mother-in-law, who was much more *mother* than *in-law*. She treated me like a son from the moment we met and always supported my writing — even when it took her baby girl three thousand miles away from New York to Los Angeles. My mother-in-law passed away before this book was completed. I would give anything to have her back.

And I want to thank Pethra's daughter, Janine. By the time this book is published, you will have given me seventeen years of your life, love, and support — not to mention two daughters so beautiful that every family photo looks like a game of Which One of These Doesn't Belong? I'm a crass, uncouth gorilla surrounded by stunning, graceful swans. I could live to be a hundred and never figure out how I got to be so damn lucky.

Finally, I want to recognize my grandfather Nicholas Joseph Santora. I was born on his birthday and it always made me feel special that we shared that day together.

Grandpa, I finished this book a few days ago, and I found out you died only ten minutes ago. I sat down and started this paragraph and I'm not sure what exactly to write. It has been twenty months since I've last seen you. I wish I still lived around the corner from your house so I could have spent more time with you. I love you so much and I miss you with all my heart already. In a few weeks it will be our birthday again. I'll miss our tradition: 'Happy birthday, Grandpa' . . . 'Happy birthday to *you*, Nicky.' And then we'd both laugh. August 4 will never be the same without you.

About the Author

After the first screenplay he wrote won Best Screenplay of the Competition at the New York International Independent Film and Video Festival, Nick Santora (a former attorney; JD, Columbia, 1996) was hired to write an episode for *The Sopranos*. After that incredible experience, he decided to leave New York and move to Los Angeles to try his hand at screenwriting full-time.

Soon thereafter he was hired as a staff writer for the CBS drama *The Guardian*, where he was promoted to co-producer in less than a year. From there he went on to write and produce a season of *Law & Order* and write and co- executive-produce four seasons of *Prison Break*.

Nick has also written feature films; he was a credited writer on the Lionsgate/Marvel feature *The Punisher: War Zone* as well on *The Long-shots*, starring Ice Cube — a film that Nick also produced.

Nick's versatile career took an even more interesting turn when his first novel, *Slip & Fall*, was published and became a national bestseller within its first week.

Nick recently completed *Sandstorm*, an original comic book series he created for DC Comics.

Currently, the majority of Nick's time is spent

as co-creator/ writer/executive producer/show-runner for the hit A&E series *Break-out Kings*.

Nick is thrilled to be able to share his life with his beautiful wife and their two wonderful daughters.

We do hope that you have enjoyed reading this large print book.

Did you know that all of our titles are available for purchase?

We publish a wide range of high quality large print books including:
Romances, Mysteries, Classics
General Fiction
Non Fiction and Westerns

Special interest titles available in large print are:
The Little Oxford Dictionary
Music Book
Song Book
Hymn Book
Service Book

Also available from us courtesy of Oxford University Press:
Young Readers' Dictionary
(large print edition)
Young Readers' Thesaurus
(large print edition)

For further information or a free brochure, please contact us at:
Ulverscroft Large Print Books Ltd.,
The Green, Bradgate Road, Anstey,
Leicester, LE7 7FU, England.
Tel: (00 44) **0116 236 4325**
Fax: (00 44) **0116 234 0205**

Other titles published by
The House of Ulverscroft:

THE ABBEY

Chris Culver

Ash Rashid is a homicide detective who can't stand the thought of handling another death investigation. In a year's time he'll be out of the department completely. That's the plan, at least until his niece's body is found in the property of one the city's wealthiest citizens. The coroner calls it an overdose, but the case doesn't add up. Against orders, Ash launches an investigation to find his niece's murderer. But the longer he searches, the darker the case gets — and if he doesn't solve it fast — his niece won't be the only family member he has to bury . . .

NIGHT WATCH

Linda Fairstein

New York Assistant D.A. Alexandra Cooper is in France, visiting her restaurateur boyfriend, Luc Rouget, but her holiday is curtailed when a young woman is found murdered. The only evidence: one of Luc's matchboxes promoting his new restaurant in New York. However, Alex is summoned back home to handle a high-profile case. The head of the World Economic Bureau stands accused of attacking a maid in his hotel. Alex is torn between preparing the alleged victim to testify — and a murder case too close to home. When a second body is found — in Brooklyn — with Luc's matchbox, Alex fears that the two cases are connected . . . and that uncovering the secrets of the city's most powerful could cost her and her loved ones everything they hold dear.

A DEATH IN VALENCIA

Jason Webster

Max Camara is feeling low. Ominous cracks have appeared in the walls of his flat; the body of a well-known paella chef has been washed up on the beach; there are rows and threats about abortion clinics; the town hall is set on demolishing El Cabanyal, the colourful fishermen's quarter on Valencia's sea-front. As Camara untangles these threads, he stumbles into a web of corruption and violence, uncovering deep animosities and hidden secrets, and forcing him to question his own doubts and desires.